I0831809

IN GOLD WE TRUST

The True Story of the Papalia Twins and Their Battle for Truth and Justice

Trafford Publishing

Order this book online at www.trafford.com
or email orders@trafford.com

Most Trafford titles are also available at major online book retailers.

Note for Librarians: A cataloguing record for this book is available from Library and Archives Canada at www.collectionscanada.ca/amicus/index-e.html

Printed in Victoria, BC, Canada.

ISBN: 978-1-4251-2289-8 (Soft)
ISBN: 978-1-4269-1668-7 (Hard)

We at Trafford believe that it is the responsibility of us all, as both individuals and corporations, to make choices that are environmentally and socially sound. You, in turn, are supporting this responsible conduct each time you purchase a Trafford book, or make use of our publishing services. To find out how you are helping, please visit www.trafford.com/responsiblepublishing.html

Our mission is to efficiently provide the world's finest, most comprehensive book publishing service, enabling every author to experience success. To find out how to publish your book, your way, and have it available worldwide, visit us online at www.trafford.com

Trafford rev: 3/16/2010

www.trafford.com

North America & international
toll-free: 1 888 232 4444 (USA & Canada)
phone: 250 383 6864 • fax: 812 355 4082
email: info@trafford.com

Original transcription by Ruth Elaine Sauder

Contents

I

Foreword

THIS IS THE story of two brothers - identical twins, who went in search of a gold mine, found one and then were forced to defend themselves against attacks on many fronts as they battled to bring it into fulfillment. This is also a story about success and failure and the ability of the human spirit to rise up from the ashes and continue to strive for excellence.

In 1957, Robert and Tony Papalia came to Canada as youngsters with their family. They grew up in a working-class suburb of Montreal and became involved in music promotion activities while still in high school. From these humble beginnings they eventually became owners of what may be today one of Canada's largest gold deposits. The story surrounding the acquisition, proving, and defending of this property is full of the intrigue and suspense of a spy novel yet everything you read is true.

Some people may think that those who invest money do it out of greed - out of a desire to obtain more wealth at the expense of others. Nothing could be further from the truth. Greed implies evil - acquiring wealth through exploitation or cheating of another. Money is simply a system used to evaluate the relative value of merit of different activities, products or services in a society. When an individual earns money, an opportunity is created to apply this wealth to achieve something better. As paper, money really has no value. But when put to work, it provides the driving force by which society can be improved. The Papalias are investors who believe in generating wealth out of wealth. They are builders and creators.

I first met the Twins in 1993. My impressions from afar had been tainted by the gossip and innuendo that have swirled around these characters since the late 1970's. Harassed by the RCMP, Scotland Yard, the Canadian Government, and many envious investors, the Papalias have survived through sheer will and determination to succeed and to do it with flair and excellence. Their reputation has been tarnished by the many charges and court cases which they have been put through but the knowledge that truth was on their side gave them the resolve to battle through to victory. Many of the rumors I heard turned out so absent of reality that I wonder how information derived from our media is really confirmable by an individual reader, listener or viewer.

Canadians tend to react uncomfortably to reports that there are members of our government institutions whose sole purpose is to investigate, interrogate, intimidate, and harass legitimate citizens, whose ideas and ways may differ from the norm. Our supposed Free Press when faced with such stories rarely push hard enough against the people or methods behind the accounts. The story itself is always more newsworthy. Insinuations derived from established sources such as the police, army or government agencies are often accepted at face value without addressing the possible real motives behind the accusations.

There are elements of this book that, at first, may seem impossible or contrived. I can assure the reader that having researched each and every strange fact; I have found the tale absolutely genuine. The integrity of the Papalia brothers is unquestionable in my opinion. They are men of their word who walk along the knife-edge between collapse and victory on many of their ventures. High risk-takers, they undertake projects that have very high payback. As a result, not all their investments prove successful, but those that do work out, pack a big punch. Failure is not a word in the Twin's vocabulary; rather they consider lack of success to be another term for postponement.

As I have come to know them, I realize that Robert and Tony possess a joie *de vivre* sadly lacking in contemporary Canadian society. Prepared to experiment with new concepts and methods, these entrepreneurs have stumbled into some amazing and sometimes, crazy ideas. Only by taking chances and attempting the impossible can civilization improve and discover new ways. Ideas do not come from a group of people; rather they are the product of a single mind, although in this case it appears to be one distributed between two individuals. The reward for the originators should be immediate and tangible and for society, it may appear in the form of new jobs, better technology, and lower consumption of raw materials or environmental improvements.

Canada needs more of such individuals and Papalias epitomize the spirit of the old-time prospectors and risk-takers who tried to do the impossible.

Vancouver, Canada   John Meech

II

Preface

THROUGHOUT THE COURSE of history, there have occurred certain infamous cases of abuse of power by governments against individuals. These individuals, when confronted by such a powerful and oppressive adversary, must reach down into the very depths of their human spirit in order to find strength of will and determination to physically and emotionally survive in their fight for justice. Unfortunately, only a very select few have such capabilities, our story is about two such people.

Robert and Tony Papalia, two young Italian Canadian businessmen who for years have become the victims of harassment, false imprisonment and physical torture by two of the most powerful law enforcement organizations in the world: Scotland Yard and the Royal Canadian Mounted Police.

These police organizations when they realized that they had made a mistake in accusing these men, instead of trying to recitify the situation, apparently chose to use their considerable might and resources to cover up their error. A course of action that might have succeeded with the average person but in the case of the Papalia's, it proved to be the wrong decision. These men had not become the owners of possibly the richest gold mine in Canada by shirking conflict.

From their dark, dank cell in the depths of medieval Brixton Prison, the Papalia's began their fight against their accusers. Propelled by the passion of their innocence, the Papalia's determined not to accept this corruption and fought the false charges against them to the highest court in England, the venerable Old Bailey. Antagonized by their treatment from the justice system, Tony Papalia, decided to represent himself and at the end of the most expensive trial in English history, obtained a complete acquittal of all the charges but at a cost to the brothers of million of dollars and their lives devastated.

IN GOLD WE TRUST is a story of amazing portrayal of personal courage against overwhelming odds.

Vancouver, Canada — Deedee Panesar

III

Acknowledgement

ROBERT AND TONY Papalia would like to acknowledge the help and support of the legal staff that were present during our trial and incarceration with a special regards to Loris Fortuna and Giuseppe Bombara whom without their help, justice and truth would have been impossible to establish.

We would also like to acknowledge the incredible effort and dedication of all the people that made possible for this book to come together.

Albert Swann
Battistino Fornero
Bettino Craxy
Bischoff & Co.
Brian Leary, QC
Carlo Colombotti
David Benham
David Offenbach
Donald Brady
Dr. A.K. Schellinger
Dr. Gabriella Smuckler
Dr. Neils Skov
Edward Nixon
Franco Desideri
Frank Feoli
Geoffrey Lines
Gerry Kirwan
Giovannino Agnelli
Gus McPhail
Jack Lovelock
John Kennedy Jr.
Judge Lawson
Loretta King
Matthew Tutino
Michael Jackson
Micheal Spencer
Mike Fernandez
Mr. Reide
Nelson Mandela
Nigel Milne
Offenbach & Company
Philip Gaglardi
Pierre Elliot Trudeau
Professor Shellinger
Ralph Feoli
Randy Jackon
Richard Nixon
Robert Craig
Robert Steiner
Robin Wood
Roy Ward, QC
Ruth Elaine Sauder
Sir Michael West, QC
Taylor Kramer
Umberto Frascati
William Stevenson

IV

Dedication

THIS BOOK IS dedicated to our families who supported and loved us unconditionally throughout the entire time of incarceration and prosecution and Deedee Panesar for publishing this book.

To all the oppressed people, all visionaries and believers in the justice and truth: Believe in yourself and God and enjoy the glory.

Robert and Tony Papalia

V

The Theft and Enslavement of a Nation

THE BOOK YOU are about to read is an account of a real event that demonstrates to what lengths a Government will go to insure that its friends have control of Money supply and wealth. I have been asked to write this Narrative so that the readers of this True Story will have some perspective as to how such a situation can, and does happen to Private Law abiding Citizens when and if they dare to challenge how the way Governments create new money supply and wealth.

I will put forward factual events in historical perspective so that the reader may review historical fact and reflect on how we have come to construct the Society that we presently live in. However, before I go on, I wish the reader to have some definitions so that he/she may understand some of the Terms that will be used in the upcoming text.

Gold: Symbol (Au) - a yellow Noble metal that does not tarnish and has been used since the beginning of time for Trade and Commerce and universally accepted as Currency / Money. This metal is reported to be rare in abundance and has traditionally and historically been the measure of wealth and the foundation of Paper currency until the latter plan of the 1900's (1968).

Silver: Symbol (Ag) - A white Noble metal, not quite so rare as gold, but sought after for its qualities and for coinage. Again as for gold, silver and its' accumulation was used to determine wealth. In the British Empire the "Sterling" standard became the standard of the Currency, hence the Term "Pound Sterling".

Money: A Piece of paper, generally with pictures of Dead Persons / Heroes or Royalty that has a denomination (a Number) that has been given Value by a Central Bank or Federal Reserve. In the past "Money" was known to be anchored or set in Value based upon how much Gold and Silver was held by the Central Bank or Federal Reserve. In today's climate, money from any Country is tied to the Value of other Money (generally from those Countries that control Economic and Political Power). In other words, the value of one currency to another is variable based purely on the perceived value as indicated by the Directors of the World Bank, the G-8, The European Common Market and any other tea leave readers associated with Central Banks and Federal Reserves. However Gold and Silver are still considered as Money in most of the World that does not belong to Religion of "World Control by Green and Multi-Coloured Paper".

CENTRAL BANK OR FEDERAL RESERVE

An organization generally operated by Private Economists / Bankers that Creates and Manages money supply for a Nation. These organizations generally control "All" Governments' Economic Planning and control internal Economic and Political activities of any Country by setting lending rates and Political Economic Policy hence controlling the availability of money, and how this money is to be allocated.

One must understand that "Money" is the focus of everything that happens on this Planet. Think about it, we all need money for rent, food, transportation, etc. We simply can't live in our Society without money. The persons that make or manufacture/create paper money know this, and in so far as they know that persons with no "money" will find a way to get it, they create safety nets within those Countries that control Money supply to the World so as to prevent any problems from occurring from those that do not have money. Some Examples - Socialized Medicine, Social Services (Welfare), Unemployment Insurance, Low Cost Housing, Strong Police Forces, Strong Taxation Collection Agencies, are just a few examples these Governments use to find ways to prevent internal conflict by the Masses. We must take note that these Programs (named above) commenced in earnest during and post the Great Depression of the early 1930's to prevent Civil Unrest during the Implementation of the First phases of "The New World Order". To understand the preceding statement we must think back to the events or the early 1930's and most specifically the Agreements and Understandings that came from "The Bretton Woods Conference" held in the United States. This "Conference" was held at the Request of those that established the United States Federal Reserve System, and set policies for management of Central Banks of Industrialized Nations. They were the most powerful Bankers of the World after consolidating their Wealth at the expense of the "World at War".

This Conference would soon set into motion all of the above programs to prevent internal Political Conflict in those Countries were power was to be Centralized. They would by their actions, start the rest of the World towards a path of War and Conflict. This Conflict would force all wealth to be brought to where the New Formed Centralization of Economic Power was to be started from. They further started a process of changing the Laws and Statues that Govern Countries so as to create new and more powerful legislative doctrines to regulate and control Equities Markets, Taxation Acts, Movements of Money and Laws of Commerce. The processes put into place by Governments that were willing participants to these changes are visible to anyone that cares to review the Legislation put forward by these Governments, post 1934. You may see how the process was put into motion and if you cannot see it go to your Library and review the Economic Press editorials of the period and you will begin to understand.

With the apathy and lack of economic knowledge available to the Masses it became possible to put their Plan in motion and Identify and Name all those Countries and Individuals that did not wish to play the game. The persons in power subsequently made those that did not agree with this new policy to become the Enemies of the Bankers and Central Banks. Later these entities were to be to made villains and enemies to the cause of establishing "Private and Selective Control of Money Supply" on a Global scale. As such, those that refused to partake in "The Cause" had to be brought into compliance by whatever means necessary.

Canadians were difficult to change over, as they enjoyed wealth and prosperity, and they had some economic knowledge. The process of bringing them into the New Economic order could not be done quickly. After all, Canadians were not stupid persons, they were literate and knew just about all they needed to know to harvest our natural resources and make money from that effort and work.

So here is how it went.

a) Those in charge had to find a way to stop the manufacturing of money from primary resources. An example; if you take something like Gold, Silver, Platinum, Copper, Oil, etc. from the ground and sell it to those that need and use it, you get their money paid to you in Canada and you prosper. So they (those in charge) had to cause legislation to cause changes in how we as Canadians develop our Mines and Natural Resources. This process of changing the rules was very elegantly performed. First you must put into place a National Energy Program, so that you have complete control on Development. Then you must remove from the Curriculum of Colleges and Universities ways and methods to affect evaluations of Mineral Ore Bodies. You must choose different Rules and Standards that permitted no creation of innovative procedures, technology and methods to generate or lead to Noble and Precious Metal development. Those in charge had to change the reporting rules and reporting procedures to Securities Commissions, for those that wished to develop Mines. And for those that made it through the New Rules and Quasi Judicial Agencies that were to obtain the means and abilities to go to production the needed to make things difficult by other means. Those that produced small quantities of Gold, Silver and Platinum, were now forced to sell their products on the Black Market and not deliver to the Bank of Canada the products they made. To be sure that these events happened the Government Agents Offices were prohibited to buy product and the Bank of Canada was to dose their buying facilities in the producing areas of Canada. "Slowly but surely they dried up supply from everyone other than their Corporate Friends and Partners". Other more serious remedies had to be found for those that dare challenge these New Rules, Regulations and Procedures, which by the way is what this book is about.

b) Those in the Timber business had to have all their harvesting protocols changed and they had to made subjects to New and more obscure Duties and countervailing Tariffs. New Legislation had to create Free Trade Agreements, that in, fact weren't.

c) Those in the Oil business had to now tow the new line of a New National Energy Policy that prohibited development of Oil and Natural Gas on Federally control Land. If the Provinces developed the now had to seek permission to sell their Oil and Natural Gas production, and if they did not comply they were to have a new Socialist Government installed with the clandestine assistance of the Federal Establishment. And if that did not work, you simply created a scandal of epic magnitude so as to implement "The War Measures Act". (Refer to the Macdonald Royal Commission, testimony on who set and Planted the Bombs in Quebec during the alleged FLQ Crisis).

d) The next step was to cause our existing wealth to be used up. This process was to be called Inflation. This was easy to do. Let's not kid ourselves, we are all greedy and such we can be bribed very readily. Pierre & Company simply had to go on a spending spree so as to use up all our accumulated wealth and create a new form of Government Finance - the new term was to be "Deficit Financing", where you and I did not have to earn the money our Government spent, we would simply allow them to borrow as much as they pleased from their Banker Friends and spend it to our "BENEFIT". To make sure there was enough money every Thursday, The Bank of Canada holds a Treasury Bill and Bond Sale, where they sell these pieces of Paper to the Banks at a discount and we (the taxpayer) through our Ministry of Finance borrow the full retail value of this created paper and pay through our taxes, the Banks, interest and principal as they desire. In short form, we pay for Money that someone else decides to create from nothing. This is the New System of Money supply allowed by our Government and their Banker Friends to create. No more, could we rely on the goods and services we as Canadians create by our efforts to set our Currency Standard and Value. We were not permitted to produce any product that was defined by the rest of the World as Money, unless we were part of the New Club. Instead we have become subject to the will of a floating Currency with new rules and regulations put into place that would prevent us from controlling our destiny.

e) Sometimes those in charge of our monetary system do more sinister things. They allow Banks to do what we are not permitted to do. But and we won't talk about them because it's illegal. Could we suspect or believe, that our Banks do things and Financings "Off Ledger and Off Balance Sheet" in Tax Havens? God Forbid, but that's a story for another book!

f) Those in our Government now having completed this wild spending spree had to find a way for all of stupid greedy people (we Canadians) to support their Banker friends by taking away our money by means of Taxation to pay for the bad debts they (Government and Bankers) created for us.

They frittered away our Birth Right and our Wealth and we now have to pay them Interest and principal on our NEW NATIONAL DEBT. Cool, isn't it, they spend the money, here, there and everywhere and we get the privilege of paying for money they created and added to the money supply (inflation) that was wasted intentionally. But this too was part of their Plan. You see they knew that we were an apathetic bunch that believed that our Government was working for us and not working to undermine our status in the World. They really just wanted us to be below the USA and not be upstarts.

In short, you have now the beginning of "The New World Order". To site a few examples so you may reflect and know how they obtained this power to control the World I will site some examples below:

- The Royal Families of Europe (Post WWI) understanding the "new conditions" came to transfer all their wealth to England, The Commonwealth of nations and the United States. Most specifically their Gold and Silver Reserves were to be transported (for safe keeping) to Banks in these jurisdictions. Banks, such as JP Morgan Bank, Bank of Hong Kong Shanghai, The Borough of Manhattan Reserve Bank, Bank of England and its' subordinates / associates etc: Federal Reserve Notes were issue to these entities in exchange for their Gold and Silver.
- Countries such as China, Germany and Italy were being taken over by Socialist. Governments and/or Imperialistic Forces. (Post the Depression & The Bretton Woods Convention). These Countries and their Citizens were now seeing War and Conflict as immanent facts. Hence, the dying Governments and their Sophisticated Citizens transferred their wealth in the form of Gold and Silver Reserves from their Private and Public holdings to the United States and the United Kingdom for safe keeping. While at the same time the Banks (in the British Empire, the United States and Switzerland) involved in the safe-keeping of those Gold and Silver assets would issue Gold Certificates to these entities (their depositors). For the most part they did not know that their Certificates would not be honoured for redemption upon their maturity.
- Post WWII large amounts of Gold and Silver was in fact found to be held, in

the previously named Federal Reserves and the Countries Central Banks. For the most part the Safe Keeping parties did not return them to their original depositors, using the excuse that there was a War and nobody knew who the rightful owners were. Holding those Reserves of Gold and Silver, the Central Banks and Federal Reserve, using in the methods created by Agreements established at The Bretton Woods Conference permitted these Central Banks and Federal Reserve to use these Assets to establish New Central Banks in the Occupied Territories of WWII. Those Gold and Silver Reserves were now set into activity to create New Capital and to recreate New Currencies for the Countries in Europe and in Asia as to be able to keep these dissident Areas in compliance with the New Order. Further these occupied Countries were now to be defined as a part of the Allies' group of Countries. If they for some reason were not to become part of this group they would simply not receive any Finance to cause reconstruction and restoration. They (the Countries occupied) were to become under the influence of the Western Democratic Alliance, or be isolated and made to be the New Enemies of the Western Alliance. Those Countries that did not come into this Democratic Alliance were to become the Enemies of the Cold War (Russia, China, etc.) and their assets that had been transferred became the custodial property of the Federai Reserves, Central Banks and Selected other Banks and Financial Institutions.

- A new way of ripping entire populations off. If you don't like their dissention to the New World Order you simply make them the enemy and they cannot use their money or wealth unless they play by your rules.

Well enough of history, the short of it is that there was a deal made at Bretton Wood, New Jersey in 1934, Those that went along with it, set up a new system of money supply and control of it, the rest were either pummelled in submission or became the Enemy, not to be included in any economic development unless they generated it themselves. Of course, Canada was one of those places that had to tow the line on this "New World Economic Order".

As a Note - Read the Book "A Visit to Jeckal Island" and you will get the truth of how the above was done.

The above brief narrative is not intended to be critical of the need to prevent War and have Global Trade work more effectively. The idea of a new and more structured way of doing things was a good one, but the old axiom - "Power corrupts and Absolute Power corrupts absolutely" - holds true. For, if you give Power to someone or something, someone or something will use that Power against you and they will do so with impunity when they have no checks and balances and because we the apathetic Masses were not aware of their plan to take over the World. If, we the Masses knew of the plan and how was to be implemented we would have (on Mass) protested and caused some checks and balances to be implemented as to make these persons accountable. But this is not the case, as these persons are above the Law of any Land or Nation.

TO THE YOUNGER CANADIAN READER OF THIS CHAPTER.

There was once a time here in Canada, when the United States Dollar was worth a lot less than our Canadian Dollar. This time was pre the invoking of Economic Policies of Lester B. Person and Pierre Elliot Trudeau. You see, (in keeping with the plans set into motion by those in charge) by 1966 there was an order constructed by The Bank of Canada and their Handlers to remove all Silver Coinage from circulation and make preparations to remove Canada from the Gold & Silver Standard. At the time our currency was the strongest in the World, we enjoyed the World's highest Standard of Living and our taxation was amongst the lowest per capita in the World. In short, we had it pretty good; high productivity, abundant natural resources, good markets, world leading Telecommunications and Aero Space Industries (remember the Avro Aero and CN-CP Telecommunications). This upstart State "Canada" was to be in conflict with the planned and designated New Economic Super Star (The United States). As such our Weak Politicians had to tow the line to their Masters (Select Bankers and Economists), as we were making them (the USA) look bad. How dare we as Canadians become other than harvesters of Wood, Oil, Fish, Metal and Water? We were making our neighbours look *very* bad in deed. To insure that we would not go to that place of superior prosperity ever again, several methods had to be put into place. That place of superior prosperity being anything other than the working servants to those that need what we were blessed with.

g) The final treat was to be in store for us and we are now living it, it is a steady diet of servitude. To explain – If you had a bright idea or a better mouse trap or a better way of doing things, you were to have your Financing ability severely curtailed. In that any idea of substance, or any development of substance, that was in need of money had to get that money from the Equity Markets, due to the fact that our Banks would no longer lend money to you. Bank Policies and regulations changed so that the rules couıd not permit speculative or equity lending. No longer could your Banker lend you money, because he knew you and believed in your ability to pay him back. They the Bankers now excused these regulations and changes in lending policies as coming from the Bank of Canada. The reason for the rules being put into place by Our Central Bank was that, the Canada banks tried this Lending Policy in Countries like Argentina, Brazil, and Columbia and wound up loosing their shirts, not to mention our money. They did not say that they (The Banks) were encouraged to lend money to these Countries by our illustrious leaders that knew that they would be sending the money into oblivion with no hope of getting it back. Hence, if this lending policy failed we all had to pay the price. Of course this too was planned because our Central Bank. "Our Bank of Canada" was always there to baiı these twit Bankers out and cause the increase of the money supply at the expense of those that live here in Canada. After all we hadn't complained yet and we were too busy trying to keep our Families together and find ways to get more income to Pay more taxes to keep more Bankers happy.

So, here we are to review this brief chapter. We went off the Gold and Silver Standard.

Our Government spent all our money and went into debt so that our money would be worthless. We started a process to produce less of anything that we could get a lot of money for. Our Banks would no longer finance anything even remotely speculative. Our primary resources industries were to have lesser and lesser amounts of highly qualified and educated persons to draw from. We now as Canadians, have to go to our Neighbours, if we want money to develop anything. Our Bright Persons leave and go to the USA and this is known as a "BRAIN DRAIN". Quebec is given Rupert Land as a bribe - *(far* those that cannot remember, this was were all the Hydro-Electric Power was to come from to export to the United States) and the money from this Energy was to create a New Cash Flow for those in Quebec's Establishment to go along with the New Order . Alberta was given the shaft by the National Energy Policy. Newfoundland had its' Fish resources given away to the French, Portuguese, Taiwanese, Russians, until they had no more Marine Resources. British Columbia, would have its' Timber Industry destroyed at the hand of Free Trade and its' Mines would run silent in the hands of the NDP Government and their newly discovered Policies. The Northwest Territories was to become stagnant at the Hands of the New Federal Aboriginal Policies and New Land Deals. Export of our Oil and Natural Gas Resources was to be curtailed at the prevention of Building the New Mackenzie River Pipeline. ETC. ETC. ETC.

Now that you have some idea of what is going on. Read this book and understand that these two guys "The Papalia Twins" had discovered something about Gold and how to remove it from an Area known as Port Douglas, in British Columbia. Their Gold was small potatoes in the overall scheme of things, but if they were to recover this Gold then others would do the same thing with the same methods and as such the Plans of those in charge would not proceed quietly. Know this - You are not in charge of your destiny and if you are to see how these people in charge work, you will begin to understand "that you don't matter much to them".

For a few of you that still carry Birth Certificate. Look at the back of it and you will see a number. In some Provinces it is still defined as Revenue Receipt. In other words you're nothing but a way for someone to define what you are worth to them in Dollars. Do not make the mistake that they care. You must work, your wife must work and not bitch that 65% of your money goes to those that piss it away in the name of Government.

Not that it matters, I, too must work and pay for the indiscretions of those that Govern us, but if I am to be a slave in their service, I, at least want to know that I am and I think you should too!

Vancouver, Canada John Carniel

VI

Prologue

MY GRANDFATHER USED to say that people are divided into two groups: the conformists and the non-conformists. Those pertaining to the first group, he used to say, are those who hold the deep conviction that the world will never change, that it is to be accepted as it is and lived in accordance to its inflexible established norms. Those pertaining to the second group disagree with this, assuring that the world can not only be improved, reliant on the overall universal effort, the will of mankind, but also by putting their words into practice, in pursuit of the biggest, most difficult and noble causes, i.e., the conquest of their dreams. It is these optimists by nature, who end up inspiring all others, disposing of preconceived ideas focused on ingrained neutrality. It is these people who aim to acquiring the knowledge of use of the global universal force, of the will of mankind, who make the most of their liberty. And not just to do as they please, but rather to reach an understanding of their true and free nature.

My grandfather, a manufacturer of hand-made toys during the trying post-civil war period in Spain, formed part of this optimistic group. A self-made man in a time of gloom and doubt who, notwithstanding, and till the end of his days, maintained his belief in the incredible capacity of the human spirit. It was he who taught me to differentiate the components of these groups.

As a result of this, the moment I learned of the amazing Papalia twin brothers, Robert and Tony, it all became clear to me.

Following the theory of the good and wise man that was my grandfather was there to exist a listing of the best and most brilliant human beings categorized under the second group, the Papalia would undoubtedly have to head such list. It is these persons whose example, so full of virtues, has served as an inspiration to others.

Many were the things, places and circumstances which came to my mind after learning of their existence. All of them magnificent, reminding me of the essence of the heroes I have loved ever since my childhood. Mythical adventurers, superheroic saviors of other words, go-getters living incredible adventures in exotic places, battlers of the human spirit or researches of a truth beyond the difficulties of the obvious. The Papalias are all of this and more, given that they never limit themselves to what could be, but rather to what should be, loyal to their principles, to their free spirits, and incessant.

It is for this reason, that the major public should be informed as to and made acquainted with their story, in order to make it clear that not only one but two – in this particular case – can make a difference, and that the power of the human spirit can break the barriers of the unimaginable. That things can change and can be made better. That dreams can become tangible, despite the impediments imposed by society. To teach us that reaching out for our goals is by no means foolish, as many would wish us to believe, but rather a huge virtue. There are those who conform to lead the reality of the life they have been endowed, those who operated in accordance with what they are dished up, and those who fear to lose what they already have and prefer not to take risks. Others prefer to grasp out at their objectives.

The Papalia twin brothers are the living example of what is apparently impossible to achieve. You may or may not find their story credible, but I can guarantee its authenticity. The experience is well worth the while, even those skeptically inclined, as it reminds us all the divine and human who inhabit our souls.

Madrid, Spain David Barto

The Arrest

ON THE EVENING of Friday, May 6th, 1977, there was no room available at the Dragonara Hotel. Tired after the long flight from Milan, with a stop-over in Geneva to attend to several business matters, Robert Papalia was unhappy to be displaced from his favorite hotel with its familiar and quiet, yet continental surroundings. After assistance from the desk clerk, Robert and his traveling companions, his twin brother, Tony, and a business acquaintance, were able to find accommodation at the Mayfair Hotel.

They were met earlier in the evening at the airport by their English employee, Richard Swinnerton who drove them to the Mayfair. It was very late when they checked in, so Robert decided to set about arranging their schedule of meetings in the morning.

The Papalias were participants in a number of business ventures. Their primary deal focused on developing a Canadian gold mine. Through interests in Metals Research SA, Nasco Mining Syndicate, Zyrox Mines Ltd. and Platinate Minerals and Industries Ltd., Robert and Tony controlled what they believed to be one of the largest known gold reserves in the West.

The ore body is not a typical placer deposits. The gold is distributed in the finer sizes of the sand and so, is often referred to as "invisible gold" by the old-time prospectors. In addition, the deposit showed important platinum and rare-earth metals potential. Metals Research also owned a license for a new chemical process to extract the precious metals. The combination of this innovative technology together with the significant gold price increases occurring in the 1970s had convinced the Papalias that innovation went together with mining and could really pay big.

Only the day before, Robert received word from Robert Craig, the company's consulting metallurgist in California, that he was about to leave for the mine site to begin erecting a portable pilot plant. Test work on the deposit should commence within the next six weeks. This was exciting news as it indicated that all the planning and preparation was advancing.

After several early morning phone calls, Robert checked his wallet before proceeding to breakfast. It contained his American Express card and several hundred dollars. He made a mental note to go to his London bank, Bear Securities, on

Monday to get some cash, while Tony would be driving around London with Swinnerton visiting the new premises for the European office of AATB on Pall Mall Street.

On a previous trip to London, Robert had met a young Italian banker, Umberto Frascati. He had persuaded Robert to use the bank he worked for, Bear Securities, which had been taken over recently by a Swiss Bank backed by some Italian financiers. Several services offered by the bank were important to Robert and so he had made an initial deposit of $100,000 dollars to cover expenses while in England. The account now contained almost $200,000 dollars.

Richard Swinnerton and Tony's conversation began with the latest London news. The week before their arrival, several London merchant banks and a number of well-known law-firms were caught-up in a major scandal. Scotland Yard had arrested some 70 to 80 foreign bank employees in one massive overnight sweep. But that was a trivia matter during the discussions.

❧

The weekend was devoted to socializing; a trip to Ascot on Saturday for an antique car show was a nice diversion. Some of the people they met there joined them later for a party that went on into the early hours. The Twins were always noticed wherever they went, in part because of their dark attractiveness and charismatic personalities but also because of their striking resemblance to each other. They were natural performers with an ability to command attention from those around them.

Sunday was enjoyed in typical English leisure fashion. They slept in but awoke in time to enjoy brunch exchanging general views on events. Later, Robert went out with his English friend Maxine to see the *Rocky Horror Picture Show*. Little did he realize how prophetic this movie title would be.

Tony remained behind with Swinnerton to work on some AATB matters, since AATB had merged with First Montreal Investment Corporation, an asset management and market specialists in international arbitrage. Firm which Tony had founded with his brothers in 1965.

❧

When Monday arrived, the real reasons for being in London finally had to be faced. At 10:30am, Robert telephoned Bear Securities to arrange a meeting with Frascati. Since becoming their banker, Frascati had assisted them in incorporating a subsidiary company to distribute a new sound system for movie theaters or cinemas in the UK. Robert was interested in how the incorporation was proceeding. The phone rang and rang without being answered.

"That's odd," thought Robert, "Why is the bank closed on a Monday? Surely it's not another bank holiday!"

He turned to other matters with a resolution to try the bank again later. Meanwhile, Tony was setting up an appointment with the London law firm retained to assist them with their corporate matters in England. They wanted to discuss establishing a branch of the Anglo-American Trade Bank, AATB. This bank was part of their overall strategy for MRSA. The bank was to serve two main functions: first as an in-house financial tool for their growing corporate empire; and secondly to market their precious metals productions. London is an important European financial center and they believed AATB would provide them with an excellent market position to maximize profits from their precious metal sales.

After arranging several other appointments for the week, Robert tried once again to telephone Bear. It was 11:30am and this time someone answered,

"Hello."

"I'd like to speak with Mr. Frascati, please," said Robert.

The voice on the other end rasped, "He's not available."

"Okay then, I will be dropping by anyway. My name is Robert Papalia and Metals Research SA has an account with the bank. I would like to cash a cheque on that account today."

The voice told Robert, "We can't cash any cheques today because we don't have the signature cards on hand. I'm sorry but I can't help you further," and with that the phone was hung up.

Robert was beginning to show more than casual concern, "The sounds like a strange excuse. What is going on with this bank?" He turned to Swinnerton and asked him to find out if there was any connection between Bear Securities and the banking scandal they had talked about on Saturday.

After discussing the matter further over lunch with Tony, they decided to drop by the bank that afternoon to find out what was up.

Bear Securities occupied luxurious premises at 11 Waterloo Place in the very upmarket St. James district of London. The building was one of those imposing 19th Century, pseudo-Grecian edifices that epitomize importance and money. There were three steps up to the pillared façade and the bank's massive wooden double doors that opened into an enormous high-ceiling foyer. The interior was dark and somber with wood-paneled walls interrupted only by high leaded-glass windows. The premises were a monument to age and substance.

They entered the bank and walked the thirty feet or so across the foyer to the receptionist. Robert told the woman who he was and that he wished to cash a cheque. The clerk sighed and gave an uncertain look, "I'm afraid we can't do that. All our papers have been seized."

So it appeared that Bear was one of the banks involved in the arrests and scandal. Tony was thoroughly disgusted and now showed his displeasure.

"How could you guys be so stupid to deal with this *Mickey-Mouse* bank? You should be doing business with a reputable institution!"

Robert tried to explain, "But Tony, Umberto Frascati was recommended to us by our Swiss bankers."

"We should go straight to our lawyers," Tony replied.

Robert asked the receptionist a few questions to identify the people in charge of the bank. As they turned to leave, Robert noticed some brochures on a sideboard. Picking up one to read he noted that Colombotti & Partners, lawyers to the Italian Embassy in London were listed among the bank directors. There was something strange here and he intended to get to the bottom of the matter. The rest of the week was a busy time. They had meetings with their lawyers, several follow-up meetings with stockbrokers and a number of discussions with several English business associates. Most of their work focused on the AATB branch and Sonoroma Corporation.

Sonoroma held the rights to a sound system for movie theaters similar to the Sensaround enhanced stereo system being installed in North America at that time. The English subsidiary was to market Sonoroma's product in Europe.

These meetings consumed their time until Thursday, May 12th. Robert was to travel to Amsterdam on Saturday while Tony and his business acquaintance were returning to Milan on the same day. Their mother and sister, Ivana, along with Tony's wife, Pattie and infant son, Anthony, had flown to Milan from Montreal and were waiting for his return planning to take a vacation in Italy.

On Tuesday morning Robert phoned Mr. Carlo Colombotti to arrange a meeting at his law office. Upon his arrival, he explained to the lawyer his trouble with Bear and asked how he could get his money from the bank. Mr. Colombotti was graciously apologetic, "There is no problem with the bank. We'll honor our commitments ..." He promised to look into the matter and sort it out quickly.

On Wednesday night, Robert and his business acquaintance, a consultant that Robert had recently hired for European affairs went out on the town to sample some of London's exciting nightlife. At the Hilton Hotel they met several beautiful American women. From there, they went on to a number of discos and they spent the balance of the evening partying. Arrangements were made to meet the women again on the weekend for more of the same. Of course, this necessitated changing their plans to remain in London over the weekend. They decided to take advantage of their extended stay by returning to Bear on Thursday afternoon. In the event that this visit was unsatisfactory, they had already arranged to see their lawyers to begin legal proceedings.

Tony was eager to leave London to join his wife but agreed to stay an extra day with Robert until Friday (the 13th!) to finish their business and work out their banking problems. None of them could know what this seemingly innocent delay was about to cost them.

Thursday morning dawned as a typically dull, drizzly London day. One final meeting had been arranged with a stockbroker named Singh. They suggested to Mr. Singh that their discussions take place over lunch. Singh agreed and took them to a restaurant in the Old City of London, in the financial district.

It was Robert's first meeting with Singh and although their primary focus was marketing the Sonoroma sound system, the conversation ranged broadly and was general in scope in order to get to know each other better. They talked about the financial situation in the world and in England. Robert told Singh about their larger corporate activities including MRSA. The discussions remained general and no decisions were reached about further business deals.

As lunch ended, Robert asked the waiter for the bill. When it arrived, in a flourish, Robert pulled out his American Express card and said, "I'll get it!" The waiter cleared his throat and informed the group, "I'm very sorry Gentlemen, but we do not take American Express."

Robert was taken aback but soldiered on, "Oh well, never mind, I will write you a cheque."

The waiter using his best stiff upper-lip style, replied, "I'm sorry, Sir, but we cannot take a personal cheque either."

The mood around the table suddenly shifted from relaxed and happy to very uncomfortable. Tony knew the group was short on cash and he rolled his eyes at Robert. All week long he had been pushing to start the lawsuit against Bear. Of all the bloody banks in London, Robert's business consultant to Euorpean affairs, Mario Berton, had to pick this fly-by-night outfit and now this embarrassment.

Singh jumped in, "Let me get the bill, please."

Robert said, "Would you? We're most grateful as we are a bit short of cash right now. I can have the money sent to your office this afternoon to cover it after we've been to our bank."

"That's fine. It's nothing really."

"Thank you so much. I will make sure you are reimbursed."

And so they parted on that basis.

Robert, Tony and Mario hailed a taxi and headed for Bear Securities. By this time, Tony was thoroughly pissed-off and rebuked his brother, "Why bother, Robert. Let's go straight to the lawyers and settle it that way."

"But Tony, Colombotti said he would take care of everything. We will go over there and if we can't get out money, we'll sue."

It was just before 3:00pm when they arrived in Waterloo Place and approached the lavish premises of Bear Securities. The door was locked and so Robert pressed the bell with the tip of his umbrella. After several moments, the door was opened by a clerk who admitted them to the bank.

They walked into the foyer. The bank appeared deserted with only the clerk and the Manager, a Mr. Mann, in sight. No other customers were present.

Robert addressed Mann whom he had met previously, "I'm here because I spoke to Mr. Columbotti. You are supposed to settle my account today."

Mann replied, "Yes, I know about it. If you don't mind waiting a few minutes; perhaps no more than twenty, one of our directors will be here and we should be able to clear up the matter."

"Fine, we'll wait then."

Mann turned and left the reception desk and returned to the administrative offices at tile rear of the bank. Tony sat down on a couch in the waiting area. Robert picked up a copy of the Financial Times and began to read.

After several minutes, Tony got up and began to pace. He had no patience to wait for this messed-up bank to put things right. He began to chat with Mario but became more and more irritated as the minutes ticked by. He looked at his watch. It was now 3:40 pm -- more than twenty minutes had passed since they had talked with Mann.

Tony addressed Robert and Mario, "I've had enough. I'm leaving right now for our lawyer's offices to begin proceedings. You two can stay here if you like. Should you finally get satisfaction, give me a call and I will cancel the suit. Otherwise, the case starts now." Tony turned and left the bank.

Almost immediately after Tony left the bank, the door to the street opened once again and six or seven burly, scruffy-looking fellows in casual street-clothes walked in.

Knowing that London can be a pretty rough place and being streetwise himself, Robert smiled at Mario and out of the side of his mouth joked in Italian, "Look Mario, I've created such a commotion in this bank that they have brought in their bouncers to throw us out!"

Mario laughed and they both returned to reading their papers.

The strangers walked by and disappeared into the inner offices of the bank. After a few minutes, Robert felt someone breathing down his neck. He turned to find himself staring into the eyes of a big, tall, white-haired, florid man. The fellow was flanked by two unkempt, pugnacious-looking characters.

Robert was annoyed that this fellow was standing so close to him that he could feel his breath. So he turned to him and in a very angry voice said, "Yes, what can I do for you?"

The man to whom Robert spoke took a step back, "We are the police. We are here to investigate this bank and we're talking with all their clients."

Robert motioned to the couch where there was plenty of room, "If that's the case, gentlemen, please sit down. I'm one of the bank's clients. I am waiting here to settle a matter with my account and have it closed. I'm expecting one of the directors here very shortly."

The white-haired fellow replied, "Our investigations are quite confidential. Our office is just around the corner from here. It will only take about ten minutes of your time if you wouldn't mind talking to us at our offices."

Robert did not want to miss his meeting with the director to sort out his account, "Are you certain it won't take very long. I don't want to miss this fellow" referring to the bank director he was expecting at any moment.

The officer assured him they wouldn't be long. The big man spoke in a kind of threatening manner as he insisted they accompany him. Reluctantly, Robert and Mario collected their coats, umbrellas and briefcases and began to walk toward the door with the apparent police officers. Mario was obviously perplexed about the situation and asked Robert what was going on. Robert explained that these men wanted to ask them questions about the bank but even as he answered Mario, he began to question in his mind why the men had not produced any ID. There was certainly nothing about their outward appearance that would suggest they were police officers.

As they approached the door, Robert could hear what sounded like walkie-talkies and radios on the other side. He walked out the door to be greeted by an extraordinary sight. The square was filled with uniformed police, bystanders and motor vehicles. There were at least five blue police vans. Helmeted police in riot gear stood surrounding each of the trucks and at various points around the perimeter of the square. Other officers were in control of dogs. It was quite the crowd. People in some of the other office buildings were looking out their windows or were peeking from behind their doors, the cackle and crackle of walkie-talkies filled the air, the scene was simply organized confusion, Robert smiled briefly, not realizing what was about to come his way.

At about the same time Robert was leaving the bank, Tony was walking briskly towards the lawyers' offices. He was only about 400 to 500 yards from the bank and the street was very crowded. Suddenly someone came up to Tony and said, "Something has happened at the bank. You'd better get back there."

"What ...?" Tony had no idea who this person was or how he knew that he'd just been at the bank but, instinctively, he reacted with concern since Robert and Mario were back there. He began to run back in the direction of the bank.

As he rounded the corner and saw the same scene in the square that had greeted Robert, he immediately thought the worst, "It's an IRA bombing!" Fearful for Robert, he ran faster. Beyond the mess of police and vans, Robert could see Tony running towards the bank. He looked to be in quite a state.

Tony gasped for breath as he spoke to Robert, "What's happened?"

Robert realized Tony was concerned and he reassured him, "I don't know what this is all about, but nothing has happened to us. Everything is okay." He motioned towards the plainclothes officers he was with and said, "These are the police. We are going to talk with them for a few minutes. They are conducting an inquiry on the bank and ..."

Before Robert could say anything more to his brother he felt himself lifted bodily off the ground by both his arms. He was shoved unceremoniously into the back of a nearby car. On either side of him were two brawny fellows with two more in the front seats.

It happened so quickly, he had no time to protest. He managed to get a quick look over his left shoulder and saw Tony and Mario being shoved into two other vehicles. He yelled out, "Hey, what's going on here?"

The response to this protest came from one of the bullies beside him who pushed his head forward to face the front of the vehicle. One of the guys in the front seat barked out. "Shut your mouth!"

Tony's situation at that moment was similar to his brother except he was out of breath from having run into circumstances for which he had no context, "What is going on? Where am I being taken!!?" he bellowed.

Each question was greeted with complete silence or he was roughed up by one of the four goons in the car who pushed him into submission and told him to shut up. Although Robert had said these people were police, it hardly seemed possible given the kind of treatment he was receiving. It flashed through Tony's mind that he was being kidnapped. But why? And by whom? None of this made any sense. These guys appeared to be rough characters. What little they did say was interspersed with epithets and coarse, threatening language.

Speeding through the streets of London, Robert was alone with his captors. There was no sign of the cars containing his brother or Mario since leaving the square. Robert was in total confusion. Nothing that had occurred prior to being tossed into the car had prepared him for this situation. None of his questions were answered by his captors. He wondered if he should be afraid. Funnily enough, he found himself becoming separated mentally from his present status.

He felt like someone who had been channel-surfing until a TV news item popped up which he now watched dispassionately. He tried to force his mind to accept what was happening as real, but his brain kept switching to observer mode, reviewing the action so far and speculating what was coming next.

They drove a considerable distance which Robert guessed at about forty minutes. He thought they must be on the outskirts of London, in an old commercial area with the streets filled with what appeared to be warehouses.

London can look bleak at its very brightest. Robert was struck by how dreary it was just then, among these old grey buildings with the overcast sky and the falling rain.

The car pulled up to the back of a building that Robert took to be a factory. He was hustled out of the car, escorted into the building, led down a long hall and then pushed through an iron doorway. The door was slammed shut with a metallic ring. Robert listened to the voices of his miscreant escorts recede down the hall. He sat for a long period of time and did nothing. He was in a severe state of shock.

Tony and Mario were undergoing similar fates.

None of them yet understood that they were in the hands of Scotland Yard's finest, the Serious Crime Squad known as the CID. This unit was specifically setup to counteract terrorist activities and other serious criminal activities such as organized crime. The treatment being dished out was reserved for the worst of the terrorists. The detectives involved thought they knew exactly what they were doing and exactly to whom they were doing it. The standard drill for extreme terrorists had been used -- CID pounced without warning, immediately isolated the individual suspects from each other and told their captives nothing, either about who they were, what their intentions were, where the prisoners were being taken or what was coming down the road.

While such procedures may be effective ways to deal with outright terrorism, it is completely devoid of any consideration for human rights. And so in this circumstance, three non-terrorist businessmen, two of them, Canadian-Italians and the other an Italian professional, sat in their separate cells and wondered what had befallen them.

Tony found himself in a cell similar to that of his brother. It is not like Tony to sit passively even in a seemingly hopeless situation. He examined his cell: it consisted of tile-covered walls and an iron door. The only furnishings were a plank for sitting or sleeping and an open toilet. In the center of the ceiling, there was a light recessed behind a wire opaque plastic cover. The cell was small, cold, dark and dirty. There was a drain in the floor. The only cleaning the cell appeared to get was when it was hosed down to remove the vomit of some drunken inmate. Tony took off his shoe and began to pound on the door yelling at the top of his lungs.

In his cell at Limehouse police station, Robert, Tony's identical twin, emerged from his state of shock to commence the same activity. His cell was like something from the medieval times. The door had a small slotted window about a foot from the top with a metal cover plate that could be open or closed from the outside. On the wall, he could see a push-button bell but nothing happened when he put his finger on it. There was considerable noise and activity on the other side of the door. He could hear people talking, yelling, doors slamming, movement. The sounds from the other side of his door could easily have been those of a busy factory. He was still uncertain whether he was in police custody. "What the hell is this?" he thought, "If these are the police then why are they treating me like this?"

This couldn't be lawful, to lock him away in a jail cell without any reason. He was very confused but the shock of the situation was now giving way to anger. He placed his finger once again on the buzzer by the door and kept it there. With his other hand, he began to bang on the door. The noise from his banging agitated him even more. It was like being inside a cave. Most of the sound came back at him reverberating off the wall. He wondered if any of his racket was penetrating beyond the door.

Suddenly the window on the door was slid open. Framed in the slot was the fresh, clean-shaven face of a uniformed man about 22 years old. He said, "Hey fellow, why are you making so much noise?"

"Who the hell are you? Let me out of here!"

The young face didn't reply. The window was shut and the face disappeared.

Robert resumed his banging. Twice more, the same officer came to the window and told him to be quiet. On the third trip, the guard yelled at Robert, "I'm not in charge of you. I can't talk to you until someone in charge comes along." That was the last visit to the door. Eventually Robert got tired of banging and stopped.

Sometime later, the iron door opened and a tray of food was slid in on the floor before the door slammed shut again. On the tray Robert found eggs and baked beans. He wasn't yet hungry enough to eat so he left the meal untouched.

For the first few hours, Robert stood at the door or paced in his cell but eventually he became tired to the point where he had to consider sitting or laying on the plank. He tried to arrange his jacket beneath him so his head was pillowed. His natural aversion to filth inevitably gave way to his need for sleep.

This scene continued for three nights and days. Meals arrived at regular intervals but the persons bringing the food would not speak to him. By Sunday Robert was very aware that he hadn't washed or shaved for four days. The waiting for whatever was going to happen next was interminable.

After observing his guards' uniforms Robert came to the conclusion that he was being held by the police. Being alone for all that time caused his imagination to race all around. His thoughts included such ideas as, "England has been attacked. There must be a war and they think I'm an enemy alien."

He tried to arrive at a rational conclusion for what was happening to him but his mind kept returning to the thought that there was nothing personal about his predicament. Something of great global importance must have occurred.

The other concern on Robert's mind was his family: his mother, his brothers and his sister. He wondered if any of them knew where he was. He had been expected in Amsterdam that weekend and Tony was to be in Milan. When they failed to show up and to communicate their whereabouts, he knew his family would become very worried.

The Beginning

IN THOSE BLEAK days of the war between 1940 and 1943, Dora Carenza Papalia would watch. She would stand at her window looking through binoculars as the Allies and what was left of the Italian Navy and the German tactical air support fought their battles in the Ionian Sea off the coast of Calabria at the toe of the boot that is Italy. She watched the battles and feared for her children.

The war had already been difficult with her husband, Raffaele, away with the Navy much of the time. Raffaele was a *Maresciallo Carabinieri*, a high-ranking policeman before the war. The family coal business founded by her husband's father was suffering from lack of management during Raffaele's absences. Good workers were almost impossible to find with all the able-bodied men consorted into Mussolini's army. Now she wondered if the Allied invasion was successful and Italy was defeated what the future would hold for her children, her two sons and her daughter.

Dora was thirty-three. Her husband was only a few years older. In 1943, they would have been married for 15 years. Throughout the war, Raffaele served with the Italian Navy in a division that patrolled the Straits of Messina between Sicily and the mainland.

Following the invasion of Sicily and the Allied movement onto the Italian mainland during the summer and fall of 1943, the Italian government was in disarray. In July, a coup d'etat replaced Mussolini as Head of the government. Shortly thereafter, Mussolini disappeared from the Italian General Headquarters. Marshall Badoglio ostensibly took command of the government and authorized signing a treaty of surrender with the Allied forces on September 3rd. But in fact, the Germans still occupied almost all of Italy and certainly controlled all activity in Rome.

Badoglio, together with the King, and several other generals managed to escape from Rome before the announcement of the surrender on September 8th. But, Kesselring, the German Commander-in-Chief in Italy, acted swiftly following the announcement, taking as prisoners numerous lesser generals and others from the Italian General Headquarters. Over 150 senior officers from headquarters were captured by the Germans.

The effect of the surrender together with the lack of administrative continuity left the Italian forces in limbo. One day they were fighting side-by-side with the Germans, the next they were supposed to assist the Allies in their occupation of the country. The Germans were now regarded as their enemies.

After the Allied occupation of Sicily, Raffaele and his troops had been ordered to withdraw to Naples to await further orders. As the Allies crossed over onto the Italian mainland, still no orders were received. Rumors abounded that Italy had surrendered but confirmation could not be obtained. Raffaele grew increasingly worried. Here he sat in German-occupied Naples while his family was in Calabria, the first area to be occupied by the Allied Forces.

Desertions over the past few weeks were prevalent as no information or directions were coming out of the High-Command. Il Duce's disappearance increased the doubts and concerns still further.

With the public announcement of the surrender on September 8th, Raffaele decided to act. Perhaps he had been foolish to wait so long. The Germans in the area were now unpredictable; if he was caught they would probably take him prisoner or perhaps he would be killed as a traitor. He was hundreds of miles from the German-Allied front and the country between Naples and Calabria was rough and mountainous with few roads. Together with all of his ship mates, Raffaele abandoned his post and went into hiding in Naples.

Two events occurred in quick succession that gave him some encouragement. On September 9th, the Allies landed at Salerno only thirty miles south of Naples. Then several days later, Kesselring announced that he would offer all Italian troops amnesty rather than taking them prisoner. The amnesty required that the Italian troops within the German-occupied territory must surrender their arms following which they would be ordered to return to their homes. It quickly became obvious however, that the amnesty was much less than absolute. Any Italians suspected of desertion or anyone considered to be assisting the Allies through the Italian underground were detained and shipped north to POW camps.

Raffaele decided to risk one aspect of the amnesty provisions; to keep his service revolver for his trip in case it was needed. He would be passing through German and Allied occupied territory but now that he was no longer engaged in direct hostilities, he believed he had a good chance to make it home.

He was very familiar with the countryside between his home and Naples. At Salerno, he was able to avoid the front lines by traveling well inland along mountain trails between the small villages where the locals were friendly and shared their meager resources and food with him. Occasionally he walked on the roads but immediately took to the mountains whenever he thought there was danger of an encounter with the Germans. The Germans had done a thorough job of destroying bridges and planting mines to slow the Allies as they advanced up the country. Eventually he was forced to remain off the roads.

During the first two weeks of the invasion, the Allies had barely moved sixty miles because of the serious demolition conducted by the retreating Germans. As he approached the Allied front, Raffaele used extreme caution. He traveled only in daylight and finally holed up for several days in a small town inland from Lagonegro.

n September 17th, after the Allies had moved further on and had secured their position at Lagonegro; he came down from the mountains. Now his journey was swift. From here to the south, the Allies has repaired the bridges sufficiently to allow him to move with ease along the roads. The Allied troops behind the front lines were friendly and did not impair his trip. He was able to walk the sixty miles down the coastal roads to his home in six days.

About 10 miles south of Pizzo, he again turned inland through the mountain passes to shorten the trip to seven miles rather than the thirty miles required to go to Reggio Calabria and around the tip of Italy. Mid-morning of September 29th, 1943, Raffaele Papalia found himself on a high ridge near the base of Mount Aspromonte. To the southeast, the land fell away from this high point a distance of about one mile to his home town, Staiti, nestled comfortably at the foot of the mountain. Raffaele could see the rooftops of Staiti in the valley and beyond that, much farther away, the deep blue of the Ionian Sea.

The town looked so peaceful from such a distance. The buildings appeared to be intact -- its isolation had kept his home from destruction or harm by either the Germans or Allied forces.

He began his descent towards the town and an hour later he walked into the town square. He saw an American Army jeep and a couple of desultory-looking soldiers talking to some children. One or two people called out to him in greeting and he waved in return but continued towards his home. He walked in the front door and called to his wife, "Dora, its Raffaele. I'm home."

Dora quickly descended the stairs and the two embraced warmly both so relieved to see that each other was unharmed. They talked for a long time telling each other about their separate experiences over the past few months during the collapse of their country. Raffaele learned that all of the children were well and except for the replacement of German troops by Allied troops in the square, the town was essentially untouched by the war.

Over the next few weeks, the Papalias adjusted to being reunited. Raffaele tried to turn his attention to working his coal, salt and tobacco concessions but he was acutely aware that the war was not yet over.

Mussolini had resurfaced in late September about the same time that Raffaele had returned home. Hitler had rescued him and placed him in charge of a puppet government in the northern areas. In the south, a coalition government ruled but the Allies continued to occupy their home and a stagnant peace prevailed. Little in the way of leadership or direction was provided by the Southern government throughout 1944 while in the north civil war was tearing the country apart.

The family was thoroughly sick of the war. Disheartened by the chaos, they yearned for real peace so they could start rebuilding their concessions into a viable enterprise and get their lives back in order.

Dora was expecting another child due by the end of January 1945. It was not the best of times for a new baby, but in their closed and ordered Catholic world, it was accepted by Dora and her husband with grace and wisdom as inevitable. Raffaele resented the difficulties in providing for his family. So many goods were scarce or nearly impossible to obtain. He continued to struggle on since to do otherwise would be the demise of himself and his family.

❧

On January 23rd 1945, Dora gave birth, not to one child, but rather unexpectedly to two healthy, identical-twin boys. Raffaele looked at his two new sons and saw that both were strong and aware. He was pleased and surprised that two babies had come along at this time but was thankful that amongst all the devastation and destruction, some joy and happiness in his healthy children had entered their lives. He marveled at the similarity between the two boys; he himself found it difficult to tell them apart at first. The couple named their two boys, Antonio and Roberto.

It was as if their birth heralded the beginning of the end to the interminable war, for within three months, the war in Italy came to an end. The Allies and the Italian partisans had pushed Hitler's troops back to Austria. At the end of April, the news reached the south that Mussolini was dead; his mutilated body hung up for all to see in a square in Milan.

A few weeks later, in May, the Germans surrendered and all over the world people issued a collective sigh of relief. In Staiti there was no immediate change except the exodus of the occupying troops in the later half of 1945.

Raffaele was under serious pressures by the changes brought about by the war on the value of his business holdings. During his father's time, the monopoly concessions were worth a small fortune and they ensured his family a place in the "borghese". But with his father's death, succession duties took out a chunk and the division of the inheritance amongst himself and his siblings further diluted their profitability. He hoped that with peace he would be able to rebuild his business into something of value.

During the year immediately following the war, life was relatively tranquil in the little town of Staiti. As the Twins grew from infancy into childhood, their characters began to develop and manifest themselves. The older children in the family doted on the Twins. They were considered to be special. As the youngest members of the family and as identical twins, they were given an uncommon and exceptional status in their home and in the town. Both family and strangers paid them much attention and the Twins in response to this attention learned to perform.

They attended a convent school and were doted on by the nuns who regarded them affectionately because they were extremely bright and so outgoing. It was a joy to teach them but at the same time the classroom could be dangerous as the Twins were little terrors. The standard trick performed by many identical twins became their standard fare and so they often reversed roles playing each other, confusing their teachers and disrupting the entire class.

Springtime in Calabria and Sicily can be astonishingly beautiful. The sea and mountains dominate. During the long, clear evenings the reflected sunlight on the hillsides gives the land a purple glow from whence the area derives its nickname "Costa Viola" -- the Violet Coast. There is a profusion of greenery and colorful blossoms in the warm weather of spring. The sea is a delicious, placid turquoise joined to the land by ribbons of white sand. Beyond the beaches as the land rises, the climate is hot and dry. On the plateaus and in the valleys on the sun-soaked hillsides are the orange, lemon and olive groves. Elsewhere one can see the vineyards of grapes for commercial wine-making and commercially grown jasmine blossoms.

One bright day in early April, 1950, the Twins were filled with the effect of spring fever derived from such splendor. They felt it was torture to expect children to remain indoors on days so lovely as these. So they took it upon themselves to inform all their classmates that a school picnic had been scheduled for the next day. Everyone went home that day filled with joy. In the morning, the children arrived at the school dressed in their play clothes in anticipation of the wonderful day ahead to romp in the hills. Their parents had packed each child a picnic lunch --it was all set to be a glorious day except for one thing, the Twins had planned the day, not the nuns.

But when the nuns learned of the pseudo-plans, they decided that rather than disappoint the children, they would take the school on the picnic. The children played all day in the sun and the nuns sat on the soft grass, watching the children and relaxing. It was such a marvelous day that the boys were never disciplined for the matter. They brought away from this episode the knowledge that sometimes it pays to take the initiative and push authority to its limits!

❧

During the two year period of occupation by the German and Allied troops, Italy descended into a state of almost total collapse. Railways, roads, bridges and communication systems were systematically destroyed by the occupying forces. In the years that immediately followed World War II, nothing happened to strengthen the economy of southern Italy. While parts of the north were beginning to recover, the south remained terribly depressed. In Naples, the slums filled with people; poverty was the worst of the Twentieth Century. There was talk of families starving to death while living in caves and cellars.

Raffaele and his family were not quite as poor as that, but it was a time of severe struggle to make ends meet. The loss of infrastructure in the south caused numerous problems for Raffaele to transport his products to market. The rebuilding of the Systems was proceeding at an inordinately slow pace. Rampant inflation was eating away at his profits and made it impossible to plan effectively. He shook his head in disgust at the progressive increase in the cost of each new order from his suppliers. Items that before the war cost fifty lira were now at three thousand lira -- an increase in the cost of living of over 60 times between 1938 and 1948.

There was also on-going worry that the economic reforms being proposed during this reparation period would actually be implemented in the south. The government was considering expropriation of his concession licenses and Raffaele knew that they did not have the ability or will to provide satisfactory compensation. He believed he was going to be wiped out and his wife watched as he became more remote and depressed. She saw the extreme worry in his eyes whenever he came home each night.

By 1948, although only 41, Raffaele began to suffer frequent angina attacks. His doctor told him to rest but he could not do so as long as he had a family to support. In the summer of 1950 after a sudden brief illness, Raffaele Papalia succumbed to his heart problems. And so at the age of 38, Dora was left a widow to care for five children aged 5 to 19 years old.

After the funeral, Dora traveled to Reggio to speak with the family lawyer about settling Raffaele's estate. But Raffaele had neglected to make a will and that meant the administration would be lengthy and expensive. Other members of her husband's family were to share in the estate. At the end of the process, she was able to retain only their home and furniture and a small land-holding containing olive and orange groves. She essentially had no viable means to provide a steady income for her family.

When Dora became fully aware of her circumstances, she quickly decided on a plan of action. She had learned from her husband that to wait for things to improve on their own was rarely useful. She called her children to her in the sitting room. The two older boys, Adolpho and Giuseppe, sat on the floor at her feet. Her daughter, Ivana, sat across from her in the large easy chair. The five year old twins were distributed between her lap and Ivana's. She explained to them that they must leave their home. Their father's brother, a successful surgeon in Catania, had offered them lodgings with him if they needed assistance. She felt at this point, she must have the comfort and support of a family, now that Raffaele was gone. Some of her sisters were also living in Sicily and by moving to Catania, she would see them more often.

The notion of leaving Staiti did not bother Dora too much. This was her husband's village and she had settled here after their marriage. In her youth, she had done considerable traveling with her family who owned a circus. She had seen most of Northern Africa and Italy while she was still very young.

Although the children had heard many romantic stories from their mother about her own itinerant youth filled with travel, they did not respond well to the proposed move. Even the older children had rarely been out of their small mountain village. Everything and everyone they had known was here in Staiti. The thought of living in a city the size of Catania filled them with horror.

The two little boys did not fully appreciate what was taking place, but they too became upset when they saw the dark looks on their brothers' faces and heard the crying of their sister. Dora was saddened by her children's unhappiness but she realized none of them understood how little choice she had in the matter.

❧

Within a few short months, Dora managed to sell her land, her home and some of her furniture. She moved her family and herself and the remainder of their worldly possessions to her brother-in-law's home in a small coastal village in the shadow of Mount Etna. Ognina located only a few miles on the outskirts of Catania.

Her brother-in-law and his family welcomed them warmly into their home. But Dora was aware that there was an extra six mouths to feed. While she could see that things here were not as stagnant or hopeless as in rural Calabria, she was not the type of woman who could be dependent for long on the charity of her in-laws. She had a strong streak of initiative and independence. Soon after their arrival, she asked her brother-in-law to help find a small business she could buy with the proceeds from the sale of her home. Thereafter, she and her children could work together to run the business and sustain themselves. Ivana, her daughter was almost twenty, while the two older boys were seventeen and twelve. It was only Antonio and Robert who were still too young to help out in making the family living.

Her brother-in-law was able to find and negotiate the purchase of a small restaurant next to a Fiat assembly plant. The eldest son, Giuseppe, took on much of the responsibility for running the business. Together with Adolpho and Ivana, he and Dora developed their road-side café into a welcome stop for many travelers through this beautiful region.

Giuseppe added a gas bar to their road-side stop; he and Adolpho oversaw a string of employees as they pumped gas, changed oil, repaired engines and fixed flat tires on the cars going to and from Catania. There was much traffic on this road as it led to Catania from the main ferry slip to the mainland. The addition of the gas bar caused many more people to stop at the restaurant. It wasn't long before they were making their own version of the wonderful Sicilian gelato (ice cream) for the tourists and travelers who stopped for gas.

The family had been in Catania only for a brief time when one of their maternal aunts suggested a possible match for Ivana. The young man she had in mind was in his early twenties and had immigrated to Canada several years before. His name was Frank Feoli. He was back in Calabria for a visit and so Dora took Ivana to meet him. They hit it off well from that first meeting. By mid 1951 after seeing each other on a handful of occasions, but carrying on their courtship by letter, Ivana and Frank were married. She moved with Frank to settle in the city of Montreal in Canada.

The restaurant became a hang-out for some of the Germans and Americans working in the area at the newly-developing oil fields. Robert and Tony would race down to the restaurant after school was let out at 1:00 pm. They would make and serve the ice cream or sit behind the cash counter and make change.

There was a big man, a Texan, who stopped at the gas bar to fill up his big, new Buick with gas on a regular basis. He would come into the restaurant each day for a drink in the cool, shaded haven away from the scorching sun. He always got a kick out of the two kids, not yet teenagers, behind the cash counter who were handling their business transactions and making change in a manner well beyond their years.

The Texan was one of the workers in the new oil fields in Sicily. There was an old phonograph in the corner where he liked to sit, nurse his drink and listen to the music. One day he came to the restaurant with a present. It was a 78 rpm record and he gave it to the Twins. He made them realize that he wanted them to play it on the phonograph.

Robert put the record on the machine. He did not understand the lyrics but he liked the tune very much. It was different reminding him of the music he heard in the American western movies which played from time to time at the theater in Catania. He would listen to the record over and over even when the Texan wasn't there. Tourists who stopped by on their way were often surprised to hear *The Yellow Rose of Texas* playing inside this small Italian road-side café.

It wasn't long before the Texan got into the habit of throwing his car keys at the boys whenever he came into the place for a fill-up and his evening meal. He would sit inside while his car was being serviced. When it was ready to be moved from the pumps, Tony or Robert would jump behind the wheel of the vehicle to move it off to the side. They fell in love with that big, beautiful car. It was huge compared to most of the European motor cars they saw every day: It had lots of chrome and plush upholstery. They learned all of the basics about driving a car before they were eleven years old.

Dora missed her daughter very much and always looked forward to receiving letters from Ivana in Canada. Things sounded very good and exciting in Montreal. Frank and Ivana already had their own house and a big, new car much like the one the boys loved so much. Within a couple of months of the wedding, Ivana was pressing her mother to come to live with them. She missed her family and wanted them to join her in Canada.

Dora resisted the move initially but eventually began to examine the life she had in Sicily with her sons. The road-side stop certainly made them a living, but what of their future? She could not see her sons waiting on tourists all their lives. There was clearly more opportunity for them in North America.

As soon as the decision was made to immigrate to Canada, Robert and Tony were sent off to a new school in the heart of Catania. Every morning bright and early, they took a bus into the city. They began English lessons at this school in addition to their other subjects in preparation for the move to Canada. This was an exciting change for the Twins --for the first time they traveled regularly into the city without someone to look out for them. They loved Catania; it was an older city, totally unique in so many ways. There was the same overwhelming sense of heat and light that prevails in all southern Italian cities but in Catania the heat was greater as the buildings were made out of the black lava rock from Etna's eruptions. The somber antiquity of the architecture contrasted simply with the vibrancy and liveliness typical of the southern Italians who lived there.

Many afternoons, when school was let out at 1:00 pm, they would stay in the city for several hours before catching the bus home. If there was a matinee of a new American film they would go to see it, trying to pick up the American words and phrases as they read the Italian sub-titles.

They often wondered whether Montreal would live up to Catania as a city. Would it be as big and bright and as exciting as Catania? They were at an age when they were ready for new adventures. From what they learned from the tourists and the movies, they believed there were many new and exciting things for them to look forward to. They could hardly wait until it was time to leave.

Virtually every family in southern Italy in the 1950s had at least one family member who had gone to North America. After the destruction of Italy during the war followed by the failure of southern Italy to rebound into any semblance of economic recovery, the Papalias became part of the massive emigration of people who left their homeland in hope of greater opportunities elsewhere.

The Interrogation

ON SUNDAY, JUST before noon, the door opened. Standing in front of Robert were two of the men he had seen in the bank on Thursday. One of them said, "My Chief wants to see you."

"Oh, yeah? Well, I want to talk with him as well. Take me to him immediately."

The two cops grunted and then led him away to a waiting car for a drive of about twenty minutes duration. The car finally came to a relatively tall building for London and the police officers took him up three or four flights of stairs. Robert was directed into a room where he recognized the white-haired man from the bank standing behind him. Beside the white-haired man was another person whom Robert did not know. The two escorting cops entered the room with Robert and closed the door.

During his short ride, Robert had been able to observe that the world had not changed since his imprisonment four days earlier. There was no sign of war or disruption in London. He began to think this must be one giant mistake. If so, there was going to be hell to pay. At this point he still believed that England was a country which respected human rights -- a place where the rule of law reigns supreme. Unfortunately, Robert was about to discover the extent to which England's private little police army, known as the CID, strays from the hallmark of British justice.

When he entered the room Robert thought it important to try to retake control. He looked at the fellow behind the desk and said, "If you are a policeman, show me your credentials. Tell me exactly what your problem … is?"

Before he could finish speaking, one of his escorts standing behind him slapped him hard across the side of his face. Then he was pushed into a wooden chair. Robert's head reeled from the blow and he clung tightly to the arms of the chair to steady himself. The man in charge came out from behind his desk and sat on the desktop facing Robert. He said, "Now then, where are the drugs? Where are the forged currencies?" The questions came from all sides but mostly from the guy in charge.

"What are you talking about? What forged currencies?"

The questions made no sense to Robert. These were questions for which he had no answers. He said, "I don't know what you are talking about. I would like to speak to a lawyer and I wish to contact my Embassy."

This comment was greeted by guffaws and smiles from the characters surrounding him in the room. They continued to pepper him with more questions and accusations. "We know you are in with Santoro and Baracchini."

Robert replied, "I have no idea what you are talking about."

The questioning went on in this vein for hours without stopping. Whenever, Robert said he didn't know what they were talking about, he was hit and slapped across the head at the whim of the two escorts behind him.

Some of the questions involved his company, Metals Research SA. When he gave them truthful answers, he was called a liar. He asked again and again for a lawyer but his request was always denied, ignored or ridiculed. Several hours into the interrogation after he had been cuffed and beat repeatedly, one of the escorts on his right momentarily moved in close to Robert's chair. Robert reached down grabbing his leg and pulled upward flipping his harasser onto the floor. As the man leapt from the floor, Robert could see hatred in his eyes. Although strengthened by his offensive action, he stiffened in anticipation of what was coming.

His arms were pinned to his sides from behind and the guy who had taken the spill came at him smashing his fist into Robert's face. Robert felt excruciating pain and a spattering of white spots covered over his field of vision. He felt his nose plug up with blood. He opened his mouth to breath but he could feel his warm blood dripping down his face into his mouth, onto his chin and then onto his clothes.

"Try that again, you fucker, and you are going to wish you were dead!"

With his nose throbbing and blood all over his face and clothes, the inquisition continued. It did not stop until 1:00 am of the next morning. During this time, each of the officers took breaks of ten minutes or so at regular intervals but there was no rest and no food or drink for their prisoner throughout the thirteen hour ordeal.

The session came mercifully to a close primarily because Robert's interrogators became exhausted. The interview had not gone well. Detective Inspector Edwin Ward was the white-haired man in charge of the interrogation. He found himself thinking what a tough little character this Papalia was. Ward was a product of east-end London -- tough part of the city in which to grow up. He had risen through the ranks the hard way, and felt himself to be as tough and devious as any of the criminals he apprehended.

He took pride in his reputation as a cynical and unpleasant person. It was helpful to have such a hard case reputation when dealing with the criminal element. In Ward's view, Robert and his brother were smart, thoroughly hardened little bastards. It was unlikely that they would ever admit to anything. The Italian, Berton, hardly spoke any English. Even with an interpreter present, they had been unable to unearth anything helpful. But that was okay, for Ward had learned over the years that when dealing with the worst sorts such as these, you don't have to get them to actually admit willingly to their crimes. Interrogations such as this one would usually persuade most suspects to open up enough to sign a confession eventually. So far, he hadn't been able to crack Berton or the Twins but Swinnerton had been very helpful.

Swinnerton was weak. After only a few hours of rough stuff, all they had to do was offer him a deal and he practically fell all over himself admitting to everything under the sun. It was obvious that he did not understand or know about some of the finer points of the fraud his cohorts had perpetrated. He had been recruited by these schemers on the basis that they were involving him in a legitimate business deal but when the police pointed out some of the problems with certain elements of these deals, Swinnerton confessed his belief that it had been a fraud all along.

There were also several documents evidencing the various transactions and corporate activities that proved beyond a shadow of a doubt that a massive fraud was being planned. Ward, himself, did not yet fully understand everything but once the interrogations were complete, he and his assistant would sit down with the Crown prosecutors and piece all of the elements together in way that would prove conspiracy.

Ward could not believe his luck in stumbling onto this scam. While conducting his surveillance of Bear Securities the previous week, these two Sicilian-looking guys walked into the picture. He had no idea who they were. Once they were identified as Canadians, he hadn't really expected much when he contacted the Canadian Criminal Intelligence Services (CSIS). But the information gleaned from the RCMP about the Papalias proved very interesting indeed.

Although they had no direct proof, the RCMP had been quite helpful in establishing exactly the sort of people the Yard was dealing with.

Last week he had been on the tail of a single bank-related fraud. This week he was about to blow an international Italian Mafia conspiracy wide open. His career was to be given a tremendous boost by these events. His superior had contacted him over the weekend to tell him a promotion was in the works to be awarded no later than Monday. The promotion would give him the required authority and credibility as he pursued the international elements of the case. The case was a major coup -- the kind every detective dreams about solving. This one had practically fallen into his lap and he was not going to let those slimy bastards get the best of him. He was going to get a conviction no matter what.

Ward left his office shortly after 1:30 am in the early hours of May 16th. He was going home to get some much needed rest before he tackled the interview with the remaining suspect, Robert's brother Tony. Maybe they would have more success with him than they had had with Robert.

❧

Tony Papalia sat looking into the pale blue, flint-like eyes of Edwin Ward. After five days of sitting in his cell, he had finally been brought to this room. They were asking him questions but none of them made any sense. "What do these idiots want?"

The man on his right enjoyed hitting Tony at each and every opportunity. He wore a heavy gold ring that caught Tony on the right side of his head with each blow delivered.

"Papalia, you think this is rough," spat out Ward, "Well, we've only just started the game."

"Fine", thought Tony, "these guys think they're tough. Well, I'll be even tougher!"

He said to Ward, "I can't answer your stupid questions. I demand to contact my Embassy and to speak to a lawyer."

Ward sneered, "You can't ask for a lawyer or an Embassy. You have no rights here, you little Wop, because I can keep you here forever and even if I were to kill you no one would know about it."

Ward narrowed his eyes and began to ask the same questions again.

Tony looked at him, "You are insane. I'm not giving any answers to anyone."

Tony saw Ward's eyes flash. He came out from behind the desk and approached Tony. Ward lifted his leg to kick but Tony was able to shift his body in time to avoid the impact and Ward ended up kicking the chair. A barrage of fists rained down on Tony from the two fellows on either side of him. But Tony silently rejoiced as he watched Ward pull back his leg in obvious pain.

Limping slightly, Ward stepped over to his desk and lit a cigarette. He took two puffs and removed it from his mouth. Holding the lit-end of the cigarette upwards he came towards Tony, "This is compliments of your friend Bryden of the RCMP."

Tony sat horrified as Ward brought the cigarette close to his face. He tried to move his head away from the hot ember but the other two men held him hard. One had him in a choke hold around his neck while the other grabbed his hair and forced his head back exposing his nostrils. He smelled the smoke first as Ward brought the cigarette up inside his right nostril. The pain seared through his body and he stiffened and then he screamed.

Even after the cigarette had been removed, the pain was unbelievable. Tony shouted, "You're a fucking idiot!" His eyes were tearing so heavily that he could no longer see the figures in the room clearly but through the blur he saw Ward move back behind the desk. Tony mind was racing, "So those RCMP bastards back in Canada are somehow involved in this. Even outside of Canada, they are still trying to destroy our lives."

He heard Ward ask again about a conspiracy between Bear Securities and Metals Research. Tony was still in tremendous pain, his nose running, his eyes streaming. He had no idea what the hell these bastards were talking about and so Tony sat sullenly and said nothing.

Ward was tired. It was obvious that he would get nothing out of this brother either. Seven hours and he still refused to talk and was still asking for a lawyer.

"Fine then, we don't need your answers." Ward turned to the fellow behind him and said, "Pawley, take this down. I'll ask the questions and then we will sort out the proper answers together."

Tony was taken to another room in the same building where he was directed to sit at a table. There was one officer who remained to watch him but he would not enter into any form of conversation with the prisoner. After some time, he was returned to the interview room where he was informed that the officers were very satisfied with his confession. Laughing loudly, one of the men waved a sheet of papers in Tony's face and sneered, "I don't suppose you would like to sign this?" The officer didn't expect a response and didn't wait for one. Instead, Ward instructed him and the other escort to return Tony to his cell.

The prisoner was returned to his cell at Limehouse police station a little after 7:30 pm. He was in pain and he was worried. The hand with the ring had come down on the side of his head many times. He couldn't help wondering if he was still in one piece. Whenever he moved his head a certain way, he felt something in his skull moving around as if loose. "Is it my imagination? Is the pain from my fried nostril and the soreness from the blows to my head causing me to imagine the worst? Or am I in danger of dying in this cell tonight?"

Well, if he was about to die, Tony decided he would not slip quietly into a coma. He took off his shoe and with the little strength he had left, began to bang on the cell door calling out for help. After what seemed hours, someone finally came to the door and peered in through the window slot. Tony looked up. "I need a doctor," he demanded.

The person left and Tony heard nothing from the other side of the door for a very long time. Much later that evening, Tony heard noises from the hallway. The door opened and in came a bespectacled, East Indian gentleman carrying a black medical bag. The door remained open while the examination took place. The guard watched from the doorway.

"I am a doctor. I am told you are ill."

Relieved that medical help had been summoned, Tony said, "Good Doctor, I need to be examined. Something may be broken in my head. I have been badly beaten by the police." Tony cradled the right side of his head as he spoke.

The Doctor looked at Tony. It was obvious to any reasonable person that he had been beaten up. He looked as if he had been dragged out of a ditch. His hair was askew. He smelled. His clothing was filthy and stained. He hadn't had a bath or a shave for five days. The Doctor looked at Tony and thought, "Why did they drag me down here so late at night to listen to the complaints of scum like this? It would appear there is no concussion. The prisoner is coherent and his eyes were focused and even. He is obviously in pain but I doubt whether he is going to lapse into a coma and die."

The Doctor looked at Tony and said, "It happens all the time. You will be all right." He stepped through the door and the guard slammed it shut behind him.

Tony sank to the bench and rested his head in his hands. He drew his legs up to his chest and finally escaped his pain through a fitful sleep.

❧

Following his interrogation, Robert was kept for an additional two nights at the building where they had examined him. The cell he was assigned at this site was extraordinarily hot, Robert wondered if the intense, uncomfortable heat was yet another way to torture a confession out of him.

On the third day, his guards came for him and took him down a long corridor to a holding area. A large number of people were seated together in a room waiting transportation. Robert spied Tony among the group; he looked terrible. It was obvious that he had been treated in at least the same fashion as he had. Robert called out to his brother in Italian, "Tony, how are you?"

Tony looked up, "How do I look?"

"Terrible."

"What's going on, Robert?"

One of the guards beside Tony barked at him that if he was going to talk to the others, he must speak in English.

Robert could now see Mario and Richard. Until that moment, it hadn't dawned on Robert that Richard would be arrested as well. He looked scared and stared at the floor when Robert greeted him.

All of them were escorted together into an adjacent interrogation room. All of the officers who had participated in the interviews were also present in the room. Additional uniformed guards stood at all the doors while others stood behind each prisoner. Tony recognized a senior officer standing behind a desk in the room. He had been present a number of times during his interrogation. He suspected this man was senior since the physical violence always ceased when he was present. He would step out for a minute, the cuffing and kicking would resume. Then there would be a knock on the door and the Big-Wig's reentrance would signal that everyone should be nice and friendly -- at least until he left again. But once the interrogators really got down to business, the big-shot did not return.

Today, he and two others behind the desk wore uniforms of high rank, with medals and marks of distinction on their chest. The remaining two men behind the desk were dressed in business suits.

Once they were all assembled, the senior officer identified himself as Chief Inspector Cator of Scotland Yard, CID Branch. He motioned to some officers in the corner by a camera, "Take the accused pictures and fingerprint them. Then we will read the charges to them."

The picture-taking and fingerprinting were soon completed and the four men were ordered to sit down in a row in front of the desk. Cator motioned to an officer beside him and the man began to read. He addressed each of the prisoners in turn and read the same series of charges to each.

Even after all of the beatings and the five days of isolation, Robert could not quite believe what was happening. When they brought him to this room and were finally getting to the point of all this, he'd been expecting something but he didn't really know what it would be. He heard the clerk saying …

"... conspiracy to defraud the Bank of England, the Treasury Department and the Department of Trade …"

"… conspiring together to defraud those people who might be induced to invest up to $365 million US dollars in Metals Research S.A ..."

What was this insanity? Conspiracy to defraud $365 million dollars! Then he heard another higher figure of $288 billion dollars. The numbers were unbelievable. Where did they dream up this stuff?

All of the tension and horror of the last few days had led to this moment; to hear these amazing absurdities being thrown at them by their accusers. All of the tension suddenly drained from Robert's body. The gods must surely be laughing at them right now. They were clearly in the hands of a "Monty Python" version of the Keystone Cops.

By the time the clerk began to read the charges for the third time to the third person being charged, the complete stupidity of the situation had become apparent to our two "Mafia" Twins. Robert looked over at Tony and as their eyes met, they couldn't help themselves. In unison, they each threw back their heads and began to laugh -- not gentle chuckles but deep gales of belly laughter that filled the room to drown out the droning clerk who was beginning to read the charges for the fourth time.

Growing Up in Canada

THE NECESSARY DOCUMENTS had been put into place and the tickets were bought. Dora arranged to send some of her dearest possessions and sold or disposed of the rest. She and her sons said good-bye to their family and friends and left the beautiful old-world city of Catania to travel to Naples in January 1957.

When they arrived in Naples, they boarded a huge ocean-liner for their trip across the Atlantic Ocean. After leaving Italy, the ship stopped in Portugal and then carried on to North America.

The Atlantic in the best of times is a dangerous and turbulent place in midwinter and this trip was true to form. The skies and seas were all tile shades of grey with intermittent storms of rain, sleet and snow. The sea was rough and, along with most passengers on board, Dora was forced to spend the major part of the voyage in bed suffering from acute seasickness. Shortly after, her two older boys, Adolpho and Giuseppe, succumbed as well.

Tony and Robert were eleven when the journey began and quickly found themselves almost the only occupants of the dining room. The crew spoiled them with rich foods and desserts, as no one else could keep down much of anything. During the crossing, the Twins celebrated their twelfth birthday; the cook made them a grand cake and the waiters and busboys assembled around their solitary table to sing Happy Birthday.

The boys truly were enjoying this trip. Seasickness didn't touch them. They were given full freedom to roam the decks including the inner workings of the ship. They even joined the Captain on the bridge to see him chart their course.

The vessel was of British registry and many members of the crew were English. The boys used this opportunity to practice some of the smattering of English they had acquired at school, but Italian would continue to be their sole language for many weeks after their arrival in Canada.

Early one morning, Tony came running into their cabin. To his brother, who was just rising, he exclaimed, "Robert, come quick. There is land out there."

Robert hurried to dress and together they went out on deck. The sharp bite of the cold sea winds hit their faces as they hung over the rail and looked at the distant brown, barren hills on the horizon that was soon to become their home. Overhead, they were greeted by the noisy calls of increasing numbers of sea gulls and other birds welcoming them to Canada.

They returned to their cabin to find their mother looking pale but sitting up for the first time in days. Their older brothers had recovered several days before as the rocking of the ship had subsided as it approached land.

With the proximity of land the ship's rolling eased and the spirits and health of the passengers began to improve. They returned to the dining room and began to take brisk walks on the deck bundled up against the harsh cold. The ship arrived in Halifax on January 28th on the dawn of a clear, bright but cold, day. They quickly cleared Immigration and Customs and boarded a train for Montreal. As the train proceeded through New Brunswick and they entered Quebec, they were able to get their first look at the landscape. The boys spent many hours peering through the frosty windows which they kept clear by blowing hot air and rubbing the ice from their small porthole.

Initially most of the country appeared uninhabited with deep snow everywhere. As they raced along the St. Lawrence River, they began to see farms and small villages that dotted the rivers edge. The first day's journey brought them to Quebec City, a city built on two levels. The older part of the city lay along the river's edge; above was a high promontory with a large plain and numerous buildings. There were many more lights in the twilight morning hours than they had ever seen in the southern towns of Italy. The site struck the boys with awe leaving an impression that would last with them for the rest of their lives.

As they approached Montreal, there were increasing signs of the new urban world that awaited them. The railway runs along the south shore of the island of Montreal and on the other side of the river they could see busy highways with cars more numerous and much larger than in Italy.

Finally they arrived at Central Station in Montreal. They made their way along the platform until they were directed up to the large hall that makes up this massive station. Dora gathered her family together and they walked through the large double-glass doors into the hall. There was a roped-off area in which many people were gathered waiting for family or friends from abroad. The oldest boy, twenty-three year old Giuseppe, spied his sister, Ivana, at the exact moment that she saw him. They all ran and hugged each other in joy. In the flash of a moment the family had been reunited. Dora was now reassured upon seeing her daughter and son-in-law, Frank. She found her surroundings strange and she could hear people talking to one another in various alien languages, although there were certainly many Italian tongues.

Frank introduced the family to his two bothers, Ralph and Joe. They had come to the station with their cars so there was room for everyone and the entire luggage for the drive home. They drove through the snowy streets down St. Catherine's Boulevard and up St. Hubert. This first glance of downtown Montreal with its snow, lights and modern buildings enthralled the Twins.

That first night in Canada was a festive occasion with a great feast of Italian home-cooking and hearty red wine. Everyone talked at once. They told their sister about the journey and about their plans for the future. Robert and Tony had everyone laughing with their exploits on board a ship full of sea-sick passengers except for themselves. Ivana and Frank began to instruct them about the way of life in Canada.

❧

For the time being, Dora and her sons, stayed with the Feolis in their duplex in the working class district of Montreal known as St. Leonard.

Frank told Giuseppe and Adolpho that he had asked around for jobs for them and had discovered a good chance for positions at a food distribution firm, loading trucks on the warehouse docks. An Italian friend of his told him to bring the young men around to see about finding them placements. Giuseppe was the oldest brother, full of adventure, and he was ready to begin his new life in this new world. Adolpho was the intelligent, quiet type who took things a little slower than his brother. Frank told him that if he worked hard and paid attention he would soon be able to find something better.

Montreal in 1957 was a vibrant and exciting city. Like most of North America, it was undergoing many transformations as the new cultural icons of television and rock and roll music began to have increasing impact. The tremendous growth rate sparked by the influx of immigrants from Europe and around the world made the city of Montreal a very cosmopolitan place indeed. Optimism reigned supreme especially among the hard-working immigrant communities.

A young reformer was elected Mayor of Montreal in 1957 -- Jean Drapeau. His campaign based on anti-corruption, swept him into power with a huge mandate from the population. He quickly succeeded in obtaining the resignation of the Chief of Police and managed to organize a badly needed road-building operation. Unfortunately, he was not entirely successful in some of his more ambitious anti-corruption projects. Many of the old-boy clubs that existed in the city hierarchy were not happy with his attempt to destroy the system of patronage and pay-offs they had setup.

The cultural makeup of Montreal is primarily English and French. In the province, French is the clear majority but in Montreal, the English represent a very substantial minority position approaching forty-five percent. At the time, they held most of the positions of power and for the most part, constituted the moneyed-elite of society. The language of business in Montreal was English, and so most people from other parts of the world who poured into the city in the 50s and 60s, sent their children to the English school systems. This created an uneasy and partisan disharmony in the working-class districts of Montreal between the French and immigrant Europeans whom the French called les autres. Later these groups grew to become a significant part of the Quebec culture known as the Allophones.

Jobs were plentiful, however. In addition to being Canada's largest city, Montreal was becoming the transportation centre on the Easter seaboard of Canada. The St. Lawrence Seaway mega-project was in the process of being completed bringing millions of dollars into the Montreal economy in addition to fueling a boom in other service-related industries.

The excitement of Montreal with its cultural diversities, its exploding economy and its vibrant youth culture was to have an everlasting effect on Robert and Tony. As twelve year olds entering a new age and world their first impressions of North American life were Elvis Presley, snow, Marlon Brando, lots of colorful lights, more snow, neon and glitter, more snow again and lots and lots of big cars.

The Twins were taken to the local English Catholic elementary school. After consultation with the Brother in charge, they were placed in Grade Three to give them an opportunity to learn English without falling behind in their other studies. So their first day in a Canadian school was rather odd and they were very glad to have each other for support. They found themselves in a room full of children all younger by several years. Tony remembers watching the nun who was their home room teacher, making a speech to the class about their new classmates but it was in a language that was not yet understood. By her hand motions, it was apparent that she wanted them to sit down and so they took their places. During that day and for several thereafter, they were bewildered, but they watched, they paid attention, and they learned quickly.

During recess and while at play at lunch in the school yard, the Twins learned the most English. Only by participation and communicating in a friendly environment can one hope to learn a new language fully. Soon what they picked up from their classmates and friends began to impact on their performance in class.

In the evenings after school, they would return to their extended family. Aldolpho and Giuseppe had each obtained work at the food distribution warehouse just as their brother-in-law had predicted. They returned home from work each day tired and with ravenous appetites. Robert and Tony assisted their brothers in learning English by instructing them in the phrases they had learned at school. Now that the older boys had jobs and with the assistance of Ivana and Frank, the burden of providing for her family was lifted from Dora. She was able to spend her days at home with her daughter caring for their home and preparing the meals for the men when they came home from work.

Tony and Robert were always very athletic as kids, and in Italy, just like other boys, they had played football (soccer) all the time. But in their first few months in Montreal, the weather was too harsh to play. The snow stayed on the ground until late March and after that there were many weeks of thaw and mud when it wasn't possible to play on grassy areas. During these cold, dreary days, Dora taught her two sons how to play the guitar. It was a fortuitous coincidence that the instrument she had learned to play over twenty years before as an accompaniment for the folk music of southern Italy had now become the number one instrument of choice for the new generation of popular musicians in North America.

Elvis Presley was at his height in 1957. He had a string of Top-40 hits behind him and he was plugging a generation into the new music of rock and roll. The Twins started to listen to all the radio stations that played his music and did their best to mimic his songs as they learned to play the guitar. That first winter, they were very content to practice their music and learn the English lyrics to Presley's songs.

By June 1958, they were well on their way to becoming fully Canadianized. They now spoke fluent English as well as some French they had picked up in the neighborhood, albeit with an Italian accent. Their teachers were very impressed with their progress through Grade Four and decided it was now necessary to push them ahead to ensure they were properly challenged by their school work. After consulting with Dora, the school passed the Twins ahead into Grade Six in the fall.

Over the next two years, the Twins continued to increase their learning pace each year. After Grade Six they were advanced to Grade Eight and after Grade Eight they were placed into Grade Ten. By September 1960, they had made up for all of the years they had been put back in order to learn English. They were now fifteen years old attending the first year of Senior High School at a new English Catholic High in their district called St. Pius X.

During their first three years in Canada, as they were always ahead of their classmates in terms of social development, maturity and intellect, their teachers allowed them great latitude in class. They were always the top students excelling in every subject and were often chosen to participate in special school projects that gave them a respite from class time. So when they walked into St. Pius for the first time in September, they brought with them a sense of their own pre-eminence in the school hierarchy.

Whenever a new high school opens, it takes a while for the standard values and exclusive inner circles to form while students measure their competition and jockey for position. Robert and Tony looked around the auditorium of the new school at their first assembly with an air of self-assurance that is unusual in fifteen year olds. They were dressed immaculately in matching crisp, white shirts, stovepipe pants, loafers, white socks, blue sports-jackets and school ties. Their hair was cut and styled in a modified version of the Elvis-look. To satisfy parental and school sensibilities, it was slicked back on the sides and combed forward and up to make it fuller on top.

The school was segregated with the girls attending separate classes from the boys on the other side of the school yard under the authority of an order of nuns. The religious order that ran St. Pius was the Christian Brothers of Ireland. On opening day several Brothers went up on the stage to instruct the students about the various extracurricular activities planned for the school year. Brother Rose explained that he would be coaching the junior and senior sports teams. When he mentioned soccer, Tony elbowed Robert in the ribs. This was their sport and they had to be on the team.

There were many Italian families in St. Leonard and soccer was played with intense passion on back lots with pick-up groups of kids. The level of play was very high and both boys had developed excellent ball-handling abilities by playing against play ground school chums with names like Petrucelli, Ferrara and Venafro. On their street, if you were Italian you played soccer and that was that. The French could have their hockey. In this aspect of their lives, the Twins stayed true to their Italian background.

By the end of the day, the Twins were placed in their classes and had signed up for the Junior soccer team. They had met some new friends and not all were Italian; most students came from an English or Irish Catholic background. As they were leaving school, Tony and Robert found themselves following behind three girls down the sidewalk. One of the girls, a pretty brunette, looked back at them and smiled as she turned to her friends. The two boys smiled back and Robert thought, "God, it's wonderful to leave the younger kids behind!"

Tony said, "Ciao!" to the girls unconsciously turning on the Latin charm that was going to make the next three years most memorable. The girls stopped walking and the one who had smiled turned and responded, "Hello." The Twins introduced themselves and the girls did the same. They discovered they were all in Grade Ten at St. Pius. The boys had to get home for a jam session with some friends but they promised the girls they would see them again. As they headed for home, Robert turned to Tony, "I think I'm going to enjoy high school a lot."

Tony replied, "Yeah, it looks like it is going to be a great year."

❧

The boys continued to develop their love for music. Their mother had taught them some basic chords and progressions; they took their instruments into the neighborhood and began to practice the guitar with friends. They were trying to develop a band. If they could learn some songs perhaps they could get to play at one of the infrequent dances beginning to take place around Montreal.

They set up a studio in the basement of one of their friend's home. Besides Robert and Tony, there was a Bass player, a Sax, an Organist and a Drummer. They called themselves "The Pirates". They were busy developing their repertoire and hoped to become professional enough to play in public.

Sometimes while practicing at home, Robert and Tony would use their acoustic guitars and sing harmony together. But, with the band they were fully electric with several small Fender amplifiers to plug into the two guitars and bass.

One day, a classmate of Tony asked to come along and watch a practice session. Tony taught him some chords and they practiced together on several occasions. Walter Rossignuoli didn't own a guitar at the time, but he really wanted to learn to play. In a few weeks, Wally had his own electric guitar and within a few years became an exceptional guitarist. He went on to a professional career as Walter Rossi playing with such performers as Buddy Miles, Wilson Pickett and Pagliaro before turning solo in the late 1970s.

As the school year progressed, the Twins were enjoying the year more and more. They were meeting girls and starting to date. The band continued to practice twice a week and they began to sound pretty good with some of their songs. The only problem was the constant need to find new places to practice since most of their parents did not want to listen to their electrified music except on rare occasions.

The first year at St. Pius was good for Tony and Robert in many ways. The Twins were very popular. They began to date. Their music had progressed to where they were now playing in public as a duo or with "The Pirates". Their only disappointment was the soccer team. The junior squad was having a losing year and neither boy liked being on a losing side. Most of their teammates were indifferent to the game and hadn't played much before high school. It was frustrating to lose to teams that were only moderately good. Tony knew if the guys from his neighborhood played with them it would be a different story, but most of them were attending the French Catholic School. He resolved to do something about the situation to improve next year's team.

That Christmas, Robert talked the Brothers and the Mother Superior into allowing him and Tony to visit the girl's school to sing and play guitar for some of their classes. They took their instruments across to the girl's side of the school and sang for them. Needless to say this enhanced their reputation. In fact, they now became the most popular guys in school. After the Christmas break, they began finding notes in their lockers from love-struck teenage girls. One girl had such a crush that she wrote a poem called *The Papalia Twins* which passed amongst her friends until it ended up in Robert's hands.

That spring, a boy who had graduated from High School the year before came to their school for a performance. His name was Andy Kim. Robert and Tony were asked to open the show in the school auditorium by playing one song. The selection they picked out was *Bye, Bye Love*. It went over extremely well. There was lots of applause and cheering and some of the girls even screamed and called out their names. When they left the stage, they were really pumped by all the adoration they had received from the crowd. Robert said to Tony that night, "The only chance we're going to get to perform is at school dances. Those only come along maybe twice a year. We should talk to the Brothers about using the school auditorium and holding our own dances."

Tony and Robert laid out a plan that night to organize a dance. The next day, they approached the Principal, Brother Slattery, to press for a school dance. The Principal was not really against the idea but he told them he would think about it and let them know. After they left his office, Brother Slattery smiled to himself and thought. "These two kids are real go-getters. They are involved in all aspects of school life and their grades are good. There are other kids in the school who in spite of being well off, get into trouble whenever they are unsupervised. Maybe we need to have someone organize dances and parties for the students under the auspices of the school so that teenagers have somewhere to go to have fun and something to do other than hang out on street corners."

Later that day, he called the Twins back to his office and told them he would allow their request on the strict condition that they took full responsibility for everything that transpired during the evening. Furthermore they must ensure that nothing would happen to embarrass the School or the Church. Tony and Robert quickly agreed to these terms and left the office glowing inside.

The dance was scheduled for Saturday, May 11th, just two weeks away. The plan was for Robert to act as a disc jockey and play his Top-100 record collection most of the evening. The records would be balanced out with several live performances by the Twins throughout the evening.

Robert had some flyers printed up advertising, *Bob's Dance Party* featuring *The Twins and Top-100 Records.* Together with several friends they nailed up flyers all over their area of the city. They talked it up at school every day.

When the great day arrived, kids were lined up outside the auditorium well before the doors opened at 7:00 pm. By 8:00 pm, the hall was filled to capacity -- 600 people, and they remained all night long. Admission was seventy-five cents while soft drinks were sold for twenty-five cents. Robert performed on stage all night while Tony, when he wasn't singing, supervised their friends who were working the door or serving refreshments. The school authorities required they close down at 11:00 pm so at the appointed time they turned on all the lights, cut out the music and cajoled the stragglers out the door. The dance had gone off very smoothly. There had been no trouble of any kind. After cleaning the hall, they headed for home feeling quite euphoric.

At home, Robert poured out the evening's receipts onto his bed while Tony watched. They counted it up and found they had taken in over $700 dollars. After paying for the flyers, streamers, banners, records and soft drinks, they had made a very, tidy profit.

The Twins couldn't believe their good fortune, they had organized the dance because they loved music and had wanted a forum in which to perform. It ended up that two sixteen year olds had made as much money that night as their older brothers each made in a month of very hard work at their jobs. So a pure act of love for music and showmanship had grown into a promotional venture that could be extremely profitable. With the luck that comes with perfect timing, they were among the first to discover this fact in Montreal.

With this success, Robert and Tony began to plan dances as regular events throughout the long, hot summer and into the Fall of 1961. Initially, they sought the use of Catholic community halls or school gyms and auditoriums; later they moved on to theaters and clubs. The events were billed as *The Dance Party* or *Bob's Dance Party* and featured a selection of Top-100 records interspersed with live performances by the Twins or other young hopefuls such as *The Del-Mars.* Inevitably the dances were sell-outs. They began to develop credibility in the fledgling Montreal rock scene as entrepreneurial kids who knew what other kids wanted.

They found themselves in the vanguard of rock music promotion in the city of

Montreal. Robert was able to get complimentary copies of the latest releases; first from record stores in exchange for a plug for the store during the dance; and later from radio stations, agents and promoters.

Although they were now making a good deal of money, neither their family nor they thought of this activity as anything but an extremely profitable hobby. It was not as yet, regarded as a business and they did not believe this was going to be their careers. The social forces around them were still channeling them into finding respectable careers with prestige and future.

During the summer, the Twins continued to play soccer with their neighborhood pals. Tony dreamed of becoming a professional soccer player and he loved to play the game whenever he could. The caliber of play at these pick-up games was so much higher than at school. His competitive drive chafed against playing on another mediocre team in the coming season. One hot mid-July day after a particularly excellent game, Tony approached several of his mates sitting on the grass in a group. He sat down in their midst and said, "How would you guys like to play on my soccer team at St. Pius this year?"

"If we all played together I bet we can be one of the best teams in Montreal."

He assembled a list of advantages of St. Pius over their French Catholic High School to help convince his friends and their parents. Tony continued to work on them over the summer and by August he had talked six of them into transferring. That year, the senior soccer team won their division and made it into the High School finals. Despite the ethnic mix in the school, the squad was predominant Italians, mostly kids from Tony's neighborhood. Their season was a marked departure from the year before; they never lost a game. Their goalie, Venafro, posted numerous shutouts. Against the weaker teams, the scores were typically 10 or 12 to 0.

The school gained a sense of pride and excitement from the excellence and professionalism of their successful soccer team. The games began events to which the entire school would come out and cheer on their heroes.

One Monday in mid-November, the team assembled for their final practice of the year. The next day would be the final game against St. Thomas Aquinas to determine the city championship. Brother Rose was putting the boys through their paces. He had to yell at Tony a couple of times this day; first Tony was standing around and not paying attention to the drills; secondly he was undermining the coach's authority with his teammates. They appeared to listen to Tony about what to do rather than to the coach.

Brother Rose liked the Papalia boys very much. He considered Robert one of the most-consistent hustlers on the team. That boy could always be counted on to be out there motivating his teammates to push just a little bit harder. Tony on the other hand, was the total soccer star but his play would vary from lackluster to outstanding depending on his mood. The coach felt Tony's natural self-confidence was beginning to move into the realm of arrogance. He decided it was time to teach Tony a lesson.

The next day as the team boarded the bus for Kent Park and the big game, Brother Rose took Tony aside, "Tony, I didn't like the way you practiced yesterday. It was sloppy. I've decided to remove you from the line-up today. You won't be starting."

Tony was shocked and very angry. He looked at Brother Rose considering what he should do or say. He felt the anger inside beginning to boil over but he fought to regain his self-control. Quietly, he took off his jersey and gave it to the second-string boy. On the bus, Tony was fuming. He could not believe he was being denied an opportunity to play in the championship game after all the work he had put in recruiting the team and then playing such a great season.

It began to rain heavily as they drove to the game. Puddles were forming on the field; the footing was clearly going to be treacherous. Even so, many students and teachers turned out under umbrellas to watch the game. Both sides were keen to win. Banners were strung out on either side of the field. Behind the St. Pius bench they read, *Falcons - Montreal's Finest* and *Red & White are No.1.*

There was much surprise and comment among the knowledgeable fans when they saw that Tony was not among the starters. For his part, Tony avoided the crowd. He was seething inside but did not want to do anything stupid. He was first-of-all a team player, and he did not want anything to reflect badly on himself or his team. He still hoped he would make it into the game. He stood on the side-line and with his fists clenched and warmed up by himself with a ball as though he was preparing to enter the game.

The game began with both teams driving hard to score the first goal. St. Thomas turned out to be the best team they had faced all season and the game was a true championship encounter. Play went back and forth, up and down the field. Both teams had the crowd on their collective feet with good scoring chances, but both goalies stopped everything that came their way.

At the start of the second half, the game remained scoreless despite the supreme efforts by both sides. The field was a quagmire; the players were tired, wet and filthy, covered in mud and in some cases, blood, as the slippery conditions led to more than the usual minor injuries.

During the second half, St. Pius began to show its greater conditioning and ball handling skills but the team was plagued by bad luck. On two occasions after Herculean efforts, a goal was scored only to be disallowed by an off-side call.

With less than ten minutes to go in the still-scoreless game, Brother Rose began to reconsider his decision to pull Tony out of the line-up. He wanted the championship as much as anyone; he didn't want this perfect season to end with a non-scoring tie (this was in the days prior to penalty kick shut-outs). He had been watching Tony at the side of the playing field. The boy had kept on warming-up throughout the game. As time was getting short and it became apparent he wasn't going to play, some of the opposing fans began to taunt him with cat-calls. Tony had ignored it all and kept his focus on the game. Brother Rose had to admit that the kid showed a lot of character. Besides, he was the only one of his exceptional players who was still fresh. "Tony", he called. "I want you to substitute for Antonecchia on left wing".

Tony responded immediately. He was determined to play the game of his life and a minute after entering the game, his opportunity came. Robert sent a comet kick flying in front of the opposing net. In the efforts of both teams trying frantically to gain control of the ball, there was a pile up of bodies to the left of the goal. The ball took a bounce and several players tried to head it but missed. Tony took a flying run and leapt over the top of the bodies in front of the goal. As he floated through the air, he caught the ball on the front of his chest. He couldn't use his hands to control the ball so he twisted his body as he descended keeping the ball with him.

The onlookers saw it as an effort of sheer will and determination. When he landed, he took two steps and fell forward across the goal line still controlling the ball in front of him on his chest propelling it into the net.

The St. Pius fans went wild while the St. Thomas supporters were devastated. When the game resumed, St. Pius regained possession of the ball. It was passed to Tony on the wing and he began to move down the field. He passed to the center to Petrocelli and took off down the wing at full speed. Petrocelli spied Tony streaking on his left and lofted the ball ahead. By the time Tony received the ball, he had passed all the St. Thomas defenders. At about 45 feet out from the goal, Tony got behind the ball and kicked it as hard as he could.

It was a dream kick.

Replaying it over and over in his head, Tony can recall how it left his foot and flew in a well-placed arc through the air. As it approached the goal line, the goalie dived to his left to stop the ball. Just before it reached his outstretched hands, the ball actually changed direction and curved to his right to enter the net above his right shoulder as he continued his dive to the left.

This time the crowd went absolutely bananas.

Tony had scored the only two goals of the game in a three minute period with less than five minutes remaining. The last minutes of the match were anticlimatic as everyone knew the game was effectively over. When the whistle blew, fans rushed on the field to shake Tony's hand or slap him on the back. His team mates put him on their shoulders and carried him from the field.

Brother Rose just shook his head in amazement. Overjoyed that the team had won the game, his resolve to teach Tony some humility had ended instead with the boy becoming the school hero. A special assembly was convened the next day to celebrate the championship and to honor the team. Tony was dubbed "The Cinderella Kid" by the school newspaper. Even the Montreal Gazette reported the game in its sports pages citing Antonio Papalia as a hero.

In later life, the lessons Brother Rose had taught Tony would not be in vain. Tony had learned the importance of humility in working together with others. He also discovered that putting all your eggs in one basket at the same time could be dangerous. By holding back his best player under adverse conditions, Brother

Rose had inadvertently provided his team with a clear advantage over the opposition in the dying moments of the game.

By Christmas, Tony and Robert were the definitive examples of Big Men on Campus -- nice looking, well-groomed, good students, top jocks, and directing a business on top of the newly burgeoning rock music scene. Nothing happened to change this situation over the next year and a half. They continued to ride the crest of the wave and their company continued to make money.

During their last year at high school, St. Pius again won the city soccer championship. Together with several of their team mates, Robert and Tony were recruited to play for a semi-professional team in Montreal which acted as a farm club for Cantalia, one of the Italian professional soccer teams playing in the European league. They received a wage of thirty-five dollars per week.

In the fall of 1962, the Mexican National soccer team stopped in Montreal on its way to the World Cup in Sweden. They requested to meet the St. Pius city champions as a practice game for their up-coming tournament. The game was played on a closed field and St. Pius won 4-1. While the Mexicans may not have taken the game very seriously, they were certainly impressed with the caliber of this team. The city champions of 1961 and 1962 were two of the best senior soccer teams that St. Pius ever produced.

So at the young age of 17, Tony Papalia had achieved his goal in life -- to play professional football. But he knew there were more for him to discover and more talents for him to apply in his life. The brothers went for the top in everything they did with respect for excellence, style, and achieving the best.

Inside Brixton Prison

AFTER BEING ASSEMBLED to hear the charges against them, Robert, Tony, Mario and Richard were held overnight in separate police cells. On the following morning, May 18th, they were brought back together and hustled into a blue police van. With escort vehicles and sirens wailing, the cavalcade proceeded to Magistrate's Court for a brief appearance. They were given no opportunity to speak with anyone and so they appeared without legal counsel. Within minutes the magistrate decided there was sufficient evidence to hold them all in custody and he granted the prosecution's motion to refuse bail. By ten o'clock, they were whisked away to another part of London to be processed for booking into Brixton Prison. Their clothes were taken from them and replaced with prison clothes.

Brixton is a prison used only for remand purposes, that is, as a holding tank for persons awaiting trial who haven't been granted bail. It is generally presumed that people waiting trial will only spend a short time behind bars at Brixton. As a result, the prison lags behind most other British penal institutions with respect to comfort and adequacy of facilities. It is situated in the poor, largely black-populated borough of Brixton often referred to as London's Harlem.

The prison was built in the 19th Century. It is seriously overcrowded and very antiquated: the cells uniformly dark, dank, drafty and cold. When it was built, no provision was made for running water, central heating, or electric lighting. When added later, these were tacked-on in a make-do fashion reinforcing the over-all effect of flawed, deficient quarters for human habitation.

When the Twins and their colleagues arrived at the prison, there was still no running water in the cells. For their toilet, a bucket was provided to be emptied after use. If they were lucky, their jailers would take them once a week to a central shower facility to clean themselves. Each cell was equipped with an electric light behind wire mesh on the ceiling and the central heating system was coal-fired providing only modicum of warmth. It is perhaps trite, but certainly true, that the claustrophobic environment in which they found themselves made them feel like characters in a Charles Dickens novel.

In the beginning they were placed in cells which housed six men on three sets of bunks, two high to a wall. Besides their beds, the cell furnishings included a spindly metal table on which a constant game of cards was being played. The

Italians formed themselves together in one cell block, while Swinnerton was placed somewhere apart from the rest of them. They never saw him again until the start of the preliminary hearing. Robert and Tony now discovered that five other Italians had been arrested, interrogated and charged as had they. These included Pier Luigi Torri from Bear Securities, Flavio Baracchini, an Italian judge, Vincenzo Santoro, a commercial lawyer from Milan, and an Italian businessman named Boccardi. Robert and Mario Berton had previously met Torri at "Bear" but this was the first time any of them had ever met Baracchini, Santoro or Boccardi. They shared their cell with Torri, Baracchini and Santoro and together they discussed their common circumstances in an attempt to make sense of what was happening. The only conclusion they could draw was that the entire situation was inexplicable and the police had made a great mistake.

While the other three had lawyers, Robert, Tony and Mario Berton were still unrepresented. They needed to obtain immediate legal council to obtain their freedom at the very least.

The legal firm of Colombotti from the Italian Embassy was already hard at work attempting to secure the freedom of Baracchini, Santoro and Boccardi. Within a couple of weeks, Boccardi was released and given permission to leave for Italy. Several days later, the Italian judge and lawyer were released on bail but were requested to remain in the UK. Despite this order they immediately left for Italy planning to clear their names from there. Needless to say, this circumstance did not help the others to arrange their own bail and release.

Torri was denied bail altogether since it was shown that he was a fugitive from Italian justice.

The Twins and Mario were completely unschooled in the British system and how to find legal counsel. Shortly after their arrival at Brixton, a fellow sidled up to Tony in the booking area and asked whether he needed legal assistance. When Tony replied that they certainly did, the fellow produced a business card of a friend of his who worked for a London firm of criminal solicitors. This fellow made arrangements for Tony to meet one of their solicitors, a man named Gittings.

When Gittings arrived at the prison, the Twins and Mario were taken to a small, windowless room to meet him. Robert and Tony attempted to explain what they could. Gittings appeared to listen intently and every once in a while, he would make a note of something they told him. His clients were still in an extremely-charged emotional state about the treatment they had received from Scotland Yard. They complained about the beatings and the failure of the police to allow them access to legal counsel while they were being questioned. They told him that an examination of their clothing worn at the time of their arrest would reveal it to be ripped, dirty and blood-stained.

Gittings advised them their most pressing problem was to secure their freedom and to decide whether or not to plead guilty to the charges laid. They instructed him to initiate an action against the police for the assaults they had suffered at the hands of their interrogators, but Gittings showed no enthusiasm for this matter and tried to turn the discussions to other issues. As to any suggestions about their plea, Robert and Tony were emphatic about their innocence of any wrongdoing. They made it clear they would never plead guilty.

Over the next six weeks, the brothers, together with Mario and Torri, were transported once a week to Magistrate's Court where the question of their release on bail was raised. Each time the prosecution made lengthy speeches about why they should be kept in custody because of the seriousness of their alleged crime and the likelihood that they would flee the country. Their legal representative said very little on their behalf. Each week they were denied bail and returned to Brixton in a blue police van.

The meetings with Gittings were becoming increasingly filled with tension and distrust. While Gittings had seen the bruises and marks on their bodies when he first met them, these had faded long ago. His interest in pursuing a civil complaint against the police was clearly nil. He told Robert and Tony at one of their meetings, "Don't bother, you will get nowhere trying to prove police brutality. It will be your word against that of the police and the court will believe them over you."

Instead of listening to their requests, Gittings would repeat his strategy, "Have you thought any more about allowing me to make a deal with the Crown in exchange for a guilty plea. In addition to Swinnerton's confession, I now understand they are about to obtain Frascati's cooperation. Once that is achieved, you are as good as convicted. It is better to show the authorities that you are not going to put them through all sorts of time and expense to prove their case. If we deal now we can look for some leniency in sentencing."

Both Robert and Tony turned red with anger. They had been fed this same line over and over again ever since it became apparent that Richard was going to present evidence against them. Tony said, "Look Gittings, we've told you before, we can't plead guilty to something we didn't do. The charges are all a setup. If Richard has anything to say against us then he is lying."

The meeting ended as did all the others with dissension and turmoil between the accused and their lawyer.

It was clear to Robert that it would not be easy-dealings with his lawyers and with Magistrate's Court. The Twins became aware that the system was designed so that the Brixton jailers would refer unrepresented prisoners to certain firms of criminal solicitors. They became suspicious that Gittings was failing to champion their cause since he had no desire to bite the hand that fed him. If he really fought for them, he would unlikely receive further referrals from the people who worked at the prison.

Gittings continued to pressure them to plead guilty. He kept reiterating his belief that sentencing would go much easier on them if they would show some remorse and help avoid a lengthy and potentially highly-publicized trial. From their side, the Twins told him they would be happy with any publicity they could muster about the case so the public could learn about the great wrong being done.

Gittings just shook his head, "Do you really think the English public will sympathize with a bunch of Italians accused of coming to this country to defraud them of millions of pounds?"

Robert and Tony were totally frustrated with this reasoning. Robert said, "Look, they've charged us with conspiring with people we never met, with people we've never even heard of, until we met them here in prison. You must be crazy, telling us to plead guilty."

❧

By mid-July, the failure in understanding and the mistrust between Gittings and his clients reached the boiling point. The Twins knew they needed another lawyer, but the problem was how to arrange for one who was not beholding to the police. The only concrete help they ever received from Gittings in two months was notification of their situation to various family members, Tony had spoken by telephone with his wife. Pattie, imploring her to return to Canada to inform his family of their plight and to see if the Canadian authorities might help out from Canada as they were receiving the silent treatment from the London High Commission. Pattie has been in Italy with their infant son waiting Tony's return for a well-deserved vacation.

Mario Berton's young wife, Martine, upon discovering what had happened to her husband came to London almost immediately. Her initial stoicism and hope had begun to wane since her husband had been in custody for two months now with still no trial date set. There was no sign he would be released on bail soon. One scorching summer day during one of her visits with Mario, he told her both he and the Twins had lost all confidence in their lawyer. While he understood very little that transpired between them because of his poor English, he was completely disgusted with the lack of action on their behalf. He asked Martine to talk with some of their acquaintances in London to arrange for legal assistance from someone who would fight for them.

Martine Berton was only twenty-four years old, considerably younger than her husband. She came from a loving, upper-middle-class Milanese family. Until now, she had lived a wholly sheltered existence. She and Mario had been married less than three years, almost newly-weds, although they had two infant daughters. At the time of the arrest, the youngest was only a few months old. Martine was concerned that Mario had been separated from their daughter for most of her young life. Nothing in her background could possibly have prepared her for the incarceration of her husband in a British prison.

She spoke a little English having studied it in school. After spending two months in London, she was only just beginning to communicate with other people. When she left the prison that day, she went directly to visit with a friend with whom she had gone to school in Italy. Her friend was married to an Italian involved in the oil business; the couple had been living in London for the past three years.

Martine poured out her tale of woe to her friend's husband. The oil man was taken with this young woman's seemingly hopeless position and he promised to see if he could help. The next morning he called his lawyer, David Benham, a partner in the firm of Bischoff & Co. He asked Benham if he would meet with an Italian lady friend of his whose husband was in some sort of trouble with the police. Benham listened to the sketchy details and, thinking there was no harm in talking with the woman, agreed to meet her the following day.

When he put down the telephone receiver, David Benham paused to reflect for a moment. As it appeared to be a criminal matter, the best he could do was direct the woman to a good criminal solicitor. His firm had always specialized in business and commercial matters and was solidly ensconced in the establishment. It was unlikely any of the partners had ever played a role in a criminal case beyond a discrete referral for a client who had gone astray of the law by way of drunken-driving or some such problem. Moreover, it was quite possible that the esteemed firm of Bischoff & Co, founded in the 18th Century, had never handled a single criminal file in its two-hundred or so year history.

Benham was one of the younger partners in Bischoff & Co. In his late thirties, he had practiced at Bischoff since law school. He was a typical product of the English class system. As a boy he had attended the best public schools and later, one of Britain's most prestigious universities where he was channeled directly into taking his degree in Law. His career, although solid, was without detour and viewed from the outside, was rather unremarkable. He had found his greatest strength over the years was client-development and his firm used him to full advantage in this role.

Tall, with thick wavy brown hair, David had an agreeable face and friendly disposition when favorably disposed towards someone. He had a very dry sense of humor and would use it at the expense of those who did not impress him. He was highly sociable with a broad circle of professional and business acquaintances. All of these attributes led him to be highly successful in bringing many lucrative clients into the firm as well as keeping them satisfied once they came on-board. His role was that of a facilitator.

Once a potential client came to his office, David would instruct his secretary, his junior and his right-hand man, his managing clerk, to carry out the detailed work in the case. If any communication was needed with the other side of the case or if the firm needed outside assistance, he was expert at paving the way for his assistants with a few well-placed phone calls.

His manner of serving his clients allowed him great leeway in managing his time. A tennis game or a round of golf was often as important to his business success as time spent in the office. It wasn't unusual in the summer months for Benham to slip out of his office at one o'clock, jump into his Aston-Martin convertible and drive out of the city to play golf with a client.

Benham also possessed an innate sense of his own superiority; believing he was completely deserving of his comfortable and patrician lifestyle. Those who are most contented are usually the least likely to become involved in upsetting the status quo. Certainly, David Benham was not a man looking for a cause on the day that Martine Berton entered his office.

When he first set eyes on Martine Berton, David Benham saw before him a young fragile-looking, exquisite and beautiful woman. After some preliminary discussion, her breeding and gentility became apparent. She was the kind of woman blessed with good looks and grace, who could soften the hardest of hearts with her vulnerability and clear need for help.

Benham listened carefully while Martine told the story of her husband with the help of her school-friend's husband. He heard that Mario was a stockbroker who was arrested while visiting London with some associates. He had been held incommunicado, was mistreated by his captors and now faced numerous charges involving all sorts of crimes. He and his associates were still in custody having been held for two months without any idea about when their trial might occur and with no prospect of release on bail. Martine's husband was suffering from the deprivations of prison life and his livelihood had been seriously damaged. As her story ended with a description of their two infant children and how their father's absence affected their family life. Martine was openly crying.

It was obvious to Benham that this woman was a person who had knocked on every door and been turned away until she ended up here, filled with utter despair and looking to him as her last hope in the world. But what could he offer her?

Benham spoke. "Mrs. Berton, I will go to Brixton Prison to speak with your husband. We will then see if this mess can be sorted out."

While it is clear he was influenced by the way he became aware of Mario Berton's troubles, it is to Benham's credit that he chose to get involved. He sympathized with the circumstances in which a professional man visiting a foreign country could be detained and then treated so badly while in custody. From what he had learned from the young wife, Benham knew instinctively that Mario's case would prove to be a most untypical criminal matter.

❧

After calling Brixton Prison to sort out what was required to see a prisoner, he turned to his managing clerk and said, "Come on, Geoff, we're going to spend the afternoon at prison."

The two men arrived outside the prison gates at about two o'clock. Benham had not been in this part of London since his university days. He was struck by how much shabbier and rougher it was than he remembered it.

"I wouldn't be found in this district after dark", he remarked to his assistant. His companion nodded in agreement.

The two identified themselves to the guards and were admitted. After signing in and being checked through two gates they were led to a small room with a door at either end. They observed a barred window high above the floor with a table and chairs in the center of the room. After entering, the door behind them was shut and locked. They waited for several minutes until noise beyond the opposite door signaled the arrival of the prisoners. The door opened and in walked three men. One was taller and fairer than the other two, who quite surprisingly, were absolutely identical in appearance.

David introduced himself, "My name is David Benham and this is my clerk, Geoffrey Lines. I am a lawyer who was asked to come here by Mrs. Berton."

At this comment, one of the identical men visibly brightened. He came forward and extended his hand, "Hello, I'm Robert Papalia. This is my brother Tony, and this is Mario Berton." Tony as is his way, kept his eyes veiled, his expression unchanging as he hung back assessing the new-comers.

Robert explained, "Our friend, Mario, does not speak much English. Generally, we assist as interpreters. His English is beginning to improve these days and he does understand some of what is said." Robert introduced Benham and Lines to Mario in Italian and he shook their hands warmly.

On that first afternoon of what would be one of many, the parties spent several hours in intense discussion. Geoff Lines took notes until his hand ached.

The prisoners explained what they knew of their situation. They were promoters of a gold mine in Canada. They had come to London for a few days in May and while visiting their English bank, Bear Securities, they were arrested for an alleged conspiracy involving the bank. The charges were absurd. Their connection to Bear Securities was minimal. They had never met any of the principals of the parent company, Magica Corvena. All of their dealings had been with the two Italian employees of the bank in London, Pier Torri and Umberto Frascati. Tony only met these people after being placed in Brixton Prison with them. As for Mario and Robert, they had first heard of Bear Securities in March and had never had previous dealings with the bank.

They had begun to do business there as they believed a bank with Italian antecedents would be a good professional connection for them in London. The bank's affairs were completely unknown to any of them and aside from a few matters entrusted to Bear Securities by their company, Metals Research, there was no further connection.

Their previous lawyers had told them Scotland Yard was alleging they had made statements which proved their guilt. If such statements existed, they were complete fabrications and totally wrong. They had been beaten by the police during their interrogations and while they had instructed their previous lawyers to launch a law suit against Scotland Yard, nothing of any sort had been done.

All of this information tumbled out in a jumble of accented Italian-Canadian English with many digressions and interruptions as both Robert and Tony sought to provide them with the entire story as they recalled it. Mario would occasionally want to say something or David would direct a question specifically to him. Then there would be a huddle while the three prisoners spoke in rapid-fire Italian until

Robert or Tony provided the answer in English.

As the story unfolded, Benham and Lines felt the paranoia that gripped the three men. Of course, it only constituted paranoia if what they were saying wasn't true. At this stage the two legals could not determine what was real and what was imagined. The prisoners were adamant about their innocence. Yet, Tony talked about being driven from Canada and the Bahamas by the Canadian police, the RCMP. Their story certainly had some fantastic angles.

Robert told them they were sharing a cell with Torri from Bear Securities and he believed if anyone knew why they had been charged, he was the most likely one. He told a crazy tale inferring that Adnan Khassogi, a notorious Arab arms dealer had some Scotland Yard police on his payroll and that the Arab had arranged this entire episode as a vendetta against Torri, whom Khassogi hated. They believed as well that their previous solicitors were basically corrupt and in league with the police.

As the meeting came to a close, it was agreed that Benham would act on behalf of Mr. Berton for the purpose of attempting to obtain his release from prison while awaiting his trial. As they left the prison, Benham turned to Lines, "Well, this case certainly has the elements of bizarre about it, don't you think?"

Geoff replied, "It's quite a story. Do you think they are telling the truth?"

"Oh, they certainly sound sincere. I think they are telling the truth about what they know. But we must be suspicious about the reasons they give for the things that have happened to them. The facts are highly speculative and even they don't know with certainty how correct they are."

Benham went on, "The merits of the charges are difficult to assess at this point but for now, our primary goal is to obtain Mr. Berton's release. He doesn't appear to represent any danger to society and with the proper sureties, to ensure his appearance I see no reason why he shouldn't be released."

Over the next few weeks, Benham filed a written complaint with the Solicitor-General alleging mistreatment of his client by the police and asking for the matter to be investigated. He also took steps to obtain the names of persons willing to act as sureties and to instruct counsel to appear at a bail application. The barrister retained by Benham was a young counsel held in high esteem at the bar, Nigel Milne.

At the next bail application with Milne representing Mario, for the first time since their arrest, a forceful argument was put forward on behalf of the hapless Italians. The Magistrate actually sat up and paid attention to Defense Counsel. Milne pulled out all the stops in putting forward the case for his client.

"My Lord, Mr. Berton is a man, thirty-eight years of age. He is an Italian national and is normally resident in Milan. He is married and has two children, infant daughters under three years of age."

"He has earned his livelihood throughout his adult life working in investments and business financing. At the time these allegations arose he was a major partner in an important Milanese stock brokerage firm. He is a man with an unblemished past. Previously, he has never been charged with, let alone, convicted of a crime anywhere in the world."

"I understand that while the prosecution concedes that this man appears to pose no danger to society, they are seeking to deny him bail because he may not appear for trial due to his lack of roots in this country."

"On applications of this sort, the Crown has the onus to prove there is substantial likelihood he will fail to appear at his trial. I have not seen any evidence put before this court that Mr. Berton might fail to appear."

The Magistrate turned to the Crown, "What say you, Mr. Morris?"

"Well, My Lord, previously three of the defendants in this case, all Italians, were granted bail, and they immediately fled to Italy, where we are without power to extradite them and, My Lord, I need not remind you of the seriousness of the charges against these men."

Milne replied, "Firstly, My Lord, the nature of my client's business requires that he be free to travel throughout the world. In the year prior to his arrest, he was away from Italy as often as he was home."

"Many of the countries to which Mr. Berton's business takes him are in the Commonwealth or are countries that have extradition treaties with the United Kingdom. Mr. Berton would have to be a fool to run away from these charges only to be apprehended at a later date while trying to earn his living."

"The second point to be made for Mr. Berton's release is that the severity of these charges is still in issue. The Crown laid these charges well over two months ago, yet, they are nowhere near bringing this case to trial. My learned friend claims the investigation is still continuing, Mr. Berton, on the other hand, maintains his innocence and is anxious for an opportunity to prove he has committed no crime. He certainly has no desire to leave a fraud charge outstanding in England. Such an unresolved issue could seriously harm, if not destroy, his business. He has given me his assurances that he will be present to defend himself against the charges when these matters come to trial, I submit that the interests of the court and the community could best be served by releasing Mr. Berton on bail with the appropriate conditions."

There was some additional argument back and forth but at the end of the hearing it was determined that Mario could be released provided he surrendered his passport and undertook not to leave England; that he report twice a week to the Limehouse Police Station; and that two people acceptable to the court be willing to act as sureties on his behalf.

The prisoners left the court that day feeling elated. After months of nothing, finally some light was shining. It appeared that Mario's release was imminent. Robert and Tony thought they would now have an equally good chance for release and so immediately upon their return to Brixton, the Twins took steps to hire new' reputable solicitors. Tony sought representation with Bischoff & Co. and the firm agreed to act on his behalf. In the interest of minimizing potential conflict of interest between clients, Robert was put into the hands of a second firm of solicitors, Offenbach & Co, who were willing to work closely with the people at Bischoff & Co.

The mood in the cell that day was more positive than it had been for weeks.

❧

During their stay at the remand center they had fallen into the routine pace of the place. Three times a day they went to the mess hall to eat. By the second week, they knew exactly what their menu was for each day of the week. The food was bad and the menu invariant but they ate it anyway to fill their stomachs and break the monotony of the day. Tuesday was boiled cabbage and some sort of colorless, odorless potato mash. Wednesday was spaghetti in red sauce that made Chef-Boy-Ar-Dee canned spaghetti look like gourmet pasta.

Their meals were supplemented with chocolate bars available from the prison canteen. They ate a great deal of chocolate. They found they could get as much as they wanted by trading cigarettes for other prisoner's rations. Cigarettes were the currency of the prison. The Twins and Mario all smoked and so they requested that their families and friends bring or send them many more cigarettes than they could use personally. They used their excess stock to purchase all their supplies --candy, soap, toothpaste, toilet paper, etc.

After Santoro and Baracchini were released, they shared the cell that summer with a French guy and a taciturn Englishman. They had a great deal of time on their hands; all of it spent in the cell block except for meals, two exercise breaks in the yard per day, a weekly shower and their weekly remand hearings. Robert paced. Mario lay on his bunk. Tony, Torri and the Frenchman sat at the table playing cards. When they weren't playing cards, Tony or Robert would pick on the guitar that had been brought into them. Mostly however, they just talked, trying to figure out how they got into this mess.

Torri was certain that he was central to the story but did not understand how the others in his cell had become caught-up in the web. The Twins were now convinced their predicament was further interference by the RCMP back in Canada. Hadn't Ward as much as told them this during Tony's interrogation? The situation was out of control and they all wondered when it would be resolved.

The Entrepreneurs

BEFORE THE END of 1962, Robert and Tony had extended their *hobby* into a full-blown business promoting rock and roll. They began to bring *Name* acts into Montreal and shortly after into Toronto, Ottawa and Detroit. Their initial ventures were relatively small but they all proved profitable; their best one at that time had been participation into bringing the Beatles for the first time in North America and participating in the Canadian part of the Tour with two concerts in Montreal.

Before they had completed high school, the Twins decided to take the plunge and open their first club at a permanent location. The club didn't serve alcohol and the age limit was 16 years or older. They called it the Cave after the Cave in Liverpool where the Beatles had started. It had the capacity of 1000 people, a location near Mount Royal, center of Montreal. It was a converted warehouse with high ceilings and balconies around the dance floor, huge stage, very loud music, movie projection on walls and all kinds of lighting; a real temple for dance music. One of the first of its kind in all North America (discos had not even started yet). They now performed less frequently as an act together concentrating on Robert to handle the music entertainment part; being the DJ, MC and also performing as a solo with an eight-piece band interspersed with professional touring acts.

The music scene was changing. Elvis was no longer the biggest star; kids were now looking for a funkier sound than the earlier music. Robert and Tony wanted to be on the leading edge of the business, so often they would drive to New York City to catch the acts at the Apollo Theater. When they see groups or singers that drove the crowd crazy, they would book them to perform at the Cave in Montreal. In this way came to know a great many people in the rock music industry on the eastern seaboard.

A typical double bill booking at the Cave might include the following: a young blind boy named Little Stevie Wonder, a group called the Isley Brothers with a lead guitarist named Jimi Hendrix and other acts included James Brown, Ben E. King, Wilson Picket, Shirelles, Triny Lopez, Dianne Warwick, The Supremes, Little Richard, Chuck Berry, Tommy Hunt, Otis Redding, Ray Charles, Icke and Tina Turner and Chubby Checker to a name a few.

The Twins graduated from St. Pius in June 1963. They continued their music promotion business but also their education as well. Robert began to attend Sir George Williams University enrolling in economics and movie production. He continued with this program until mid-1965 as the music side of his life look on increased importance.

Tony took over management of the club business while both boys continued playing for the farm-team soccer club and started karate school. They began to feel torn between soccer, music and school. For the paltry sum of $35 dollars per week, soccer was taking up an inordinate amount of their time. The coaches expected them to be available for practices and games full time. Eventually, music and their growing business won out and the Twins quit the team.

Dora wanted her sons to pursue conventional careers. As long as Robert was attending university, he was OK to continue with the music business, but Tony was told, "Get a respectable job!"

The Twins were now averaging about $10,000 per month from their club and music enterprises but to please his mother, Tony was hired as a clerk in the Collection Department at the Head Office of the Canadian Imperial Bank of Commerce (CIBC) for the meager wage of $37.50 per week. With the many late nights from their dances, this salary was often used as taxi fare to get him to work on time in the morning at the bank.

In late summer of 1963, Tony and Robert opened a second club, larger than the Cave. They named it the Apollo after the famous theater in New York. So naturally, most of the performers from New York would perform at the Apollo in Montreal. All the top performers of the time would appear in this new club of the Twins. Opening night of the Apollo was a scene that will always be remembered in Montreal; six hours before opening there was a line-up twelve city blocks waiting to get in, over 10,000 people. The city of Montreal had to dispatch more than hundred police officers to keep order the capacity of the club to only 1200 people. The top radio station, CFCF, was broadcasting live from the Apollo that night. The performers were Little Richard, Everly Brothers, Chuck Berry, Tommy Hunt, Shirelles, Joe Tex and Robert also performed with The Persuaders as the back-up band; the place stayed opened for 48 hours non-stop. After that, the Apollo became the hottest place in North America from where a syndicate of three hundred radio stations would broadcast live from the Apollo on Saturday night and where in the years that followed almost every performer of the era in North America performed there. The Apollo Theatre in New York and the Apollo Club in Montreal were responsible for the mergence of rhythm and blues music in North America.

Shortly after the Apollo opened, major record companies in North America and England would use the club to launch their artists. One example, a DJ from England named Lord Timothy, came to Montreal to have Robert listen to the first record of a new group in England called The Rolling Stones. The record had Heart of Stone on the A side and Little Red Rooster on the B side. The Twins liked the songs and agreed to bring the Rolling Stones to Montreal.

At the time of the Rolling Stones appearance at the Apollo, the song Heart of Stone was getting released in North America. They were not yet well-known and would take awhile to catch on because of their rough appearance and sound. Six months later, the Stones began to take off with a succession of hits such as: Time Is On My Side, I Can't Get No Satisfaction, and Hey You, Get Off Of My Cloud. By 1965, they were the hottest band since the Beatles, selling out in concert halls all over North America.

Timing and luck are large parts of the music business as in any other business, the Twins would learn on more than one occasion. As the rock scene grew and bands began to play larger and larger venues, the Papalias began to book much larger spaces both in Canada and the USA and create concerts in stadiums, indoor hockey facilities or airport hangars to be able to fit the tens of thousands of people that attended these events for groups like the Beach Boys, The McCoys, The Seeds, The Rolling Stones, Young Rascals and others. This part of their business grew gigantic proportions and included their participation in the creation of the biggest event ever in the world; the legendary Woodstock (over 800,000 people) and ending with the last event: The Monterey Pop Festival in California, 1969, where the Rolling Stones with other famous groups performed. 247,000 people attended this event. This event marked the end of an era mainly because of a tragic incident where the Hells Angels, a biker gang, were attending and a fight broke out and a person was killed. After this, Robert and Tony looked at each other and said, "Where are all the flowers gone?" And decided 'No More Rock & Roll'. The whole scene had become too rough on account of civil unrest, especially in the USA on account of the Vietnam War and large crowds such as these could not be kept safe and peaceful anymore.

At the peak of their Club business, it had grown by 1968 to include nine separate clubs around the Montreal region: the Cave (1962), the Apollo (1963), Club-33 (1965), Pierre LeGrande (1965), Hullabaloo-A-Go-Go (1966 - 3 clubs by this name), the Cheetah (1967) and Harlow's (1968). The Hullabaloo discos and concerts establishments from 1966 to the of 1968 became a chain of franchises under the same name in cities throughout the eastern of Canada and the USA, 147 clubs opened from Montreal to Miami with the same concept in all places and centralized entertainment programming.

Other ventures the Twins had diversified in included: Marmalade Productions (record, movie and TV advertising productions), First Montreal Investments (financial investments and holdings, 1966) and a chain of 18 boutiques in Quebec under the name "Blow-Up" where a customer could go and within five minutes get a poster of himself made from a photo taken of him in the boutique's photo studio or from any picture that would be supplied by the customer. After the photo was taken or supplied, the customer would have to go to the cash to pay and while getting there, would have to walk through the boutique where very hip clothes, music records, celebrity posters, rock n'roll paraphernalia and gadgets were for sale. This concept proved so successful that in twelve months from start, eighteen boutiques were opened in Quebec, including one at Expo 67 in Montreal. The boutique at Expo 67 proved to be the most successful because the exposition had millions of visitors from around the world and hundreds of people everyday would line up non-stop to get their poster made. They had a clothing manufacturing factory which manufactured hip clothes of jeans, dresses and jeans. The trademark "Hardware" grew sales in three years to 7 million dollars with sales in Quebec, Ontario and New York State. Hardware was started shortly after Blow-Up.

The Twins also had three hotels, two in Montreal and one in Ottawa. One of the hotels, a landmark building in the heart of the city of Montreal and the other a sixteen-story building on Sherbrooke street. They were also participations in eight movie theatres in partnership with their brother, Adolfo. It was not unusual for the Twins to have special showings of their favorite films at the theatres for hundreds of their friends after the closing of their clubs in the wee hours.

On the personal side by 1968 Robert and Tony were also recording artists with Warner Brothers/Seven Arts and their own TV show called Eureka on every Monday night from 7:00pm to 8:30pm (prime time) plus numerous appearances on television and radio shows monthly. While all of this was being done, they still made time to work and learn in the financial markets, practice music, karate and participate in peace rallies to stop the war in Vietnam. They had managed to have great people on their staff of the various ventures and had excellent personal assistants, art creators and advisors. With 15-16 hours of work per day was the norm for the Twins. They said, "For us, it was fun, not work."

How Blow-Up was started is a perfect example to show the intuition and lightning speed Robert and Tony operate with. Tony, on one of his visits to New York was walking in the village, saw a shop that made posters of a client in five minutes. Being curious he walked in and made himself one. When he asked how they were able to do that, the people at the store were secretive and Tony could not get any information. When Tony went back to Montreal, Tony, Robert and Alex Farhood, art advisor to them, conceived the concept of Blow-Up Boutiques. The concept of the boutiques was centered on the personal poster concept. The concept looked great but there was a problem: How do you make a poster 3 feet by 2 feet in 5 minutes? This was is 1966 and technology was not what it is today. So they got on their phones and started calling the major companies, Kodak, Polaroid, etc. but still could not find such equipment. After a week, the Twins were getting frustrated and were about to give up on the idea of Blow-Up when Tony got an intuition and said, "Let's try Japan!" On their sixth telephone call, they found a man at Fuji films that solved the problem for them. Two days later, the man traveled from Japan to Montreal and after tens days, the Twins had the equipment needed: a combination of equipment from three different companies to assemble together, one part from Polaroid USA and two parts from Japan. One month later, the first Blow-Up boutique opened in Montreal on Maisoneuve Street in the heart of the city. The concept also included the hip clothes, music records, celebrity posters, rock n'roll paraphernalia and gadgets.

Corruption in the City of Montreal had been running rampant throughout the 1950s and although the election of Jean Drapeau as Mayor had helped reduce the problem, there was still a long way to go even in the mid-1960s. It wasn't long after the opening of the Apollo club that the Twins received a visit from members of the Montreal Police Force. It was suggested to them that they should hire off-duty police to work the door at $100 dollars per night per officer.

While the Twins felt this idea was an implied threat rather than a simple suggestion, they decided to comply. For several years thereafter, two officers were paid every night at each club; the monthly fee per club approached $5000 dollars for this service. It was considered by Tony and Robert to be one of the costs of doing business in much the same way that they paid 12% tax to the city on the admission charged each patron. In the long run, it turned out to be a very wise investment because it kept out their clubs and lives all criminal elements and trouble related to it of which Montreal was notorious at that time.

By now the Twins had a number of contacts in the music business in Montreal. They were advised it was best to give the police full cooperation or police raids would result. During a raid, the club was closed, patrons rounded up and sometimes, taken to the police station for questioning. Raids were bad for business and so the boys did what was required to avoid them. With off-duty officers on the door, the uniformed police would be told -- things are, cool and so they would leave without a raid.

Sometimes trouble was inevitable. There were not yet enough clubs to meet the demand and so line-ups would occur that were often blocks long, particularly on weekends. Occasionally not everyone would get into the clubs and this led to short tempers. When people did get in sometimes their nerves would be frayed and fights would break out. The music would have to be stopped while the rowdies were evicted. One night a bus load of Marines from the Plattsburgh Air Force Base came to the Apollo. Tony and his assistants found marijuana all over the club.

Soon fights began to breakout all over the club between the Marines with their razor-cut hair styles and the long-haired youngsters who resented the American military presence in Canada. It was obvious that the soldiers had come up to Montreal for the sole purpose of making trouble and kicking some long-hair butt. Tony and his bouncers managed to throw the Marines out of the club and they were banned from the premises for life. Throughout all the mayhem, Robert continued to deliver his patter, to play his records and to introduce the acts in the true spirit of the-show-must-go-on.

Such occurrences were only occasional however as most nights the kids came to the club to dance and have fun.

The clubs provided a continuing involvement in the Montreal music scene. They got to know the Vanelli brothers. In fact, the youngest brother, Gino Vanelli, first fronted a band as lead singer in one of the Papalia's clubs. The Twins jammed with Pagliaro and a young girl who often hung out at the Apollo later became a premier disco queen; her name was Patsy Gallant.

Tony did well at CIBC. In January 1964, he was promoted to an accountant's post at St. Laurent branch and then was made Manager of a St. Leonard branch in March of that year. After leaving Sir George Williams in April 1964, Robert had taken a day-time job as part of an audit inspection team with CIBC. In mid-summer, Tony decided to test the wrath of his mother and quit the bank to concentrate on their enterprise. Robert took over his position at the St. Leonard branch. Both brothers picked up considerable knowledge about high finance and bank administration but a banker's life was not for either of them. In fact, it was so far removed from the excitement they were having at night that Robert stayed barely a year with this job. Both he and Tony knew their real talent lay in their entrepreneurial instincts.

One night in 1965, a well-known and somewhat notorious promoter on the Montreal Stock Exchange visited the club. He was the kind of person who recognized his business opportunity whenever he saw one. Impressed with the cash flow being generated through these clubs, he knew these Papalia boys had the pulse on what the public wanted in the way of music and entertainment. He suggested that the Twins and he enter into a partnership in a couple of these clubs. They agreed to do this and the clubs setup were also highly successful. It was clear that demand for dance clubs in Montreal was insatiable.

But this partnership with Irving Kott was to lead the Twins in a new direction away from the rock and roll scene and into the stock market. Kott knew these young Italian brothers were making a lot of money and had the intelligence and drive to do even better. He took it upon himself to become their mentor. He wasted no time in telling them how proper investment of their money in the right places in the market could make them very rich indeed.

Robert and Tony had already begun to expand their teen club business into related fields. They invested in shops selling blow-up photographic posters, t-shirts and other rock-and-roll paraphernalia. Together with their older brother Adolfo, they opened an art movie house, the Empire Theater, which screened Bergmann, Fellini and Truffaut films.

As their enterprise continued to expand, they were becoming well-known and well-connected with other influential young people in the city. They counted among their friends some of the younger generation of the Simard Family (Power Corporation), at that time considered to be Canada's Kennedys, the Nixon Family, founders of Richardson Securities (David Nixon), the Sullivans and others. These associations also encouraged the Twins to raise their field of vision to the stock market and financial world.

At the urging of Kott, they plunged into the market a great deal of money in a new company about to be listed on the Montreal Stock Exchange that he said was going to win big-time. They convinced several of their well-heeled friends to invest heavily as well. Within a period of one week following its listing, the stock became worthless and together with all their money and that of their friends, the company quickly disappeared.

This was the first time that something they had touched had not turned to gold. Of course, they realized that the invested money had not vanished; rather it had merely changed hands. It was an expensive initiation into the cut-throat investment world but they took solace in the knowledge that their clubs were still making money. Even as 1966 dawned, they were organizing several new clubs: Club 33 opened in Rosemount and then the Hullabaloo-A-Go-Go franchise chain was started. Later, they opened the Cheetah in Expo Year, 1967. The Cheetah has particular significance to Tony as he met his wife, Pattie, for the first time at this club during one rather hot afternoon of this exciting year.

As the Twins recovered from their first foray into the market, they knew they must learn more about its inner workings if they wanted to avoid the clutches of promoters and businessmen who might not have their best interests at heart.

Despite being burned once, they didn't give up their liaison with Kott. They were bitter about their losses and felt some responsibility for the losses of their friends as well. But the Twins subscribed to the policy: Don't get mad, get even, and so, Tony approached Kott on the basis that he owed them a favor. He said, "We would like you to open some doors for us with the purpose to learn the Stock Market." And so; Kott, in his ever-so-charming way, gave them the help they needed -- he liked these two Italian charmers and believed they were going to be highly successful.

In late 1966, just before their 22nd birthday, Robert became an assistant trader on the floor of the Montreal Stock Exchange while Tony worked in the cages of the brokerage firm, LJ Forget. The Twins enrolled in the Investment Dealers Association course learning to become stockbrokers. By early 1967, Robert had his broker's license, but Tony had changed his mind. Instead he decided to focus on becoming a knowledgeable investor once he became aware of how the market worked, Robert, knew as well, that hustling to buy and sell stock for others just to make a commission was a mere stopover for him. What he really wanted was to bring an idea to fruition as a successful business venture. The Twins realized they were builders and that through their guidance they could put together companies that would become creators of wealth.

❧

Unknown to Robert and Tony, there were events occurring in the 1960s in Canada and Quebec that would have a significant impact on their lives.

Some 400 miles south-west of Montreal, there lived a man in Hamilton, Ontario who had garnered a great deal of police attention. He was a second-generation Canadian who had been born and raised in Hamilton many years ago. His father had arrived in Canada as a young immigrant from Italy in 1900. That immigrant was named Antonio Papalia, and his son was called Johnny Pops

Papalia, a.k.a. The Enforcer. By all accounts, Johnny Papalia was the reputed head of the Mafia in Canada in the mid-1960s and later.

The surnames are spelled the same, and both families came from the southern part of Italy to different parts of Canada some fifty-seven years apart. There the similarities stop since the two families are completely unrelated. Robert and Tony have never met Johnny Papalia nor spoken to him. They have no connection with the underworld, Italian or otherwise. But later events would cause their names to be linked with that of the Hamilton Papalias on a number of occasions by certain misguided zealots from the RCMP and other law enforcement agencies.

Attached to all Canadian stock exchanges is a Compliance and Security Branch which senses to ensure all investors and listed companies comply with the laws and rules of the particular exchange and to the trading of securities in each jurisdiction. Any person who seeks to become licensed to work as a broker on an exchange or who seeks to work in an exchange itself must file security clearance documents containing personal background and information.

In the first few years that Robert and Tony were involved in the business world they were unaware of any difficulty with their names or their reputations. They both worked for CIBC without incident. When they left the bank to enter the stock exchange community, they were able to take positions in brokerage firms and, in Robert's case, to work briefly on the trading floor of the Montreal Stock Exchange again without any problems.

The other issue to affect the course of their lives was the Cultural Revolution underway in the province of Quebec -- often referred to as the Quiet Revolution. Since 1759 and the Battle of the Plains of Abraham, the defeated French had lived quiet and subtly-oppressed lives in Quebec under the authority of their English-speaking conquerors. They retained their language and certain aspects of their culture and, in the main, lived quiet rural lives.

After the Second World War however, French-speaking intellectuals, professionals and political leaders began to take their places in the public life of the Province. The French outnumber the English in Quebec by almost four to one. In Montreal, where the English community was concentrated, the French still held a majority position with persons of Italian descent forming the third largest group behind the English. The Italian community was the largest ethnic group in Montreal at that time and still is today.

The situation in Quebec became increasingly politicized in the 1960s. Slogans such as Maitre Chez Nous (Masters in our Own House) were being used by the leading political parties. Other political parties were being formed with even more radical platforms -- to create Quebec as a separate French-speaking nation apart from the rest of Canada. In May 1968, a series of bombs went off in post boxes in the elite Anglo-districts of Mount Royal and Westmount in Montreal. A group advocating the liberation of Quebec called the FLQ (Font de Liberation de Quebec), claimed responsibility. Walking past a post box became a courageous act in Montreal in those days.

An outspoken Cabinet Minister in the Quebec Liberal government, Rene Levesque gave an interview to the New York Times in 1965 in which he made the comment, "We (Quebec) could get along better without Canada than Canada could get along without us."

In 1966, the Liberals were defeated in the provincial elections and the Union National came into power. This was the death-throe of what had once been the most powerful political force in Quebec politics from the 1930s through to the late 1950s under Maurice Duplessis, a Premier who ruled Quebec for almost 30 years as a patronizing autocrat. Now led by Daniel Johnson, the Union National with its conservative policies, ruled for only two years and did not wake up to the political realities sweeping across the province. Within a few short years, the Union National disappeared into political oblivion.

At this time, a group of powerful and influential Liberals began to meet on an informal basis to discuss policy issues on the future direction of their party. These included Levesque, Robert Bourassa, and Eric Kierans. Discussions began to move more and more toward the need for special status for the province within the Confederation of Canada because of its non-English-speaking nature. Apparently, Levesque first presented his vision of a sovereignty-association between Quebec and Canada at one of these meetings.

In early 1967, the direction of the group under Levesque's leadership turned toward separate status for Quebec. Eventually, this emphasis led to a split in the group with great many of the center-line Liberals leaving to return to the fold of the Liberal Party. The Parti Quebecois was formed out of these early discussion groups under Levesque. This party was to rise into prominence during the 1970s to replace the ever-diminishing Union Nationale.

In the 1976, as leader of the Parti Quebecois, Levesque would become Premier of the Province with the goal to separate Quebec from Canada. After two referendums, one in 1980 and a second under the leadership of Jacques Parizeau in 1995, delivery of this idea has yet to be achieved. But the results of the 1995 poll show virtually equal support for separation and unity. With Lucien Bouchard assuming power in the province in 1996, the future of Quebec remaining part of Canada is tenuous.

On June 24, 1967, Charles DeGaulle, President of France, visited Canada to participate in the Canadian Centennial celebrations. He stood on the balcony of the Montreal City Hall and in a speech to the assembled crowd uttered the now infamous statement, "Vive le Quebec! Vive le Quebec Libre!"

The reaction to this utterance was explosive. It hit every newspaper, radio and TV station in Canada as THE STORY of the day. The Prime Minister of Canada, Lester Pearson, was infuriated and DeGaulle cut short his visit to return to France the next day.

There were more manifestations of the French desire for liberation. Other terrorist acts continued to take place in Quebec. There were news stories about how young Quebecois were being trained as guerrilla terrorists in Cuba. Probably in the minds of most Canadians, the unrest reached a crescendo with the kidnapping of James Cross, a British Diplomat, followed soon after by the kidnapping and murder of the Quebec Cabinet Minister, Pierre Laporte. These two events occurred in October, 1970 and caused the Prime Minister of Canada, Pierre Elliot Trudeau to declare a state of emergency in the Province of Quebec. This time became known as the October Crisis.

Over 400 innocent Quebecois were swooped down upon and put into detention without cause for several weeks and, in some cases, for months by the Canadian security forces brought to bear on the situation. Eventually, Cross' hiding place was discovered after some six weeks of uncertainty. The apartment was surrounded and negotiations resulted in the hostage-takers being driven to the airport for a flight to Cuba. Cross was then released.

None of these issues had yet touched upon the lives of Robert and Tony directly. They knew the unrest was there and they followed the stories in the press each day, but it wasn't any part of their lives.

The law enforcement agency which had primary responsibility for national security in Canada at the time was the RCMP. Unfortunately, the laws governing their behavior did not spell out a clear statutory mandate for the Force to implement counter-terrorist activities should they be deemed necessary or useful to ensure national security. As a result of this lack of direction and guidelines, it is now known that the RCMP reacted to the threat of separatism in ways that are excessive and illegal.

So, the problems that Tony and Robert were about to enter into with the RCMP were initiated during this climate of unrest, terror and violence that was swirling around Montreal at the time.

In late 1966, the Twins were approached by a representative of Warner Brothers/ Seven Arts. Robert and Tony had continued to perform from time to time in their clubs and they sometimes appeared on music programs on radio and TV geared to the youth market. They had become quite well known in the Quebec music industry and were extremely fluent in three languages English, French and Italian.

With this in mind, Warner Brothers negotiated a contract with the Papalias to cut a record. In the past they had sung under the name The Twins but now they were to become a French recording duo known as Robert et Tony.

Over the winter of 1966 and into early 1967, the boys spent two and a half months in a recording studio where they produced several songs that included La Vie Ensemble and La Joie Dan Le Coeur. A record containing these two pieces was cut. After its release they began a tiring round of personal appearances and performances.

For instance, on Monday, they might start out in Sherbrooke, taping for CHLT-TV at 3:00 pm. At 4:00 pm, they performed live on the same TV station. On Tuesday, they traveled to Quebec where at 1:30 pm they appeared on CFCM-TV's *Entre Nous* show. Then they went to CFLS radio at 3:00 pm, to CJRP radio at 4:00 pm, and back to CFCM-TV at 6:30 pm for the *Allez-Y* teen show.

On Wednesday they were in Chicoutimi, where they appeared on CMT radio at 1:30pm and at CJPM-TV at 2:45pm. They left there and drove to Jonquiere to CKRS-TV and radio at 4:00pm for taping. This circuit would continue for the rest of the week. On the weekend, they would return to Montreal only to begin the cycle again the following Monday. They kept up this schedule for almost a year and a half.

La Vie Ensemble did very well and reached the Top-10 of French pop-songs in Quebec that year.

Inevitably, these two representatives of Quebeçois youth would be asked the question on everyone's mind and lips. It happened on live TV in Quebec City: "So what do you guys think about a free Quebec?" This was the first time the question had ever been asked of them. They were unprepared and had not really thought out their answer. Almost spontaneously, Tony gave the V for victory sign and replied, "Vive le Quebec Libre!"

It was delivered in a way to express sympathy for and to jokingly mimic DeGaulle's public remark. Tony never expected or intended to become a spokesperson for the separatist movement but, he was not averse to expressing publicly his opinion. As the tour continued and he was asked the question again and again, he began to give more considered responses.

Neither Twin had ever been particularly political, but they found themselves siding with the position of newness, change and upheaval like a great many other young people of the day. They saw nothing remarkable about this position as the matter was being debated daily in all parts of the province.

But Tony was about to find out that, indeed, people were paying attention to his views. He appeared on a Montreal TV show and spoke in favor of separatism when asked his opinion. This time he was heard by a number of people who knew him on the street in the Montreal financial community. Some of these people were shocked that a non-Francophone immigrant, with significant ties to the English-speaking business community of Montreal would hold such beliefs. Tony was beginning to show his talent for being controversial.

Both brothers, of course, wanted to keep their hands in at the market. But the controversy, generated by Tony's statements and their heavy touring schedule played against them. They were forced to find pay phones while on the road and sometimes, with only moments between appearances, they were trying to close deals with their brokers on the phone. Clearly, their pop-music life styles did not enhance their ability to follow the market as they wanted.

Their physical appearances also created a problem with certain members of the financial community. They wore their hair rather conservatively by rock-music standards, but rather long, by the norm of the financial arena. Several associates and brokers asked them to cut their hair to look more conventional.

They were regarded as freaks by some business associates. Some of the old-guard felt threatened by these brash, young, long-haired Italians who were becoming prominent players on the MSE. They were considered pariahs by many of the financial establishment because of their style, political views and their involvement with rock-music. Because they were not yet big-time players and not yet involved full-time in the financial community, the Twins were unaware at this stage how deep the animosity actually ran.

In 1968, they finished the promotion of their record. Robert and Tony had to make some choices. They fully realized that the financial and business world did not mesh well with the music industry. It was time to decide which direction to take, and to devote all of their energy to one or the other. Robert had days now where he would come home to face over a hundred messages on his answering machine. Some of the clubs were not doing well when the Twins were not there to look after them. Some of their employees were pocketing money for themselves. The clientele was becoming rougher; there were more fights breaking out, more hassles to solve.

The music business had its perks, but in 1968, it was not yet as lucrative as it would eventually become. Even with a hit record, they had not made exceptional money and their schedule to promote it had been grueling and disruptive. Constant touring to small towns and living in hotels became very wearing. Their recordings had been in French and were aimed at the Quebec market alone. Real success required that they cross-over into the much larger English rock-music market. Outside of Quebec, they were virtual unknowns despite their constant TV and radio exposure.

In retrospect and in light of all that has happened to them since, the Twins often reflect on whether they would have been better off to stick with their music but they did not. They decided instead to enter full time into the business world. The economy was still expanding, the markets were buoyant and the possibilities for people with drive and imagination seemed limitless.

They began by liquidating their holdings in the teen clubs and rock-music paraphernalia shops. As 1968 closed, their efforts became more concentrated in stock speculation and investment. They were doing fewer rock promotions. That business was becoming dominated by people such as Donald K. Donald who, today, is still the largest and best-known event promoter in Montreal.

When the Twins left the music world, they also left behind a forum for expressing their political views. It wasn't long before they were once again just interested bystanders in the Quebec political scene.

For the first year and a half after moving into the stock market, Robert worked as a broker for ET Lynch & Co. while Tony concentrated on investing full-time. Initially, they both found their golden touch to be working again for them as several highly favorable trades came their way. They became part of a highly successful group of young investors working the Montreal Stock Exchange.

Their reputations as knowledgeable investors continued to grow as they and their group of friends made a number of masterful speculative investments. This had a compounding effect upon their later investments as more and more people sought to get in on stocks that they had marked as picks. Robert admits that sometimes this led them to act somewhat irresponsibly at times. When they got onboard a stock that began to really fly, they would sometimes cash in early rather than wait to see if the company would perform as anticipated. They were not in any sense of the word, insiders or promoters of these stocks. They purchased only on the basis of public information available to them and on rumors on the street.

In one instance, Tony learned of a stock on the New York Exchange called Jupiter Enterprises trading at about $7.00. Tony bought some shares and told several friends about it. When the stock shot up to $17.00, those who had listened to him thought he was a kind of whiz-kid. Shortly after that at a social event in New York, Tony meets Dr. Dodick who started a company with a new product called Bausch & Lomb. The shares were trading at $3.80 and Tony liked the product, lenses for eyewear. Together Tony and Robert invested and bought 30,000 shares. In the eleven months that followed, the shares sky-rocketed and reached the price of $198.00 per share.

While Robert was an assistant trader on the Montreal Stock Exchange, he heard about a small Canadian company called Velcro that had gone public at less than $1.00 and was trading around $25.00 dollars. Robert bought some shares and so did Tony and some of their friends. Later, the product of Velcro was used in the space program and made the cover of Time magazine and the shares reached the astronomical price of $800.00 per share. These investments made a lot of money for Tony and Robert and their friends but most important it made their reputation as whiz-kids grow large and made them well-known and admired by their friends. Both Tony and Robert acknowledge however, that there is extreme luck in making picks like these.

Incidents like this, led Tony and Robert to the conclusion that they should get into the deal-making, promotional end of the business. In early 1969, Robert gave up his broker's job allowing him the freedom to participate fully in the promotion of public companies.

At the same time, Tony was offered a position in the corporate financing department of the brokerage firm, Bouchard & Co. His first venture required raising one-half million dollars. He completed this financing in three days and the stock increased in value by 120 percent.

One day, Robert acquired controlling interest in an MSE listed company, Pacific Nickel Mines Limited. He sought to become President, but there was some concern about this position because of his young age. A formal hearing was held as to his suitability for this lofty post. At the end of the hearing, the regulators involved congratulated him on becoming the youngest President at 24 years of age, of a publicly-traded company anywhere in North America.

It was this company which was to put Tony and Robert on the path toward the gold mining venture that to this day, has become their life's work.

Little did they realize however, that forces outside their control were about to drop down on them heavily. Their name, past life style and open political statements were to come together in ways that would haunt them as they could never have imagined at that time.

In Toronto, where the largest and most important exchange in Canada is located today to the loss of Montreal after the events of the Quebec Separatist issue of the early 1970s and the systematic destruction of the Montreal Financial Markets perpetrated by agents and police forces of the Federal Government in order to show Quebec depressed because of its Separatist sentiment during this period. These horrible illegal activities by agencies of the Federal Government, RCMP and CSIS can be seen in the books and reports of the MacDonald Commission.

Head of the Commercial Securities branch of the RCMP at that time was a man by the name of Kesley Merry. He was also one of the main players to the illegal sabotage of Quebec as later proven, organizing sabotage, frame up and outright terrorism to make the Separatists look bad. He had been watching the Twins for some time and started to prepare his plan to have the Twins work for this new force he was putting together to sabotage Quebec and the Twins seemed to him perfect choices since they were extremely popular and their friends included the 'who's who' of Quebec at the time. They could be his perfect agents, so he started to compile files on Robert and Tony to give them the image for what he had in mind for them. He had compiled a file which linked the Twins to organized crime (the Hamilton connection), to separatist activities (Tony's public comments) and to suspicion about their financial activities (their flashy life style and methods).

Despite the intense examination of Robert by the Securities Commission in Montreal regarding Pacific Nickel Mines Limited, this merry gentleman would continue to hound the Twins for the next decade. It should be noted that whenever they have been subjected to a properly-conducted scrutiny, the Papalias have always received the highest security clearance by government agencies in the USA, in Italy and in other parts of the world.

Diabolical Behavior

SHORTLY AFTER RESOLVING their Lawyer's problems, the Twins and Mario were introduced to two other men who would become substantially involved in the conduct of their case.

Loris Fortuna, a member of the Italian parliament, and Giuseppe Bombara, his law partner, went to London in July 1977. The newspapers in Italy were filled with the story of Torri's arrest and the massive fraud case being built against him. At the Italian Embassy, Bombara and Fortuna were briefed by a senior attaché assigned to monitor the case for the Italian government.

The diplomat told them. "I've been following the case very closely in the papers. While reported as the Torri case in Italy, here the emphasis is not solely on him. There are several prominent businessmen involved, including two Canadian-Italian brothers with an interest in a Canadian gold mine. It is very unclear how all the pieces fit together."

Bombara had been Torri's lawyer in Italy during his previous legal problems and asked if he could visit him. The attaché offered to make the necessary arrangements for them to go to Brixton. He then added, "Would you mind looking in on the others as well? They are all Italians, although the two have dual citizenship. I'm sure they would appreciate knowing we are aware of their circumstances."

The following morning at Brixton, a jailer came to the Italians' cell. "There are two lawyers from the Italian Embassy here. They want to meet you lot. They say they will speak with Torri first, and the rest of you afterwards."

As the group waited for Torri's lawyers, they wondered if the Italian government might be able to help them. "Thank God," thought Robert. Then turning to the others, he said, "One of the Embassies is finally willing to get involved. Maybe the Italians can exert some pressure for our release."

For weeks, the brothers had left message after message with the Canadian embassy that they were in a British jail and could use some assistance. All their requests were met with stony silence. But the Twins had not been forgotten, the Canadian authorities were deliberately ignoring them.

At the time, memos and telexes were flying between Canadian diplomats in London and their counterparts in Ottawa. The correspondence shows grave concern that the case might become a major story in the British Press. The Canadian

Embassy was instructed by Ottawa to provide the best excuses possible as to why they had not visited nor contacted the Papalias in prison. It is clear that the Canadian government wanted to do nothing to assist these particular Canadians while they were in the hands of British authorities.

Correspondence later obtained under the Canadian Privacy Act shows that the Department of External Affairs took great interest in all press reports about the case. Tony Papalia was viewed as a fugitive and the Canadian authorities asked for his extradition as early as September 1977. Comments about Robert suggest he was a person with criminal intent and the English case was a potential embarrassment to Canada.

The Foreign Legal Office of the Department of External Affairs made its position very clear in September 1977: "we do not-repeat-not believe it appropriate to raise questions of bail and intervene on their behalf."

The Canadian authorities in Ottawa were under the mistaken impression that bail had been set in the case at £10,000 pounds each and that the Papalias were asking for assistance to have this amount reduced.

A copy of a submission by the defendants to the European Commission on Human Rights in Strasbourg was sent by Bischoff and Co. and Offenbach and Co. to the Canadian High Commission requesting that Canada indicate its interest in the outcome of their application. The reply from the Consulate stated that as long as they were under arrest in Britain there was little that could be done. Canada was not a party to the European Convention although the United Kingdom was. It was presumed the British would abide by their signed treaties.

One ridiculous excuse given for the lack of consular support was that "Papalia brothers have not-repeat-not advised Brixton authorities that they are Canadian citizens ... no record of any formal request for a visit by consular officer."

This ludicrous position was put forward despite the huge flow of letters from family members and lawyers in both Montreal and London. A telegram was even sent to the Prime Minister's Office from Tony and Robert detailing their difficulties in arranging a consular visit.

They waited patiently for Torri. When the jailer came to take them to their meeting, Torri returned with him. He entered the cell with a big smile on his face and they presumed things had gone well.

When Tony, Robert and Mario met Fortuna and Bombara for the first time, they were surprised by the extreme dissimilarity between the two men; Loris Fortuna was a tall, dashing gentleman about forty-five years old with premature steel-grey, wavy hair, piercing dark eyes and healthy tanned skin. He was a forceful, charismatic man. Guiseppe Bombara was a diminutive, balding fellow with a pale, waxy complexion and a prominent nose that echoed the generous area of his ample stomach. But when the shorter man opened his mouth to speak, he was instantly transformed into a person with authority from the resonance of his voice and the eloquence of his flowing Italian language.

The visitors introduced themselves. Fortuna told them he had been asked by the Italian government to look into their situation. The three prisoners were awed by the status of their visitors, but the two lawyers showed such warmth and concern that the meeting soon became one between equals.

After Fortuna and Bombara had heard their story, Fortuna immediately said, "I believe in your innocence. Torri confirmed your story in many respects, and he tells us you had nothing to do with Bear Securities. He also admits he knows almost nothing about your business."

"I suspect you have been framed. The British police have been taken in by Torri's diabolical international reputation to presume that if he is involved with a particular banking concern, then it must be illegal. From that base, they have drawn in every Italian who has done business with Bear Securities. They claim to have uncovered an enormous conspiracy. The case seems far-fetched to me."

Tony asked, "What do you mean by Torri's reputation being diabolical?"

Fortuna smiled, "What do you know of Torri? Anything?"

They all shrugged. "Very little. He told us that Khassogi hates him but other than that, he keeps his past to himself."

Fortuna winked at Bombara. "Why don't you fill them in a little, Giuseppe?"

Bombara began, "Mr. Berton, do you remember the Number One scandal in Rome that happened about eight years ago?"

"I didn't follow it too closely, but I remember there was a huge scandal," replied Mario. Then he looked at Bombara with lit-up eyes, "Do you mean the Torri with us in Brixton is the same man involved in the Number One story?"

Bombara nodded, "Exactly!"

Mario shook his head and cursed under his breath. By now, Robert and Tony were on the edge of their seats, wanting to know more. "Well, go on then -- tell us." And so Bombara began the tale of Torri.

Pier Luigi Torri was a fixture in Roman society in the mid-to-late 1960s. He was a young, eligible bachelor from an aristocratic family. As a young man he had become involved in the production of several soft-porn Italian movies.

Whenever his picture appeared in the Italian gossip pages, he was listed as "Torri, the movie producer". In reality however, Torri was one of those people who were mostly famous for being famous. His background, style and propensity for trouble all made him an eminently reportable personality.

Torri was known as a grand playboy, a jet-set figure. He seemed to spend his time in the most glittering and expensive casinos and nightclubs in Italy and Monte Carlo. He drove Rolls-Royces and Ferraris. He won and lost millions of lira at the gambling tables. He owned a villa and his yacht was reported to be one of the largest and fanciest in the world. In public he always appeared with beautiful women on his arm. Marissa Mell, the gorgeous Austrian actress, had been his companion for several years at the time of our story.

His first moment of notoriety occurred in 1963 at a Monte Carlo nightclub called Cabala. Torri gratuitously insulted a woman who approached him in the club. When he didn't get the appropriate response to his insult, he escalated the abuse further until a gentleman in her group threw a punch at Torri. To escape the attack, Torri, who was a lover, not a fighter, fled by leaping over people and tables, as he went, all eyes in the club were upon him. Once across the room he climbed some stairs to a small door and lunged through it. The door however, was not an exit from the club but rather an access port to the building's chimney. Torri re-emerged covered in soot, dizzy from smoke and with singed hair. The clientele roared with laughter and applauded his comeuppance. The incident was reported in all the newspapers next day.

From that day, Torri became the star of the Italian Press, despite the revulsion of most of their readers; there was always great public interest in his antics.

Several years later, Torri and another "movie producer", Bino Cicogna, decided they wanted to run their own nightclub, one that would be truly unique. They located an obsolete war ship and planned to place it fully-refurbished with all amenities in the harbour at Basilia, an Italian resort on the Adriatic. Their plan was to create an exclusive gambling casino for the European trash/cash set.

Although the idea never got off the drawing board, it gave a great deal of press coverage to Torri and Cicogna as they attempted to put the deal together.

One of the fancier clubs in Rome at the time was called Number One located on the Via Veneto, near the American Embassy in Rome. This was the height of the dolce vita period in Rome and Number One became the place to hang out. Italian principessas were always there with publishers, playboys, and princes some of the habitués of the club mingling with starlets and socialites. This is where Torri and Bino spent much of their time.

The man who managed this trendy club was named Vassallo, himself a playboy rumored to have bed the wife of the Aga Khan, among several other famous women. Vassallo attended artfully to the whims and fancies of his want-for-nothing clientele. He pioneered the practice of roping off part of the club for the exclusive use of those who qualified as VIPs. As the drug scene began to grown in Italy, someone at Number One began to ensure that whatever the customer wanted, the customer got. Cocaine was a very sheik drug in those days. It was used by an enclave of the jet-set who believed it enhanced love-making. Of all the recreational drugs available then, cocaine was viewed as a fashionable plaything to enhance the wide-open sexual practices becoming prevalent.

People seated in the VIP lounge could signal their desire for some white powder by ordering certain code drinks. A request for a gin fizz for example, would bring the drink to the patron's table but also a packet of coke costing an additional fifty-thousand lira.

Understandably, there were some casualties as this open experiment in recreational drug use took place. Bino Cicogna, Torri's close friend, became totally involved in the 'coke' scene. His addiction became so great that his nose and mouth began to show signs of collapse and disintegration.

Bino was so far gone that he made a final desperate attempt to divorce himself from the drug and the entire scene that was destroying him. Curiously, for whatever reason, the place to which he decided to flee was Rio de Janeiro.

But shortly after his arrival in Brazil, Bino was found dead, with his head inside a plastic bag in an oven. The official conclusion of the much publicized investigation into his death was that he committed suicide in despair of his failure to cure himself. Was it really suicide? There was much speculation that Bino had been murdered because a clean, rehabilitated and sober Cicogna Bino would return to Italy to expose or denounce drug distribution at Number One.

Torri was devastated by the loss of his best friend and firmly believed he had been murdered. Not content to grieve alone, he went to Number One one night and positioned himself in a prominent place in the club. Calling for silence he announced to the assembled throng, "Bino Cicogna is dead. Bino was my greatest friend." He did not stop there. On and on he went with his rhapsody of grief accusing his listeners of being the cause of Bino's death. Finally, in a histrionic frenzy, he raged at the crowd, "I will destroy all of you!"

The link between Bino Cicogna's supposed drug-related death and Torri's accusation at Number One solidified the rumors flying around Rome that drugs were being served in the club. The police finally decided to act. One night while Vassallo was away in Paris, the nightclub was raided and cocaine was found on the premises. A great many people in the club were arrested, many of them rich, influential and famous. A police investigation was commenced into all regular patrons of Number One.

The police anxiously awaited Vassallo's return to Rome. They staked out all the airports hoping to apprehend him. He arrived at Fiumicino Airport and the police followed him as he drove his yellow Volkswagen to his lawyer's office. When Vassallo went inside, the police removed his car and conducted a search. Under the car battery, they discovered a sizable quantity of cocaine. Subsequently, they claimed that the chemical composition of the drug in Vassallo's car was exactly the same as that found in the nightclub.

He was immediately taken into custody for questioning. He had an exculpatory explanation for the drugs. He told the police and the media was, "I've been framed. Torri hates me. He planted the drugs in my car and at the club to make good on his threat to destroy me."

In Italy, the system of justice is different than English common law. Whenever a criminal allegation is made, an investigation is begun by an official who combines the powers of a magistrate and prosecutor. All other inquiries that arose from finding drugs at the club had to be suspended until these new allegations about Torri could be resolved. For if Torri was guilty, then everyone else was innocent and he had simply planted the drugs in a vain attempt to frame them.

Actually the prosecutors were rather reluctant to proceed with the initial charges as they implicated a large and influential segment of Roman society. The potential defendants, over 300 people, included many important people in Rome and around Europe who were reported to have done cocaine at the club.

The list included journalists, actors, magistrates, politicians, and at least, one member of the British royalty.

The accusations caused a media sensation. The city buzzed with gossip about the case. Public opinion, as might be expected, was divided into two camps: Everyone is guilty or everyone is innocent. The latter group believed Torri was behind the frame-up of all these influential people.

Soon after the investigation against Torri began, it was determined that he should stand trial on the allegations that he planted the drugs. Bombara, Fortuna and two other lawyers presented a defense which sought to prove that Number One was a place where the spoiled and degenerate-rich went routinely to drug themselves. The strategy proved successful as they drew out evidence through cross-examination and otherwise about the overpowering role that drugs played in the social lives of many of the prosecution's witnesses.

It may seem strange that Torri should be put on trial for such a charge but as the case progressed, it took an even more bizarre turn. Torri made himself hated wherever he went. He even enraged one of the judges by parking his Rolls-Royce in the judge's personal parking space. Then one day, a young, beautiful woman arrived at the courthouse. She said she had evidence to give.

She was led into the chambers to make her declaration but instead of talking, she produced a tape deck. She advised the court that her evidence was recorded on tape and she wished to play it for them. On the tape was a voice which everyone in the courtroom recognized immediately -- the chief judge/prosecutor of Rome. The court was hushed as all the assembled heard the voice say, "If you love me again one more time like this, very soon I'll let your boy out."

This was too much. The Italian papers had a field day, trumpeting the scandal upon scandal on this case. The prosecutor's office was in turmoil. The officials were very embarrassed and angry, not at the chief prosecutor, but rather, at the persons who would go to such lengths to bring the prosecutor's office into disrepute. It took little time for the prosecutor's office to announce their official response to the tape -- it was a trap designed specifically to destroy the reputation of the chief judge. There was evidence that Torri had instigated the making of the tape and he was now charged with "defamation of a judge".

In 1968, after a full year of trial on the original drug charge, Torri was acquitted. On the defamation charge however, he was convicted and a prison term was imposed. Bombara immediately appealed the decision and Torri was allowed to remain free while the appeal was heard. Bombara called Torri into his office and told him he would fight like a tiger for him but he must be prepared for the worst as the politics of this case were clearly against him.

On the day of the appeal Bombara went before the judges and argued the case with everything he had. During a break in the proceedings he telephoned Torri to update him on how things were going but Torri had left Italy. He could not face the prospect of jail.

Bombara knew that unless the appeal was successful, Torri would probably remain a fugitive. Later that day when the proceedings came to an end, the appellate court voted to uphold the conviction. Bombara left the courthouse and steeled himself for the following day. He knew he would be inundated by reporters once word got out that Torri had fled the country.

Of the many prominent people awaiting trial on the drug charges arising from the Number One case, all had their trials stayed indefinitely once Torri's appeal was upheld and he had fled Italy. Torri was about the only friendly witness for the prosecution's case about drug activities at the club. With Torri's conviction he was now a criminal, and could not be a credible witness. And, with his absence, there was no chance of his testifying at all. It was a most convenient result for the beautiful people who had been under investigation.

❧

At this point in his story, Bombara paused. He looked at Robert, Tony and Mario's wide eyes. "Would you like a cigarette?" he asked. The brothers and Mario each took a cigarette from the proffered pack.

"Well, as you can imagine," continued Bombara, "when the Italian Press got wind of Torri's arrest in London, they went crazy. In addition to rehashing the old news about Torri and Number One, they are reporting every fine detail they can get about this case."

Fortuna laughed, "Yes, in their usual way, they have done everything they can to obscure the truth and make the story as fantastic as their imaginations allow. One report had Torri conspiring with a group of Colombians with strong hints at drug connections. These Colombians were claiming to own a mine that not only had an unlimited supply of gold, but also produced emeralds. We can presume that the people who wrote these stories thought that a Columbia emerald mine was more exotic and would sell more papers than a plain old gold mine in a Western province of Canada."

Bombara asked, "Do you know why Khassogi and Torri hate each other?"

"Not exactly", replied Robert.

"It has the same basis as Prince Rainier's dislike for Torri."

Robert looked disbelieving, "The Prince of Monaco? What does he have to do with Torri?"

Bombara was enjoying this. "Oh, nothing really -- just another of Torri's escapades. About a year after Torri left Italy, I received a postcard from him. On the back of the card was written: The sun in Monte Carlo is stupendous but, I'm very tired of seeing it in squares. So shake your ass and come free me."

He continued, "So I went to Monaco immediately and found him in an ancient prison right under the Prince's palace. He had been arrested following a Customs search in which a sizable sum of undeclared currency had been found. His yacht is one of the biggest and most sumptuous on the European coast. He told me Rainier had asked to buy the boat on several occasions but always he refused. When Torri arrived in Monte Carlo on his yacht following his latest refusal, the boat was boarded by Customs agents who didn't stop searching until they found something. What they found was one-hundred million undeclared liras in a safe."

Bombara obtained the services of three prominent French attorneys as French laws apply in the Principality of Monaco.

The trial was held in Nice. At the trial the lawyers were able to show that Torri had been denied the required statutory time limit to make a proper declaration. His yacht had entered the harbor at 1:00 am in the morning. The raid and seizure occurred in the early hours of the same day before he was legally required to complete his declaration. Torri was found not guilty.

Several years later, while living in London, Torri met Adnan Khassogi, a new but important player in the international social scene. Khassogi was reputed to be an arms dealer who had apparently accumulated a vast fortune.

He heard about Torri's beautiful yacht and he asked Torri whether a friend of his, an Arabian Prince, could use his boat for a week's cruise out of Gibraltar. Khassogi was prepared to pay a very handsome sum to charter the vessel and so Torri agreed to the proposal. Unfortunately, a significant cultural gap existed about the proper activities that could occur on board his yacht. When it was returned to Torri, it had been desecrated.

Mahogany cupboards and drawers had been ripped out to feed the open fires made on the teak deck to cook meals of goat and lamb. Several animals had been brought on board to be kept in a stateroom until they were slaughtered. Accoutrements such as the fine cutlery, dishes and glassware had been lost or broken. When Torri surveyed the damage he was appalled and outraged. Torri was a man given to extremes at the best of times. Doubtless the blowup between himself and Khassogi was a memorable one. Eventually he sued Khassogi for the cost of repairs to his vessel and was awarded damages.

But Khassogi, despite his reputed wealth, simply refused to pay. The two men became bitter and openly hostile to one another. They developed a hatred toward each other that ran deep. Each would slight or insult the other whenever they accidentally crossed paths in London. It was not surprising then, that Torri believed Khassogi must have a hand in these current troubles.

Bombara finished recounting the story and as he did so, Robert, Tony and Mario found their minds drifting back to the four walls of their meeting room. For over an hour they had been transported mentally to the racy European lifestyle that in its breadth and freedom was reminiscent of their own until the time of their arrest. They felt as if they had been allowed to walk outside the walls of Brixton for a short while and now had returned to the gloomy, grey, barren little room where they were sitting.

Tony turned to Robert, "You know Robert, despite the fact that Torri is one of the most arrogant, obnoxious people I have ever met, I could almost feel sorry for him after hearing this stuff. He's sure had his share of trouble."

Robert nodded and then replied, "Yeah, but the man is a fugitive from justice.

Being on trial with him isn't going to make our lives any easier. He looks like a three-time loser."

Robert turned to Bombara and Fortuna. "We appreciate your coming to give us this background information, but more importantly, can you help us?"

"Yes, that is why we have come here -- to help you," said Fortuna, "We cannot act as lawyers for you here in England, but we can offer our professional support for those aspects of the case that need looking after in Italy. We can help gather evidence for your defense there and in other parts of the world."

"As well, we can offer the usual support that the Italian government would offer its citizens in your circumstances. We will ensure that diplomatic channels are put to use to lobby for your release from prison. We will instruct the Italian Embassy to assist you to find sureties acceptable to the British courts. We plan to do everything we can to help."

"We appreciate very much what you are offering to do," said Robert and then he added, "It seems strange that a man of your stature would become involved in a case like this one."

Looking very serious, Fortuna replied, "I know what it is like to be locked away and persecuted for no good reason. My life is about helping people caught up in injustices such as yours." With that, he arose from his chair signaling an end to their meeting. "We will return when our investigation is completed on the matters you have discussed with us."

The prisoners thanked the two lawyers, shook hands and banged on the door to be returned to their cell. Upon entering their cell, Tony looked at Torri and exclaimed wryly, "Torri, you never told us what a diabolical character you are."

Torri who was lying on his bunk, smiled. His natural reserve and aristocratic demeanor had prevented him from confiding in his cell mates, but he was pleased that they now knew how infamous he was back in Italy. He had a perverted sense of pride in his many escapades.

Robert asked Torri, "These fellows, Fortuna and Bombara, are they serious about helping us?"

Torri replied. "They are good men. Fortuna never shies away from an unpopular or difficult cause. They helped me when everyone in Italy was against me. And Fortuna went up against the Vatican on the divorce issue in Italy. He is the number one reason that divorce is legal in Italy."

Tony was walking the cell. "Well, this is looking better. Hopefully in a few days we will have all our sureties and we can be released from this hole. I think I'll go crazy if I have to spend much longer in here."

The others concurred and they settled down to their routines to pass the time and wait for their next court appearance and freedom.

It was the first week of August and David Benham was in his office trying to clear away all of the pressing matters on his desk. Everything that had looked like it might be a problem over the next few weeks had been resolved and he was looking forward to his vacation.

He was reviewing his files with Geoff Lines, ensuring that his staff knew the current status of each case. They came to R. v. Berton, Papalia and others.

"Ah, yes. Well, I don't anticipate anything arising here during my absence. Nigel is fully instructed and sureties acceptable to the court are ready to be put in place. After the hearing next week, Messrs. Berton, Papalia and Papalia should be released on bail. After that it's simply a matter of preparing for the Committal hearing and that looks to be months away."

When they were done reviewing the files, David picked up his pipe and prepared to leave for his vacation. "Geoff, if anything unexpected should arise, be sure not to call me," he said with a wink.

Geoff knew he wasn't serious and replied, "Oh, I don't think there is anything here we can't handle. Have a good holiday and forget about the office."

Five days later, the prisoners were brought before the court again. This time they anticipated being released on bail. They sat in the holding cell at the Magistrate's Court waiting for their turn, all of them anxious, not a word being spoken. Finally, mid-morning, their case was called. As they entered the court, they saw their barrister already on his feet. He looked very angry. His face was red and he was reading a piece of paper.

"My Lord, I must protest the behavior of the Crown in this case. They gave me no notice that they were planning to lay a completely new set of charges. The first I knew of this was when my learned friend handed me this paper only two minutes ago. I've had no opportunity to seek instructions from my clients. I request this matter be stood down long enough for me to talk with my clients."

The request was granted and almost as soon as they had entered the courtroom, the prisoners were led back out to await their lawyer in the holding cell. Nigel Milne, his robes flying and his wig slightly askew, came marching into the cell. Behind him followed the diminutive figure of Geoff Lines.

"Well, fellows, the Crown is doing everything in its power to ensure you are not released. They've instituted seven new charges. They are now alleging that your supposed scam was a fraud in the range of two-hundred billion pounds. It is being touted as the biggest attempted fraud in the history of England."

"They are also hinting at something else, only hinting, but I think the Magistrate got the message. They are suggesting that you have ties to organized crime. The implication is that you are dangerous characters and it would not be in the community's best interest to release you. What do you say to these allegations?"

Tony erupted. "What is this? If you are Italian, you must be Mafia? I thought judges and lawyers were supposed to be intelligent people, not idiots!"

Nigel had a lengthy discussion with his clients and then returned to the courtroom. He argued with great force for release for his clients but it was not to be. They were not going to be released from prison for a very, very long time. The court canceled the terms of bail established for Mario the previous week and ruled that the accused were to be held in custody indefinitely.

❧

Another surprise awaited them upon their return to Brixton. They were sitting about the cell in a group funk of depression and anger, when who should be led into the room but Umberto Frascati, outfitted in Brixton attire.

Robert exclaimed, "What are you doing here?"

Downcast, Frascati replied, "I've been charged as well. They literally grabbed me off the street and shoved me in a car. At first I thought I was being kidnapped or was about to be killed."

Robert retorted, "Welcome to the Club!"

Frascati stated. "For months since your arrest, the police and, even my own lawyer have been telling me that I must testify against you about what I know of the conspiracy. They have hounded me. I told them a million times, there is no conspiracy; that you simply came to Bear Securities because of my efforts to recruit you as clients. Torri had nothing to do with it, I told them. I can't get on the stand and testify about a conspiracy when there wasn't one. I can't lie. It's not right. So, now I am a conspirator too because of my failure to cooperate."

Robert bounced from his chair and with heavy irony began to speak, "I've just figured it out. It all makes sense now. All Italians are in the Mafia and so if a group of Italians are doing business together, then it must be a conspiracy."

"Have you noticed that all the people in jail are Italians and other foreigners? Even Torri's poor little nineteen year-old receptionist is in jail. Should we come clean and admit she is the mastermind of the whole plot?" he said sarcastically.

The others smiled.

"And the Englishmen, Mann and Maude, nothing has happened to them. They of course, being British could have nothing to do with the conspiracy. Even though Richard has been charged, he has been let out on bail. The only reason they've charged him is because he's viewed as some hopeless, naive colonial who can be manipulated to testify against us. The police work in this case has been nothing short of brilliant."

Tony sat and listened to his brother's attempt at humor but he could manage nothing more than a wan smile. His brother and Mario were dealing with their incarceration better than he was -- he needed his freedom. He missed his wife. He missed his son. Today's disappointment was almost more than he could take. He found himself withdrawing mentally from his surroundings. He felt himself slipping deep inside himself. He felt as if he were falling into an immense black hole -- a hole so deep and so dark that he wondered if he would ever re-emerge.

Pattie's Story

PATRICIA BOLTON WAS raised in St. Laurent, a quiet multilingual suburb on the Island of Montreal. The daughter of Irish-Catholic immigrants, her father died when she was two years old but soon after her mother remarried a Protestant businessman. Her upbringing was strictly Catholic with a tight rein exercised by her mother and step-father.

In her early teens, she was only allowed to socialize during the day, never in the evening. One Sunday afternoon in 1967, as a young 14 year old, she accompanied several girl-friends to the Cheetah Club in nearby St. Leonard. A band was performing made up of several boys with whom she was friendly at school. During one of the sets, the lead singer became quite ill and was assisted from the stage to the Club Manager's office.

Tony happened to be working that day on the Club's record collection when his bouncer brought in the sick singer. In the hallway, he spied a petite red-headed beauty with a concerned took on her face. She inquired about her friend's health and was invited into the office. Tony was arranging to drive the boy home and he began a conversation with this young beauty.

He was instantly attracted to Pattie; perhaps it was her lack of interest in him, perhaps it was his mood at the time. Generally, Tony found it easy to meet and talk with women but in this case, the girl was aloof and not particularly enchanted with him. This was a challenge. He instructed his doorman to drive the boy home and Pattie asked if she could have a lift as well. Tony tried to convince her to stay but she refused. After dropping off the singer, instead of driving to her home, the doorman told her, "I have instructions to bring you back to the Club." And despite all her protests, he proceeded back to the Cheetah and left her with Tony.

Tony used all his skills to convince this colleen to go out with him but to no avail. She didn't really care for him and knew her parents would never agree to her dating a 22 year old man. In frustration, Tony drove her home releasing her to her fate with the advice, "Give me a call when you grow up."

Over the next few years, Tony saw her several times at his clubs but they never really talked again until one day when out for an early morning drive, he spied her walking along the street. He stopped and offered her a ride and they went for coffee and a talk. Pattie held an attraction for Tony that he found difficult to understand and explain. She did not react to him like other women. He could not manipulate or control her in any way. She did not appear to care for him at all but something inside him wanted to pursue her.

He asked her for a date and after much convincing, she agreed. But a part of him viewed this infatuation with disdain and he decided to have some fun with this little vixen. He arranged for Robert to go in his place, a game the two of them had played often in the past. It didn't take long for Pattie to recognize she was with another person despite the similarity in looks. She laughed at this trick and enjoyed herself that night despite the charade.

When next she met Tony, she rubbed his face in this deception until he felt very bad. This made her all the more attractive to him and so the pursuer became the prey -- he found himself falling deeply in love with the pretty woman and they began living together in 1974.

Pattie provided Tony with a stabilizing force in his life at a time when the world seemed to be crashing down around him and his brother. Her resolve, honesty, and love gave Tony the quiet counsel he needed in his life to survive this very difficult period.

The police began to hound the Papalias and their family members on a systematic basis. Strange things were happening all the time. They were being watched and followed and their phones appeared to be tapped. Privacy was no longer a part of their lives. One evening, Pattie was driving their Volkswagen van to pick up a bottle of wine in preparation for a dinner engagement at Robert's home. Another car came up rapidly on the rear of her vehicle. It tailgated her for blocks, moved close to the rear of her car, and kept flashing bright headlights as if to blind her. Eventually, in panic she hit the brakes and the car behind slammed into her car. The driver refused to identify himself to her but after the Montreal police attended the accident, she was informed the other driver was a member of the Canadian Secret Intelligence Service.

Pattie returned home completely freaked out.

Needless to say, this period placed extreme strain on everyone and their relationships with each other. Tony and Pattie had initially planned to marry in August 1974. A traditional Italian wedding was being put together by members of the Papalia family. The turmoil of the time and the pressure for a large wedding caused Pattie to have second thoughts. The wedding was canceled in July much to the chagrin of her Latin suitor. Tony was devastated but understood his fiancée's position. She needed to make some input into their future lives together; she wanted to be his partner not just a pretty wife.

Tony spent most of the remaining summer pursuing her again, trying to patch up their differences. Eventually he succeeded in convincing Pattie of his love and promised her some control in their future lives together.

Finally in October, they were married in Our Lady of Fatima Church in St. Laurent. It was a small affair by Italian standards but Pattie and her family organized the wedding she wanted, not the big one her Italian in-laws favored. They honeymooned in Stowe, Vermont -- a three day sojourn together without anyone else around, a trip that would have to suffice for many years to come.

Pattie discovered that marriage to a Papalia required extreme patience and trust. Tony traveled considerably. There would be long periods of separation as the Twins began to organize their attack on their British Columbian gold mine. Whenever, Tony returned, he would debrief himself by discussing the details of his work with her into the wee hours of the night.

Pattie took solace in the fact that she was pregnant and soon would be joined by a child who would give her the close companionship she yearned for. In May 1975, Anthony was born. Tony was there for the birth but soon after flew away for more work. One might imagine the birth of your first child to cause a father to change his ways and become more attentive, but the business of Pacific Nickel was at the boil and Tony had to move fast to stay ahead of the 'sharks'.

Shortly after Anthony's birth, Tony left Canada with Robert to set up their base in the Bahamas. Pattie stayed behind in Montreal to raise their child and maintain their connection in Canada. Eventually, the separation would become unbearable and Tony soon returned to retrieve his wife and son.

The harassment by the police and RCMP also became intolerable to Pattie. She and their child were under 24-hour surveillance. Her car was stopped on many occasions for no apparent reason to check her vehicle documents. One day she approached the men watching her apartment and invited them in for a talk. She asked them what they wanted from her and why they were bothering her. They asked her many questions about Tony and Robert but eventually left her home when they realized she would tell them nothing. Despite this incident, they continued to follow her and watch her apartment. Finally she convinced Tony that the situation had become too dangerous and he resolved to remove his family from this threatening atmosphere.

So, Tony asked Pattie to load all their valuables into the Volkswagen van and one night under the cover of darkness, she and young Anthony left Canada and drove into New York State. Tony had purchased a small farm in upstate New York at Saratoga Springs and Pattie and her child could live in peace there on the old farmstead. Finally the family was out of the jurisdiction of the Canadian authorities and the intimidation ended.

Tony stayed with Pattie in Saratoga Springs for several months but eventually the separation from Robert became very inefficient. The Twins had decided to spread their corporate wings and develop a global strategy. Their company was now incorporated in Panama and headquartered in the Bahamas. Robert was developing plans to open up opportunities in Europe while Tony would take care of the North American scene. Miami was a good location for this activity in the USA and was close to Robert in the Bahamas as he continued to organize his plans for a Bahamian Stock Exchange.

So, Tony returned home, sold the farm and, once again, he and Pattie packed up the van and this time drove down to Florida. They rented an apartment in

Miami where they lived in bliss for about six months as Tony managed the North American interests of Metals Research.

Pattie remembers this period as being a very happy time filled with stability and hope for the future. She really enjoyed Miami; they developed many lifelong friendships and she saw Tony much more frequently. New Year's of 1977 was a particularly enjoyable occasion as she and Tony were joined by Robert and Mario Berton and his wife and young child for a two week holiday.

But constancy is not the normal state for a Papalia, and their lives were soon to change significantly.

In early May 1977, Pattie went to Italy to vacation with Tony at Robert's apartment in Milan. Tony was in London with his brother on business but was to join her in several days to begin their holiday. But he never showed up.

At first this was not recognized as a problem. Often, Tony would be delayed on business and Pattie had been forced to change her plans on many occasions. But there was a difference this time. In the past Tony would always let her know where he was and what was going on. This time, there was no communication -- not a phone call, not a telegram, not a letter, not a message. After three days of waiting, she was extremely worried. No one knew where they were. Pattie had little money. After one week she was frantic. She had met Martine Berton in Miami at New Year's and called her for advice.

Although Pattie did not speak Italian, both women could communicate in French. Having received no word from Mario, Martine was as worried as Pattie but after another week of waiting, Martine learned of their husbands' arrests and incarceration. She quickly, informed Pattie and arranged to get her some money on instructions from Tony through her husband. The two women were shattered by the news. They wondered how this could have happened. They each had extreme faith in their husbands and knew they were honest businessmen who would never cheat another person.

Pattie remained at Robert's flat for several weeks existing on the money she had received from Martine Berton. Eventually she received a phone call from Tony who was now in Brixton Prison. He told her not to worry; that he and Robert were alright but there was going to be some tough times ahead. The charges being laid against them were all crazy figments of the hyper-active imagination of some over-zealous policemen. He had no idea when they would receive bail and the Prosecution was fighting hard to prevent their release.

He advised her to return to Canada and find a job to help support herself through the next little while. Tony was worried about Pattie coming to see him in England. He was concerned that her employment in some of their subsidiary firms could put her in jeopardy of arrest. After all, Scotland Yard had charged nearly everyone at Bear Securities including the receptionist and secretaries.

But Pattie went to England and did visit Tony at Brixton. She wanted to see for herself the conditions under which he was incarcerated. She was horrified with what she found; the conditions of filth and depravation were appalling. The stories of harsh treatment and torture were unbelievable, Tony had lost weight and looked much paler that normal. She was devastated.

During her brief stay in London, Patti arranged for a supply line to provide Tony with what he needed and what the authorities would allow the prisoners to receive. Each week there was hope that bail would be granted but as time went on, it was clear that the Crown would never allow these 'Mafioso' criminals to be set free. Hope began to turn into despair as bail denial followed on bail denial week after week.

So with insufficient funds on which to live, Pattie was forced to return to Canada to attend to her infant son, Anthony, and to obtain employment. At first she lived with her parents in St. Laurent and found work with a Graphic Artist firm in Montreal designing posters, brochures and other documents.

Tony wrote to her almost daily to keep her informed on what was happening with their case and how they were dealing with the Brixton environment. Tony was embarrassed and angry about the grief and anguish caused for his wife and for the rest of his family. With the Papalias in a London jail, the RCMP harassment of their family stopped. But all requests to the authorities in Canada by Pattie and the Twin's family members were rejected as being a problem under the jurisdiction of the United Kingdom. There was nothing Canada could or would do to help. Pattie was now Tony's lifeline back to Canada and he needed her to address several of his business activities.

One of the issues Pattie could handle was to maintain the mining leases held by Metals Research on the Lillooet property. Pattie traveled to Vancouver to ensure that payments on their leases were made each year. During her visits, she became enchanted with this beautiful city and later suggested to Tony that perhaps she should move their family to Vancouver to be closer to the company's major asset.

Pattie carried on working in Montreal until Tony's release on bail in April 1979. The news of his liberation was so wonderful, she immediately booked a flight to London and together with Anthony and they spent two marvelous weeks of freedom with Tony. When she returned to Canada on this occasion, she and Anthony moved to Vancouver permanently to await Tony's return in 1982.

Today Tony and Pattie still live in the Vancouver area where the activities of Metals Research occupy much of their business lives. They have four children: Anthony born in 1975, Robert in 1982 shortly after Tony's return to Canada; Melanie came on the scene in 1985 while Ashley entered their lives in 1988.

The Escape

(August 1977 - September 1977)

DURING THE LONG summer, the prisoners had considerable spare time. Once their bail was revoked, there was no point in finding proper sureties for the court. It seemed hopeless that they would gain their freedom by legitimate means.

One day when Robert, Tony and Umberto discussed their situation with one of the prison old-hands they had come to trust, the old guy shook his head and said, "The best thing for you would be to go!"

At the time, they shrugged the suggestion off. The idea of a breakout seemed ludicrous, more in keeping with a James Bond movie than real life.

Countless hours went by with nothing to do but read and talk. Their families brought them newspapers and books. The papers kept them abreast of world events and aware of the strange way their case was shaping-up.

In the dog days of August, the police investigation was continuing. Edwin Ward had gone to Italy and Switzerland looking for evidence. He managed to get a Magistrate in Italy interested in starting an investigation. Presumably this would allow parallel investigations of the alleged fraud in Italy and England and the sharing of information between the two jurisdictions.

In Italy, Ward tried to ascertain the names of MRSA shareholders who had been duped. He spent three weeks becoming increasingly frustrated as his efforts failed to find anything of substance. Instead of unhappy investors, he met people such as Dario Marruchi and Baron Locatelli, knowledgeable, sophisticated investors who stood behind the promoters of MRSA and who believed in the legitimacy of the company and their gold mine.

Ward made the mistake of conducting his investigations in Italy without notifying or cooperating with the Italian police. After ten days on his own, the animosity between himself and the Italian police had grown to the point where it was being reported in the Italian press.

The Italian newspapers were very interested in the case because of Torri. They were anxious for any information that Ward would give them. And Ward was only too happy to comply. He was quoted in the Italian newspapers on a daily basis. As his Italian investigation continued down a dead-end, the newspaper reports sunk to great depths of yellow journalism. The allegations became wilder and wilder with the papers no longer quoting Ward directly instead relying upon an "unnamed" source in Scotland Yard.

At that point in Italy, a large scandal had erupted involving discovery of some six-hundred million Lira in fake Italian government bonds. Within days of Ward's arrival in Italy, he and the magistrate were jointly feeding out stories about secret bank accounts and an unnamed real estate agent in possession of fake bonds. Ward was quoted as saying, "these documents will probably be very useful in my investigation". They were careful however, to qualify the allegation by noting there was no evidence yet to link the two matters.

The papers loved it and wanted more. Headlines appeared daily in all major Italian major newspapers with new fantastic assertions: "Torri, the master-mind behind fake South American Gold and Emerald Mine"; "Torri believed connected to fake government bond scandal"; and finally, "Torri's bank and company, MRSA, connected to International Mafia money laundering".

These particular allegations came to light in both the Italian and English press on September 12th. This appeared to be the hidden agenda behind the charges. The justification for putting these people out of business was that they were Mafia. An unnamed source from Scotland Yard indicated they had uncovered a fraud of massive proportions and their investigation had led them to a connection with the International Mafia, and recycling of dirty money from the proceeds of drug profits and international kidnappings.

In England, the story was prominent on page one of the Evening Standard, the Daily Telegraph, the Guardian and the Home News. The emphasis here was less on drugs and more on a connection to Meyer Lansky, "the Godfather of the American Mafia". It was alleged that he was the brains behind the creation of these banks and companies for the purpose of laundering profits from organized crime. Only the Guardian mentioned that "whatever links to the Mafia exist, they are tenuous at this time."

As for the rest, they seemed wholly content to print exactly what unnamed sources fed them without question. Scotland Yard were painted as heroes, "No investor in England, or anywhere, as far as we know, had parted with funds because thanks to their diligence, the organized crime squad had nipped the scheme in the bud."

And so, Ward's failure to find a single disgruntled investor was turned into a triumph by Scotland Yard's public relation men.

In the Italian media, the failure to find anyone who had been bilked was dealt with somewhat differently. The papers were advised that a number of people had been defrauded but were ashamed to come forward since they were embarrassed to have been cheated by these con-artists. The purported investors had supposedly failed to comply with Italian currency laws.

At Ward's final press conference in Italy, he was unhappily surprised by the Milanese lawyer, Santoro. He came forward at the press conference and announced that they had started a defamation suit against Ward and Scotland Yard for the lies being propagated about him and the others. Immediately upon commencement of the civil suit, Ward left the country never to return.

❧

In Brixton, the prisoners were aware of what was being printed about them. Torri, Frascati and Berton were particularly puzzled by the link to the American Mafia. "Who the hell is Meyer Lansky?" asked Berton.

Tony and Robert had a vague idea, having grown up in North America, "Some old guy in the American Mob and he's not even Italian!"

It's one thing to be charged with a crime and to be certain you can prove your innocence at a fair hearing. But since their arrests in May, they had been beaten by the police; held incognito for a week; denied bail; betrayed by their first lawyers; and been made to feel they were already convicted. Their situation was becoming bizarre. The latest charges had no basis in reality; complete fabrications. They were now convinced the Serious Crimes Squad wanted to secure a conviction at any cost, even if a Kangaroo court was needed.

What chance did they have in a jury trial in England? They were publicly reviled foreigners characterized as dangerous and evil men of the most unsavory reputation and associations; linked by the police to every organized criminal activity in the last forty years. A juror who read such things in the papers was going to fear and loath them before hearing any evidence.

The words of the old man -- "The best thing for you would be to go", echoed again and again to Tony and Robert. Perhaps the only way out was to escape.

Indeed, there was another man, an ethnic Chinese, who tried to sell them on the notion of escape. This fellow had arrived in their wing of the prison shortly after them. He told them he was awaiting trial on drug charges.

The Oriental gravitated toward the Italians. For reasons known only to him, he chose this group as his friends. But, there was something mysterious and threatening about him and Robert and Tony did not trust him.

Not long after befriending them, the Chinese told them of his plan to escape. He wanted them to join him and asked them to meet him the next day during their exercise period to discuss the details.

The next day during their walk in the courtyard he told them of his plan. They would blow up the courtyard wall of the prison and escape to the outside where they would flee in a helicopter that awaited them.

From his manner and some of the things he said, they believed he had the capability to blow up the courtyard walls. However, to dash for freedom to a helicopter on the other side in broad daylight seemed immensely daring and foolhardy. The plan had elements of a suicide mission to it.

The hazard of the plan combined with their distrust of him put the Italians in an awkward position. There was something not quite right with the guy. Either he was a very hard case with serious criminal connections or he wanted them to believe he was, in which case, he was probably a police plant. Why had he chosen them as friends out of everyone else in their wing? There was no rational explanation for it and considering the hazardous nature of what he was proposing, they became convinced that he was working for the police. They discussed the implications very seriously in their cells.

Frascati said, "You know, if this guy is crazy enough to think up such a plan, he's crazy enough to do anything. What is he going to do when we tell him we want no part of his great escape? He may want to harm us if he thinks his plan is threatened by our knowledge of it."

Tony concurred, "He's either crazy or he's a police plant. I don't like the guy. He comes in here and right away he wants to be our friend. Now he wants us to take part in an escape that would be suicide. Maybe killing us all in a daring escape is the police way of getting rid of their problems."

"Each week we're told the investigation is continuing. They probably haven't worked out how to put together, or should I say, fabricate, a case against us.

Our lawyers say it might be two years before we go to trial. And while we're sitting in here, our families are out drumming up public sympathy for us. The police don't like to look stupid in a highly publicized case like this one. They would rather have us dead than to admit they made a mistake with our arrests."

"Yes," said Frascati. "They're looking at a public embarrassment of international scope now unless they can get rid of us or frame us. My girlfriend already has 5000 signatures on a petition objecting to our continued imprisonment and my father has talked to several Ministers of the Italian government."

"And also there is Fortuna and Bombara's efforts," interjected Robert.

Tony continued to talk with Frascati, "I always believed in the system -- that democracy works. England was always the hallmark of justice. Things like this don't happen to people in a country like England -- I thought. But I've seen what these police are capable of. Look what they have done to some of our sureties. They have threatened those people who wanted to stand up for us."

Frascati replied, "I've come to the conclusion these people are capable of anything. When I was on the outside the police wanted me to testify against you and tell the world about the huge conspiracy. When I told them there was no conspiracy, they tried blackmail, 'Say it's so, or we'll arrest you too.' That's why I'm here now, because I wouldn't lie for them. It wouldn't surprise me if, as you say, Tony, they are planning to have us killed."

Umberto finished, "So then, what we should tell our Oriental friend?"

Tony answered, "For the time being we'll let him think we're interested. His plan requires time to work out the details. This will at least buy us some time."

Over the next couple of weeks they walked in the courtyard with the Oriental and helped him plot his escape. They dismissed the helicopter part of the plan as too dangerous and substituted instead several motorcycles.

Slowly, as the group thought about an escape they knew wasn't going to happen, there was an evolution toward the subject. They began to feel the only viable way out of their dilemma was an actual escape as they moved closer to the moment when the Oriental expected them to carry through with their plan.

One of Robert's favorite comics in the Italian newspapers was the adventurous character. 'Diabolik'. Diabolik was famous in Italy, for his daring-do. Week after week he would plot amazing escapes from a variety of tricky situations. One week as Robert read the comic strip, he turn to the others and said, "Do they really have such things -- files concealed in a shoe that can be used to cut through metal bars, or ropes with diamond chips embedded in them?"

Torri spoke up, "Sure, we used to use these things in the movies all the time."

Robert's interest increased, "Really? Could you get some of these for us?"

Torri sat up on his cot, knowing the implications of their discussion. "They won't be hard to obtain. The difficulty is getting them into our possession."

Intuitively in tune with his brother's thoughts, Tony said, "Find someone to get these things. We'll take care of the rest."

A week later while returning from remand court, Torri triumphantly pulled files and ropes from his sleeve to show to the others, "They were passed to me in the courthouse right in front of the police. They didn't see a thing."

They each looked at the metal files. They were surprised by the ease with which Torri had obtained them. They now began, for the first time in their lives to think seriously about the possibility of escape, an action that could place their lives in serious jeopardy.

They were intelligent and observant businessmen and it showed in the care and thought they put into carrying out their plan of escape. Tony and Robert had already discussed the basic elements of their plan and now they brought in the others to help them execute it.

Torri claimed to have connections on the outside that could get them false documents, including passports. They would also arrange for get-away cars and organize a safe house in London.

For the inside work, most elements were put together by the Twins. They determined that the best opportunity to break out with the least risk would be during one of their weekly visits to Thames Magistrate's Court.

Each week before their court appearance, they were held in the same detention cell, sometimes for several hours.

This cell was about fifteen feet in length and ten feet in width. The room itself was brick from floor to ceiling with one entrance into the room in the center of one of the shorter walls, blocked by a massive, impregnable metal door. The furnishings consisted of two benches, one on either side of the long walls, bolted to the wall and the floor.

There were no windows in the cell. On one end of the room directly opposite the entrance, was another doorway which led to a small, private lavatory area with a washbasin and toilet. Above this washroom, the designer had made provision for some light and ventilation. There was a skylight at the top in the ceiling. The face of the skylight consisted of thick, heavy-glass set at angles. On the inside of this opening were a series of metal bars. The skylight was so high; the bars seemed merely a precautionary measure for an otherwise impossible climb. It was through this skylight that the prisoners intended to go.

As they began to implement their escape, they began to notice little things that could assist in their plan. One of the group realized at lunch one day that the cheese in their sandwiches was similar in color to the mortar between the bricks in their cell at the Magistrate's Court. They began to hoard the cheese.

On their next trip to Magistrate's Court they began to work in earnest. One of the Twins climbed up onto the washbasin. Tony was able to scrape away the mortar around three separate bricks with an item of cutlery liberated from Brixton. The bricks were staggered at spots upon the wall from between six and fourteen feet in height. Once the bricks could be removed, it became possible to use them as footings and handholds to stand on the wall below the skylight, holding onto the window's bars. They replaced the bricks and pressed cheese around the bricks to simulate mortar and to hide their holes in the wall.

When they returned the following week, they were pleased to see that the loose bricks remained as they had left them, apparently undetected. Once the bars were taken out and the window slats removed, they could climb out to freedom. It was necessary to coordinate what would happen once outside.

The Twins could see that the skylight opened onto a street beside the courthouse building about 10 feet from the roof edge.

They knew from observing their surroundings on arrival and departure in the prison van that the courthouse adjoined a police station. This station, unlike the detention area of the courthouse, was more than one storey high, many of the windows on the second storey of the police building looked out directly onto the roof of the court's detention center.

The housing for the cell's skylight jutted up about three feet higher at its highest point than the rest of the detention area's flat roof. Although they had no way of checking with certainty, the group believed this frame offered enough cover that upon climbing onto the roof and staying low they could crawl the six feet directly across to the roofs edge, and drop over that side undetected. When they would go over the roof's edge, they would have to hang by their arms and then drop the remaining eight or nine feet to the ground.

To get up and out onto the roof and across down to the ground required a considerable degree of athleticism. Robert and Tony, at thirty-two years of age, were the youngest and most agile of the group. Torri and Mario, the oldest were forty-three and thirty-eight respectively. Frascati was in his mid-thirties. Luckily, all of the men had led relatively active lives and none of them were severely out of shape. Even so, they began a rigorous training program of daily calisthenics and stretching.

On their outings to court they began to work on the metal bars on the skylight. Each week, upon their arrival at the detention cell as they awaited their court appearance, the bricks would be removed and one of the Papalias would climb the wall and start filing at the metal.

The fancy ropes embedded with diamond chips broke almost immediately. Initially, they had placed their hopes on these ropes but they proved useless.

If they were going to cut through the metal it would have to be with the tiny, flimsy metal files. The work was painstaking, Robert and Tony were the only ones with the physical stamina to hang by their arms and saw for any length of time. They would spend almost every moment from the time they arrived in this cell to the time they were removed, taking turns at the job. Half standing and half hanging from a metal bar, one of the brothers would achingly and methodically rub the little piece of metal across the bars.

It was much slower and more difficult work than they had anticipated. The files were tiny and flimsy and they broke often. They found themselves working, slowly, rubbing bits and pieces of file across the bars to what seemed like little effect, but they had time on their side.

They measured their advance in millimeters and after many hours, they could see that progress was being made. Each of the bars in the window was cut more than halfway through and there was no sign that anyone suspected anything. They began to calculate when they would be ready to go out the window. They told Torri to ready the arrangements with his friends on the outside to ensure that the getaway cars and documents would be waiting for them.

Each week they quickly went about their preparations for the day when they might go through the roof. In mid-September the frenzied reports on their case reached a peak in the British Press. Allegations of their organized crime connections were hitting the front pages of the major newspapers daily.

Frascati looked at his cell mates after reading some of the newspaper articles. "Until today, even though we've planned for escape, I never really thought I would do it. I thought in the end, when the time came, I would stay behind." He waived the paper he was holding in the air, "But, I don't see any choice any more. If we don't go, we'll be convicted of whatever lies they wish to print."

Tony added, "Did you notice last week, how David Benham and Geoff Lines were looking at us? They're not sure about us any more after all they've read in the papers. When our own lawyers don't believe in us, we're in trouble."

Torri, whose previous problems in Italy, helped to color his views, added, "There is no justice. Those who believe in justice are fools. They will convict us of whatever they want to. It is definitely time to get out of here."

The others sat in silence. For once they felt that Torri was absolutely right. So long as they remained in prison in England their situation was hopeless. All of them except Torri hoped to do as Santoro, Boccardi, and Barrachini had done before them --- to go to Italy. From there they hoped to put normalcy back into their lives and work on establishing their innocence.

Robert spoke, "We're definitely being squeezed from all sides right how. The Chinese is putting pressure on us to follow through with his crazy plan."

He looked at the others and said in low tones, "It should be this Thursday, Torri make the arrangements with the people on the outside to be there this week. We can be ready then. It would be stupid to wait any longer."

That night, Robert lay awake in his bunk, thinking over and over how the day would go when they went to court this week. It played like a movie in his head. In some versions of his daydreams things went well and he imagined himself safe in a villa in Northern Italy sitting down to a fabulous meal, laughing and joking with his friends. In some versions, things did not go so well but he tried to put these thoughts out of his mind. He refused to allow himself to think of failure. He was still reviewing the endless possibilities that the next few days might bring when, exhausted, he fell into a fitful sleep.

❧

The morning of September 22nd, 1977 began with their well-known routine on remand day. They awoke early and waited for the guards to allow them out of their cell block to lead them to the washroom where they could wash, brush their teeth and shave. Frascati found some difficulty in shaving that morning. He wasn't scared but he was definitely keyed up. He had to concentrate to hold his hands steady so he didn't cut himself.

Next they went to the mess hall for breakfast but their appetites were worse than usual. Had anyone been watching them they would have seen that none of the Italians did more than pick at their food this morning.

They returned to their cells after breakfast where they waited until the guards came to get them for their trip to court. On court days, the prisoners were encouraged to dress up for the occasion. Long ago their families and friends had brought them a variety of outfits to wear on their trips to remand court.

This morning each of them chose two sets of clothing to wear, one layer on top of the other. The idea was that once they were away from the court house they would strip off the outer layer in an attempt to confuse their pursuers.

When the guards came by at 8:15 am, they were led out of the cell block and beyond a locked and barred gate to a holding area. Two armed guards were to take them out to a van waiting in a courtyard. The outside gate was opened and the van emerged from the prison and headed toward Lambeth Magistrate's Court about a half-hour's ride away.

At its destination the van pulled into a locked courtyard area at the rear of the courthouse. Just before 9:00 am the prisoners were escorted out of the van and directed into the back hall of the courthouse. They were led to the same detention room as always. Once inside, the metal door was slammed shut behind them. They heard the lock tumbling shut and then the sound of the guards' footsteps as they walked away. The prisoners were alone.

The group immediately set about their final preparation for their deliverance. One stood by the door while the bricks were removed and Tony climbed up to the foothold for his last turn at sawing through the bars. They knew there was at least an hour before anyone would come to take them into court.

Frascati didn't say anything to the others as he still held a small hope that he would be saved from doing this desperate act by the successful outcome of this morning's court application. His lawyer, David Offenbach, was bringing yet another bail application this morning with a new set of sureties. Maybe he would walk out the front door this morning instead of breaking out the back.

After about forty minutes Tony descended. "I think it's ready to break, probably another few minutes of sawing before we're ready to go."

Robert boosted himself up and examined their work. He came back down and concurred with Tony that the bar was holding together by a mere thread of metal. It should be a quick job when the time came.

They waited nearly an hour and a half until being summoned to the courtroom. That's the way their weekly appearances went. If there was a long list of cases, they sometimes waited into the afternoon to be called to court. Other days they were in and out and back to Brixton by lunch time.

Today was going to require some patience. It was hard on their nerves waiting. A good deal of pacing was done -- more in anticipation of the moment than anything else. They didn't want to make a break before their court appearance because of the chance that someone would come to get them while they were escaping and sound the alarm.

They had decided to wait until they were finished for the day. The guards never hurried to put them in the van for the return trip to prison. If their court appearance went past noon, invariably they were left for a couple of hours and taken back at the end of the day. This allowed the possibility of a clean break. Hopefully they would be long gone before anyone realized they had escaped.

A little after 10:30 am, finally a guard came to get them. They were brought into court and placed in the prisoner's dock. They nodded to their lawyers and the lawyer's assistants, and settled down to listen to the ritual. Today it was Frascati's lawyer listing all the reasons why he should not be held for a moment longer without bail.

After four months of the same arguments, as their lawyers, week after week, pressed their case for release, the process had become meaningless. Only one of the five men before the court that day retained any interest in the proceedings -- Frascati. As he heard the discussions taking on the same character and tone of the previous proceedings, his thoughts joined the others and turned to the time they would be out of court and back in the detention room.

It was after 11:30 am before the case was finished. Frascati's application was turned down. He and the others would be kept in jail for however many months or years it took for their case to come to trial. Just before the guard took them from the courtroom, David Benham came over to prisoner's dock and said to Tony, "Geoff and I will be in to see you in a little while; we'll take a quick lunch and then be over to see you."

Tony nodded. He wished he could tell them not to bother coming to see them, but he knew that might arouse suspicion. Besides he knew Frascati's lawyer would be coming to see them today in any case to discuss the day's events.

When they were returned to the cell, they waited until the guards brought them lunch. Today was liver and onions. Once the trays were set down and the guards had left the cell, the prisoners didn't look at the food again. They had too much on their minds to think about eating this prison slop.

At about 12:10 pm there was some noise at the door and the two lawyers, David Offenbach and David Benham, entered the room trailed by Offenbach's junior, and Benham's Geoff Lines.

Usually, the lawyers were greeted with some anticipation by their clients. They were normally full of questions and glad to talk face to face with someone on the outside. But, today, the mood was very different. The Italians were sullen and distant. Both Offenbach and Benham tried to start a conversation but were greeted by silence. Their clients would simply nod their heads and glare at the visitors. The lawyers assumed they were all terribly disappointed at the failure of yet another bail application. Offenbach gave them a little pep talk about not getting disappointed. He told them it was just a matter of time before they would be successful in getting them bail. Their clients listened; they weren't impolite, but they hardly said a word in response.

Finally, at 12:30 pm the lawyers gave up and said they would be going. As Geoff Lines turned to leave the room after the others, he nodded toward Tony and thought he saw the hint of a smile playing around his lips.

When they were outside the detention area Geoff said to Benham, "You know, I swear they were glad to get rid of us today. They couldn't wait for us to go."

Benham replied, "They're upset at the whole world today. You can hardly blame them for getting depressed now and then after all the months they have been in custody and no end in sight."

At that moment, at the other end of the courthouse, in the detention room that housed the Italians, Robert was climbing up to begin sawing through the bars on the skylight. When the first bar was fully cut, Robert pulled at it and dislodged it from its place in the opening. He felt a rush of adrenaline. Two more bars and they would be climbing out to freedom.

It wasn't long before all the bars were out. Now he was faced with the panes of slatted glass. He tapped on one with a piece of metal bar, but, it was essentially unbreakable with the resources available and he didn't like the clanking noise of the bar against the glass.

He grabbed hold of one of the slats and tugged. He felt one give to the right. He pushed to the side and was pleased to see the glass slide out of its frame. He thought to himself, "for once part of this plan is easier than it first appeared."

Quickly, he removed all the glass slats and laid the panes on top of each other beside the window. There was now nothing between him and the flat tar roof. He could see clearly the short expanse they would have to crawl across before dropping over the side to the ground below. He climbed down for a last minute discussion before they went out the opening.

He said to the others, "Stay low! That way we'll all get out of here safely."

Torri stepped up to the base of the wall. "Let me go first. Those are my people out there waiting for us. If they don't see me right away they may get worried."

The others didn't see any reason to object to this. Someone had to be the first one out. They helped boost Torri up to his first footing in the wall and watched while he scrambled out the hole.

Robert turned to the others, "Come on, Frascati, you are next." Umberto began to climb up to make his way to freedom.

❧

Unknown to the men still in the cell they had already been betrayed by Torri, who took the easy route to his car and left. The second he emerged on the roof he made a decision that was to cost the rest of them dearly. Instead of moving across the roof in an undignified and crab-like, stealthy manner, he immediately stood upright and moved quickly to the top of the roof to drop over the side down a drain pipe. When he landed he stepped into the Jaguar saloon car waiting below and instructed the young driver to take him to Heathrow Airport. Before 1:30 pm that afternoon, Torri was on a flight out of Heathrow to Paris and from Paris he caught a connecting flight to New York. Once he stepped into the Jaguar the rest of his cell mates never saw him again.

At the moment when Torri, all six feet of him, stood up on the roof, several police officers in adjacent offices of the Harbourview police station were gazing out the window across the expanse of the courthouse roof.

One of the Bobbies looked on in shock and amazement as he saw the top half of Torri's body pop up above the skylight frame. He called out to the others around him, "Look out there, those bloody Wops are escaping."

There was general scrambling and confusion as all the officers sprang into action to stop the escape and spread the alarm.

Frascati emerged from the hole and took a few tentative steps on his haunches. He was suddenly startled to hear a window opening across the street and an anxious voice yelling, "Stop them, before they get away!" He immediately ran to the edge of the roof where he dropped over the side.

Right behind him was Tony. As his face came up to the opening, he felt the brush of a pant leg on his nose as someone went tearing by. He looked up and saw a plain-clothed policeman run across the roof in pursuit of Frascati.

Tony hesitated for only a second. There were only two ways to go, and he wasn't anxious to drop back down the hole when he was this close to freedom. He stood up on the roof and immediately saw that in addition to the officer who swept past him there was another guy about ten feet away on the other side. The second cop yelled to the first, who then turned back to face Tony.

They came towards him slowly from either side, intending to pounce on him together. One of the officers called out "Hey there fellow, stop where you are."

For his part, Tony stood in a martial-arts stance of readiness, arms out at his sides, knees loose and ready to spring, watching out of the corners of his eyes as both of the cops approached him.

Seconds passed and just as the officers were almost on him, Tony sprung at the first cop knocking him off balance. He managed to use the man's falling momentum to rush him around to block the other cop.

The two policemen were off-balance for only a moment but it was all the time Tony needed. He sprinted to the edge of the roof and jumped. As Tony jumped and was airborne, he looked behind before he landed as he saw the policeman on the roof getting up and putting a hand in I breast pocket. It flashed through Tony's mind that they would be shooting at him when he landed.

His feet hit the pavement hard. Even though he landed well, feet first, knees bent, from that height the impact was too much for his feet to absorb. He heard a crunch and felt a shooting pain in his ankles. In the same moment he rolled to his side expecting to hear shots or to fight off any officer who followed.

But no gunshots were fired as he rolled out of the way. Glancing up, Tony could see the police were still on the roof. None had followed him. It was too high. The officer who he thought was pulling out a gun was now standing with a pen in one hand and a pad of paper in the other. He was writing something.

Tony stood up and saw Frascati about fifteen feet away, standing with his arms across his chest. Beyond him was a Fiat car with a youth sitting in the back.

From that distance Tony couldn't tell if Umberto was cool, collected and waiting. Tony ran toward him and saw that Frascati was immobile with fear. In the time that he had waited for his compatriots, terror had got the best of him. Tony slapped Frascati's face hard and said, "Come on." The slap got him moving again and he ran to the car jumping into the driver's seat.

Before he got into the car, Tony looked up at the roof, cupped his hands and yelled, "Robert, I'll be back." He hoped his brother heard him. Then he hopped into the passenger seat and the car got away while the herd of policemen and guards ran towards them. As they drove towards Trafalgar Square, sirens were blazing and they could hear the faint noises of a helicopter in the air .

The second he was in the car, Tony turned to the young boy in the back seat. "Have you got our money and documents?"

The boy responded, "I don't have any papers but, your money, I got at home."

"What is your name and where is home?"

They boy told them his name was Stefano and reported his address. Tony asked Frascati if he knew where that was and Frascati nodded yes.

"All right, we will see you later. Go."'

Stefano didn't waste any time. He jumped out of the back seat and took off down the street.

Frascati, although he had started the car made no immediate move to go, so

Tony yelled, "Let's go." Umberto fumbled with the gears and then proceeded to back up and smashed a car behind him (it was the Magistrate's car of the morning's court proceedings).

Tony slapped Frascati again hard. This finally seemed to get him functioning. Frascati slammed the car into gear and took off down the alley. From that moment he was like a Formula 1 race car driver. Just past the courthouse complex they turned left into a busy street. About a thousand yards down the road they saw and heard a police 'Panda' vehicle coming toward them. All the vehicle's lights were flashing, and its sirens were blaring. The police van with a SWAT team went right by them racing in the direction of the courthouse. Frascati turned their car into one of London's innumerable round-abouts and they emerged on the other side to disappear into the streets of the city.

They knew it wouldn't be long before the police began looking for the car, Tony flipped off his dark turtleneck sweater to reveal a shirt and tie beneath. Within ten minutes they found an inconspicuous place to leave the car. Frascati took off his outer shell of clothing as well.

They left their car and set out on foot. They had £80 which was all the money they were allowed to have on their person in prison and they went inside a 'Boots' drugstore to purchase hair dye and shaving implements.

They emerged to the street with their packages and heard the sounds of a helicopter flying low over the city. Sirens blared at a distance as more police converged on the site of their escape. They decided to lay low for awhile; to find some place to change their appearance before continuing their plight.

Tony saw a movie theater about a half block away up the road. The marquee showed there were matinee performances all afternoon, "Let's go there for now, Umberto." They hurried across the street to the purchase tickets and went into the theater. There they stayed for the rest of the afternoon.

❧

Meanwhile back in the cell, Robert and Mario sat waiting for something to happen. It was fully ten minutes since Tony had climbed out the skylight and although they could hear yelling, people running, sirens and helicopters in all that cacophony of noise and activity, still no one had come to check on the cell.

Initially as Tony climbed out on the roof, Robert had started up after him. But he heard Mario call below him, "I can't make it up, please give me a hand."

Robert dropped down and helped boost Mario up to his first footing. He was waiting for Mario to pull himself up through the skylight when suddenly Mario tumbled down on top of him.

"What happened?"

Mario picked himself up off the floor and said, "They're fighting with Tony."

"Who?"

"The polizia."

Robert started to go back up the wall intending to help his brother, when he heard Tony's voice at a distance, "Robert, I'll be back."

He peeked out and saw, the five officers looking over the side of the building after Tony. He knew he didn't stand a chance to get by all these guys, so he quickly climbed back down. Then he and Mario left the lavatory area and returned to the main part of the cell. They could hear all-hell breaking loose outside, Police were yelling, alarms were going off, people were running on the roof and in the corridor outside their cell.

Mario said to Robert, "What should we do?"

Their liver and onion lunches were still in their trays on the bench. Robert said, "Sit down and put your tray on your lap. Look like you're eating."

After a seemingly interminable wait, suddenly the door came crashing open. The biggest, burliest guard in the courthouse all but fell into the room, being pushed from behind by a gang of other guards and police. The fellow roared at Robert, "Where did they go?"

Sitting hunched over his now-coagulated lunch on a tray, Robert gave them a blank, innocent look as if to say, "Is something wrong, guys?" and then he pointed in the direction of the lavatory.

The big guard let out a bellow of frustration and immediately Robert and Mario were lifted bodily under both arms and carried out of the cell. They were thrown into separate cells and the doors slammed shut behind them.

Robert knew he was in for a rough time and began to formulate a plan. Removing his spare socks and shirt he stuffed them underneath the bench. He then sat and waited. Within half an hour, several guards came in to conduct a complete strip-search of his body but they neglected to search the cell. When finished, the guards left him alone for quite a long while.

Around 4:00 pm they came to get him. He was under the heaviest security he had yet seen. There was a guard on either side of him holding him under his armpits, with several more guards in front and behind, some of them carrying weapons. He was half-carried in this fashion into the courtroom. Mario was already there and he, too, was surrounded by guards.

Robert looked at the people around him and saw something in their eyes that he had never seen before. He saw shock, uncertainty, even a bit of fear on the faces of some of the guards and the police milling around the court.

He realized now that, perhaps only momentarily, they had redressed the power structure between themselves and the authorities. A blow against Scotland Yard had been struck from which the Yard was reeling. For all these months, they had taken every piece of shit the police and prison authorities cared to dish out. As he looked across the court and saw Ward standing near the prosecutor, eyes glazed, barking at his minions, his face beet-red, Robert felt elated. Tony was free, and they had managed to shovel some shit back at their persecutors. He felt some power return after months of being under the control of others.

The application being made to the court was to return Robert and Mario into police custody in order to interview them about the escape. Robert could see the police were livid. He knew they would take out their anger on him and Mario. Because Mario still spoke very little English, Robert knew he would take the brunt of the questioning and attendant violence. He needed an insurance policy.

When the prosecutor paused in his speech, Robert managed to get the attention of the Magistrate, "Sir, I wish to address the court."

"Yes, Mr. Papalia, what is it?"

Robert, standing in the prisoner's box said, "Sir, if we must return into the custody of the police, would you please take a close and careful look at us, because we want you to be aware of the changes that are liable to occur when we're put back in the hands of the Serious Crimes Squad. We expect to be beaten up and mistreated again. We want you to be aware of that."

The Magistrate looked discomfited. He thought to himself, "Bloody, audacious Italian -- suggesting in open court they would be beaten by the British police."

"Fine, Mr. Papalia, while I doubt your concern has any real foundation; it has been noted in these proceedings."

Minutes later, the application was granted by the court. Robert and Mario were led out and taken directly to a van for transport to a police station. On this trip there were armed guards accompanying them inside the van. Outside was a cavalcade of vehicles, carrying heavily-armed guards. The procession rushed through the streets of London in tandem, sirens blaring and lights flashing.

Robert thought some more about all the activity surrounding them. Everywhere there was heavy, heavy security. This had now gone beyond the stage of being merely a criminal matter. The police had created this "Mafia" scenario themselves. And now that some of the prisoners had escaped, it looked like these guys really believed they were under attack by a force they hadn't reckoned with. They appeared to believe that the tentacles of organized crime had reached well into England to take retribution against the police and the State. "Well," Robert thought, "let them believe it. It can only work in our favor. Let the police run around scared for awhile. Let's see how they like it."

Once at the police station, Robert was taken directly to a room for questioning. They wanted to force him to talk very badly. But this time they were unsure of themselves; their arrogance was gone. The squad was scrambling, panicked by the escape. They manhandled him. One policeman picked him up by his lapels and ripped his jacket, but this interrogation was nothing like the last one. Although they threatened him, they didn't assault him badly. In response to all their questions Robert remained silent or told them he wanted his lawyer. The "interview" was mercifully short and eventually he was thrown into a cell.

They placed him in a cellar cell. It was very dark and cold and Robert noticed a disagreeably wet, rotten odor about the place.

He sat in the dark for awhile and wondered about Mario. He was infinitely smarter about prisons than a few months before. There was a toilet in one corner. He walked over and stuck his head close to the bowl and yelled. After a couple of moments, he got a distant response from Mario. They had done nothing to him, but he had been alone for hours. In the darkness he imagined he could hear Robert being tortured. He was very relieved to learn that Robert was okay. Having found comfort in the knowledge each other was alive and well, they each managed to catch a few hours sleep on their hard cold beds.

Next day Robert was taken for a second interrogation. This time after refusing to speak and asking several times for a lawyer, Detective Pawley took out his gun and put it to Robert's head. It was a terrifying moment, but scared as he was, Robert kept his wits about him. He said, "Get serious, Pawley. The whole world knows you've got me here. You can't blow my brains out."

Robert could see the hate and frustration in the cop's eyes. The only thing holding back the police from killing them was the highly public nature of the case and the repercussions should they disappear.

Pawley recognized the truth of what Robert said. He knew what a media circus the case had become. It wasn't only the British press. Now, the Italians and the International press corps were following all aspects of the story. After a moment's hesitation Pawley removed the gun, but not before he delivered a swift kick to the chair Robert was sitting on.

For three days Robert was kept in police cells. He was taken out many times for interviews. It seemed as if everyone in Scotland Yard wanted to talk to him. He was brought before many high-ranking police and intelligence officers. On one trip to another police station for an interview, one of his guards asked the driver to stop the car at a park. He pulled Robert from the car. "Come on," he said, "I'm going to take your cuffs off and then you and I are going into the park to have it out. Just our fists, may the best man win."

Robert looked at the guy. It was obvious how frustrated these cops were and some of them were so stupid. "You think I believe you're going to let it be a fair fight. You're just dying for an excuse to beat me up and I'm not going to give you that opportunity. I'll stay right here in the car. You do whatever you like in the park, by yourself."

The officer gave him a disgusted look. He wasn't used to dealing with crooks like this. Most of the petty criminals he'd dealt with were stupid and relatively compliant. He hated this smart-assed, defiant little shit. He pushed Robert back in the car and they continued on to their destination.

While he and Mario were kept at the police station they were unable to wash, bathe or shave. On the second and third days, whenever he spoke to a guard or a police officer Robert would say, "I guess the English are really dirty people. They don't like to bathe." He would say this to piss them off -- and it did!

Rather than maintaining total silence, Robert began to tell the same story over and over again. Torri had planned the whole thing. None of the others knew anything about it until the day of the escape. They had merely taken advantage of an opportunity that presented itself. He tried to stop them from going, but was unsuccessful. This version was totally useless to Scotland Yard. The officers became exasperated, but continued to try to get something out of him.

On the Monday following the escape, when all their interrogation attempts had proved futile, the police placed Robert and Mario in a van with heavy security for a return trip to court.

Upon their arrival at Magistrate's Court, there was a mob of reporters. Before they stepped from the van, the press had to be held back by police as they tried to move closer. Robert could see there were TV crews with cameras and microphones. He heard a question yelled at him in Italian from a television reporter but his guards weren't going to let him stop to talk to these people. For just a moment he would have the attention of the world. How could he use it? He wanted to do something symbolic to let his brother and the people who mattered to him know that he was physically and mentally okay, that his spirit had not been broken by the events of the last few days. He would have only a few seconds before they made their way through the crowd into the courthouse proper. Upon emerging from the van, surrounded by police, Robert held a defiant fist straight up in the air. Then just as suddenly his arm was grabbed and pulled back to his side. He was whisked into the courthouse.

Once inside the court, Robert noticed immediately that the lawyers were all in their Sunday best. Only a few barristers, who routinely worked in the Magistrate's Court, ever bothered much about their appearance sometimes looking outright shoddy in their usual dress. Today, however, there were cameras present. Today they might be interviewed by the media. And today they were all sharply dressed and beautiful. Several even wore boutonnieres. Robert's lawyer came to talk with him. The application before the court was routine -- a remand hearing yet again. The Crown would take the position that Robert and Mario should be kept in custody until their trial. They would be returned to Brixton Prison.

They chatted for a bit, because a great deal had transpired since they last saw one another. Robert told Mylne that he had asked for his lawyer throughout the ordeal of the past four days, but his request was ignored.

Mylne told him that after the escape, the solicitors who had visited them were immediately under suspicion. Benham and Lines were taken from the courthouse to be questioned at a police station but, of course, there was nothing of substance to link them to, the escape. Still, it was a nasty business, as no lawyer enjoyed being under such suspicion.

Robert was surprised, "Surely, Nigel, the police don't think we'd involve our lawyers in anything as risky as an escape. The whole notion is absurd. We wouldn't trust them enough to involve them in such a plan."

Nigel had to smile at this. He thought he had better get to the business at hand, "In the circumstances, I suppose your instructions to me today will be for me to agree that you be remanded in custody to Brixton. That way we'll all be out of here a lot quicker."

"No," Robert said firmly, "I want you to make an application for bail. As I told the police, Torri planned and executed the whole thing. Tony and Frascati were merely taking advantage of a window of opportunity that opened up to them. I didn't go, and I tried to stop Tony from going. I want the court to know that. I want you to try to get bail."

His lawyer was a bit surprised by the request but he followed Robert's instructions and did his best in court to put an appropriate complexion on a difficult argument. Not surprisingly, the request was denied. The reporters covering the case rushed back to their newsrooms and the afternoon's headlines in the English papers read "Brother Tries to Stop Escape" accompanied by a picture of Robert being led into the courthouse with his fist high in the air. The gesture was interpreted by some media as giving the 'Red Brigade' salute.

Robert and Mario were remanded to Brixton prison but they were not returned to familiar surroundings. Instead, they found themselves transferred to the Maximum Security wing of the prison. Here they were isolated further from the general population. The only other residents were a famous British bank robber, a weird and menacing American black guy who everyone treated with great respect and a group of alleged IRA terrorists awaiting trial.

❧

That first afternoon of the escape, Tony and Umberto tried to find time in the theater washroom to shave their faces or dye their hair. But, the movie house was constantly busy. It was impossible to spend more than a minute or two in the lavatory without being interrupted by someone. They were wary of going back and forth too many times for fear an usher would become suspicious.

They planned to hide in the theater to change their appearance, but this didn't work out. After the last show, the lights came on and an usher came through to clear out the stragglers. They found themselves out on the street. It was late evening and they felt comforted by the fact that it was dark. Even so, the Square was filled with people and the news vendors were yelling, "Read all about it! Read about the Great Escape!"

Tony approached the vendor and bought a paper. At the newsstand he was shocked to see that the story of their escape was on the front page of every afternoon paper. In most cases it was the only story on the front page. In a couple of papers the headlines were three inches high -- a type face usually, reserved for the advent of war or the end of the world.

As he walked quickly away from the newsstand he felt very vulnerable. In addition to the headlines and the story with the picture of the roof top, the article contained a picture of each of the escapees on the left-hand margin of the front page -- Torri, Frascati, and himself, each below the other. Both he and Frascati feared they would be recognized any minute.

As they walked down the street, Tony held the newspaper in front of his face as though absorbed in reading but in reality, he was using it to hide behind.

They saw an empty cab coming along the road and Umberto hailed it. The cab came to a stop, and the duo jumped in the back. From behind his newspaper Tony gave the man their desired destination.

The cab moved off and after a few seconds, Tony said to the cabby, "I'm reading about this prison escape. It's really something, don't you think?"

The cabbie, like so many London taxi drivers, was a friendly, loquacious sort. This comment set him off on a long, rambling commentary, which neither of his passengers wished to interrupt. He had seen special police units all over the city. Heathrow Airport was shut down for a few hours to install proper security. It must have been a Mafia job to break these blokes out. Frascati remained silent with only an occasional nod of agreement to the cabbie's eyes in the rear view mirror. Tony only had to interject occasionally with stock phrases, "No, you're kidding" and "That's really something" to keep the man talking.

Within fifteen minutes the cab let them out at Stefano's neighborhood. They rang the bell to his apartment and were relieved to discover he was waiting for them. He gave them the money he was holding for them, about £2000.

Tony said, "We've got to lay low for awhile. Where can you hide us?"

The boy gave it a few seconds thought, then said, "I work for a construction firm. I know about an apartment that's being renovated. No one lives there and no one is working there right now. You can stay there for a couple of days."

The three of them left Stefano's flat. As they began walking down the street, the boy saw his local priest getting into his car.

"Good evening, Father."

"Good evening, Stefano."

"Father, I'd like you to meet my two cousins. They're visiting from Italy."

The father greeted Umberto and Tony warmly and they returned the greetings.

"Father, could you give us a ride, please? We're going to visit friends."

"Sure. Get in."

They told him where they wished to go and on the way the priest said, "Have you heard. Pier-Luigi Torri escaped from prison in London today."

"No, we hadn't."

Both Tony and Umberto were thankful they were not yet as notorious as Torri, Stefano had the priest drop them several blocks from their final destination. They waved good-bye and set out on foot. Tony's feet by now were badly in need of rest. Finally they arrived at a building where there was an apartment.

Stefano led the way upstairs. The flat was semi-furnished with beds and chairs and everything they needed for cooking in the kitchen.

Stefano told them they could stay in the apartment. They could cook, lay on the beds and use the bathroom. During the day, they would have to stay in the attic to hide themselves because the people running the store were liable to come up to the apartment if they heard movement. They found the access to the attic and pulled themselves up to their lofty perch.

Tony gave Stefano some money. He said, "Buy us some spaghetti, bread, coffee, tomatoes and cigarettes." The boy returned with the goods in about half an hour.

Tony asked the boy, "Do you have your money?"

Stefano nodded yes.

"Fine, now you should leave the country immediately. Go to Paris or Rome for awhile. Stay out of sight until things calm down."

When they were all sure they had everything they needed, the boy bade them, "buona sera" and then disappeared.

They were alone now and for the first time in many hours, they began to relax a bit. Tony took off his shoes to examine his feet. They were aching badly. He lay on a bed with his feet up. They cooked some food and ate it. They smoked and they napped.

In the early morning hours they put everything back as it had been. Tony discovered his feet had swollen up too much to get his shoes back on. They took their things and their bag of food with them and climbed up into the attic through the trap-door. There were boards up there that they were able to arrange to lay upon. They spent sixteen to seventeen hours each day, talking about everything and about nothing. They found, too, that there were cracks in some parts of the walls of the attic around them. Occasionally, one of them would get up and peck through a crack to catch a glimpse of the outside world. From the heights of the building, they could see quite a distance.

Whenever, they heard sounds from below, someone coming up to the apartment, they remained absolutely still and quiet until they heard the footsteps recede down the stairs again. In the afternoon of that first day, they became aware of police lights at a distance.

This situation carried on through Friday, Saturday and Sunday, living in the apartment at night and hiding in the attic in the morning. Each day they could see the police lights moving slowly, inexorably closer to their hiding place.

❧

Scotland Yard, after their initial shock and confusion, mobilized a massive task force to recapture the fugitives.

Barely five hours after Stefano had left Tony and Umberto, the police came crashing into his apartment to arrest him. They had tracked him down without too much difficulty through the car he had used in the getaway; they found him in bed with a young woman he'd picked up in a London nightclub. He had not left the country as he'd been told to do.

They took him in for questioning. The boy proved mostly unhelpful as he was unwilling to say much. However, acting on the assumption that someone in or around this neighborhood had knowledge of the escape or had seen something, the police began questioning many Italian people who lived in the area. To a large extent, their selection of people to question was indiscriminate but eventually they found the lead they needed.

One of the people brought in for questioning was the priest, who had given the two escapees a ride. He was shocked when they placed the photos in front of him and he discovered that he recognized the two men from last night. He couldn't tell the police where the men had gone, but he could tell them where he had dropped them off.

Once this location was pinpointed, and acting on the hunch that they hadn't yet gone far from the drop-off point, the police cordoned off a section of the city about a square mile in diameter around the last known whereabouts of the fugitives. Once the area was secured they began a meticulous house-to-house search using police dogs.

It was this slow methodical process that Umberto and Tony were witnessing, as they saw the police lights move closer to their hiding place each day.

❧

On Monday morning, the police finally arrived in the neighborhood of the grocery store hide-out to conduct a search of the premises. About mid-morning, as Tony and Umberto lay motionless on their boards, barely daring to breathe, they heard noise and the footsteps of several people ascending the stairs toward the apartment.

They could hear the shopkeeper telling the police that the apartment was vacant until some repairs could be done. They continued to hear movement and talking for some ten minutes as the police went from room to room and examined every corner. Then the noise receded and the police were gone.

This was good. They began to feel better. Now that the police perimeter was beyond their hiding place, perhaps they could leave tonight.

Tony's feet had improved considerably with the rest they had received over the past four days. The two men began to think that their ordeal would soon be over once they were in a position to travel. They would leave this place tonight and make arrangements to leave the country.

So they were surprised that same afternoon, when they heard the police return to the apartment about four o'clock. It sounded like there were a great many people below. They could hear the exasperated shopkeeper saying, "I told you, there's nothing here."

Right below them they heard someone stop, "What's up here, then?"

"That's the attic."

They lay there helplessly and watched as the trap-door opened. They saw a man cautiously peek his head up through the hole. He held a handgun ready for use.

Tony stared into Chief Inspector Bennington's eyes, and the barrel of his gun. It was over. Tony and Umberto knew it and so did Bennington, but Bennington was obviously adrenaline-pumped having found the two men in this way. The last thing Tony wanted was to give him an excuse to use the gun. They were only about a foot and a half from each other. As Tony raised his hands to his head while he lay on his side, with his right hand he very gently pushed the gun barrel so that it pointed into the air. He said, "Don't be silly Inspector, there's no need for that."

The Inspector lowered his gun and yelled to the others that he had found the fugitives. He climbed up, and told them to drop through the trap-door slowly. Frascati went down first and immediately found himself grabbed from behind, spun around, hands put behind his head, and Inspector Ward's gun thrust into his mouth. It was a moment of pure terror. He looked into Ward's eyes and saw murderous hate, Frascati thought the man looked insane. He tried not to choke, or panic or move suddenly as he tasted the acrid flavor of old gunpowder and cold steel. There was no question in Frascati's mind that Ward would have shot him if all the other police and the shopkeeper had not been present.

Tony followed Umberto down. They were handcuffed and led away to a police station for a strip-search and interrogation. After several days, they appeared in court where they were again remanded into custody, this time with an additional charge of escaping lawful custody. Eventually, they were re-united with Robert and Mario in the Maximum Security Wing of Brixton Prison.

Tony and Robert Discover Gold

(1966-1972)

OF THE ENTIRE world's commodities there is probably more romance and adventure attached to gold than to any other. The word gold conjures up images of glittering coins and sparkling jewelry, items of personal wealth and adornment having value beyond enumeration.

Virtually every society has found intrinsic value in gold. In countries where inflation is rampant, the populace will turn from paper currency and debased coin to hoard gold and shore up their personal wealth. Governments rely on the metal to back their currencies. Men and women contemplating marriage symbolize the continuity and strength of their mutual love by wearing a band of gold on their fingers.

The metal is a warm, bright-colored, malleable, glittering substance in its pure form. It is one of the densest metals found in natural form; its weightiness and nobility giving the metal its broad appeal. Many people have given up their lives in pursuit of it.

When he began to work at Bouchard & Co., Tony was forced to take a more analytical and sophisticated approach to investments. He specialized in mining ventures and found himself being drawn more and more towards gold.

Since the 1930s, the USA had fixed the price of gold at $35 USD per troy ounce and until the late 1960s, the world's monetary system had operated on the basis of this standard unit of currency exchange for the US dollar.

Tony's interest was sparked in 1968 by the French and German government buying gold in such quantities that a price increase occurred on some markets to $37.50 USD. In response to this European assault, US monetary policy was drastically revised; the dollar was no longer tied to the price of gold. Tony, like many other currency and commodity traders, believed this move would cause the metal's price to rise rapidly because of its artificial constancy for the past forty years. He was not to be disappointed on this point.

Gold began a steady rise on all markets. In May 1973, it cleared $100.00 USD on the London Metal Exchange for the first time. By the end of the 1970s, the price hit $400 and briefly skyrocketed in the month of February 1980 to nearly

$800 mainly due to the Hunt brothers, two Texan oil tycoons, who tried unsuccessfully to corner the silver market. Throughout the 1980s and 1990s, the gold price has been relatively steady at $360 to $400 per ounce.

Tony and Robert as well, developed a fascination and obsession for gold. They predicted to each other and to their friends that the precious metal would increase in value. They read about it, they talked about it, they visited mines and they tried to learn everything they could about gold from the late 60's onward.

At the time of the Twins exploits in the music business, thousands of miles from Montreal, in British Columbia, Canada's most westerly province, a group of individuals came together to form a mining consortium in hope of finding and developing a commercial mining operation. The key men in this venture in 1966 were: Albert R. Swann, a lawyer actively involved in the mining industry as a consultant; Dr. Neils A. Skov, a PhD; and Donald S. Thompson, a local businessman.

They had seen a report by a British scientist named Pitt, prepared in the later days of the Second World War when the Allies had an interest in finding platinum reserves. Pitt reported showings of platinum in the Lillooet River delta located about 120 miles north of Vancouver. Their syndicate obtained or staked approximately 70 claims. Forty-six of these claims were in the area of the Lillooet River delta, comprising some, 3680 acres along the course of the Lillooet River and Sloquet Creek where they feed into Harrison Lake.

The group assigned most of their claims to two corporations; Zyrox Mining Co. Ltd and Platinate Mineral Industries Ltd, both companies set up to explore and develop the area's commercial potential. The mining group understood their project was highly speculative. At that time, they did not know with certainty, whether their leases contained anything of value. But they were experienced enough to believe the sand might carry significant potential.

Part of their optimism derived from the historical significance of the region. British Columbia had played a prominent role in the gold rushes of the 19th Century. Significant strikes occurred in a number of places within BC and further north, in Yukon. In BC, the rush had centered on the Cariboo region following the famous Barkerville discovery to the north in the 1850s. The Lillooet River is situated at the southern end of the Cariboo and for a while, in the late 1850s and early 1860s, a community of several hundred people sprang up along the north shore of Harrison Lake to service the placer miners in the area and those passing through to the Cariboo.

This thriving town was called Port Douglas, but it lasted only a short time. Soon after, an alternate route was established up the Fraser River canyon to the east of the Lillooet. By the turn of the Century, Port Douglas had become a ghost town and by 1920, no further placer activity was reported in the region. Since then the remaining buildings were destroyed by time, neglect and fire. Except for a community of Indians who lived in this remote and tiny valley nestled between blue-misted mountain ranges, Port Douglas became a footnote in the local history of the great gold rushes.

In addition to its history, the area's geology showed considerable promise. The tributaries and creeks feeding into the Lillooet drain a two-thousand square mile basin and the sands in the delta are estimated to have accumulated over some ten-thousand years. The base rock over which this drainage system runs is considered a strong host for precious metals. Over the course of time, significant values may have been deposited in the delta.

Two geologists, Gerry Kirwan and Robert Steiner, independently found quantities of gold dust (often called invisible gold by the old-timers) at the mouth of the river before any claim-staking had taken place. Steiner says neither of them acted on this information, since miners in those days generally considered nuggets and fine grains of gold necessary for conventional placer mining to be feasible. It hadn't yet occurred to the conservative mining community that a property on which surface samples contain invisible gold, may be as valuable as one on which the gold can be seen with the naked eye.

Two possibilities exist: first at depth, one may find the gold is coarser in size, particularly at bedrock; and second, a viable method might exist to recover the invisible gold from the entire deposit.

Exploitable gold occurs in nature in one or more of the following forms: as pure particles or nearly so in sizes ranging from several millimeters to perhaps, several microns in diameter; as alloyed grains with silver, copper and mercury; as a compound with tellurium (tellurides); and as solid-solution in sulfide minerals like pyrite. None of these appeared to be significant at Lillooet.

When the Zyrox/Platinate group staked the area in 1966, they did so almost completely on speculation. After staking, they proceeded to discover what minerals of value, if any, were on the property. The group raised over $200,000 amongst themselves, their family and friends to invest in developing these properties. This is when Tony got involved.

Late in 1967, the group obtained samples from several leases and attempted to have then assayed locally in the Vancouver area. The partners found great inconsistency in their initial results. The commercial labs in Vancouver claimed they weren't properly equipped to deal with these types of samples.

A gold assay is a process used to determine the amount of gold in a sample using a high-temperature melting technique called fire-assaying. This method collects the gold into a metallic lead button at the bottom of a mold into which the melt is poured. Fluxing agents are added to hold the rock material in a slag which is typically quartz-based. The method is an art-form requiring considerable skill and experience. Often, the flux recipe must be adjusted to avoid problems in producing a suitable button.

The precious metals are recovered directly from the lead metal by oxidizing and volatilizing the lead. The gold content is determined by weighing or by other modern methods that employ atomic absorption spectrophotometry.

Fire-assaying is the accepted state-of-the-art process to assess the correct quantity of gold, silver and other precious metals in a rock sample. The method has been around for centuries and has not changed much throughout the past 100 years.

In early 1968, Bert Swann requested assistance of the Mineral Sciences Laboratory of the Mines Branch in Ottawa in assaying the Lillooet sand. He asked them to undertake a study into conventional fire-assay methods to help them improve the consistency of their analyses of the sand material.

Unfortunately, whenever conventional fire-assaying methods are questioned, images of scams and unsavory practices are conjured up. Most conservative assayers will raise their eye brows and roll their eyes whenever the term unassayable gold is used. As such, the Mines Branch was unable to offer much help in developing a consistent assay procedure.

The first assays in 1967 and 1968 ranged anywhere from a value of $2.25 per ton to a high of $36.50 per ton based on the market price at that time of $30 to $35 per ounce. In gold quantity, this translates to 0.07 to 1.05 ounces per ton. In 1995, with gold at about $350 per ounce, we are dealing with an ore now worth $23 to $365 per ton. This range is truly outstanding for a conventional placer deposit or, for that matter, for a hard rock deposit! In addition, significant amounts of platinum were reported -- also ranging into the ounces per ton range.

Swann and his consortium felt confident they were onto a find of substantial importance but they were becoming frustrated in their search for an accurate way to measure the precious metals content of the sand. They knew that to have their project accepted by the mining community, fire-assays would be mandatory. There are many examples of deposits with non assayable gold. Such 'ores' invariably are barren of valuable metal. Furthermore, the BC Securities Commission tried to discredit famous scientists' work on the project by ruling that only standard fire-assaying would be acceptable to them – science was denied.

Over the next two and a half years, they continued to search for the secret of the sands. Samples were sent to respected labs in California, Colorado and London. The International Nickel Company of Canada Limited, one of the largest mining concerns in North America and a major producer of nickel and platinum, reported that the results of their assays were of considerable interest. They obtained 1.28 ounces of gold per ton as well as significant measurements of platinum-group metals and silver from a concentrate sample.

To find a deposit in which the gold is present as dust particles unlocked with the rock at concentration levels approaching one ounce per ton is extremely unusual. Bert and his colleagues could hardly contain their excitement. They continued to search for an accurate analytical method and as they looked they turned toward the new technologies of applied chemical metallurgy.

Samples were sent to a Robert Craig in California; Craig was a metallurgist, well-known to those in the mining industry in western USA and Canada. He had facilities to undertake a variety of assay methods. He was also able to plan the pragmatic aspects of creating a new mine -- from determination of the best extraction method to the choice and design of equipment necessary to make the mine and processing plant a reality.

In early 1970, Craig reported, "... a standard fire-assay ... did not produce results anywhere near the recovery obtained by the wet chemical method ..." Craig's chemical assays showed results in the range of ounces of gold per ton on numerous samples.

The economics of a gold mine depends on many factors but when the assays are this high and a high tonnage is present and can be measured, a great deal of interest should result from knowledgeable people in the industry.

In this case, there are 1760 claimed acres in the mining leases of interest. Drill holes were pulled at a variety of locations around the property to depths as great as 100 feet. Not one hit bedrock. The geological reports indicated that the sand existed to a depth of at least 150 feet or more. Using a cautious estimate of 1000 useable acres of sand to a depth of 100 feet, Craig calculated 336 million tons of ore. He conservatively estimated a net profit after taxes of about $10 USD per ton of ore. Using these figures, one obtains a NET profit of $3.38 billion dollars US from mining the sands. At a rate of 25,000 tons per day, an annual profit of over $90 million dollars could be expected with enough ore to last for over 38 years. This was an amazing sum in the late 1960s; at today's gold price; we are looking at almost fifteen times this profit.

The mining consortium's next step was to undertake a year-long bulk sampling research program conducted by a local firm in BC called Delta Smelting & Refining Co. Ltd. The firm used fire-assay to analyze the samples but they also studied several variables in the procedure to determine their influence on the results. They tried different flux recipes and used much higher temperatures than in the standard procedure. The research proved that, when using higher temperatures for long periods of time, consistent assays were possible.

The modifications to the standard fire assay method used higher temperatures, special fluxes, larger batches and slag reruns. These are not particularly remarkable changes and had produced greater consistency in their assay results. The latest assays correlated with the earlier assays that showed surface material and drill hole samples with gold between 0.53 and 1.21 ounces/ton, as well as significant silver and platinum group metals.

But fire-assay is only an analytical tool; it is not a method to recover the gold commercially. So although the inconsistency problem was beginning to be understood, a viable method to extract the gold was not in sight.

Bert Swann sat in his office on Clyde Avenue in West Vancouver. Through his window, the panoramic view of the harbor and the downtown core of Vancouver stood out in all its spectacular brilliance. Across from him sat Neils Skov, his business associate peering at a copy of the Northern Miner.

"What do you think, Neils? The article claims this Schmuckler has developed a chemical extraction process to recover fine gold from ore concentrate."

Although Neils held a PhD, the article described a patented process of an Israeli scientist that was difficult to understand.

"I don't know, Bert. It looks legitimate, but we're into the realm of very specialized, obscure and wholly, new research into the chemistry of noble metals. It will be quite awhile before we see if it proves itself. The awarding of a US patent gives it some credibility and it may be exactly what we need to process the metals in our sand."

They had spent nearly all their seed money and were still a long way from having a producing mine. Now there was new hope. This article talked about a new, cheap, low-energy process to recover gold. In its simplest form, the method involved concentrating the ore, dissolving the concentrate in weak acid and adding a resin developed by the Doctor. The resin was able to attract the gold and separate it from the rest of the concentrate. Apparently, the resin could be reused over and over again. The article claimed it had extracted virtually all of the gold contained in the concentrate tested. Maybe this was it -- the answer they needed to make all their previous work worthwhile.

Bert was putting the finishing touches on an agreement with a public company listed on the Toronto Stock Exchange to bring the property into production. They needed more money and new partners as they had spent the last of their privately-obtained funds. These eastern financiers had sent out their own geologist and he had reported back on the favorable findings of commercially workable quantities of precious metals. The report noted however, that the metals were present in micron and sub-micron sizes and that the sand composition was complex. The presence of certain components appeared to interfere with detecting the precious metals, The report concluded that research was needed to determine the best process for metal recovery.

Swann made a number of inquiries and found that Schmuckler was a Professor at the Technion Institute in Israel. The address was encouraging. Technion was a large, well-respected university, with good facilities and background for research. He wrote a long letter explaining their project and dropped it in the mail. Then he waited anxiously to hear the response.

On December 28th, 1970, Gabriella Schmuckler sat down in her lab and wrote to Bert Swann. In early January, Bert received her letter. He could see from her reply that she took the systematic approach of the researcher, well-schooled in the scientific method. The point she addressed first was, "it is necessary to clear up discrepancies ..." referring to the wide array of results and the early problems with conventional assay procedures.

She went on to suggest a way to clear up the inconsistencies -- to react the ore with a chemical solution and then evaluate the amount of gold dissolved. She wrote, "... there are at least five ways to dissolve your samples, but to my knowledge, none are within the capability of ordinary testing laboratories ..."

She suggested that her research lab could do some fundamental tests upon samples from the property. She concluded her letter, "... If this preliminary work is without results, it will mean no precious metals of importance are in your samples and you will be spared further investment ..."

Bert called a meeting of the Board of Directors to discuss the Professor's letter. The directors unanimously agreed to invest in the Israeli doctor's work. She sounded very knowledgeable and certain of herself. If she could provide the answer about how to extract the precious metals in the Lillooet sands, then that would solve the major problem regarding commercial viability of the property.

Before the end of January in 1971, Bert had shipped a sample of surface material labeled "Chem. Bulk" to Israel.

In the meantime they continued to follow other routes of inquiry. They began working with a renowned North American metallurgical engineer, Dr. A.K. Schellinger. Schellinger was tops in his field with a long career in academia at Stanford University and in industry with Cerro de Pasco Corp, Kennecott Copper, Hanna Mining and the Iron Ore Company of Canada. He worked as in industrial consultant with the Colorado School of Mines Research Institute and was listed in American Men of Science.

Swann and Skov arranged for Schellinger to fly to Vancouver and visit the property. They drove for an hour and half out of the city to the north-eastern part of the Fraser Valley to the resort of Harrison Hot-Springs at the southern end of Harrison Lake. From there they traveled sixty miles up the lake by powerboat into ever-increasingly cloud-shrouded, mountainous terrain, to the remote northern tip of the lake.

Part of the mining property bordered the north shore of Harrison Lake. When they arrived, Bert beached the boat on the sandy brush-covered delta and the three men walked inland for a bit traversing the brush until they came to the banks of the Lillooet River.

Swann bent down and scooped-up a handful of wet sand. He ran it through his fingers into his other palm. He held it out for Schellinger's inspection and poured some of the grit into the scientist's outstretched hand. The two men worked the earth between their fingers.

"This stuff is quite a bit different from 'standard' placer gold deposits," said Swann. "It's unlikely, even magnified, that you'll actually be able to see the gold or other metals, but our assays show us they are there."

Skov added, "We need your expertise, Dr. Schellinger, to help us develop an on-site extraction method for these sands. We understand that when it comes to conventional methods of extraction you are a man who is state-of-the-art."

Schellinger, a distinguished-looking man in his mid-fifties looked the part of the serious scientist, but like most men who spend much of their lives in god-forsaken parts of the planet developing new mining projects, he had elements of the geologist plus frontiersman and adventurer as well.

"Well, boys, I can see how this material would pose problems. We are looking at very minute particles of precious metal to be taken out of this sand. But, I can do a number of tests and, if there's a way of getting gold and platinum out by conventional means, then I will find it."

He continued, "I'm just guessing at this point, but, I think we are looking at developing a two-stage process. We'll see if we can physically separate some quantity of the precious metals by placer methods and then we'll look at putting together the best extraction method for tile rest of the metal in the ore."

The men talked about sample sizes, testing methods and money, and by the end of the day they came to an agreement to retain Schellinger. When their meeting finished and they had made the long trip back to the city dropping Schellinger off at his hotel, Swann and Skov relaxed over a drink.

"Well, Neils, here's hoping that by this summer, Schellinger will have developed a pilot plant to put in place on the property, and to top it off, Dr. Schmuckler will write us a favorable report. Then we'll come to an agreement with her about using her resin process on the sand."

Neils smiled at Bert. He hoped for the same thing, but said, "C'mon, Bert, you should know things are never that simple and straightforward in this business."

Bert smiled back, "I know! I know! But I'm excited and encouraged by our plans at the moment so -- Here's to the Lillooet Project!"

The two men raised their glasses and toasted their imminent success.

Over the next few months Dr. Schellinger began his work on the property. He returned to Port Douglas in late February 1971 in terrible weather with an ice-cold wind blowing down the river valley across the lake. He collected his surface samples from the property carefully bagging and labeling them for the trip to the testing facilities in the United States.

It was one of those rainy spring mornings with the sky a sheet of steel grey and the mist hanging over the mountains and amongst the evergreen trees. The inhabitants of the Pacific Rainforest wonder if they'll ever see the sun again. Bert Swann arrived late at his office. The morning mail was already in the slot.

One of the envelopes caught his eye and he realized it was a letter from Dr. Schmuckler in Israel. He had already spoken to her by telephone on many occasions. During those conversations a seed of mutual respect had been planted and a warm professional friendship was beginning to emerge. He no longer thought of this woman as a faceless scientist halfway around the world. Regardless of her professional credentials and her incisive mind there was personal warmth about the good doctor that was almost motherly. Bert had begun to think of her, not as Dr. Schmuckler but, as Gaby.

As he looked at the letter, he had a pretty good idea of its contents. He ripped open the envelope and reviewed the report. Yes, there were no surprises. She had devised four methods to dissolve the ore sample. Two of the methods showed measurable amounts of noble metals; the most promising dissolution occurring in a hydrochloric-nitric acid solution known as Aqua Regia.

Dissolving the sample by this means recovered 2-5 parts per million of gold as well as measurable amount of platinum. This amount of gold was not as extraordinary as some of their previous assays, but Bert knew these sample were solely surface material scooped right off the top of the claims. The assays at depth had shown greater amounts of precious metals.

Gabriella ended her letter by saying:

"These methods must be tested more rigorously, and quantitative analytical results must be obtained. Samples must be prepared and sent for comparative analysis to a recognized testing lab in the USA. One such lab is that of Mr. Robert Craig, whom I believe you know. "

Bert Swann felt really good about this letter. Gaby had told him over the phone that initially she expected the tests might show little in the way of precious metal content, as is most usually the case. She herself was surprised by her findings and was very interested in doing further work on the sands. The letter confirmed this. They didn't yet have all the answers, but for the time being, metallurgical experts in the field of precious metals from all over the world were working together on the problem. Gaby was made aware of Robert Craig as a result of their work. Schellinger was having his samples concentrated at the Colorado School of Mines and would be shipping some of the concentrate to Israel so that the two research labs could compare results.

Recently there was an inquiry from a scientific research group in New York and he had referred them to Dr. Schmuckler. Perhaps by being in the vanguard in this type of research, their group would develop a patent process for on-site precious metal mining using Ion Exchange that could be sold to other mining groups. That possibility, however, was part of the unforeseeable future.

But right now, Bert had a less pleasant reality to deal with. There was still no money from Chemalloy, the public company in Toronto that had optioned some of their claims on the basis of providing financing to production. Almost from the moment the contracts were signed, Chemalloy was in default on their financial commitments. What a bunch. When Bert first met the principals of company, everything was absolutely first class. They flew first-class, they stayed in the best hotels, and they wined and dined in the best restaurants.

Their attitude was, "Forget the car and boat trip to the mine. We'll charter a floatplane." If any company appeared to have money behind them, this one did. Yet now things had come to the point where when Bert called Toronto and asked to speak to someone, the secretary, would invariably come back on the line, and say, "I'm sorry, he's in a meeting," or "He's just stepped out of the office, can I have him call you back?" And of course they never did call back. He was getting too old for this kind of garbage.

It wasn't that he'd given anything away. He had spent too many years in the mining promotion business to ever sign something that would allow a con-artist to get the better of him. If Chemalloy didn't come up with the money soon, the Board of Directors would have to meet. In all probability it would mean canceling the contracts and starting over to find new financial backers.

Not long after that spring day in 1971, the Ontario Securities Commission intervened and declared a cease-trading order in the shares of Chemalloy.

The day the cease-trading order became public, for the first time in a long time Bert was actually able to speak to the President on the phone. He promised Bert it was just a minor matter. As soon as the order was lifted there was going to be no end to the things they would do. The cheque was practically in the mail. Bert got off the phone and immediately called Neils to ask him to assemble the Directors. He wasn't going to waste any more time listening to promises. The only way to stay on schedule was to look for new financial backers.

He finished talking to Neils and put down the phone. "Dammit" he thought, "It's almost June and we're still not planning for commercial production." Another summer was going to pass them by without processing facilities on the property. He desperately wanted to be beyond the testing stage of this project. It had taken four years to get this far. He was going to get his financing and he was going to bring this mine into production if it was the last thing he ever did.

The Board of Directors met and the company lawyers were instructed to notify Chemalloy that the Zyrox-Platinate group was canceling Chemalloy's options on the property pursuant to the non-performance clauses of the contract.

Although a lawyer by training and a businessman by vocation, Bert rarely dressed up to go into the office. The standard of dress for mining promoters tended toward comfort rather than formality and a shirt and pressed khaki pants generally sufficed. Bert scanned his closet for his "begging-for-money" suit. He was going into the financial heart of Vancouver, into Howe Street, to talk to some brokers and see if he could excite some interest in the project.

That day Bert made the rounds visiting brokerage firms and others he knew in the Vancouver financial community. Most everyone was aware of the basics of the Lillooet Project. He had spoken of practically nothing else for years. They commiserated with him about the bad luck in getting involved with Chemalloy, and how this had delayed his plans to proceed to production yet again.

But the answer was the same all over; they would get back to him if they heard of anyone in the market who could become a financial backer to what was still regarded as a very high-risk mining venture.

Driving home, Bert felt desolate. He thought he'd gladly sell his interest in Lillooet to get back the money he had put into it and be finished with these headaches. If they were ever going to find a way to get the gold out they must do research. But, without funds to back Schmuckler's proposed program they were stalemated. All his adult life Bert had pursued mining as a means to make more than just a living. He always believed the next mine or the next claim was going to be the big one. He'd had interests in producing mines before, but none had the extraordinary potential of the Lillooet claims. And even though the metal was there, still it eluded him. No money and no extraction process added up to no means of getting the gold. Maybe he just wasn't meant to be rich.

A few days later Bert was sitting in his office between phone calls to Toronto to canvas possibilities there, when the telephone rang. He picked up the receiver, "Zyrox Mining, Bert Swann speaking."

"Hello, Mr. Swann, my name is Tony Papalia. I am one of the shareholders of the Company. I was speaking to an underwriter friend of mine at Continental

Securities and he told me that we are still looking for money. I'm in BC for the express purpose of examining promising mining properties. I'm closely affiliated with a mining company in Montreal known as Pacific Nickel. I wonder if I can meet with you to find out more about our problem with the mining."

Although Tony was a shareholder, Bert had never met him before. Bert noted that the speaker had an accent and that he sounded relatively young. "Sure thing, I'd be glad to talk to you."

They established a time and place for a meeting. Bert thought he would prefer neutral territory. He wanted to size this fellow up before spending a lot of time showing him the particulars of the mining claims and the work done so far. He chose the lounge at the Hotel Vancouver at 3:00 pm the next day. If it turns out this kid is a mover and shaker from Montreal, it wouldn't hurt to be seen with him. A large part of the financial world operates on the basis of rumor. If you're seen talking to a heavyweight about a business deal, all of a sudden the phone starts ringing with interested people from all over.

The next day was one of those fine spring days when the snow-covered mountains stand out in relief against the pristine blue sky, as a backdrop to the city and the ocean, with its dozens of sailboats roaming amongst the freighters in the bay. It was one of those days that make smug Vancouverites wonder why anyone lives anywhere else in the world. Bert drove his car across the Lions Gate Bridge and into the heart of the city. He arrived at the hotel at about ten to three. The valet took his car and Bert headed inside.

He stood in the doorway of the Timberman's Club lounge, taking in the mock woodsy theme of the room. "Presumably meant to make robber-barons feel at home," Bert thought to himself. He allowed his eyes to adjust to the dimness of the light, and surveyed the room. He didn't see anyone who looked likely to be Papalia. He took a seat at a table by the window and watched the door.

At almost exactly 3 o'clock, a young, dark, white man with longish hair and intense dark eyes appeared in the doorway. The fellow conferred briefly with a waiter who pointed in the direction of Bert's table. Bert rose from his seat and extended his hand as they introduced themselves to each other.

Tony sat down and Bert waved a waiter over to take their drink order. They talked informally for a bit while both men sat sizing up the other, and then their talk moved onto the purpose of their meeting.

Bert, casually dropped the comment, "You're pretty young to be handling deals of this size, aren't you." He was testing the waters for defensiveness.

Tony smiled, "I guess you could say my brother and I are classic examples of immigrant kids in a hurry, we've been involved in business in one way or another since we were fifteen years old." No defensiveness there.

He told Bert a little about their background in music. "We became interested in the market several years ago as a way to invest our money, and we've done well. But, being passive investors isn't our style and we've gradually moved more into the corporate development side of things. "

"My brother Robert is President of Pacific Nickel and we plan to develop it into a dynamic force in the Canadian mining industry." He went on, "I've been spending much of my time over the past year or so, looking for interesting gold mining properties. My brother and I are convinced gold is going to be a fabulous investment now that it is no longer pegged at $35 by the US government. With the US easing up restrictions on private ownership in the States and gold trading freely on the open markets, we think the sky's the limit for gold. Some people talk about it reaching $100 US or more per ounce."

Bert finished his drink and ordered another round. Grinning broadly he agreed, "Exactly." He knew that he had found a soul mate on the topic of gold.

As far as Bert was concerned, gold was magical. Even in the richest of ores, gold was present at extremely small quantities -- parts per million. When you finally dug out the ore and processed it to recover the values, you were left with a small, beautiful piece of glittering yellow metal, enough perfection to please the gods. He thought it absurd when so-called investment gurus stated that gold was an obsolete commodity except for its use as an item of adornment.

The current wisdom in the modern world of international trade and high finance, believed gold had no further role to play. Only primitive societies would hoard gold. It had no intrinsic value and modern man will put his money in bonds and stocks or trade in currencies. The monetary system was too sophisticated to need gold as a benchmark according to this line of thought.

When it came to gold as an investment you were either a believer or you were not. Bert knew immediately he and this young-man were on the same side of the question. Both of them would stand behind gold as a commodity that would make the gloom-and-doom talkers eat their words.

Bert liked Tony. The young man was confident and laid his cards on the table immediately with a confidence that belied his age. He had an air of veracity that the principals of Chemalloy, with all their flash and pomp, had lacked. Bert began to explain the Lillooet claims to Tony. When he mentioned some of the more favorable assays, 1/2 ounce of gold per ton and up, he saw Tony's eyes widen and then narrow with increased interest. He could tell this young man wasn't naive and sensed that Tony was thinking, "So why do you need me, and why aren't you already producing this gold?"

Bert began to explain about the minute size of the precious metals particles and how physical separation hadn't proven feasible or even possible, and how they were working on a system of chemical extraction. He explained about the Israeli chemist with her patent in noble metals recovery and how financing was needed for her to continue her research. To a large degree she had already refined her methods but what the project needed now was a pilot plant on the property to define the process on a scale larger than that available in a lab.

Tony was intrigued. He would have to take steps to verify what Swann was telling him. He would need copies of the reports and the correspondence with the Israeli scientist to verify her credentials and he would need to speak to her on the phone. And most importantly, he must visit the property where they could take samples for independent analysis.

Tony loved the innovation of this project. The idea of a better way to process gold and precious metals was the part he really liked. Here was something new and incredibly big. They'd be in on the ground floor perhaps, to own part of the rights to a process which could revolutionize gold mining.

The two men talked for several hours. Tony suggested they go for dinner and continue their discussions. At 9:30 pm that night, after dinner and some more drinks, Tony and Bert parted ways. They had discussed in general terms the business side of a potential deal.

Tony phoned Robert the minute he got back to his hotel room. He told his brother he had found the most interesting project he could ever imagine. One aspect that intrigued him immediately was the size of the project. Often the decision to bring a mine into commercial development was made when the available quantity of ore was defined. In this case, it was clear that the volume of the sand could be estimated with incredible accuracy. According to Swann, the tonnage was estimated in the range of six hundred million tons. At that level, if the grade of the deposit could be quantified properly, they would be taking out tremendous quantities of gold for the next fifty years.

Robert was curious and wanted to know more. Tony had a couple of drinks in him and was slightly bleary. He was happy with his meeting with Swann, he knew he hadn't yet done his homework, but he wanted Robert to understand how excited he was over the possibilities. "Let's put it this way, Robert, this is the BIG one. If we own a large piece of it and it's half as good as Swann says, we'll never have to worry about money for another day of our lives, your biggest problem will be to figure out how to spend it."

Robert's interest was piqued, and Tony continued, "Look, I'll phone you again after I've seen the property and I have read the reports. Right now, I'm supposed to meet Gus and Murray at Oil Can Harry's."

Robert laughed. Tony's upbeat mood was contagious, even if he had been woken from a sound sleep at 1:30 am in the morning Montreal time. "Well, brother, if you meet any attractive women tonight, keep their phone numbers for me. I'm the one without a steady girlfriend and they won't know the difference between me and you. It sounds like I'll be making a trip to Vancouver soon."

"Ciao."

Over the next few months, Tony, Robert and another director from Pacific Nickel Mines, Jack Lovelock, all made trips to Lillooet and began to review the reports; they held many meetings with Bert Swann and Neils Skov. Robert and Jack took samples from the property and returned with them to the University of Montreal where the material was analyzed and assayed. They also hired a Vancouver-based geological consultant, William Stevenson, to conduct tests on the project. It was obvious that a great deal of testwork had already been done. The assays commissioned through Stevenson were not very favorable but he had employed conventional methods. In light of the earlier reports, they presumed that such assays failed to elicit all the gold in the samples.

The University of Montreal test gave positive results at elevated temperatures and they decided to get involved to take the project through to the development stage. They approached Swan and Skov to see if they could work out a deal.

By November, 1971, the parties had hammered out a written agreement. The principals of Pacific Nickel didn't want to option the property in exchange for development money; they made it clear to Swann they wanted a hands-on position of control if their company was going to provide the needed capital. It was agreed that the project would be undertaken as a joint venture with Pacific Nickel overseeing development of the mine through to production, in consultation with the Zyrox/Platinate board. The first step after the contracts were signed was to re-hire Dr. Schmuckler to undertake further research.

But as Robert and Tony were busy planning expansion of Pacific Nickel into the west-coast, several bizarre incidents took place in Montreal which was to change their lives in many ways. The first occurred just prior to Tony's meeting with Bert Swann. He dealt with it immediately and believed it was finished.

In the summer of 1971, Tony received a phone call from a Toronto stockbroker. At the time Tony held an account at this fellow's firm.

"Tony, I just had a rather strange visit that I thought you should know about."

"Yes Fred, what's it all about?"

"Well, some guy was just here claiming he was with some special Security Branch of the RCMP. He says his name is Kesley Merry."

He asked me if I knew that Tony, a.k.a. Antonio Papalia, was a member of the Mafia. Then he told me I'd have to close your account."

"That's craziness. Do you know how to contact this guy? I'll talk to him and straighten this out."

"Apparently he's got an office in the Toronto Stock Exchange. Maybe if you phone Compliance you can track him down."

"Thanks for calling, Fred. I'll take care of it."

After a few calls, Tony was able to contact Merry in Toronto. Tony explained who he was and why he was calling. Angrily he said, "A terrible mistake had been made. I am not Mafia, and have never had any such association. I came to Canada as a 12 year old in 1957 with my widowed mother."

Kesley Merry listened to Tony. Then he apologized. He explained they thought the brokerage account had belonged to the Antonio of the Hamilton Papalias.

The call ended on a friendly note with Merry promising to rectify things with the broker and saying that the next time he was in Montreal he would like to meet Tony and his brother. Tony was amenable to this, "Sure, whenever you're in Montreal give me a call."

The rumors seemed to end, his trading account stayed open, and Tony thought no more about it.

The Committal Hearing Begins
(October 1977-December 1977)

AFTER THEIR RECAPTURE and return to Brixton, Tony and Umberto, along with Mario and Robert had to adjust to a more rigorous form of imprisonment than they had previously known. Now they were held in the Maximum Security wing of the prison. With the exception of Torri, who seemed to have made a clean getaway, they were more than ever under the watchful eye of their keepers.

The special high-security section was well away from the general population of the prison. They were issued special orange coveralls marking them as high-security-risk prisoners. When any of them were escorted outside of their wing -- to the mess hall, to the showers, to their meetings with lawyers -- two guards tagged along on either side.

Their time in the exercise yard was taken with the other maximum security prisoners and apart from the rest of the prisoners. There were not many detainees at Brixton who warranted this special treatment. The two main groups were the Italians and the Irish. The latter were a group of Irish nationals awaiting trial on charges of having committed terrorist bombings in London several months earlier. Then there was an infamous old-timer who was the reputed head of an organized group of bank robbers who had pulled some of the largest and most elaborate jobs in England in the 1970s. And, finally, there was an American who kept himself apart from all the others. This man had an impenetrable, ominous and threatening air about him. The little contact the Italians had with this man gave them the impression that he was a sociopath. They respected his standoffishness and made no effort to get to know him.

For the rest though, they all got on very well which surprised them since the outside world generally regarded these men as comprising an extremely dangerous segment of society. Among other activities, the Italians and Irish began a good-natured rivalry on the soccer field during their exercise breaks, carrying out their own ongoing international tournament, Italy vs. Ireland. The bank robber, Eddie, was regarded as a sort of elder statesman, who was always willing to share his street-wise ways with the new kids on the block and he occasionally acted as referee in these games. With the exception of the American, it was an amazingly cohesive community.

The most significant change in their status however, stemmed from an altogether different source. The sensational way in which their case and escape was reported made everyone treat the Italian group differently than before. Immediately following their arrest they were generally regarded as a group of anonymous businessmen facing fraud charges. Now, both the guards and the prisoners, having followed their story in the newspaper for weeks were thoroughly convinced that these men were very important Mafia capos. Generally, this meant that the guards were more careful in their dealings with this group of prisoners, while the general prison population began to treat them as returning dignitaries.

On those occasions when they brushed past other prisoners in the mess hall or on their way to or from a meeting with lawyers, the most hardened criminals sought their favor or showed respect by means of small signs. They were offered cigarettes or other substances of their choice, without obligation, only that the giver could seek some recognition from this illustrious group. They found themselves both feared and admired and they did nothing to promote or dispel this impression on the inside of the prison walls. This unsought reputation was the one thing they had going for them on the inside that allowed them to be left alone or treated with respect.

❧

Once back in Brixton, the newspapers had nothing new to report about them. The prison routine began to impinge upon them once again as the center of their reality. They continued to go before the courts on a weekly basis, but, now, things transpired by ritual. The prisoners put forward their contention that they should be released on bail prior to their trial, but everyone knew there was no chance that any bail application would succeed.

They began to focus their attention on getting a hearing. A hearing would give them something to fight against, instead of the ongoing limbo that their lives had become.

Most people charged with a crime are given a brief description of the evidence that will be presented against them at the hearing. This process allows an accused and his lawyers to make a reasonable assessment of the case they will face. But, this case was so extensive, so technical and obtuse, in most of its many elements that the evidence against them continued to be a puzzle. Documents and dates were pasted together in an arbitrary fashion.

They were told that the Metals Research group was actively engaged in a conspiracy with Bear Securities to defraud the investing public in England by selling MRSA shares. And this conspiracy was tied into a smaller and only marginally related conspiracy whereby Bear, in concert with the ICB bank, attempted to defraud Cessna Financial Corporation of $1.5 million US dollars.

Since the accused knew that the dealings they had with each other were both nominal and wholly legitimate they found the steady stream of lawyers coming to speak to them about each new tidbit in the case, to be a constant source of fascination and concern.

Geoff Lines told Tony that Scotland Yard had visited the Lillooet property and a forensic scientist was going to present the findings of his own assay. He would testify that the amount of gold and platinum in the Lillooet sands was almost non-existent.

The previous week Geoff had been cornered in a hallway at the courthouse by Inspector Julian Bennington, the top man in charge of Scotland Yard's case. He was forced to listen to Bennington's gloat "You may as well take a load of builder's sand and try to sell it as a precious metal property, for all the gold that's in those Lillooet Sands."

Tony was exasperated as usual. How were they ever going to make the lawyers understand everything so that they could conduct a proper defense? "What?" he said, "Have the police bothered to look at the other thirty or forty reports done on the sand over the last ten years?"

"Well, I understand that the Crown thinks they're all fraudulent."

"How can that be? That's nonsense. We and our predecessors were dealing with respected, world-renowned laboratories."

Geoff just shrugged. The prosecutor's office was not giving the Defense complete discovery of the case. For the most part there were huge gaps in the evidence supplied to them. As well, the highly technical aspects of the case that included metallurgy stock share-pricing and international banking, left their lawyers struggling to understand what was relevant, what would need to be proved and what could be discarded as non-consequential. Until the Defense saw all of the Crown's case, there was no way to assess accurately possible defenses and chances of success.

❧

As the Fall of 1977 began to fade into Winter, the group was relieved to hear at one of their weekly remand hearings that the Crown was ready to proceed to trial and wished to set a date. The Defense lawyers and their clients were in agreement that there must be a committal hearing. They would learn about all the evidence that made up the Crown's case. Then they could develop a theory of defense and hopefully assemble evidence to refute the charges.

The clients wanted the case to go ahead as soon as possible and their lawyers understanding their desire, cleared up their calendars to get the earliest date. The committal was to begin on December 19th, 1977. There would be a week of hearings before Christmas, then a break over the holidays and a resumption of proceedings in January. Despite the fact that some witnesses would have to be brought from other countries, the lawyers hoped to complete the hearing by late January 1978.

The Crown was concerned that Torri was not before the court, but they had no lead on his whereabouts and they couldn't continue to delay the proceedings against the other defendants indefinitely.

After completing most of their investigation, the prosecution was attempting to extradite Paul Harris from the Caymans. They included him as one of the alleged co-conspirators in their theory of events. His presence in England would bolster the share-price rigging allegation of their case.

Over the course of the next month and a half, all the imprisoned defendants worked unrelentingly with their lawyers to clarify their response to the charges. Almost on a daily basis, the solicitors' clerks would arrive at Brixton with instructions to find out the clients' responses to some newly revealed aspect of the Crown's case.

On these occasions Tony, Robert and Mario went on hour after hour explaining their personal backgrounds, the history of the Lillooet Project, their involvement in the mineral deposit and their admittedly-convoluted corporate structures and dealings. The clerks took copious notes. These handwritten notes were taken back to their offices to be transcribed into typed memos of proof. The solicitors would then review these memos and instruct the barristers as to their clients' responses.

This process became a source of extreme frustration for the prisoners. There were many times when the typed memos upon being returned to Brixton for review, were wrong in some important particulars. Somewhere communication between the parties would break down and so, they would have to go through it all again to correct the mistakes.

As things progressed toward Committal, Tony and Robert could see there were some clerks who suffered from inattention, who jumped to wrong conclusions and who did only what was required. But there was also one clerk who showed a dedication and commitment to getting it right and doing his utmost; this man was Geoff Lines. He emerged in these months as a life-line for Tony and Mario, his clients in particular, but, also, he acted to ensure that all four of the accused men knew there was someone on the outside in England who was doing everything in his power to ensure they got a fair trial.

The prisoners began to rely on him above all others. And as Geoff spent more and more time with his clients, arriving early and leaving late, returning to his office and working late into the evening, he began to like and then, to respect his clients. He came to believe in his clients' innocence, despite all the damning evidence against them.

As the first day of the committal hearing loomed near, the Defense remained in the dark about many important aspects of the case. David Benham knew that Scotland Yard's investigations had taken them all over the world. The police had been to Italy, the Bahamas, Panama and they had been to the mining property in British Columbia. Supposedly, the Crown had uncovered significant evidence from around the world of a gigantic international conspiracy to defraud. The defense lawyers waited anxiously to see how the evidence would unfold.

❧

It was a cold, windy, grey December day in the City of London when the prisoners were brought before the Court to start their hearing. They were transported in a manner that had become the norm since Tony's and Umberto's recapture. They were placed together in a prison van with police escort vehicles, front and back carrying a battery of armed police. All of the vehicles sped together to their destination, sirens blaring and lights flashing. Robert was always struck by this display of force. He was quite astonished at the trouble the police took for them. It was clear that this odd band of Italian and Canadian businessmen posed an exceptional threat in the minds of the police.

At the Magistrate's Court that day there was much added security. The courthouse personnel were tense in anticipation, of the endless possibilities that might be available to this powerful group of criminals; these foreigners who had, God knows great influence within the secret world of organized crime. There was a heightened sense of expectation in the air that morning at Lambeth Magistrate's Court.

Normally, Magistrate's Court is a forum for fairly routine criminal matters. It is the drunks, the miscreants, the petty thieves and minor assaults that are the daily bread of the Court's work, with an occasional nod to more serious crimes such as murder, manslaughter, armed robbery and embezzlement, at the committal stage of proceedings. There was no question that today's case was different -- a crime of great magnitude with international implications. The court personnel vied for an opportunity to be part of this case. Those assigned to other court rooms loitered around the doorway to Courtroom Two, or they stuck their heads in at the door, trying to catch a breath of the excitement that hung in the air before going off to their more mundane fate down the corridor.

Extra security measures were in place in the public gallery with prohibition on bringing in carrying cases and compulsory cursory searches of all persons seeking access to the gallery. Interest in the case was extremely high -- and public seating severely limited. In the end, only close friends and relatives of the accused and some of the more significant London newspapers and BBC were assured of seats.

When the veritable army of lawyers was assembled, the gallery was full, the clerks and security personnel were in their places, and the Magistrate had entered the courtroom to preside over it all, the last people to be brought in were the defendants. With the exception of Richard Swinnerton, Renata Harris and Madeline Blot, who were out on bail, and who had all come forward when the case was called, the remainder of the defendants, the four Italians, were led in from the lock-up. Beside Richard Swinnerton sat the diminutive and pale figure of the pretty young Frenchwoman, Madeline Blot. Next to her was an older, harder and much more streetwise woman, Renata Harris, and then came Frascati, Berton and finally, the two Papalia brothers. They all sat down and the proceedings began.

The Crown's case was being led by one senior counsel; a man with years of experience in prosecuting criminal cases in the courts of Great Britain. He had a reputation for winning the most complex of cases. Little did he realize he was embarking on the most difficult case of his career. He hoped, perhaps expected, to add to his list of achievements. He would put these Mafia chiefs behind bars, bringing their nefarious schemes in England and elsewhere to an end.

Michael Worsley was brought in by the Attorney-General's office to take conduct of the case very soon after the original arrests. He had worked day and night with the Scotland Yard detectives to gather the paper trail that made up this case. It required fitting together the jig-saw puzzle pieces of a maze of corporate dealings on several continents over a period of years until finally he had irrefutable proof for his conspiracy theory. His job was to present these convoluted facts to the court in a coherent and convincing manner.

Mr. Worsley began by preferring fresh charges before presenting his opening speech to the court. This had happened several times since the defendants were originally charged in May. Whenever Scotland Yard or the prosecutor's office would develop a new hypothesis about some part of the alleged conspiracy or whenever they recognized flaws in the wording of the charges, new charges would be drafted and laid. In this instance, prosecutors had identified a potential jurisdictional problem with one of the "Cessna" charges.

In essence, the new count read that Frascati, Blot, and Harris had attempted to obtain Cessna aircraft by fraudulent means. Since the aircraft themselves were never in Britain, and under jurisdiction of British courts, it was necessary to change the charge. The new charge was amended to indicate that the noted defendants had attempted to obtain certificates of ownership of those aircraft by fraudulent means. The Crown felt that this charge was appropriate since the aircraft ownership certificates had been delivered to Bear Securities in London.

Once the charge sheet was amended, Mr. Worsley began his opening. To no one's surprise he went on at length for a total of four days, explaining the nature of the criminal charges and the evidence he would bring forth to prove the guilt of the accused. His delineation of the case sought to "marry-up" a vast and diverse array of people and events to prove the Crown's conspiracy theory.

He told the court that the people involved in this conspiracy included the seven defendants before the court; Mr. Torri, who had escaped; the three other Italians who absconded after being released on bail, those being Boccardi, Baracchini and Santoro; and Paul Harris of the Cayman Island, who the Attorney General was attempting to extradite to Britain.

The case consisted of two major frauds. There was the smaller scam involving issue of three bank drafts from the International Commerce Bank for a total sum of just over $1.5 million US payable to Cessna International Financial Company. Worsley stated that it was intended that these drafts would not be honored and so the defendants Torri, Frascati, Blot, Renata Harris, Boccardi, Baracchini and Santoro had intended to defraud CIFC of the said moneys.

The second part of the case alleged that Metals Research Société Anonymous

(MRSA) had no gold, no valuable assets, and a worthless mining claim in British Columbia and that the principals in MRSA knowingly misrepresented the affairs of their prospects to defraud public investors of up to $300 million US dollars. In advancing this fraud, the defendants conspired with persons at Bear Securities to use the bank to deal and promote bogus MRSA shares. Those facing these charges were Robert, Tony, Mario, Swinnerton, Frascati and Torri.

❧

One would think when Scotland Yard's Serious Crime Squad took up a case, the investigation would be the work of professionals. They would have on their team at least one expert in commercial law who would sift through the acres of paper and reports and assemble an ironclad case of fraud and conspiracy. But, as Mr. Worsley spoke at length and began to delve deeper into his elements of proof, it appeared to Tony that the police had done no such thing. They had simply brought mounds of paper to his office for him to sort out the niceties to prove the case. Their investigation was based on one fundamental premise:

The Serious Crime Squad had it on good authority from their Intelligence network with the Canadian authorities that the Papalias were Mafia and this assumption would not be questioned. This premise would serve as the foundation for putting together the case.

This kind of thinking resulted in a blind spot on the part of the police and prosecutors in their conduct of the case. It made it impossible for them to see serious defects in the evidence. Because they could not consider the possibility of innocence, they relied heavily on many fallacious assumptions. Having labored mightily to develop a theory of the case for himself, Mr. Worsley gave a masterful performance in the courtroom. He slotted each item of evidence into his own configuration of how it fit with the other elements of the case.

To everyone listening, with the exception of the few men who knew the real truth, it seemed these charges were very serious and the Crown certainly had a great deal of evidence to prove their case.

Mr. Worsley attacked the Papalias and Mario Berton on several fronts. First the Crown alleged they were involved in rigging share-prices of MRSA. The quoted price for MRSA shares on the Reuters Monitor Service of $12.00 US per share "was purely artificial."

The Crown prosecutor explained it as follows: having created an artificially inflated price for the shares, the accused were in the process of increasing the share capital of the company to 25 million shares at $1.00 US per share. If these shares were fully subscribed by investors, $300 million US dollars would exchange hands from investors to the treasury of the Company.

Mr. Worsley concluded on this point, "And that is one way, then, in which money was to be obtained by, the issue of shares in a company whose prospects -- the mining of noble metals, were entirely falsely presented to the public."

He then moved onto the aspect of the case that tied Bear Securities to MRSA.

"The principal aspect ... in this main part of the case... is the proposed sale of shares in MRSA ... that involved setting up, what is sometimes known as a 'Fringe Bank' to assist in the share dealings ..."

He alleged that the conspirators had set up two such banks, in "sumptuous premises in the West End." These banks were Bear Securities and ICB.

Having named these banks, Worsley then returned to the 'Cessna' part of the case to show how the two were tied together. According to the Crown, the false bank drafts in the amount of $1.5 million US dollars came about as a result of the following machinations, "certain accomplices of some of the defendants wanted to take over an Italian company which had interests in the airplane business - a company called CAST. The plan was that the debt of the company should be paid and that the company would acquire further aircraft from Cessna ... paid by a Banker's draft, issued by ICB."

"The plan was to date the bank drafts a year hence ... but when the conspirators ... thought, more about it, they decided to let ICB drop out of the picture altogether and its place taken up, for the purpose of the mining fraud, by a new bank called Anglo American Trade Bank (AATB), which would take over the premises of ICB at 60 Pall Mall."

"ICB would drop out of the mining part of the fraud and ... simply disappear. When the drafts that had been issued by it, in favor of Cessna for the aircraft, fell due ... the holders of the drafts would find the bank no longer existed."

But the conspirators were caught when Mr. Van Drunen, Cessna's agent in Brussels, tried to discount the drafts but could not do so. So this was how these two matters, which appeared to be separate, were tied together.

"The three banks, Anglo American Trade Bank, International Commerce Bank Limited, and Bear Securities Limited, having been set up for the purposes of the mining fraud, took advantage of the existence of one of the banks, ICB, to use it for the aircraft fraud -- a much smaller matter. Then it was thought that since that small fraud had been perpetrated, the bank better disappear and its place be taken by one of the other banks, the AATB."

The only two defendants who could be linked to both purported frauds were Torri and Frascati. These two were the common elements, the 'lynch-pins' that tied the two frauds together.

Worsley then explained to the Magistrate how he saw the evidence being organized. The first category of evidence would show the involvement of particular defendants. This type of evidence consisted of four sub-categories. First, there would be those persons who had dealings with the various conspirators in setting up the frauds and would include such diverse elements as the people in the British Post Office who assisted Torri to set up telex machine at ICB, and the lawyers and accountants in Panama who incorporated MRSA on the instructions of the Papalias and Mario Berton.

Secondly, there would be evidence consisting of all the documents found in the possession of the defendants. This included everything from share certificates to doodles written on hotel stationary.

Thirdly, there would be "confessions" related to establishment of these banks as typed up and signed by the relevant members of the Serious Crime Squad.

The fourth sub-category of evidence would be police observations of some of the defendants. With Worsley's public admission of "police observations" he then dropped what he hoped would be a bombshell on the defense lawyers. It had the desired effect. He saw several lawyers squirm in their seats and highlight their notes at this point as they visibly began to wonder what, indeed, the police had observed.

"Unknown to the defendants in the aircraft part of the case, Torri and Frascati, police were observing movements at ICB and Bear Securities. They had been observing movements at those banks from early February of 1977 onwards ..."

As Frascati heard this and watched the discomfort of his lawyers, he wondered what the police could have observed that was so damning. Certainly there was nothing unusual going on at 'Bear'. The most interesting part of this revelation for Frascati was the timing of the investigation. It followed almost immediately upon Bear's solicitors sending a letter to the London Sunday Times demanding a retraction of libelous statements made about the bank.

Worsley then described the second major category of evidence; documentation and testimony which would show the falsity of the information being prepared about MRSA activities and assets. This category was broken down into five areas. There would be scientific testimony which would explain "what actually existed upon the land in British Columbia."

The evidence would compare Robert Craig's report from the spring of 1977, with the information contained in the 'Black Brochure'. Worsley pointed out that Craig was a scientist working for MRSA at the time he wrote his last report on the Lillooet property which showed considerably less noble metals on the mining claims than the amounts set out in the 'Black Brochure'. The 'Black Brochure' was a corporate document printed in Milan in March 1977. The brothers and Mario Berton had brought about six copies with them on their last trip to London. Worsley alleged that the figures in this brochure were grossly inflated, and that this brochure was to be disseminated to the public to be used to trick unwary investors into this sham corporation.

Worsley made light of the details surrounding the proposed process to recover precious metals from the ore. He indicated the principle method to be used was "Iron Exchange" and compared the group of promoters to alchemists who tried to change iron into gold. It seems ludicrous that an experienced lawyer such as Worsley would make such an error in a case such as this one but this was just one of many instances of bungling on the part of the police and the prosecutors.

The third sub-category of evidence was the 'Black Brochure' itself. The Crown would lead the court through a close reading of this prospectus and expose, paragraph by paragraph, the lies and misinformation contained therein.

The fourth sub-category of evidence would be testimony of those members of the Serious Crime Squad who visited the actual mining claim site in BC.

Finally, the last sub-category of evidence would be "admissions" by certain of the accused that would prove the falsity of what they were planning.

Having given a bare-bones outline of the Crown's case, Worsley returned to discuss some of the particulars of the Crown's conspiracy theory which established jurisdiction in the English courts.

The true purpose of ICB, AATB and Bear Securities, was to be vehicles in London to sell shares of MRSA to naive English investors. Having made this allegation, he paused to anticipate a possible defence response and then asked the question, "Why sell shares of MRSA to English investors through fringe banks, rather than to Canadian or American investors?"

Worsley saw two answers to this question. The first was that English currency control laws require English investors to pay a surtax when they exchange pound sterling for foreign currency to invest in securities such as MRSA. Setting up 'fringe banks' in England for the purpose of avoiding this surtax, by buying direct in sterling within Britain was a common practice at the time of this hearing. The prosecutors reasoned that a person investing through a 'fringe bank' to avoid the Foreign Investment surtax would be less likely to go to the authorities to complain if they were defrauded.

The second reason was that English investors would have, more difficulty in discovering that the mine was a sham than would people who live near the site.

At this point, Worsley, having established a criminal motive for establishing these banks, took the opportunity to throw in some gratuitous remarks about the character of the persons on trial.

"Well now, I've said enough, perhaps, about the general principals in this case. When you look at the details in the case, it's quite apparent that the work of the defendants is that of a team of 'INFANT INTERNATIONAL CONFIDENCE TRICKSTERS.' Some of the defendants ... are in fear of the man who has run away -- Torri -- and his associates." Worsley declined to give details of the cause for this fear but he told the court, "... we shall come to it in due course."

He continued "... it is quite apparent that ... the activities in which the defendants are involved can be regarded as being activities of the Mafia."

Having said this, Worsley now qualified the statement of Mafia involvement making it apparent he had no intention of proving the matter, "... whether it be the Mafia, whatever that may be, is not for me to set out to prove. All I can say is that on the evidence, Mafia or not Mafia, the activities in this case are the work of a very highly organized criminal team."

Michael Spencer, Tony's barrister, considered getting on his feet and objecting to these gratuitous comments. Worsley was careful in setting up this part of his speech to make sure he got the Mafia innuendo before the court, before making it apparent there was no proof of this particular allegation. Spencer felt it was probably too late to object to it now. He would never let something like this go unchallenged in front of a jury, but he felt certain that the Magistrate wouldn't need this lapse pointed out to him. If it became necessary, Spencer decided he would point out the Crown's over-statement of the case in his summation.

To establish a conspiracy, Worsley had to show a 'common purpose' -- an agreement to commit the frauds alleged. There had not been actual frauds committed, in either of the two basic conspiracies alleged, so Worsley had to show that the defendants by their acts and declarations formed a common intention to defraud. So he moved into those aspects of the evidence whereby he would show a conspiracy, particularly, as to the conspiracy between Torri and Frascati of Bear Securities and the principals of MRSA.

While listening to Worsley drone on and on, Robert and Tony couldn't restrain themselves from looking at one another and rolling their eyes and shaking their heads. Without speaking, they were able to communicate their mutual disgust with how the Crown had patched together wholly unrelated events, and placed importance on matters of insignificance.

"There was a vital meeting of conspirators in the Cayman Islands at the beginning of 1977. The meeting began with the arrival of Anthony Papalia and Mario Berton on January 2nd, 1977. They were joined by Swinnerton and Robert Papalia on the 4th of January."

"Swinnerton left the Caymans on January 8th but the others remained until the 11th ... with this information he concluded, "... that was an important meeting of the conspirators for shortly thereafter, Bear Securities applied to the British Department of Trade and Industries for a Principals License under Section 3 of the Prevention of Fraud Investments Act. This document is necessary for any company dealing in securities such as MRSA shares."

To nail down this part of the conspiracy, Worsley noted that only two days after the meeting in the Caymans, Mr. Torri met with two of the Italian directors of Bear Securities, Pellizone and Silvera, in London. At this meeting in England, these men stayed at the best hotels in Britain at the expense of Bear Securities.

The Papalias and Frascati were dumbfounded by the Crown's aggressive fabrication of conspiracy by interweaving unrelated events. Their Defense Counsel sitting several rows in front of their clients and taking notes, could see that Worsley was talking about two separate groups of people in separate countries attending entirely separate meetings at various times. Spencer turned to the lawyer beside him and scribbled, "Where's the common link?"

His colleague scribbled his reply, "There must be more to it than Worsley's saying at the moment."

Spencer made a note to himself that they must find the evidence that connected these two events. He was hoping they would find out at Committal, but perhaps, Worsley was going to keep this up his sleeve until the trial.

Worsley continued with his "evidence" of conspiracy. Another primary connection between the two groups of defendants was that lawyers for Bear Securities sent a letter to their client bank on April 29th, 1977, wherein they advised that their application for a securities license had been turned down by the Department of Trade until such time as the minority interests of the parent company, Magica Corvena, were disclosed.

This April 29th letter, according to Worsley, had a great deal to do with a memo found in Torri's home, dated May 2nd, 1977, reading, "could you telephone Mr. Berton or Robert Papalia in Milan. This is very important." There is nothing in this May 2nd note to say what was the subject of the very important matter, but, pointedly, Worsley never bothered to tell the court that Robert Papalia and Berton were busy on that date trying to sublet the ICB premises from Torri for the AATB, a matter that had nothing to do with the issuance of a security license for Bear Securities.

While Worsley went on at length delineating the supposed fraud, the remainder of the evidence consisted of the many corporate documents found in possession of the Papalias and Berton. These documents were wholly bogus stated the Prosecutor. Since the documents showed efforts being made by the accused to comply with corporate legal requirements such as audits and underwritings, Worsley concluded "they wanted to maintain the appearance of legality for ... the time being, until substantial proceeds could be gotten into their pockets."

For this purpose, said Worsley, some of the letters of account and expenses claimed were obvious forgeries brought into being and backdated by the defendants. These forged documents would assist the directors in siphoning off money from MRSA when the time came to do so.

The Crown insisted that not only were the documents bogus, but so, too, were the many scientific reports prepared from examination of the Lillooet claims.

The basic theory behind this allegation was that in all cases where samples were provided to the geologist or scientist preparing the report, the results of tile assays tended to be more promising. In those instances where the person preparing the report collected their own samples, the assay results were not nearly so good. Thus, it was that Dr. Schellinger's samples showed only trace amounts of precious metals, while Dr. Schmuckler's tests on the same batch of samples sent to her in Israel showed very promising amounts of gold. Likewise with Mr. Craig's reports -- this man was the Defense's own metallurgist. He was the person hired to develop a process for commercial exploitation of the sands.

In 1969 Craig wrote a report from samples provided to him. In 1977 he visited the property for the first time and obtained his own samples. The 1969 results were much better than the later results.

Mr. Worsley makes much of this, "... in Mr. Craig's 1977 report it states ... the writer was much impressed by the results obtained from the random samples. It was far better than we had hoped for at the depth the sample material was obtained from' ... This is contrasted with the reports made in 1969, where the analyses conducted on samples provided to him were much more favorable than those in this letter. Yet, in this letter the much reduced figures as compared with his 1969 reports are said by him to be much better than hoped for. So what he had been provided with in 1969, one can only wonder."

Mr. Worsley had the disconcerting habit of talking around an issue but never really saying what he meant. He implied that all promising reports on the property were based on salted samples. A salted sample is one in which quantities of precious metals from an outside source are added to produce an artificially high reading for the precious metals.

Perhaps Mr. Worsley avoided being forthright about the salting allegation for a reason. If he came right out and made such a statement, the Magistrate or Defense Counsel might ask for proof that the samples were salted. This was yet another example of the Crown's reliance on innuendoes rather than proof.

Another thrust of the Crown's case against the Papalias, Berton, and Swinnerton were their "confessions". Mr. Worsley detailed for the court how each "confession" came into being. He noted the dates of the arrests and the times and duration of each interview with the accused.

He made a point to tell the court that the typed versions of these statements were taken from the notes of the police officers present at each interview.

These notes were written at the same time as the "confessions" made by each accused.

These statements were signed by all of the officers present at the interview but not by the accused. There was no legal requirement in Britain at that time, for the court to be satisfied that the so-called confession was accepted by the accused as his own, as evidenced by his signature upon the statement.

Worsley concluded his comments on the "confessions" by saying, "Now, that's all I wish to say about the interrogations and the written statements to the police ... It is my submission that if you're satisfied that the evidence given by the officers about the interviews and the taking of statements, is prima facie credible evidence, it is my submission ... the admissions made by all defendants, would justify apart from any other evidence, in committing them to trial."

He then admitted to the court that the Crown's case against Madeline Blot and Renata Harris was weak. He submitted however, that even if the evidence was insufficient to commit these two to trial on the basis of the primary charges, they should be committed to trial because they "knowingly assisted a person or persons to prevent apprehension or prosecution."

As he wound up his speech, the Magistrate interrupted him, "Mr. Worsley, with respect to the share-rigging aspect of your case, will you be calling some sort of expert evidence of share price valuations?"

"Sir, I can call evidence if necessary ... from one of the big stockbrokers who deal in foreign currency securities ... but ... what I am saying about Robert Papalia and the others, is that when they rigged the price on the wire service they were simply feeding to the wire service, through Frascati, such prices as they chose to make up in their heads. The prices weren't based on any genuine dealings, and indeed, they have admitted as much ... plainly the quotations were bogus."

"So that is the basis, then, on which I put it. And, as I say, if at any later time you want me to call attention to the detail, the very words that were used in the admissions, I am in a position to do so at any time you would like me to."

Then, perhaps thinking better of his resistance to the Magistrate's request he said, "Sir, having heard what you have said to me, I may try to procure some evidence, I think, from somebody like Merrill Lynch or other big stockbrokers, if it may assist you. I'll take that step certainly."

It was late in the day at the end of the first week of the hearing, when Worsley finished speaking. The Magistrate adjourned commencement of evidence until the following day. Following Worsley's speech, the greatest gap in faith occurred between the Defense lawyers and their four Italian clients. The defendants felt it was clear that the prosecution was trying to frame them. The conspiracy allegations were quite simply made up. The claims of fraud in the scientific reports were wholly untrue. Worsley had manipulated documentary evidence such as the 'Black Brochure' to give it a perverted meaning.

Their lawyers, on the other hand, were taking a "wait-and-see" attitude. Their experience of how the system and the world worked, was that the Crown didn't bring charges of this nature unless they were relatively satisfied a crime had been committed. The Crown's case would be complex. The Committal was an opportunity to see the Crown's case, to become familiarize with it, and to develop an attack strategy for the trial.

In the morning Worsley began to build his case with a relatively minor witness. The man on the stand answered Worsley's questions for little more than ten minutes. When he was done Worsley offered the man to his learned friends for cross-examination. Each Defense Counsel in turn rose to say he had no questions of the witness.

Tony became livid. "No!" he thought to himself, "No way are these guys going to have a polite little session and then hang us at the end of it."

He spoke very briefly to Robert. They both concurred that there were at least a couple of questions they would like to ask the man. Tony whispered to Geoff to get his attention. Geoff came back to speak to them. Tony was very forceful. He wanted to speak to Michael Spencer – immediately!

Geoff scribbled a note to Michael and took it to the front tables; Michael glanced at it briefly and then rose to his feet. The next witness had not yet been sworn in. "Sir, I wish to request a brief adjournment. My client has asked to speak with me. He says it is urgent."

The Attack of the RCMP and their Merry Man
(1971-1975)

DURING THE EARLY 1970s there was continued political turmoil in Quebec. Unknown to the citizens of Canada at that time, but now part of the public record of events as documented by the McDonald Commission Report, some members of the RCMP Security Service after the "October Crisis" of 1970 embarked upon a course of surreptitious conduct which can only be characterized as ill-conceived, totally lacking in judgment and illegal.

Between October 1970 and early 1973, actions such as coercion, attempted blackmail, breaking and entering, and one known bombing by members of the RCMP became standard operating practice. The stated purpose of this illegal activity was to infiltrate the FLQ separatist organization with the objective of destroying it and ridding the country of this terrorist threat.

One method used by this group of RCMP officers was known as Human Source Recruitment. The unit would target an individual they believed was connected to persons involved in the separatist movement. They would apply serious pressure as they tried to gather intelligence. Not everyone approached agreed to cooperate, but many reported feeling threatened. They believed that failure to cooperate would have dire consequences.

In one documented case, a man who refused to work with the RCMP was fired from his job within days of his refusal, after a visit by the police to his employer. Around Montreal at the time, rumors were circulating that the RCMP had set up a kind of "dirty-tricks" squad to discredit the separatists.

On Tony's return to Montreal following discussions in Vancouver with the Lillooet group in early part of 1972, he had a message that Kesley Merry was in town and would like to meet with him. Innocently, Tony contacted Merry and made a date for lunch. On Merry's suggestion, Tony brought Robert along.

Kesley Merry was an enormous man. He had a booming voice which together with his 400+ pound frame posed an intimidating presence. His deep voice and reporting skills acquired at Ryerson Polytechnical Institute in the field of television and radio communication had quickly landed him a job as a police reporter for CKEY radio station in Toronto. Later, he covered the police beat for the Toronto

Telegram newspaper.

He became a member of the Metro Toronto police auxiliary unit during this period and often packed a police revolver on occasions. After the demise of the Telegram in 1971, he moved to the Toronto Stock Exchange to become its chief intelligence officer. This position put him into contact with the RCMP on a regular basis at a time when the intelligence community was pursuing members of the Quebec separatist movement.

Merry exercised a sharp mind behind his yellow-rimmed glasses and during his 13 years on the Exchange, he developed an impressive reputation for "sniffing" out stock swindles. At this point in his career, he had just begun to investigate fraud cases. Pacific Nickel and the Papalias were among his first; one which appeared to have many intriguing aspects: Mafia connections, separatist elements and mining stock fraud potential.

At lunch, Merry made a proposition the Twins found astonishing. He told them he was attached to the Intelligence Division of the RCMP Security Service. At first Merry didn't give them too much information but suggested they could help him conduct a commercial investigation. He wanted Robert and Tony to become spies and act as informers against specific individuals, promoters and members of the Montreal, Vancouver and Toronto Stock Exchange. In exchange for their cooperation, he offered financial inducements.

The brothers looked at one another incredulously. They didn't turn Merry down immediately; instead, they told him they needed to digest the idea and talk to one another. Merry agreed to wait and arranged to meet them in a few days.

At their next meeting, Robert and Tony told Merry that they had not yet made up their minds. Merry responded to this delay with several veiled threats. They were led to believe that failure to comply might cause them problems.

The Twins left this meeting and spent considerable time discussing the matter. They knew they didn't want any part of the operation being suggested but they were afraid to turn him down outright. They decided to stall him again until they could figure out some strategy of appeasement.

The meetings continued. The Twins hemmed and hawed while Merry tried to convince them. He began to make reference to the political unrest and the separatist movement in Quebec. He suggested that there were people in high places who felt it was against the best interests of Canada for the Quebec economy to become too strong, especially as it looked like René Lévèsque's separatist party might be coming into power. He told them he was aware of their Lillooet Project and that he felt it might be detrimental to Canadian 'unity' for such a large project to go ahead through the vehicle of the Montreal Stock Exchange. The time was not opportune for a boom on the Quebec market.

Merry now made it clear to Robert and Tony that they were being recruited for more than a mere commercial investigation. He told them the RCMP believed certain individuals in the Quebec financial community were financing the separatist movement and they wanted to identify such people. Secondly, they were planning to interfere in the business life of Quebec with an aim to undermine the economic well-being of the Province. Presumably the rationale for this idea was to make Quebecers believe that political unrest and separatism would lead to economic instability and perhaps, a recession. If the economy suffered, this would discredit the separatists.

Tony was very bothered by these bizarre meetings and went to Jack Lovelock, Vice-President of Pacific Nickel for advice. He asked Jack if he could get him a body-pack to tape one of the meetings with Merry. Jack was struck by how strange the whole matter seemed and how disturbed Tony was by it.

Eventually, after several meetings and before Tony could arrange for the tape recorder, Merry's threats became more strident. Tony and Robert were unable to avoid an answer any more. They both stated unequivocally "No!"

Merry's harshest threats failed to persuade them. "You will never have peace again -- we will destroy you financially," was what he told them. They walked out of their last lunch saying, "Kesley, you are a criminal and a fat pig! You are committing acts against Quebec and we want no part of you or your criminal team. As far as you going to destroy us, you just try it. And one more thing, Kelsey, go fuck yourself." And they got up and walked away.

The effect of this acrimonious break was not immediate. They tried to forget about Merry and they immersed themselves in the Lillooet Project and in living their normal lives.

The scientific work on the Lillooet Project had continued. A great deal of progress was being made to understand the Lillooet sands. Some findings continued to frustrate the team while other data caused elation.

Dr. Schellinger had arranged for a complete analysis of the sands by the Colorado School of Mines Research Institute (CSMRI). In Colorado, the sand was pre-concentrated using standard gravity techniques for placer-type ores. CSMRI performed standard fire assays on the concentrate produced. As had been shown previously, such results were disappointing. Only trace amounts of gold in the samples were analyzed – 0.005 ounces of gold per ton of ore. CSMRI noted that the concentrate consisted mainly of magnetite, an iron-based oxide material. The report concluded that magnetite could be recovered for commercial production but no significant precious metals were in the sands.

But CSMRI also sent some of their concentrate samples to Dr. Schmuckler in Israel and a Professor Williams at Stanford University. Williams performed some limited tests on the concentrate utilizing an electron microprobe and a Superpanner. This latter device is a type of shaking table used to remove small quantities of very fine heavy mineral particles.

The microprobe analysis is insensitive to amounts of gold below 14 ounces per ton of material and so no valid conclusion about the presence or absence of gold in the sample could be drawn. The Superpanner extracted one nuggety speck of gold from the sample. For micron-sized material however, even the Superpanner is ineffective.

In contrast, Dr. Schmuckler's lab was able to report some exciting data on the CSMRI concentrate sample. Her laboratory at Technion used an analytical technique based on dissolution and resin-extraction. With the well-prepared concentrate samples from CSMRI, Schmuckler got her most promising results to date. She had reported to Bert Swann that she had found 205 parts per million of gold in the CSMRI concentrate, the highest value yet determined on a sample from Lillooet -- equivalent to 6 ounces per ton.

Bert Swann and Neils Skov knew immediately the importance of this finding. Bert could hardly contain himself, but he knew he must establish the reason for the discrepancy between the results of CSMRI and Schmuckler. They contacted Dr. Schellinger and arranged for CSMRI to retest the concentrate utilizing Schmuckler's methods.

The retest using Schmuckler's techniques although not exactly the same as that found by the Israeli lab, showed a much higher gold content than previously reported. Where initially they measured only 0.005 ounces of gold per ton, now their analysis read 3 ounces of gold per ton of concentrate, certainly not a trivial amount.

After Schmuckler's extraordinary results and the confirmation by CSMRI, there was no surprise when Dr. Schellinger issued a revised report in March 1972, concluding that because of the complex nature of these sands ..."FIRE ASSAYING is inappropriate ... because ... the presence of gold can only be confirmed by complete digestion and ION EXCHANGE gold extraction ..."

The Board of Directors at this point felt they must continue to fund Dr. Schmuckler's research until she had fully overcome the problematical aspect of the sands. The fundamental research was complete. It was now the Israeli scientist's mandate to develop an Ion Exchange resin and technique for wholly eliminating the interference of IRON in ION exchange recovery of precious metals from the Lillooet sands.

As 1972 came to an end, Dr. Schmuckler had been engaged in specific research on the Lillooet sands for over two years. Much progress had been made and Pacific Nickel, as the financial backers of the project during the past year, was in favor of continuing to fund her program and had done so.

Then on March 12th, 1973, the world turned upside down for Robert, Tony, the other members of the Board and the investors in Pacific Nickel. Without notice the Montreal Stock Exchange announced they were de-listing Pacific Nickel Mines Limited for breaching the rules of the Exchange.

De-listing a public company is a most serious matter. Robert, as President, immediately contacted one of the regulators. He understood the problem was related to a failure to file a financial statement on time. But, when Robert checked this out, he discovered that the statement had been filed, and in a timely fashion. He then asked Jack Lovelock to see what he could find out.

After several conversations with people at the MSE, Jack told Robert the Exchange claimed Pacific Nickel had improperly traded in the stock of another junior mining company listed on the Toronto Exchange. Jack pointed out that the alleged infraction had occurred the previous year and the particular transaction in question had been disclosed months ago in company documents filed with the Exchange.

The response to this was that they were acting on the matter now because they had only just become aware of the infraction. Jack then met with the company lawyers. Later he spoke to Robert, "I don't know what to make of this. Technically, I suppose there was a breach of Exchange rules, but everyone I've spoken to seems dumbfounded by the fact that it has resulted in a de-listing. Everyone says that the punishment doesn't fit the 'crime'. This kind of infraction is regarded as minor and not the type of thing for which they de-list a company. The usual practice in this situation is to sort out the problem by consultation with officers of the company."

When Robert and Jack again approached officials at the Exchange, they were told this reason for the de-listing was the official reason. From the way this was stated, Robert felt there was something more, and so he asked, "What is the unofficial reason?" This question was greeted by denials, "No, no, we didn't mean it that way. The official reason is THE reason."

Robert generally relied on Jack's years of experience as an administrator and replied, "Well, Jack, what do we do now?"

The people at the Exchange refused to explain why Pacific Nickel was being treated different from other companies. "I'll arrange a meeting with the Quebec Securities Commission (QSC). We'll find out why they did what they did and what they want us to do to make things right."

At their meeting with a key member of the Commission, Mr. Lusignan, he agreed with Robert and Jack that the de-listing without notice was puzzling. This type of infraction did not warrant a de-listing. At the end of the meeting he turned to the Compliance Officer who was present and asked him to talk with his superiors to see what could be done to rectify the matter. Lusignan also suggested that if they did not get a satisfactory answer they could appeal the decision of the Exchange to the courts.

Robert and Jack left the meeting feeling reassured. But when Jack passed on Mr. Lusignan's comments to the people at the Exchange, their only response was, "Tell him to talk to his boss." Days passed and they heard nothing from the Exchange about reinstatement or about the steps required to be returned to good standing. They were now phoning continually, seeking to meet again with the officials of the Stock Exchange but, more and more they felt stonewalled.

Mr. Lusignan originally had been sympathetic, but now, was apologetic and evasive, as though he knew something he wished he didn't know. Still the de-listing continued. He hinted there was another reason for the halt besides the one they had been given. The implication was clear that the problem lay with Robert rather than with the company.

After a couple of weeks of getting absolutely nowhere using the less formal channels, the lawyer for Pacific Nickel requested a hearing and one was scheduled for late spring 1973. Meanwhile the company limbo continued.

The suspension was very costly for Robert and Tony. Both had invested heavily in Pacific Nickel. Since the company had bought into the Lillooet Project, Robert had concentrated most of his work and resources into the company.

Tony's commitment was monetary and he was beginning to feel pinched financially. In late April, for the first time in his adult life he was strapped for cash. During the last couple of years the Quebec economy had gone from bad to worse on account of the Separatist issue: terror in the streets with bombs going off at various times; the Stock Exchange in Montreal being systematically destroyed by intent from the Central Government's illegal sabotage; people, especially the English part of the population was moving out of Quebec en mass; head offices of major corporations and banks were moving to Toronto; real estate value had dropped over fifty-percent; all business was in shambles. Also the US markets were at an all time low on account of the Vietnam fiasco and Social unrest.

On account of these events Tony and Robert had suffered large financial losses. All their other investments were not liquid and would take some time to sell even at a loss and now Pacific Nickel's shares were not liquid. In late April, for the first time in his adult life, Tony was strapped for cash. He received a call from a Toronto broker, Jack Meier, about some shares in another company he had bought on margin which had now declined in value. Tony promised Meier he would take care of it. Meier was good about it, but Tony knew how the market worked and he didn't have many days to cover his position. At this juncture, he wasn't terribly worried. He still had a couple of other things happening in the market and felt confident he could cover his debt with Meier.

Tony's other major investment at that time was in a company called 'Karou'. This company had developed an all-terrain recreational vehicle. Around the time that trading in Pacific Nickel was halted, Tony had discussed with Robert the possibility of assuming management of Karou. They had invested heavily because they liked the product and the company, but recently they were becoming disillusioned with the company's direction.

Since they believed the de-listing of Pacific Nickel would be temporary, the Twins attempted to carry on as usual. Tony went to the Quebec Securities Commission to speak to Mr. Preu, Head of Surveillance, about taking over Karou. Tony was angered by Preu's attitude as he refused to discuss the matter seriously. He dismissed Tony with, "Do you think we want you running another public company in this Province?" Tony believed 'you' meant Robert, since Tony was not running any other company at that time.

The Twins began to receive phone calls from many of their friends and business associates. Members of the RCMP were appearing in brokerage houses around the city and flashing photos of pictures of Robert and Tony. The police were questioning people about whether they had ever seen Robert and Tony with these other people. Were they aware that Robert and Tony were related to Johnny Papalia? In some cases, it was suggested that he was their Father, in others their Uncle.

Tony and Robert were furious. Under the guise of an investigation the police were attempting to connect them to organized crime. They thought of their 'friend', Kesley Merry. Robert immediately got on the phone to him.

"What are you trying to pull, Merry? You know we're not connected to the Hamilton Papalias, but, there are police going all over this city planting the suggestion we are related to them."

Merry didn't confirm or deny involvement in the investigation. Instead he chuckled and said, "See what that can happen when you don't cooperate."

Then he told Robert that this was just the beginning. "It will be interesting to see how far you guys get with the Lillooet Project."'

Merry hung up, leaving Robert listening to the dial tone on the other end. "Unbelievable," he thought. "Who could imagine that the police can think and act like this? Was Merry behind the halt-trading in Pacific Nickel? Hopefully we will find out at the hearing in a few weeks."

While these bizarre events were going on, Pacific Nickel's lawyer advised his clients he was getting the impression that the Exchange wanted them to drop their appeal to the Courts. The lawyer convinced them it was better to sort things out through a joint meeting with members of the Commission and the Exchange. At such a meeting the concerns of the Exchange could be openly aired and dealt with. So the Company dropped their appeal subject to an agreement there would be an informal meeting where the parties could discuss the issues and resolve the matter.

At that meeting, once all the preliminary niceties were finished, Jack Lovelock looked at the regulators across the table from him. "How about starting off by telling us the real reason for the de-listing?"

The Exchange and Securities Commission people looked at one another and then Mr. Belanger, President of the Exchange, pointed at Robert and said, "You're the problem."

This started a lively discussion in which the parties argued back and forth about the legitimacy of de-listing a company in this manner, for reasons other than those being given as the 'official reason'. Their lawyer sought to get at the heart of why Robert was not an acceptable person to run the Company. But they got nothing of any real substance. The point was made that Robert was very young to be running a public company, but that didn't really stand up since the QSC had looked at the matter formally and decided to allow his appointment when he had been proposed as President of Pacific Nickel in 1969. Since that time he had become older and more experienced.

It was suggested that without the Papalia 'problem', the matter could probably be resolved favorably. The Pacific directors decided to adjourn the meeting to discuss these revelations with their lawyers.

In their private discussions, Robert, Jack and the lawyers decided their first priority must be to get the Company trading and active again. They could then fight with the Exchange about whether their objection to Robert had any merit.

One attorney observed that reporters had noted the de-listing and were anticipating a story. He felt a scandal might arise from a formal hearing and the newspapers got their hands on what now appeared to be unsubstantiated allegations of Mafia connections coining out of the proceedings.

Once the officers of the Company had examined all their options Jack Lovelock returned to talk to Mr. Belanger of the Exchange and Mr. Preu of the Commission. He suggested that Pacific Nickel would be willing to put together a new board, approved by the QSC, if it meant that the Company would be activated again on the Montreal Stock Exchange. Jack came away from meeting thinking he'd come up with a plan acceptable to the Commission.

The first new Board member appointed was Sidney Phillips, Queen's Counsel and President of the Montreal B'Nai Brith, who agreed to become Company President. He then went to Mr. Prue and Mr. Belanger, and asked, "If the Company puts in place a new board, is there any reason why the company won't be reinstated?" He received assurances that once Robert Papalia no longer had a place on the board, they could expect no further problems.

Time was passing. It was June and the de-listing had persisted now for three months. Robert resigned his directorship and stepped down as President. The new board consisted of Jack Lovelock and a number of prominent members of the Montreal and Toronto financial communities: Mr. Sidney Phillips; Sam Etcheverry, a former Canadian Football League quarterback (a CFL Hall-of-Famer) and now a well-known Montreal stockbroker, a Chartered Accountant partner for a large Montreal accounting firm; and a prominent Toronto lawyer who would eventually become senior in-house counsel for a well-known Fortune 500 company.

With the new board in place, Jack took it back to the authorities. They refused to re-list the company on the basis that the Papalias could still exercise de-facto control of the company by virtue of Robert's controlling share of voting stock.

Robert offered to put all his stock in a voting trust but this was also rejected. The backers of the company began to look at other alternatives to obtain immediate re-listing. They attempted a Rights Offering but were immediately served with a Cease and Desist Order by the Quebec Securities Commission.

After this failure, Sid Phillips and Jack Lovelock, now very anxious to get the Lillooet Project on track and needing a means to raise development money, sought to do a 'private placement' of shares in the amount of $100,000 in favor of a listed Toronto company. The QSC claimed jurisdiction over this type of financing as well and responded that they didn't think the proposed Toronto company was acceptable either.

Jack Lovelock was completely exasperated. Once they knew that the Papalia control was a problem for the Commission he'd acted as intermediary and instigator to put together proposals they hoped the Commission would find acceptable, but they were stymied at every turn. He went to see the Commission people again with another of the company's new directors. Jack talked about the merits of the

Lillooet Project and how anxious they were about the delays.

This time Jack was talking to the Head of the Commission, Mr. Demers. Demers interrupted him as Jack discussed the Lillooet, "We're not questioning your project -- this is in complete confidence -- You may have one of the best properties in North America, but as long as I am Head of the Commission, the Papalias won't do any public financing in the Province of Quebec."

"Does that mean you're willing to wipe out all the other shareholders just to get to the Papalias?"

"If we have to, yes."

It was summer 1973 and Pacific Nickel remained inactive. Dr. Schmuckler's most recent contract had run out. The company wanted to continue her research program but had to wait until they had a corporate vehicle to raise the capital and continue development. Meanwhile since Pacific Nickel could no longer meet its obligations, Robert took on an assignment of the Lillooet leases from Zyrox and assumed all of Pacific Nickel's financial obligations personally under agreement that he would retain ownership of the project.

Tony's problems had recently become compounded by activities at Karou.

Karou was one of several companies in Quebec trying to take advantage of the emerging field of All-Terrain Vehicles exemplified by the enormous success of the Bombardier Company with their 'Ski-Doo' snowmobile, the first of its kind. The Karou company had developed a prototype off-road vehicle but had not yet managed to sell it anywhere in the world.

In May 1973, a German businessman, the Principal of a German Corporation called Incontrada, appeared at the Karou offices in Montreal. He was already known to the Karou people through a previous meeting in January 1973 where he agreed to act as a sales agent for the Karou ATV in Africa.

Frederick Jaeger swept into the Karou offices in Montreal with great news. Incontrada Zambia Ltd (a wholly-owned subsidiary of Jaeger's Incontrada) was on the verge of making a sale of 120 ATVs to the Government of Zambia. Several vehicles were already in Zambia and the government was prepared to pay $30,000 per unit. He told them Incontrada Zambia Ltd. was in possession of a letter of intent from the Zambian government, but before the contract could be signed Karou needed to post a performance bond at the Foreign Commerce Bank in Zurich. The amount of money required to get the contract and import permits in place would be about $50,000 dollars.

The managers of Karou listened, their eyes wide with interest. Their company was currently unlisted on the exchange. It was traded over-the-counter and the market for its shares was quite limited. The Company was cash-strapped, having spent its seed money to develop the vehicle and now, here was Jaeger playing Fairy Godfather, waving a government contract in their faces, for over a hundred ATVs worth millions of dollars. It was as good as money in the bank once it was signed or so they reasoned.

Tony was called to the Karou offices to meet Jaeger and discuss the contract.

Jaeger stated he was prepared to post the $50,000 dollar performance bond if he was rewarded for arranging this contract by being sold some Karou stock. He said he knew the stock would increase in value significantly once the deal was announced. He wanted, to participate in the wealth that would flow into the company. The problem was he had no accounts available in Canada to close such a trade. Tony agreed to help out by selling him some of his Karou shares.

Tony helped Jaeger set up a bank account at a branch of the Royal Bank where he was well-known. He agreed to transfer 12,000 Karou shares to Jaeger in return for a post-dated cheque. The fair market value of these shares totaled $51,000 or $4.25 each.

Later that week, the two of them met for lunch at the home of a business associate of Tony. Tony had received a call from a friend at the Royal Bank, informing him that Jaeger had sold the shares the day before at the same price he had purchased them from Tony. This seemed strange to Tony but he had thought no more about it until this meeting.

During lunch Tony became very suspicious of Jaeger. He discovered that Jaeger was quite angry with certain members of the Karou board and was trying to get back money that he felt he was owed. Tony realized he might be caught in a trap and needed some additional security.

Jaeger was traveling to New York that afternoon for other business so Tony confronted Jaeger and asked him why he had sold the shares so quickly. He demanded another cheque payable immediately on the Royal Bank account. Initially, Jaeger refused but after some persuasive discussions with Tony, Jaeger finally agreed to issue a second cheque. Tony offered to drive him to the airport.

During the ride, Jaeger and Tony discussed the cheque and its amount. Less the bank's commission, the money available from sale of the shares would be about $45,000. So Jaeger wrote a cheque for this amount on his Royal Bank account and they agreed to settle up the difference when next they meet and knew the exact amount. Tony just wanted to cut his losses and get this guy out of his hair. He dropped Jaeger off for his 3:00 pm flight to New York and headed back into the city.

Arriving at his office, Tony found a phone message from the Royal Bank branch and one from his friend Gus McPhail of Continental Securities in Vancouver. He called Gus first where he learned that through his open market buy order on Karou stock with Continental, he had actually been the purchaser of Jaeger's shares which were originally his own. He now had a debt with Continental for $51,000 plus commission.

Then he called the Royal Bank. It seems a few minutes after Tony had left the airport, the bank received a phone call from Jaeger advising them to stop payment on a cheque payable to Tony Papalia. Furthermore when the proceeds of the sale of the shares were received, the bank should transfer the funds immediately to Jaeger's Swiss bank account. Tony was very appreciative they had called him. He told the bank employee, "It looks like the bastard is trying to scam me. Don't transfer that money out of the account; it's mine."

The banker replied, "I thought he might be up to no good but I'm afraid we will have to honor the transfer order when we receive written confirmation of the request from Jaeger. He said he would courier a letter to us from New York. We'll probably get it tomorrow. You better get a lawyer right now, Tony."

So by 9:00 am the next day, Tony's lawyer had obtained and served an injunction on the bank restraining Jaeger from transferring the money until matters were settled between the parties.

That morning, Tony sat in his office, "Well,"' he thought, "Another lesson learned! Never trust anybody with your own money. All it gets you is suckered." He knew it was unlikely the Zambian government contract was real.

Tony surveyed his situation and it was not good. The market had been in the doldrums and a lot of his deals were going sour. Combined with the continued halt in Pacific Nickel, it was becoming impossible to operate. He owed about $19,000 on his account with the Toronto broker, Jack Meier. He also owed $10,000 on an account with a brokerage firm in Montreal and that was about to come due. This deal now left him with another brokerage debt of $51,000 plus commissions with his friend Gus McPhail at Continental Securities.

His lawyer didn't think it would take long to settle the matter with Jaeger. It wasn't likely he'd file a defense to a indefensible action, but even so, the money available was now less the selling commission and the legal cost of getting the money back.

Within three weeks, Tony's lawyer negotiated a settlement and it became available to him after his lawyer deducted his fees. As a result of this fiasco with Jaeger, Tony was out of pocket roughly $20,000 from the proceeds of the sale of his Karou shares.

It took several weeks, but once he had the remaining money in hand, Tony had to make a decision. He did what he thought best with the resources available to him. Rather than having three creditors on his back he paid off Meier and the brokerage house in Montreal.

This left him with under $5,000 cash available and the Continental Securities debt wholly outstanding. He contacted Gus McPhail and advised him he had been caught short, explaining how Jaeger had tried to rip him off. It had cost him quite a lot of money. He instructed Gus to sell the 12,000 Karou shares at whatever price he could get for them. He made a small payment on the outstanding debt. He also arranged to open another small trading account with Continental. All profits made on this account would be applied towards the short-fall on his debt with the firm.

Finally, he gave Jaeger's post-dated cheque for 139,000 DM to Continental to see if it would be honored by Jaeger's German bank. He told the people at Continental not to expect the cheque to clear. To no one's surprise, after a month or so, it returned NSF from Germany.

Meantime Tony knew if Pacific Nickel was re-activated on any stock exchange he could immediately sell enough shares to cover his debts. Jack Lovelock had recently been turned down by the Alberta Stock Exchange on very vague grounds. It appeared the company would never be re-listed in Quebec. The only possibility left was the Vancouver Exchange. The VSE specialized in junior mining and resource-based companies such as Pacific Nickel. He had to try.

After discussions with Robert and Jack, he went to Continental Securities and explained the Lillooet Project to Gus McPhail and his partners. They examined the project and agreed to underwrite the initial offering of the company on the VSE. The proposal was put before the VSE listings committee.

On a Friday, Gus phoned Tony with jubilant news. The committee had agreed in principle to the new listing. So development of the project could proceed. With the company's new listing on the VSE, Continental Securities could expect to cover Tony's outstanding debt from the proceeds of the sale of some of Tony's non-escrowed shares in Pacific Nickel.

There had been no buyers for the Karou shares so Tony's debt still existed. Karou's own tenuous circumstances were suddenly worsened by the international oil crisis in the Summer of 1973. What limited market there was for Karou shares dried up completely once the oil shortages and subsequent increases in OPEC oil prices occurred. Needless to say the Zambian contract never materialized.

On the following Monday, Gus called Tony once again.

"Tony, I'm afraid I have some very bad news. The listings committee has revoked approval of the new listing for Pacific Nickel."

"Jesus, Gus, why would they do that?"

"The official line is that your company isn't the kind of company they want on the VSE. Unofficially, I have learned that every member of the committee was visited by the RCMP over the weekend. They claim you and your brother are under investigation for suspected criminal activities of a serious nature. It wouldn't be wise to let you have control of a public company in Canada."

"Gus, I know what you must be thinking, but whatever the RCMP is saying - - it's all lies. I've got to advise my brother and the other board members; we may want to appeal this decision. In the meantime I'm doing everything to pay my debt with you. Thanks for all your help, Gus, I'll get back to you soon."

By October 1973, Pacific Nickel had been turned down for listing by every stock exchange in Canada. Karou had failed to get any market for its ATVs. Over the summer it became insolvent. By September, Karou was bankrupt and all the Karou shares that Robert and Tony held, including those in the hands of Continental Securities, were worthless.

There was only one thing left to try before the Papalias and the Directors of Pacific Nickel would give up. Everyone involved had come to the inescapable conclusion that the RCMP was behind their inability to find a forum for public financing in Canada. They had been turned down in every jurisdiction in Canada; always after the RCMP appeared on the scene and always for very unclear or inadequate reasons. Tony and Robert called the Minister of Justice of Quebec, Jerome

Choquette, which they knew personally and asked to meet him. That same afternoon they were in his office at Palais de Justice in old Montreal. After the first fifteen minutes bringing Jerome up to date to what they had been doing for the last few years and about old times, Tony and Robert get down to tell Jerome what was happening to them. They told him about Kelsey Merry and what they had learned about their sabotage of the Quebec economy and the dirty tricks squad of the RCMP, especially formed to perform crimes against Quebec and that they suspected that they could also be the ones planting the bombs in the city. Jerome listened with much attention and became very upset. He said, "I can't believe this right under my very nose."

He was shocked to hear what he had been told but he believed that Tony and Robert were telling him the truth and besides he knew them since their teens. He had followed their amazing careers. They shared common friends in the elite of Quebec. He knew their brother, Adolfo and he also appeared on their TV show. He also knew why they loved Quebec and the Twins were idols with their music with tens of thousands of fans. He knew the Twins were not in any way part of crime, after all, he was the Minister of Justice and he knew who was what. So he told the Twins, "I'll be on this as of tonight and we touch base daily."

And so, Jerome started to raise questions and started to uncover the truth. He talked to Tony on a daily basis and it looked like things were getting done. But twelve days later, the Quebec government changed Jerome from Minister of Justice to Minister of Education. He told Tony, "This is way above my head."

Three of the board members of Pacific Nickel arranged a meeting with the Solicitor General of Canada, Warren Allman. A meeting was set in thirty days from the request; while the directors were waiting for this meeting, Tony and Robert had met with Jerome Choquette. The directors were called by the Attorney General's office and complained about Tony and Robert's meeting with Choquette. Warren Allman was the Canadian Cabinet Minister responsible for the national police force.

In the late Fall of 1973, Warren Allman had only recently been appointed Solicitor General. It is probable that the information he had at that time with respect to Robert and Tony Papalia and their activities, was wholly based upon the advice of the RCMP. The essence of what Allman told the directors at this meeting was that there was no problem with the company. The problem lay with the Papalias. To paraphrase, "They are not the type of people that anyone wants to see running a public company in Canada. There's nothing wrong with the Company. It's the Papalias that are under investigation."

There was nothing left for Pacific Nickel. The new board members, particularly those prominent in the community, began to feel very uncomfortable with the situation. While they knew that the intrigue surrounding Pacific Nickel's delisting was based on gossip and innuendo, and none of it had ever been substantiated, they were understandably worried about their own reputations. The hint of unsavory associations could do nothing but harm them.

In mid-1974, when it appeared there were no miracles available, a meeting of the directors was held with Robert and Tony present. It was clear the company was up against something that could not be fought effectively. You can't fight what you can't see. The board decided to disband itself and the Company was allowed to lapse. All investors in Pacific Nickel lost their property. Robert and Tony lost more than anyone, but Robert was able to emerge from this meeting, with the rights to the Lillooet claims.

They no longer had a public company; the vehicle needed to develop their mine. Robert still held some assets -- the mining claims, but Tony's problems continued to worsen.

❧

One day in February 1974, a man by the name of Ernest Bryden, visited the offices of Continental Securities in Vancouver. He identified himself as an RCMP officer with the Vancouver Commercial Crime Squad. He told the office personnel he wanted to examine some of their trading accounts. The people at Continental Securities were very cooperative and a secretary was assigned to show him where to find the current account files. Bryden was only there for a few minutes as he zeroed in on one particular file and pulled it from the drawer. The file was Tony Papalia's trading account. He skimmed it and then asked the secretary for copies of the documents in the file. He left soon after he received the photocopies.

Two days later Bryden returned. He asked to speak to Gus McPhail. When he sat down with Gus, Bryden got right to the point. He wanted to bring a criminal charge against Tony Papalia as a consequence of his failure to pay for his Karou shares. Bryden put it to Gus that Tony had ripped him off for $50,000. But Gus told Bryden, "Look, I've done business with this guy for a long time. I've seen his kind of thing happen to market players before, especially when there's a downturn in the market. Tony told me when this happened that it was because a Mr. Jaeger had succeeded in ripping him off and that he hadn't been paid for the shares himself."

It wasn't that Gus had forgotten or forgiven Tony for the $50,000 debt. Over several months Tony had repaid only about $2000. But Gus was a pragmatic man. He really could not believe Tony was stupid enough to participate in such an obvious scam as this cop was suggesting. Furthermore, if Tony was convicted of a criminal offense and put out of business or sent to jail, Gus could sure kiss his $50,000 good-bye.

"Sergeant Bryden, I know you mean well but charging this guy with a criminal offense won't get my money back. As far as I'm concerned it's a civil matter."

Bryden told McPhail he wasn't anxious to let the matter drop and that he would be in touch in a few days.

Shortly after Bryden left, McPhail telephoned Tony in Montreal.

"Tony, I thought you should know an RCMP guy named Bryden, came to my office and made a bee-line for your account file. Now he wants me to bring a criminal charge against you for defrauding me of $50,000. He says you were wash-trading[1]. Maybe you should call and tell him your side of the story."

"Thanks for calling. Gus. You know the problems I've been having. The market is in the doldrums; Pacific Nickel is in the toilet, no one will let us re-list anywhere; and now, you're telling me, I may be prosecuted because this guy Jaeger, tried to steal $50,000 from me. I'll talk to Bryden and see if I can straighten it out. Maybe if he's willing to lay a criminal charge against Jaeger, that will motivate Jaeger to pay back the money he cost me and apply it toward any debt with you. I deeply appreciate your patience and friendship."

Tony decided that rather than phoning this RCMP officer, he would face him man to man. The next day, he was on a plane to Vancouver. He had made arrangements to speak to Bryden at his office. Tony arrived at Vancouver International Airport and took a cab directly to the offices of the Commercial Crime Unit of the RCMP in Vancouver, Sergeant Bryden was waiting for him when he got there.

"Come on into my office, Mr. Papalia." He shook Tony's hand and directed him into a small cubicle, standard-issue, mud-yellow walled government office.

Bryden was very polite and explained that he went to Continental Securities to investigate the trading of Karou stock in May 1973 in Montreal and Vancouver. He had some concerns that Continental had come up $50,000 short when Tony failed to produce the money for the shares. He also said, "You aren't required to tell me anything, Mr. Papalia, but if you think it might help establish your innocence feel free to tell me your version of events. Of course, if a charge is brought, your statement can be used in court as evidence."

Tony was not yet totally cynical about the police. He said he understood and proceeded to explain himself to Bryden. Tony honestly believed Bryden would realize that a combination of unfortunate circumstances together with Jaeger's duplicity had led to his financial problems. He intended to repay Gus in full when he had the ability. He recounted the problems with Pacific Nickel and the rumors being spread around that he was related to the Papalia crime family. At this point Bryden interjected, "I've heard that rumor, Mr. Papalia, and I want you to know that I know you are not related to those Papalias."

It was an awkward moment. Bryden had meant to put Tony at ease with this statement; to get him to continue to talk openly. For Tony however, it came as a surprise. At that point, he knew Bryden's comment made him uncomfortable, but he didn't put together why until he was on the plane returning to Montreal.

Tony finished his story and asked the officer to investigate Jaeger. He reasoned that the German businessman should be the subject of criminal charges as it was his scam that put things in motion to cause the loss on the shares.

Bryden thanked Tony and escorted him to the door, promising to look into

---

1 Wash trading refers to the practice of selling and buying shares in a company to yourself on the same day of trading. The purpose of this manipulation of stock is to attempt to drive the price of shares either up or down depending on your objectives. Later on you can either buy or sell shares at the new price thus making a substantial profit. The practice is illegal.

the Jaeger situation and let him know the outcome. He asked Tony how to get in touch with him and Tony gave him his office and home phone numbers.

On the plane home, Tony went over his meeting with Bryden. Had he done the right thing? Was Bryden's investigation wholly independent, arising because he happened to discover the outstanding debt to Continental? If so, an explanation of events should suffice to thwart criminal suspicion. But how was it that Bryden sounded so sure, so firm, "I know you're not related to those Papalias."? It was as if Bryden already knew all he needed to know about Tony. He hoped Bryden was a decent cop who would conduct a complete investigation with an open mind. Surely things couldn't get any worse.

Back in Vancouver, Bryden was going over the notes of his conversation with Tony. He was disappointed. He had hoped the guy might slip up and say something that would amount to an admission of fraud. But he hadn't. This Papalia had his story down too pat and it was surprisingly detailed and complex. If he didn't have the background on this fellow from the National Criminal Intelligence Branch of the RCMP, he might have believed him.

As for this guy Jaeger, he wasn't going to investigate him. He'd already spoken to him and his version differed substantially from Papalia's. Bryden thought Jaeger seemed shifty - probably relating only part of the story. Most likely the truth lay somewhere between these two statements. Jaeger was West Germany's problem, not his but he had let Jaeger know that if he didn't cooperate, he would be named in the indictment too. Bryden wanted to nail Papalia.

He had told Tony that he knew he wasn't related to Johnny Papalia. What he hadn't mentioned was that even though they knew there was no blood relation, Tony's name appeared on the NCIB's list of people suspected of having criminal associations with known organized crime figures. The word from the top was the Papalia brothers were probably being put in place by organized crime to perpetrate stock frauds and launder money, and those in authority wanted them out of business. He had been instructed to look into Tony's affairs in Vancouver and this Karou situation was all that came up.

Bryden looked at what he had in this case. He didn't have an admission of guilt but there was Jaeger's testimony and the outstanding trading account. He could show that Tony sold and bought the same number of shares in a twenty-four hour period. That alone was suspicious.

Even though the $50,000 proceeds had originally gone to Jaeger, Tony was ultimately able to regain most of it and use it to pay other debts, not the one with Continental. He had the brokerage transactions and the motivation. He didn't know if he had enough for wash-trading but he though he could prove a simple fraud charge. If Tony were convicted of fraud he could never be a director of a public company in Canada again. He, Ernie Bryden, would put this guy out of business.

It was Friday afternoon. On Monday he would sit down and carefully formulate the charges against Tony to appear on the criminal information. He'd also brief the prosecutor and recommend they proceed towards an indictment. If they were lucky, maybe they could put this guy away in jail for a good long while.

Soon afterwards, in the Spring of 1974, an RCMP officer came to Tony's home one evening in Montreal. He and Pattie had just arrived home from dinner. Tony answered the door and found two uniformed officers there.

"Are you Mr. Antonio Papalia?"

"Yes."

"Well, this is for you then." The officer slapped a paper in Tony's hand, grinned and tipped his hat.

"Apparently you're in a bit of trouble in Vancouver," and he walked away.

Tony looked at the papers in his hands. It was headed "In the Supreme Court of British Columbia -- Regina v. Antonio Papalia." The writ alleged that he had ..."by deceit, falsehood or other fraudulent means defrauded Continental Securities of the sum of $51,000 on or about the 15th day of May, 1973 at Vancouver, British Columbia."

Tony had never needed a lawyer until then except for business purposes. Neither had any of his friends or business associates; the people he associated with had no need for criminal lawyers and no one he knew had any criteria for assessing who was a good criminal lawyer and who wasn't.

Several days later, after speaking to some trusted friends, he eventually got the name from a friend of a friend of a fellow who had an office in downtown Vancouver and whose specialty was criminal law. Tony made an appointment to see him and flew to Vancouver. He found the lawyer's office in Gastown, a renovated, trendy part of the city.

Gastown previously consisted of old factories and derelict hotels along the downtown waterfront. It was close to the tough east side of Vancouver and the criminal courts, but thanks to urban renewal, it was now a place where winos and lost souls were receding on the tide of new restaurants, chic shops and a massive influx of tourists and day-trippers from the suburbs.

The law office itself showed the proprietors to be up-to-date -- not stuffy at all; lots of wood and sand-blasted brick with large, potted plants and Rolling Stone magazines on the tabletop in the waiting room. The lawyer who greeted him was youngish, probably Tony's contemporary. He wore a fashionable suit with wide lapels, a wide tie, longish hair with semi-conservative side-burns to the bottom of his ears. He presented the image of a guy on the cutting edge. He might work by day as a lawyer but his first allegiance was to the new age; the kind of guy Tony could relate to -- hip, not traditional.

Tony told his story and they agreed to a retainer. His lawyer felt his version of events with supporting testimony from McPhail and independent evidence about Jaeger and his activities would result in an acquittal. He suggested they proceed by way of a preliminary hearing. This would allow them to see the fundamentals of the Crown's case and assess the government witnesses. At this stage, it looked as if the case could be dealt with quickly and effectively.

Tony left the office feeling relieved. They would ask for a trial by judge with jury and get a look at the Crown's case at the preliminary hearing. If it was weak enough, the case might be thrown out early. Tony returned to Montreal.

Weird things now began to happen to the Papalias. They were being followed and watched. They felt their phones were tapped as well. One day, Tony's fiancée, Pattie, was involved in a strange accident in which her car was deliberately hit by another one being driven by a member of CSIS.

Was this an isolated incident? They didn't know but all of the family were becoming very shaken. The Twins were developing a persecution complex.

One day, the brothers went to the Provincial Legislature in Quebec City to talk with people in the Attorney-General's Office about their problems with the Quebec Securities Commission. As they emerged from their meeting and descended the steps to their car, they discovered all four tires had been slashed.

Robert looked at Tony, "Since when do tire-slashing vandals hang out in front of the Attorney-General's Office and slash car tires in broad daylight?"

Tony shook his head, "And look at all the cops and security people around here. How much will you bet that none of these crime-fighters saw anything?"

"No thanks, Tony, I won't take that bet."

The final straw came in late 1974, a few months before Tony's preliminary hearing in Vancouver was to proceed. While both Tony and Robert had their own apartments, they continued to use their mother's home address for many purposes. They each maintained a room in her home and had a number of personal effects there.

One evening when Dora was home alone, there was a knock on the door. She opened the door to find several men, some in uniform, some not. One waved a paper in her face. He spoke to her in English. Her English was still very poor. They shouted something about 'police' and 'Tony' and then barged into her house. She protested in Italian. The man with the paper waved it again. She looked at the document but it was in English and she didn't understand.

The man in charge motioned for her to sit down. She saw some of the other men go into the other rooms in the house. She was a woman in her sixties, alone. She couldn't physically stop these people. She was afraid. "What are they going to do with me?" she thought.

She spoke again to the man who stayed in the living room. "Who are you?" she managed in English. She understood only part of the response, "RCMP"

They said they were police, but what did they want. She tried again, "Tony, he is not here."

The man spoke again. She didn't know what he was saying. It wasn't long before one of the officers came from the bedrooms carrying a box of papers. She yelled at the man not to take these things, trying her best to make herself understood. The fellow beside her put out a hand cautioning her to settle down.

He said something to the other fellow who then left the house with the papers. Dora was very upset. It reminded her of the banditry and lawlessness in Calabria that had prevailed when she was a girl. Until now, she had always felt secure in

Canada. She wondered what they were planning to do with her when they got what they wanted.

The rest of the gang came from the back of the house after several minutes. Some were carrying papers. A few minutes later the man in charge arose as the remaining officers returned from the back of the house and after a few words they walked out the front door closing it behind them.

Dora sat for a minute. She had the feeling they would be back at the door any second. While the men were present she showed no fear. She berated them and chided them although they didn't appear to understand her. They probably thought she was a pretty feisty old lady. Now that she was alone, she felt renewed fear and a wave of anger. Her hands began to shake as she dialed the phone number of her eldest son.

A few hours later Robert and Tony got word by telephone of what had happened at their Mother's home. Their brother was at the house with their mother and she was very upset. They both raced over to see and console her.

They were glad that apart from being visibly upset, she appeared physically fine. The brothers questioned their mother and checked their rooms. Robert could see his things were disturbed but couldn't find anything missing. Tony, however, determined that all his market activity papers were gone. The family all agreed that it was the RCMP who had invaded their Mother's home.

Over the next few days Tony and Robert discussed this incident with their lawyers in Vancouver and Montreal. They were advised that if the police had raided their home they would have had a valid search warrant. Dora had seen the fellow wave a piece of paper at her but she didn't know what it was and he hadn't left a copy of it with her. Strangely, all inquiries to the RCMP about the execution of a search warrant at their Mother's home came up blank. Everyone the Papalias or their lawyers spoke to in the RCMP denied involvement in or knowledge of any such search. The papers were mysteriously returned to Tony one day in 1986 long after all of these affairs following his being charged with tax evasion.

It was clear to Robert and Tony; they were finished as businessmen in Canada. They were convinced their problems with the police and the various securities commissions were traceable to one source. All roads led to Kesley Merry. Before him they never had any trouble; after he had sworn to destroy them; that exactly had happened. An RCMP officer three-thousand miles away could tell Tony who he wasn't related to. Every Market in the country treated them as if they carried the plague. Their reputations were ruined. Their financial affairs were in tatters and now Tony was fighting for his business life against a criminal charge.

So the Twins decided to promote the Lillooet Project from outside Canada.

It takes a massive infusion of capital to take a mine from the claim stage through to full production. Development of most mining properties normally can't be achieved through private funding sources. Public financing is the norm to develop a high-risk, high-cost, but potentially highly-rewarding mining property. Robert and Tony had word from the top that there wasn't going to be any public financing of the Lillooet Project from within Canada.

In the late sixties and early seventies, the brothers had traveled to various parts of the world. Both had been to the United States on business and pleasure. Robert with his older brother Adolfo, had attended the Cannes Film Festival in France. And both brothers, on occasions, had escaped the harsh winters of Quebec by vacationing in the Bahamas.

The Bahamas were suggested to them as a place to go. Following introduction of a new capital-gains tax in Canada in 1972, many tax lawyers were advising that if a business person was serious about avoiding taxes he or she should move themselves and their assets to a tax haven. This was some of the advice the brothers received from lawyers and accountants. If they had to leave Canada to conduct their business, it made sense to go to a place like the Bahamas. They would go there and start a Bahamian Company.

The Bahamas was an island paradise. When they weren't working, they could be swimming, snorkeling, sailing with friends or sitting beneath a palm tree drinking a concoction of fruit juices and rum. They made a few preliminary trips and decided they had nothing to lose. Robert liquidated all his assets in Canada. They were waiting for Tony's preliminary hearing to conclude in the Spring of 1975 and then they were going to re-build their lives.

They traveled to Vancouver in March 1975 to deal with Tony's fraud charge. The preliminary hearing was unremarkable lasting only two and a half days. The key evidence was that of Frederick Jaeger; Gus McPhail; the Royal Bank employee in Montreal who had opened the account for Jaeger and accepted instructions to sell the Karou shares; and Sergeant Ernest Bryden.

The purpose of a preliminary hearing is to determine whether the prosecution has sufficient evidence upon which a criminal charge can reasonably be based. A high standard of proof is not required and normally, unless some element required by the prosecution is omitted, a defendant will be committed to a trial at the conclusion of the Crown's evidence.

The Crown's evidence was weak in this case in many key elements. Jaeger came across as a less-than-credible witness. He was unable to provide all explanation or proof of his version of events. In cross-examination he was often evasive in some of his responses and unreasonably obstinate in others.

He insisted the contract to purchase the ATVs had been legitimate as evidenced by a letter of intent from the Zambian government. But he possessed neither an original nor a copy of the letter and had no idea of its whereabouts. As to the $45,000-cheque he gave to Tony, his only explanation was that Tony had demanded a cheque for this amount and he felt so intimidated he complied. But if he feared Tony so much, he never explained how he could then Stop Payment on the cheque barely two hours after writing it and request the proceeds of the sale be transferred directly to his own Swiss bank account.

On the other hand, Gus McPhail, the alleged victim of the 'crime', did not hurt the Defense. He related in a fair and even manner his dealings with Tony immediately after Continental purchased the Karou shares for him. Tony's efforts to work things out with Continental as well as his account of why he couldn't pay were consistent with the lack of a guilty mind or criminal purpose.

At the end of the hearing the judge said he had some concern about some of the evidence and would advise counsel in due course of his decision.

The last words between Tony and his lawyer suggested the situation was quite hopeful. Usually committal to trial occurs directly after conclusion of the Crown's evidence. Since the judge wanted to review the evidence he must doubt the adequacy of the case. Tony thanked his lawyer and then fired him.

During the hearing, he discovered his pseudo-and-establishment lawyer wasn't really what he had expected. Often Tony had to whisper furiously or scribble notes to push his lawyer to ask questions. Being a strong-willed person who does not back down from a fight, Tony cannot understand any hesitancy to join the fray. He wanted a courageous fighter, an advocate that would be a tiger. Instead he got a man with a soft-spoken manner. Tony felt there were questions and moments missed which could have produced a more decisive victory. He knew he was innocent and wanted that shown in court. He was unhappy with the ambiguous results, even at the preliminary stage.

Before leaving Vancouver, Tony contacted another law firm to act on his behalf. The firm was Gardner & Snartch, a group of litigators in downtown Vancouver gaining the reputation of a firm unafraid to go to the wall for their clients. He left the matter in their hands and returned to Montreal. Two months later he had sorted out his affairs and was ready to leave for the Bahamas.

During this trip Tony and Robert were able to spend some time with each other and analyze the events that had taken place and what they had learned; at this point they feared that their life was in danger; they just knew too much but they still had not understood the magnitude of the situation. They hated the fact that police officers from the RCMP and agents form CSIS were committing horrible crimes in Quebec and no one wanted to stop them all to the discredit Separatist movement. So they decided that something had to be done: the information they learned from Merry and others in "Merry's Gang" needed to be given to Rene Levesque, head of the Separatist Party of Quebec, the present opposition in Parliament. Asking a few questions to friends they learned that Rene Leveques would dine a couple of nights per week at the Alouette Steak House, a restaurant on St. Catherine Street near the Montreal Forum. So the Twins after going for a couple of nights to the Alouette met up with Rene Levesque on two consecutive nights following and filled him with they had learned. Rene Levesque knew the Twins since the days of Tony's public statements on Free Quebec that had been highly publicized on television. He asked them if they could help in the coming election but the Twins declined explaining that their lives could be in danger and that they had decided to leave the country in the very near future. When they parted, the Twins said to Rene, "Vive le Quebec Libre."

The information given by the Twins to Rene Levesque was very important because if proven could change a many things for the Separatists; it could prove that the Separatists were not terrorists and that the Federal Government had interfered with proper democratic procedures of a Democratic country by destroying the economy of Quebec and committing terrorist act, bombs, kidnappings, etc to make the Separatist movement look bad. This information was very important indeed.

Three months later after an explosion at the Steinberg's house, the owner of the famous chain of supermarkets in Quebec, there was blood found on the scene of the crime but no there were bodies. Three days after, a RCMP officer checked into the hospital with his arm blown off.

A couple of months later, Levesque wins the elections of Quebec and the Royal Commission of Inquiry into Certain Activities of the RCMP, better known as the McDonald Commission gets started. The McDonald Commission was a Federal inquiry on the events in Quebec and it was proven after the long hearings, that the RCMP were behind the terrorist in Quebec. The McDonald Commission ended in 1981.

Tony and Robert arrived at Dorval airport, north of Montreal, and checked in for their flight to Nassau. There was one last bit of business they wanted to attend to before leaving Canada. They found a pay-phone and made a long-distance person-to-person call to Toronto.

After the connection was made, they heard the operator announce, "Yes, I have a collect, person-to-person call for Mr. Kesley Merry from Robert and Tony Papalia."

"Just a second, please."

Then, "Kesley Merry here."

Robert spoke first. "We thought you'd like to know, we're leaving the country. So, you can shut down the dirty-tricks department you set up for our sake."

Tony yelled into the mouth piece, "Yeah, Kesley, you bastard. You will never be able to bother us again where we're going."

On the other end, "What do you mean you're leaving? Where are you going?"

"Why don't you use some of your brilliant investigative skills and find out?"

Then laughing, one of the Twins said, "You will end up in jail. It's a shame that the death sentence has been abolished in Canada because you really deserve it. You are a traitor to law and justice and if we never see you again, it'll be too soon. Good-bye, you fucking asshole." Both Tony and Robert were laughing as they hung up the phone and headed to board their plane. They were still naive enough to believe they had the last laugh on Merry and his band of men.

They settled into their seats and as soon as the plane was airborne and drinks were served, the brothers toasted one another on the start of their new lives. Tony sat back in his seat. He hoped he was leaving the problems of Canada behind. The only unfinished business was the unresolved charge in Vancouver. He hoped the news would be good. If not, he would return to Vancouver and fight the charge. As they headed south toward the sun and a clean slate in another country, the brothers could feel the tension draining from their bodies.

Father Raffaelle Papalia (*right*) and brother Giuseppe (*front*) with family friends in Staiti in 1935. Robert and Tony were shortly born after his return from the war. Their father passed away shortly after.

Tony (*left front*), Robert and classmates in 1950. That year, the twins decided the school needed a picnic. They told their classmates that "Tomorrow is Picnic Day!" The next day, all their schoolmates arrived with picnic lunches and the teachers could not refuse to hold a picnic. Robert remembers it as one of his greatest achievements of that time.

Falcons: The 1963 St. Pius City Champions. Tony (*first photo, upfront*) and Robert (*second photo, passing the ball*). After beating the Mexican National soccer team (who were on their way to the World Cup in Sweden) by a score of 4-1, Tony, Robert and other teammates were recruited to play for a team which acted as a farm club for Catalia. At the young age of 17, Tony had achieved his dream of playing professional soccer.

Family wedding: (*right to left*) Tony, Robert, Ivana's husband Franco, brother Giuseppe, brother Aldopho and bride Vita, Mama, sister Ivana and Giuseppe's wife, Matilde, (*front*) nieces Dora and Anne Marie.

At a concert in New York, Robert, manager Robert Nickford, Beatle Paul McCartney and Tony, backstage, in the dressing room. New York clubs featured the hippest music at that time. Robert and Tony had often traveled to New York to purchase tracks for their clubs in Montreal.

Tony and Robert with historic Music Promoter, Robert Nickford during the signing of their recording contract with Warner Bros. Robert and Tony were the first to record in French with Warner Bros. Robert Nickford also acted as their music manager.

Robert and Tony, at a photo shoot for the cover of their record album: *Tony et Robert*. The album included the singles *Le Vie Ensemble and La Joie Dans Le Coeur*

Robert and Tony with their mother vacationing in Cape Cod. They spent their one-month vacation swimming and playing their guitars.

Robert and Ben E. King fooling around at The Blow Up Shop. That evening, at Cheetah's King performed one of his several hits that made the Hit Parades, *Stand by Me*. He was a regular attraction at Cheetah's and the Apollo.

Robert and Tony at the monument that commemorates the 1850 to 1858 gold rush in Port Douglas. This was their first visit to the Lillooet Valley at the age of 24.

Robert with his girlfriend, Bonnie Bernier, and Tony and Pattie vacationing in the Bahamas. Robert spent his holidays in the Bahamas before moving there.

Robert with Mama, holding grandson Anthony while visiting with Tony and Pattie in Saratoga Springs in the seventies.

Tony and Robert, with lawyer Charles McCartney and Bahamas Minister of Interior Phillip Pinder, attending a Cassius Clay boxing match in Nassau.

$288bn fraud 'based on gold mine'

By Corinna Adam

Five men were yesterday accused at the Old Bailey of what the prosecution described as "probably one of the largest frauds ever planned in the world." The men, all but one of whom are of Italian origin, are charged with plotting to swindle investors by pretending that a gold mine in Canada was on the verge of making a fortune estimated at more than $288 thousand millions. Mr Marcus Worsley, for the Crown, said that the conspiracy failed only because Scotland Yard's organised crime squad stepped in.

The five men, Robert Washington Swinnerton, (36), of Mather Avenue, Allerton, Liverpool; twin brothers Robert and Anthony Papalia, (32) financial consultants, of Nassau; Mario Berton (41), financier, of Milan, and Umberto Frascati, (35) bank manager of Pembroke Road, Kensington were arrested in May last year. All plead not guilty.

In September 1977, another man arrested at the same time, Pier Luigi Torri, escaped from custody. In court yesterday Mr Worsley described Mr Torri as "probably the key man in London." He also named two other Italians who had jumped bail and could not be extradited.

The company through which the fraud was allegedly operated was called Metals Research SA, registered first in Panama and then in the Cayman Islands. Mr Worsley yesterday produced a thin black brochure describing the untold riches to be found in British Columbia, just off the old Yukon trail.

The brochure was, he said "a tissue of lies." A photograph supposedly showing a gold nugget found on the imaginary development, had been lifted from the May 1968 issue of National Geographic Magazine. Another impressive-looking photograph showed an oil rig, which is of no use in mining noble metals.

Also in the dock yesterday were two women, Renata Sorrentino Harris (49), of St Martin's Lane, London, and Veronique Vincete Madelaine Blot (21), of Monaco and Pembroke Road, Kensington. With Mr Frascati they plead not guilty to separate but related charges involving a short-lived bank called the International Commerce Bank—established it was said, to issue shares in the non-existent gold mine. Mr Frascati and Mrs Harris, it is alleged, also attempted to purchase aircraft ownership certificates from the corporation.

A Belgian official of Cessna became suspicious and decided to visit the International Commerce Bank's premises in the West End of London. But by then the name of the bank had been changed "They had to rush out and screw the nameplate back on," said Mr Worsley.

A few days later, on May 5, 1977, the two women and Mr Frascati were arrested as they were about to leave for Italy from Heathrow Airport. The four men in the dock, and others who have since disappeared, were arrested five days later.

The trial, which continues today, is expected to last up to six months.

The Guardian, September 15, 1978. Tony and Robert were accused of conspiracy to commit fraud for the amount of $288 billion US dollars. At that time, the United States Budget was $146 billion dollars.

The Great Escape at Scotland Yard: Umberto Frascati, Pier Luigi Torri and Tony Papalia. Torri had his own escape plan: He left in the first car directly to the airport. Tony and Umberto hid in London until they were caught. There was a door-to-door manhunt for them that lasted five days.

London: Tony and Robert, outside enjoying the sun during their final trial. After the "Great Escape" from Scotland Yard, which resulted in the largest man-hunt of the time, they had to endure 18 months behind bars before they were granted bail. Their court case was the most expensive in England's history costing the English tax-payers millions and millions of pounds.

Tony with Giuseppe Bombara in London returning from court, photographed here with their Rolls-Royce. They were driven to the courthouse daily in this car by women chauffeurs who wore silver lamé military suits with matching hats.

Lawyer-geologist Bert Swann with Evergreen University Professor Neils Skov doing assessment test work on the Lillooet Project in 1967. Bert Swann was the person who originally started the Lillooet Project.

Robert, with Professor Gabrielle Schmuckler and the Honourable Alessandro Locatelli de Hagen Auer, the President of MRSA, taking an afternoon break from meetings at Piazza Duomo in Milan. Leading world scientist Schmuckler form Technion Institute in Israel has over forty scientific publications to her credit and patents in the field of chemical recovery of noble metals at the time of our story.

Tony, Canadian Minister of External Affairs Mark McWhiggin (*center*) and lawyer Giuseppe Bombara (*right*), with media personnel at a State Visit at Hotel Quirinale in Rome.

In the valley of Lillooet, Robert walks with the Vice-President of Italy, Loris Fortuna, towards the gates of the mining pit of the Lillooet Project.

Tony and Robert in the Lillooet Valley today. The Lillooet Project still remains as one of their mining projects.

Tony and Pattie's children: Actress Melanie (*left*) and equestrian Ashley (*right*). Sons Anthony and Robert (*center*) are active in the mining companies.

Tony Papalia, Rumpole of the Lambeth Magistrate Court

(December 1977 – January 1978)

THE MAGISTRATE GRANTED Defense Counsel a ten minute adjournment and Michael Spencer, Geoff Lines and Tony went to a meeting room for a chat.

"Look Michael, Worsley doesn't have a case. I want you to attack on all fronts, and that means cross-examining witnesses to put forward our side of the story."

"Tony, that's simply not the best way. This is a very complex case and we don't know the Crown's evidence yet. If we expose all the weaknesses now we'll simply give the Crown an opportunity to bolster their case for the trial."

"No, Michael. The case is bogus. They can't keep it simple and straightforward because it will be too easy to prove our innocence. They're throwing these papers, documents and witnesses at you because they think if they include everything and the kitchen sink they can baffle everyone with their bullshit!"

"Now look Tony, I cannot approach this case on the basis that the Crown is acting in bad faith and hasn't any real evidence. I have to assume that they are going to bring a good deal of evidence which could result in your conviction if it goes unchallenged. And if I dig too deeply now it will give Mr.Worsley a lot of information about our possible defenses. The more information he has the better he can anticipate and, perhaps, close down our available defenses."

"You'll have to trust me, Tony. I know what I'm doing and it's for the best."

Tony considered this. He was deep in thought. His hands were folded behind his back and he was pacing the floor. He didn't want to get his lawyers angry at him, but neither was he willing to do things their way. "What if I told you, as your client, that I demand that you conduct an active and positive plan of defense at this stage of the proceedings?"

"Well, Tony, that's your right. But, as I can't concur with that manner of proceeding, then I can no longer act on your behalf. But, I'll tell you, I doubt that you are going to find a competent barrister who will agree to conduct this case in the manner you are suggesting."

Tony thought about this too. After a moment he said, "Can I represent myself in an English courtroom?"

Geoff looked stricken while Michael just sighed. He had seen clients try to handle cases before and just make a mess of it. "Certainly if you wish to act on your own behalf you may do so, but I can't recommend it."

Geoff added, "I'll have to check with David Benham. I'm not sure we could continue to act as your solicitors if you choose to act on your own behalf in the courtroom."

Tony had already made up his mind. He offered his right hand to Spencer in a gesture of friendship. Spencer took it and they shook hands.

"No hard feelings, Michael."

"Certainly not, Tony."

"I tell you what. I respect you. I just don't agree with your approach here, when the committal hearing is over if we go to trial I'd still like you to represent me."

"Sure, Tony. Just leave some defenses for us to use at trial."

"Sure thing."

The three men left the room and went back to the courtroom, Geoff was saying under his breath, "Oh, dear." At his first opportunity he would have to get to a phone to speak to David Benham.

When they returned to the courtroom, as Tony sat down, Robert whispered to him, "Is he going to do what you asked?"

Tony turned to his brother, winked and said, "I'm going to do it myself."

Robert was only slightly taken aback. "Can you do it?"

Tony nodded in the affirmative.

This answer was good enough for his brother. Robert patted his brother's shoulder to let Tony know he was with him on his decision.

Michael Spencer got up from his seat to address the court. He could have saved himself some measure of indignity by simply withdrawing from the case. But, if he did this, it could create prejudice in the Magistrate's mind by giving the impression that some ethical issue had arisen which prevented him from acting for his client. No, he wasn't going to prejudice his client's case by being vague and mysterious about what he was about to do.

"Sir, I'm afraid my client and I have had a disagreement over how we wish to proceed in this case." He paused for a second and his face reddened as he said, "as a result, my client, Anthonio Papalia, has fired me."

The Magistrate harrumphed. He didn't like this one bit. If indeed Mr. Spencer was fired this would probably mean a significant delay until alternate counsel could be found. It had taken a good deal of cooperation for all the lawyers involved in this case to get this matter on for its scheduled time through December and into mid January. Now, there would likely be a requested adjournment of several days or weeks to retain and instruct new counsel.

The Magistrate looked at the defendants. "Which of you is Anthonio Papalia?"

Tony stood up. "I am, Sir."

"Mr. Papalia, would you approach the bench."

"Yes, Sir." He started to walk to the front of the courtroom. When he arrived beside Michael Spencer's table, the magistrate continued.

"I suppose, Mr. Papalia that you want some time to find new counsel."

"Well, Sir, I understand I can represent myself."

"Surely, Mr. Papalia, you realize you would be better served by competent counsel such as Mr. Spencer."

"No disrespect to Mr. Spencer, Sir, but I don't agree with him as to how the case should be handled."

"Oh, you don't." The Magistrate knew it was going to be more difficult to run a case of this sort in the courtroom with a layman trying to represent himself. But, he couldn't force the man to use counsel, especially a defendant as stubborn as this man obviously was. The Magistrate questioned Tony some more until he resigned himself to the fact that Tony was not willing to budge from his decision for the time being. Perhaps after he had a taste of fumbling about in the courtroom for a few days he would see reason.

"Mr. Papalia, if you wish to represent yourself, you may do so. But, I'm telling you right now, I will not allow you to use this as an opportunity to be an instigator or a troublemaker. I expect you to conduct yourself in a proper manner in this courtroom and to observe the principles of proper decorum at all times. I will not grant you anymore leeway than I would counsel in these circumstances. Is that understood?"

Tony was the picture of compliant respect, "Yes, Sir."

The Magistrate decided to adjourn the proceedings until the next day. This would allow Mr. Spencer to collect his things and leave the courtroom with a minimum of disruption. It would also allow Mr. Papalia the opportunity to prepare his questions for the next group of witnesses.

As court adjourned for the day, there were a number of people milling about the courtroom, talking, asking questions, bracing themselves for the next day's events. Not the least of the hangers-on was a large contingent of police officers. Most of them had come to court anticipating giving testimony; some were simply there because they were interested in the trial. Now as word spread down the hallways about what was transpiring, most of the police officers in the building were converging on this court to have a look, to discuss it with their friends and to make their own gratuitous and sarcastic comments on this new and interesting development. The police were really enjoying it. Tony was trying to have a brief discussion with Geoff Lines to sort out some things before tomorrow morning when he heard a voice behind him, "Oh look, there he is, Perry Mason ..." followed by several men laughing.

He looked behind him. He saw two cops he knew, three he didn't. All of them looked at him smiling or laughing. They were enjoying this immensely; the police were positively gleeful about the news that he would be handling his own defence in the courtroom. They felt sure he was going to make a fool of himself. Tony just looked them up and down, and then turned back to Geoff to finish their discussion. He could hardly wait to get started.

Back at Brixton that night, Tony ran into a couple of minor, but irritating matters, that were going to make his task more difficult,

When the prisoners emerged from the van on their return to prison that afternoon, Tony was carrying some pens, pencils and notepaper. One of the guards immediately took notice of this and confiscated these items from him. As a Maximum Security prisoner who had previously escaped he needed special permission from the Warden to have such items in his possession.

When Tony sought the Warden's permission to have pens and paper, his request was denied. He contacted Benham's office and by that evening Geoff was advising him they would be forced to appeal the Warden's decision to the Solicitor General. Benham was writing a letter to the Solicitor General which would go out the next day. Until the issue was sorted out, Tony couldn't do any writing or note-taking while at Brixton.

Later that night, another incident occurred which Tony suspected might be related to his decision to take on his own defense. Ever since their escape and return to prison, both Tony's and Umberto's cells in the Maximum Security wing were outfitted with red lamps in the ceiling. Always at night these lamps were turned on briefly at intervals to ensure that they were still in their cells. Now, however, whoever was operating the light for Tony's cell was leaving it on for extended periods of time. Then it would be turned on and off, flickering a dozen or so times before being left on again to shine in the cell.

After watching this light show for a bit, Tony decided whoever was doing this was specifically trying to disrupt his sleep. Indeed, whoever was doing it was very successful in disrupting his sleep. He sighed, wondering at the petty perversity that motivated their keepers to perform stunts like this. It was a constant battle not to allow them to get to you, to maintain your dignity and to feel you still had some control over your life.

Tony climbed up onto his cot and after wrapping one of his shirts around the light he took a good whack with his shoe and put out the light for good that night. He returned to his cot and slept soundly until morning.

The next day Tony arrived at court ready to begin. He had a rough idea of how he wanted to proceed, but it wasn't until he'd returned to the court that he was able to take notes and organize his thoughts.

The aspects of the case that were before the court right now were mostly preliminary matters regarding the set-up and conduct of Bear Securities in England. Tony had no personal knowledge of this part of the case so he would be asking a lot of his questions in the dark. He would have to confer with Frascati before the court convened to ask his advice about possible questions.

Tony was sitting at the prisoner dock getting organized when Mr. Worsley strode into the courtroom, both his junior and himself weighted down by stacks of paper. Worsley handed copies of some of these documents to all of Defense counsel. Then he turned to Tony and when handing the papers to him said something about the papers being clearly admissible, having given proper notice. He hoped Tony wouldn't be making an objection to their admissibility.

Tony looked at the cover of the booklet he'd been handed. Perhaps Worsley was trying to be helpful. Tony didn't think so though. He immediately thought that this was another example of the constant psychological warfare they were engaged in. Worsley was trying to intimidate him by bringing up a procedural matter right off the start. He was pointing out to Tony that he knew nothing of courtroom procedure or evidentiary law, hoping to scare him by making him feel lost before he even got up to ask any questions.

Tony didn't like Worsley. So far as he was concerned, the prosecutor was making up things to destroy the lives of himself, his brother and their business associates. And Tony was definitely not the type to hide his true feelings. He looked from the bound documents he was holding to Worsley and said "Mr. Worsley, this case is based on ignorance and bad faith. Before this case is over I am going to make you swallow 800 million tons of sand because I will not allow you to win this case."

Worsley blanched. After returning Tony's defiant stare with a contemptuous look of his own, he turned to discuss something with his junior. Several of the other lawyers involved in the case had witnessed this exchange. They said nothing, but it became apparent over the next many months that from that point on Mr. Worsley took this case very personally. It was all-out war between the prosecutor and Tony Papalia. There was no way Worsley was going to allow this stubborn non-British, lay-man criminal, to beat him in the courtroom.

Although Tony had much to learn, the nay-sayers waited in vain for Tony to mess up his defense. But he was completely focused and learned very quickly. Tony had an incredible memory for detail and it was this memory together with his quick mind that would come into play in the days ahead.

On the stand was a witness who was a director of the English company that had sold the shell company, Bear Securities, to its current owners. When the man was turned over for questioning Tony almost immediately started arguing with the witness.

Mr. Worsley rose to his feet to make an objection while concurrently the Magistrate interrupted, "Mr. Papalia, if you wish to put your position before the court on these matters you must do so through your own witnesses at the appropriate time."

Tony started to say something.

The Magistrate all but hissed at him, "Do not interrupt me when I am speaking, Mr. Papalia. Now, as I was saying, the time to bring your own evidence is at the conclusion of the Crown's case. What you are supposed to be doing with this witness is asking him questions on those matters about which he has personal knowledge. If you elicit an answer that you do not like, you do not then engage in an argument with him about whether this is so. You must accept his answer, subject to your right to cross-examine him further with respect to his ability to observe or know that his answer is the correct one. Do you understand me?"

Tony stood there, "Yes Sir."

Tony asked the man a couple of more questions and then told the court he had no further for this witness.

There was another minor witness that morning, a hotel desk clerk who gave evidence on the arrival and check out times of one of Robert's and Mario's visits to London. Tony again got up and asked a question or two. It wasn't so much because this man said anything objectionable to the defense, but, rather, Tony wished to hone his skill at handling witnesses under cross-examination. He was able to establish that when the clerk said that Messrs. Papalia and Berton had checked in he really didn't remember anything about their arrival or departure. He was relying solely on the Hotel Register to show that they had arrived on the date alleged and that he was the one who had registered them.

This evidence mattered not at all for the purposes of proving guilt or innocence. Neither he nor his brother, were going to deny the true facts. It was important, however, since it allowed Tony to see how he could attack the credibility of Crown witnesses without Worsley springing to his feet or the magistrate chastising him.

Tony was pleased that he'd asked a series of questions that hadn't elicited objections from the bench or the Crown. He turned to the Magistrate and said, "I have no further questions of this witness," and sat down.

The Magistrate immediately recommended an adjournment for lunch before the next witness was called. Tony used this opportunity to take some notes, look at the Crown's list of witnesses, to anticipate the next series of questions and to talk with Robert, Mario and Geoff Lines about the case.

Geoff had been pleased to announce earlier that morning that Benham had seen no reason to terminate the solicitor-client relationship for the time being. This could change, of course, if they should have a falling-out about Tony's conduct of the case as things progressed.

Frascati who had been off speaking to his counsel approached the group as they were conferencing, "I'm going to join Tony and take on my own Defense."

"What are you talking about?"

"I just had a discussion with my barrister. I told him I wanted him to attack the 'Bear' side of the case the same way that Tony is taking on his case. He was very put out at my suggestion that he should assist Tony in the courtroom to ask questions. So I fired him."

All but Geoff were smiling all around. He was worried that perhaps they had begun something that was going to get out of control. "Wait until David gets word of this latest development," he thought.

Tony said, "That's great. I'll concentrate on Metals Research and you can focus on the 'Bear' stuff. And we can both help each other."

After lunch when the court reconvened, the first thing to be dealt with was

Frascati's advice to the court that he had fired his counsel and would now be representing himself too.

Surprisingly, the Magistrate took this news in stride and chose not to exhibit any sign of losing patience. He gave Umberto a lecture similar to the one he had given Tony then told him he could take his own Defense. Frascati sat next to Tony. Then the Magistrate lifted his gaze to survey the remaining defendants at the back of the room and said, "I will not take kindly to any further disruptions in this courtroom. Before we proceed, are there any more defendants who wish to terminate their instructions to counsel and represent themselves at this hearing?"

No one responded in the affirmative. They simply returned the Magistrate's cold, hard stare with blank stares of their own. Robert knew that now was not the time to irritate the Magistrate so he suppressed his urge to smile.

The rest of the afternoon proceeded uneventfully; Worsley was still calling background witnesses that the defense had no real quarrel with. Both Tony and Umberto asked some questions, and when either of them went too far Mr. Worsley would object. Tony was more persistent than Frascati and he began to see that he was able to say almost anything to the court if he couched his words properly. If the Magistrate did not leap to sustain Mr. Worsley's objection, Tony would argue the point always using respectful phrases such as "With the greatest respect, Sir ..." or "... I disagree with my learned prosecutor ..." He always made sure that he made his point even if the Magistrate required that he change the substance or form of his questioning.

At the end of the afternoon, most of the defendants were buoyed by how things were going. The Crown was merely building the background of the case; placing each of the defendants at certain places at various times through the testimony of people they had dealings with. This approach to the introduction of evidence was giving Tony and Umberto the time and experience they needed to prepare for the really important parts of the case.

Now, fortunately the Christmas break had arrived, and as Christmas fell over a weekend this year, it meant that court would not reconvene for six days. Then there would be one day of testimony when Worsley slotted in some more minor testimony. Then a three day break over the weekend and New Year, until finally they would reconvene on January 3rd, 1978 for a prolonged assault on the mountains of evidence to be put before the court.

It is doubtful the prosecution rested much over the holidays. Certainly the defense didn't. Every day, Tony and Umberto, with Robert and Mario acting as their assistants and researchers would pour over the documents in the case. When they needed some outside assistance to obtain copies of papers or briefings of witness statements, Geoff would come to Brixton to bring them the documents and to assist them in their strategy sessions.

When court reconvened on January 3rd, Tony and Umberto were ready for battle.

It was at this stage of the proceedings that the evidence turned to one of the key issues in the case for both the prosecution and the defense; the scientific evidence of what precious metals if any existed on the MRSA mining claims in British Columbia. As Mr. Worsley had already stated, it was the Crown's contention that there was really nothing of value in the company's mining claims. He had tendered the bulk of the scientific reports on the property as part of the documentary evidence available to the court. But, at the preliminary stage, at least, he sought to deal quite briefly with this aspect of the evidence.

He would call Scotland Yard's own forensic scientist who, in the course of the investigation, had performed his own assay on the Lillooet sands. This was to be followed by William Stevenson, a British Columbia geologist who had done work for the Papalias in 1974 and who, during the course of the investigation, had prepared a report for Scotland Yard wherein he examined the work of Schellinger, Delta Smelting and Schmuckler, and had given an opinion that there was little precious metal present in the sand. And, perhaps as a nod to her eminence in the field, Mr. Worsley would call Dr. Schmuckler as the final scientific witness to give evidence on behalf of the Crown.

When the forensic scientist took the stand, his evidence was presented in the matter-of-fact manner of the professional expert witness. With little prompting from Worsley, he set out his credentials and the nature of his duties with the Scotland Yard Forensic Unit. He described how he had received a kilogram bag of sand from a Sergeant George, who had visited the mining site with Mr. William Stevenson, and collected the sample from the surface of one of the claims. Thereafter he had performed a standard fire assay on the said sand and had obtained a result which showed 2 grams of gold per ton. The forensic scientist concluded from this that there was nothing more thin trace amounts of precious metals in the Lillooet sands.

When Mr. Worsley was finished with this short and succinct bit of evidence he asked his witness to please answer any questions put by his learned friends and then, he sat down.

When the Magistrate asked if anyone wished to question the witness, Tony was the only one who spoke up to examine the man. He had prepared for this moment with a vengeance. In the previous months as he reviewed the evidence with his solicitors, he had read and re-read the scientific reports and the Statements of Witness affidavits of the various scientists tendered by the Crown. He knew the contents of the reports inside out and backwards and forwards. And while he had been knowledgeable for years about the basics of metallurgy now he was conversant enough on the subject to joust with the experts. When he asked a question about assays or the contents of one of the reports, he knew what the answer should be.

Tony's view of the scientific reports was quite simple and it would remain consistent throughout the course of the court proceedings; that is, because of the complex nature of the Lillooet sands, standard fire assays had always failed to produce the best results. The true values of precious metals contained in the sands could only be determined by means of non-standard fire assays or chemical assays.

In the two weeks since he had taken over his own defense he had specifically focused on this part of the case. He knew he must show the fallacy of the Crown assumption that many of the reports were fraudulent. What he intended to do with this forensic man was to review some of the basics of fire assay with him and then seek his comment and agreement with respect to some of the other reports. In particular, he wanted the man's expert opinion on the Delta Smelting test results as these results became much more promising when the assay lab moved from standard fire assays to non-standard methods incorporate different fluxes and higher temperature.

As Tony began his list of prepared questions, things went in a way that he had not anticipated. The witness stated that he could not speak with authority in response to Tony's second question about standard fire assay on the subject without reference to a standard text in the field. Tony then made a stab at getting the man to comment on one of the Delta reports. The witness so qualified his answer that it was all but useless to Tony. Just for a second Tony thought the fellow was being evasive. He wondered if he should soldier on with this line of questioning when it had yielded so little. He was taking a moment to collect his thoughts and to determine how best to ask his next question when he realized that Worsley was starting to look a little red in the face.

It occurred to Tony that the prosecutor's discomfiture must mean he was making some points even though he felt stymied. As he stared at the paper in his hand it came to him in a flash what he must do. He dropped his prepared list of questions on the table folded his hands behind him and turned to stare directly at the witness.

"Mr. Facey, what is your mining training in metallurgy?"

"I have no formal training in that field."

"And your formal training in geology?"

"None."

"How many times have you performed a fire assay?"

"Just this once, my results are set out in my report that is before the court."

"How did you determine the proper method for performing a fire assay with your lack of training in the field?"

"Upon receiving the sand sample from Sgt. George at the forensic lab, I obtained a standard textbook on the subject and followed the directions therein for conducting a standard fire assay."

"So you followed the instructions in this text as you would a recipe in a cookbook?"

"Well, not in so many words. I am, after all, a trained scientist and was careful to follow the scientific method when carrying out the assay."

"Did you deviate in any respect from the instructions in the textbook?"

"Only in one particular, I was unable to utilize a sand sample of the same bulk as set out in the textbook example, because of size limitations in the equipment available to me."

"So you're saying that you were forced to improvise with your equipment, that you didn't have the facilities or equipment of an assay laboratory available?"

"Well, yes, but not so it would affect the outcome of the procedure. I was careful to pare down the whole of the experiment accordingly."

"Uh, huh. Would it surprise you, Doctor, to know that the size of the sample used in a standard fire assay is a variable that can affect the assay results in the sands you examined?"

"Yes, it would."

"But you can't say with certainty whether the proposition I just put to you is correct or not?"

"No, I can't."

"Thank you, I have no further questions."

Tony had taken the Crown's first major scientific witness and had effectively demolished him as an expert.

In the Devil's Triangle - The Bahamas

(1975- 1976)

ARRIVING IN THE Bahamas was like emerging from a nightmare.

The Bahamas have a legacy steeped in romance and adventure with more than a little larceny laced through their past.

It was on the shores of a Bahamian island that Christopher Columbus first stood and found indigenous people when he arrived in the New World. Fewer than forty years after Columbus' arrival, the islands were wholly devoid of human habitation, due largely to Spanish incursions in search of slaves for their holdings in other parts of the New World.

In the 17th century, the Bahamas became a refuge for British Puritans and later, due to its proximity to the American southern colonies and the trade routes to Europe, an operating base for a wide array of notorious pirates. It was during this era that Nassau with its safe harbor and good moorage became the center of the Bahamian settlement.

The pirates reigned almost unimpeded until the early part of the 18th century when they finally succumbed to the rule of a British-appointed governor who was himself a hard-headed rogue privateer.

The Islands remained sparsely inhabited over the next 50 years. After the American Revolutionary War, the predominantly European-derived population was to be altered significantly by the arrival of families of United Empire Loyalists, replete with slaves, from the American Carolinas. In the course of a little over four years in the mid-1780s, the population of the islands more than quadrupled, with a large portion of the new arrivals consisting of slaves.

Fifty years later, the slaves were emancipated when the British abolished slavery in Britain and her colonies. It is from this slave population that most present day Bahamians are descended.

From the time the Bahamas was opened to law and order the country oscillated between a boom and bust economy. For over one-hundred and fifty years the islands moved between prosperity as a trading center whenever there was strife in nearby America and a depressed state during times of peace.

In 1918, the Bahamas was in serious decline. Many of the white settlers had emigrated elsewhere in search of work and prosperity. The remaining largely black population lived by means of subsistence agriculture, fishing and the time-honored enterprise of 'wrecking' -- the business of salvaging goods from the numerous ship-wrecks caused by the treacherous and shallow shoals and reefs surrounding the islands.

Then in 1919, American Prohibition began and the Bahamian economy took-off. Fortunes were made out of the production and illicit supply of rum to booze-starved Americans. The new-found wealth began to attract more money. At least one of the rum-runner millionaires built a large and lavish estate for himself in Nassau in the 1920s.

The Palm Beach set began to frequent Nassau aboard their yachts. Many of the wealthy built villas along the beautiful beaches of New Providence and Hog Island. In the atmosphere of the Roaring Twenties with Prohibition, millionaires and rum flowing like water, the Bahamas developed into a destination for the thoroughly spoiled well-to-do elite. During this decade the islands had transformed into a glittering resort. Tourism became the number one industry and sustained the Bahamian economy throughout the next fifty years.

By the mid-70's, Nassau and the adjoining "Paradise Island" had reached their heyday. It was a resort of international renown, its beaches were strung with lavish hotels, with casinos and nightlife incorporating the elements of calypso music and limbo dancing. On every corner there were garden restaurants or bars in the shade of lush palms, multi-colored Bougainvillea and orchids.

The other side of the Bahamian world was its fiscal policies. Since those who ruled the country in the early 20th Century were the British-moneyed elite with input from influential American and European nobility, the Bahamas developed very favorable tax and banking laws. There are no capital gains, corporation, death, inheritance or income taxes in this nation.

The rich and famous, the unrenowned rich, the legitimately wealthy and the corrupt; all were attracted to this haven. Many stayed, bringing with them much of their wealth.

Ten years before Robert and Tony arrived; the Bahamas gained its independence from Britain under the leadership of a young black lawyer, Lynden Pindling. This young, black government was feeling expansive in its new-found freedom. The possibilities for the Bahamas seemed endless. Hundreds of banks from around the world sprung up to accommodate the money being brought to the islands.

In early 1975, Robert and Tony arrived in this city of 100,000 souls. At first they stayed at the Britannia Beach Hotel but soon decided to look for a place on Paradise Island. As they crossed the bridge leading from Nassau to the island across the harbor they saw a newly erected sign reading, "Welcome to Paradise". They hoped this was an auspicious omen of their new circumstance.

They had been at the "Britannia Beach" only a few weeks when a villa apartment became available to them. A friend, Dottie Atwood, offered it to Robert as she required someone to "house-sit" the residence in her absence.

The central portion of this small beautiful island lies just north of the bridge to the city and consists of a lagoon with hotels, casinos and shopping centers around its perimeter. To the coast is the Paradise Island Golf Course and to the west a narrow strand of land on which sits a series of private villas side by side. Each property extends across the width of the spit from the harbor-side beach area to Paradise beach on the north. None of these private residences are accessible by road and the only means to arrive or depart is by boat or by walking along either of the beach-front paths that lead from central Paradise to the western lighthouse tip of the island.

Dottie Atwood's villa was in the Moorish style. It was cool and bright, with thick white-washed walls and many areas open to the sunlight. For a pittance Robert was able to hire occasional help to come in to clean their home and tend the flowering tropical plants surrounding the house.

In many ways their time in the Bahamas had the air of an extended vacation. But to begin their business activities, they sought out legal and accounting advice to create a Bahamian corporation. The company was named "Complex Metals Corporation" and it entered into new agreements with Zyrox and Platinate to develop the Lillooet claims.

The professionals they retained were influential people in the admittedly small Bahamian business community. Their lawyers were the firm of Dupugh & Turnquest. Dupugh, QC was the senior counsel. In addition to being an English Lord, he was a recipient of the Order of the British Empire.

Turnquest was also an English Lord and an MP in the Bahamian Parliament. Through these gentlemen and their accountant, also an MP, they were introduced to the Rotary Club. At the Rotary luncheons they were introduced to the broader Bahamian business community and came to know Phillip Pinder, the Minister of the Interior of the Bahamian Government.

In a world where up to 10,000 people arrive and leave each week, within two months of their arrival Robert and Tony were regarded as old hands. They were welcomed into the social scene of their new business associates and found themselves constantly making the rounds. On almost a weekly basis they would be ushered through the main gate as invited guests into black-tie events in the exclusive preserve of Lyford Cay, the home for the titled, famous, influential and wealthy people who frequented or lived in the Bahamas.

Rotary luncheons, meetings with their professional advisors and socializing with their business associates took up only a portion of each day. They found themselves slipping into 'Bahamian time', carrying on at a relaxed pace and devoting most of their efforts to play.

Robert, in his twenties, with the pressures of the Montreal business world and the rich family dinners cooked by his mother, had developed a tendency to gain weight. Now in the mornings he would go for a walk or jog on the beach. Whenever he got the urge, he would run into the surf and swim in the aquamarine water. If he had time or felt the impulse he would go snorkeling, diving amongst the coral and old ship-wrecks that littered the shallow waters beyond the beach. This outdoor life of walking, swimming and partying, in combination with the live seafood and fruit cuisine of the islands found him at the age of 30, returning to the same weight he had carried in high-school. He was tanned and fit. Both brothers looked great and felt fabulous. They felt at the height of their powers.

Tony however, is not one to spend much time basking in the lap of luxury. He also had significant family responsibilities. Pattie and their infant son initially stayed in Montreal but the harassment by the authorities continued on a daily basis were becoming intolerable. After several months, Tony returned to Montreal to move his family to a small farmstead in Sarasota Springs, New York. As time went by, it became important for the two brothers to be closer together so he moved the family to Miami just a one hour flight from Nassau. He would address the North American aspects of their business while Robert would manage the long term development of Complex Metals.

It was a golden time for Robert. Neighboring villas were the temporary homes of such famous people as Eric Clapton and Richard Harris. The presence of these creative people meant the coming and going of numerous international jet-set types. Parties were constant, always with an interchangeable crowd of beautiful people. An endless supply of attractive women arrived weekly to the Islands, almost all of them looking for adventure and romance and the company of a handsome male escort. Robert took full advantage of it.

He acquired a white 1956 English taxicab which he kept at the resort area of Paradise Island. In the afternoons he would head across the bridge with one of his latest friends toward one of his favorite haunts. Sometimes they would pull over when they saw someone try to hail the 'cab'. If they liked the people they'd picked up they would often invite them along wherever they were going. Otherwise they would take their 'fares' to their stated destination and charge them, laughing at their private joke as they went on their way.

Robert's favorite bar in Nassau was a place called The Cumberland House. The Dutch proprietor had renovated a historic building to create a garden restaurant and bar in the inner courtyard. The interior of the restaurant had a festive, relaxed atmosphere with colorfully set tables and exotic flowering plants. There was ivy growing in profusion along the walls, and tropical palms in huge ceramic pots set about the flagstone brickwork of the floor.

While Robert and Tony were in the Bahamas, the 'Cumberland' became a popular hangout. Many of their business associates would drop in knowing they could find them with a collection of old and new friends. It wasn't unusual for the owner to close the place to the public, to leave room for a private party that would expand as more friends and acquaintances would congregate as the evening developed. Impromptu jam sessions occurred. Often the revelers would include professional rock musicians who loved to perform, even on vacation. When this happened, Robert, always the frustrated entertainer would grab a guitar or tambourine and join in the music-making. The parties went on into the early hours of the morning only to start over again the next day.

At one party a young Englishman working for the Bahamian Government on contract as a building engineer introduced himself to Robert. Over time he would turn up at the same night spots every evening and eventually became a regular friend. His name was Richard Swinnerton.

Richard was a big, bluff Liverpudlian. He enjoyed a drink with the boys and was good at telling stories. Swinnerton's background was rather humble and was impressed with his new Canadian friends. They seemed to have the ear of many important people in the Bahamas as well as a knack for attracting the famous and beautiful to their circle of friends.

While it was possible to go on for months in the Bahamas socializing with people and not knowing what they did for a living or really knowing their social status. Richard became enthralled with the Twins. Their villa on Paradise Island, their social connections and their talk of a gold mine in Canada made him think they were very rich although he never actually asked. He didn't feel his own situation was too impressive so he embellished his story just enough to create a more favorable image.

From what Richard said, Robert had the impression he was a British architect, living in the Bahamas to supervise the design of some new, large buildings. Robert accepted what Richard told him at face value, but really didn't worry about it. Robert simply liked Richard and didn't care what he did for a living. The brothers incorporated Complex Metals Corporation, but it remained a private company. It wasn't really the vehicle they needed to finance their mine. Robert had been in the Bahamas only a short time before he began to discuss the possibility of a Bahamian Stock Exchange with his friends in Rotary. Virtually everyone thought it a brilliant idea. In fact, with the encouragement of Rotarians and Parliamentarians, he was appointed to a Committee formed for the purpose of developing a stock exchange in the Bahamas. Over the balance of 1975 when he wasn't partying, Robert worked with Tony in Miami to put together the new exchange.

By Christmas 1975, everything was proceeding according to plan. Another month or so and there would be a functioning Stock Exchange in Nassau. They could get started with their plans to turn Complex Metals into a public company and use their skills to obtain the financing needed to continue development of the Lillooet property.

In late 1974, before Robert had wholly given up hope on Pacific Nickel, he had agreed with the Zyrox and Platinate groups to bring the Lillooet Project into full production. This agreement now gave Complex Metals 51% ownership. Robert had managed through all the problems of 1974 and 1975 to enter into contracts for the purpose of continuing development of the property.

Pacific Nickel had also contracted an American company, Scientific Gold and Platinum Recovery to assist in developing a viable process for the deposit. The principals of this company read like a veritable Who's Who of American academia, most of them leading scientists. The purpose of the contract was to do work at

Princeton University in parallel with Schmuckler in Israel. If the group were successful in scaling-up the chemical process for separating precious metals from the sand and magnetic concentrate, the group would get a 90 percent interest in any patents developed and used on the Lillooet sands. The remainder would be assigned to Pacific Nickel.

In May 1974, Scientific Gold had hired Gordon Bacon from BC Research, an establishment on the campus of the University of British Columbia, to collect bulk surface samples. He was to send part of each sample to Dr. Schmuckler in Israel. However, after Pacific Nickel began experiencing problems with the Quebec Securities Commission, Scientific Gold never completed its contract obligations nor did they send many of their samples to Dr. Schmuckler's lab.

Dr. Schmuckler remained interested in the Lillooet sand. She felt these complex sands represented a unique scientific challenge. The work done to date had furthered her understanding of some of the complexities of Ion Exchange for recovering precious metals. In March 1975, while on sabbatical leave at Stanford University, Dr. Schmuckler met Robert for the first time at his request. He explained the logistic difficulties they were having and asked her if she would be willing to conduct further research when the financial side stabilized. Dr. Schmuckler thought Robert an enthusiastic and sincere young man. She told him she wished to continue with the Lillooet sand test work.

But it certainly wasn't feasible during Pacific Nickel's demise. Scientific Gold's metallurgist, Gordon Bacon, issued a horrendous report on samples he had assayed showing only trace amounts of precious metals. Bacon was aware that Pacific Nickel had once retained a geologist named William Stevenson, to do some work on the sands and so he reported his negative results to him.

What Bacon didn't realize was that after Stevenson completed his earlier work for Pacific Nickel in 1972, he had not been employed again by the company. The poor results obtained by Bacon on behalf of Scientific Gold were never an issue with the principals of the Pacific Nickel. Robert attributed the poor results to the same type of problems that Stevenson had experienced. Simply put conventional fire assay fails to reveal all the gold present in the samples.

Stevenson's assays had shown gold between 0.005 to 0.114 oz/ton. These same samples when assayed at the University of Montreal were considerably better at between 0.026 to 0.288 oz/ton. The Montreal tests also attempted to extract gold from the magnetic portion of the sample by means of cyanide digestion -- a conventional chemical process for gold recovery. These results were negative. Refinement of the Schmuckler process remained the only feasible economic method to pursue. That meant research; and research meant money.

Robert had enough funds to support himself and Tony in a very comfortable fashion for a considerable period of time, but they wanted to get the Lillooet project rolling. It would give them the ability to rehabilitate Tony's financial situation. Then they could resume their stock market activity.

Over coffee one morning in December 1975, Tony looked across at Robert,

"How was Mama when you spoke to her?"

"She is fine; except she's unhappy we won't be home for Christmas."

"I know, but we're so close to getting the Stock Exchange up and running here. When that's done we'll both have more money to take trips to see the family. Did she hear anything from my lawyers in Vancouver?"

"No, nothing yet."

"God, it seems to take such a long time. This thing seems like it's been hanging over my head forever."

Christmas was spent in a party atmosphere. If anything the constant rounds of socializing intensified as the Bahamas geared up to handle the Christmas and New Year's vacationers. Even so, Robert and Tony had kept the opening of the new Stock Exchange on track. It was expected to open on January 26th, 1976. During the first week of January, they were recovering from New Year's and helping to plan the opening day ceremonies for the proposed Exchange.

On the 16th of January, the government had everything in place to allow public trading in securities. Six days later a license was granted to Complex Metals to trade publicly. Robert was very pleased, and when the business of the day was finished, he and Tony went out to celebrate with a group of friends.

Early the next morning Robert received a telephone call from Phillip Pinder. His voice had an edge of concern as he said, "Robert, there's something I must discuss with you and Tony right away."

Robert thought the ominous tone was odd. He'd seen Phillip only the night before at Dottie Atwood's home and he'd been very jovial and relaxed. "Sure, Phillip, what is it'?"

"I can't discuss it over the phone, Robert. Can you be here in half an hour?"

"I guess so. Tony's gone to Miami today but I can be right over."

Robert got himself dressed and mobile in ten minutes. He drove himself over to Lyford Cay to Pinder's residence. Phillip was still in his dressing gown pacing the floor of his study, and holding a paper in his hand.

Phillip looked at Robert's face, presumably for signs that he knew what was coming. But Robert just looked back at him, "What is it, Phillip?"

Pinder thrust the paper at Robert.

"Read this letter and then tell me what its all about."

Robert looked at the letter. It was written on official Canadian government stationary. It was from the RCMP attaché, an officer named Anderson, to the Canadian High Commissioner to Jamaica. It was dated January 21, 1976 and stated that the Canadian government had some concern that Robert and Tony Papalia might be in or on their way to the Bahamas and that the Bahamian authorities should be on the lookout for these two brothers because ...

"...the Papalia brothers ... are involved in fraudulent stock promotions and stolen securities .... and they are fugitives from Canada, having failed to appear in a court of law on January 19th."

Robert stared at the letter. He read it once and then read it again. He was having difficulty digesting it. This was completely unexpected. There was no basis for any of these allegations. Everything contained in the letter was a lie.

Robert was filled with embarrassment and anger. Phillip was his friend and had risked a lot by giving him this private interview and allowing him to see the letter. Robert knew this wouldn't be straightened out with a quick phone call.

"Phillip, I hinted before to you about some of the reasons we left Canada. The RCMP seem bent on a slander campaign against Tony and me. I am not a fugitive and neither is Tony. They say we're con-artists but they have kept us from our plans for the gold mine. They won't let us do business so we've never had an opportunity to show we're legitimate."

Phillip looked at Robert, "Robert, I don't know what's behind this letter, but the Bahamas has very strong diplomatic ties to Canada. If you stay you could become an embarrassment to the government. Certainly we're going to have to withdraw your license to trade in shares for the time being. We may cancel our plans for an Exchange entirely since the plan was put together almost totally on your initiative. Unless this matter can be sorted out immediately with the Canadian government, you're just too closely associated with the Exchange to have it open with the diplomatic and controversial incident this might become."

Robert wondered what he could possibly say to Phillip. Chances were the January 19th court date was the trial date for Tony's 'Karou' case. He hadn't known of the date, but if Phillip found out about this it wouldn't be easy to explain. It complicates matters terribly.

"Phillip, can I have a copy of the letter. I've got to speak to my lawyers."

"Yes, Robert. This one's a copy. Take it."

Robert spent the rest of the morning in conference with his lawyers at Dupugh & Turnquest. He told the partners as much background as he knew about the matters in the letter. He told them about Kesley Merry, and the RCMP rumor mill. He told them about Tony's outstanding fraud charge.

Turnquest advised him of some things he hadn't thought about. If the Canadians had any legitimate basis they could seek to extradite Tony from the Bahamas. If that happened their reputations would be ruined. It would be unlikely that they could have any association with a Bahamian Exchange. For now, the Exchange was dead.

The worst part of his advice was the amount needed for a retainer. It was a phenomenal sum of money. Turnquest told him this matter would require diplomatic intervention at the highest levels. It was a serious affair and would take a great deal of effort on an international basis to resolve it.

Robert left the lawyer's office and drove home. He went inside and began to consider his options. The ability of Complex Metals to trade in shares was now on hold. He looked at the letter -- 'con-artists' ... 'stolen securities'. He didn't know what to think. Could it be the police in Canada were so anxious to ruin their reputation that they had put together some frame-up about 'stolen securities'? It didn't seem possible, yet neither did this letter. Kesley Merry reached further than

Robert thought possible. Perhaps, Merry's work now had a life of its own. He had done such a good job spreading rumors, even cops with no malicious intent now believed Robert and Tony were heavy-duty criminals.

While he was trying to sort things through, the telephone rang. He picked it up and found it was Tony phoning from Miami. He sounded happy.

"Tony, the impossible has happened."

"What's that?"

"The RCMP has sent a letter to the Bahamian government saying we're con-artists and fugitives from Canada. Were you supposed to be in court in Vancouver yet?"

"I don't know. I haven't heard anything. My lawyers were supposed to tell me the dates. As far as I know there hasn't been a decision yet about whether there will be a trial. I swear I haven't heard a thing."

"Okay, I think you should stay put in Miami. Phillip implied that if you come here you could embarrass the Bahamian government. I'll figure out what I'm going to do. Call me tomorrow and let me know your plans. I'll wire you some money this afternoon to carry you for awhile."

"It looks like the Exchange here is dead. I've got to decide what my best option is. If I stay here and fight I'm liable to be broke before I get anything accomplished. I don't know what I'm going to do yet."

Within two days, Robert found his calls to Phillip were not being returned. An official government announcement suitably vague, was put out that the opening of the Stock Exchange was being postponed indefinitely -- a new date would be announced in the future. Sadly the idea of a Bahamian Stock Exchange never regained its impetus and to this day, has never come into being.

Robert knew he was in the same limbo he had known in Canada. There was no point continuing his business here in the Bahamas. His friends looked at him differently. Word had gone around fast. People who had known him for months now looked embarrassed or uncomfortable when he approached.

Turnquest came around to visit and was quite supportive, encouraging him to put up a good fight. Robert appreciated there were people who believed in his innocence, but he didn't have the kind of money or time to fight this thing. He couldn't hang around for a year or two, spending money on lawyers in the Bahamas and in Canada; and to what end? He knew how the financial world worked. He'd seen markets in Montreal, Toronto and New York rise and fall on the basis of rumors. You can extract all the apologies you want. It changes very little. Once a suspicion is made public, no one will ever do business with you again with the same degree of confidence.

He decided he must operate differently. Whenever he met anyone with whom he would attempt a business relationship he would explain himself. They would hear about Canada and the Bahamas and the interference of the RCMP. Then if they didn't think he was crazy or crooked, he could do business without this thing lurking in the background waiting to emerge and destroy his plans.

For now, it was important to establish a base where he could get the plans for Lillooet moving along. There must be somewhere he could feel comfortable; where he could expect a minimum of interference from Canadian subversion. He knew one place where he had a few tentative connections and where he spoke the language. Before the week was out, Robert was on a plane on his way to Rome.

The Two Hundred and Eighty-Eight Billion Dollar Fraud

WORSLEY WHISPERED FURIOUSLY to his junior while the junior scribbled equally frantically as he spoke. Tony's cross-examination of Scotland Yard's forensic scientist had created a hole the Crown would want to plug before the trial. Unfortunately for Worsley, he totally overlooked one of the main reasons this witness and his report damaged the Crown's case. Later, the defense would use this report to great effect.

The Crown's next scientific expert was William Grimsdall Stevenson. He was a Consulting Geological Engineer who worked out of Vancouver, British Columbia. Mr. Stevenson, had been hired by Pacific Nickel when the Papalias first became involved in the Lillooet Project. Robert had asked Stevenson to review a previous geologist's very promising report -- the "Kirwan Report". Later, Stevenson collected some samples himself and after having his samples assayed at a Vancouver lab, prepared a report dated November 4th, 1974.

Stevenson relied on standard fire assay procedures and his report's conclusions reflected this. Of the eighteen samples taken by him, most showed negligible amounts of gold, but five did reveal measurable quantities of 0.005 to 0.114 oz per ton.

For Pacific Nickel, these assays merely confirmed what Bert Swann had told them; standard fire assays were ineffective at detecting the precious metal content of these sands. As conventional methods were not the way to go with the project, they dispensed with Mr. Stevenson shortly after his 1974 report.

When Scotland Yard's detectives arrived in Vancouver in the summer of 1977 to conduct their investigation, they spoke to Stevenson. He stated on the basis of his assay results and several of the other conventional assay reports made available to him that "I see no possibility that the past exploration has proven the tonnage and grade of ore reported by Metals Research SA."

Stevenson's views fit well with the theory Scotland Yard was trying to develop so he was hired as an Expert witness to collect more samples, review some of the other analyses and prepare a report for the police. He was now in London to defend his conclusions in court.

Although Scotland Yard gave Stevenson all scientific data from the property his report ignored the Delta Smelting work and Dr. Schellinger's tests in the Colorado School of Mines. While his report referred to Dr. Schmuckler, discussion of her work was not mentioned in reaching its conclusions.

Under examination by Mr. Worsley that first day on the stand, Mr. Stevenson didn't say anything more damaging than the information contained in his report written for the police. In particular, Worsley was interested to get his opinion about the 'Black Brochure'.

He was asked about the brochure's estimate of 'proven reserves' stated to be approximately 890 million tons of alluvial sand containing on average 0.585 ounces per ton of gold, in addition to other precious metals. Stevenson carefully confined himself to his own work, "... in the passage ... proven reserves, there is nothing in any report I sent to Robert Papalia or his company to justify the figures shown. In fact, the reports I sent him contradict those in the brochure."

Since his samples and those collected for the police were taken from within 3 feet of surface, he was asked whether values would increase it depth. He responded that there might be increased precious metals only it the very bottom of the deposit at or near bedrock. In his opinion "... I would expect ... the amount of gold at the bottom ... to be of the order of 0.01 to 0.10 ounces per cubic yard of material." A cubic yard weighs about a ton and a half. So even its depth, he believed the gold content was well below that in the 'Black Brochure'.

He was doubtful about the three planned stages of mining set out in the brochure. According to Stevenson even the initial stage of operation, which was to process 1000 tons of material per day, would not be possible. In response to Mr. Worsley he said, "As a geologist ... I have 32 years experience ... in British Columbia, Eastern Canada, the United States, Central America and Africa. In my opinion, even the tonnage of 1,000 tons per day, envisaged in Stage A, could not be done ... within the ecological laws of British Columbia."

Presumably, the Crown was satisfied with this answer because he was not asked to elaborate or explain how he reached this conclusion.

But there was one area where Mr. Stevenson got into difficulty even before cross-examination. In his 1977 report prepared for the police and on the witness stand, he expressed an opinion regarding the amount of available tonnage for mining on the claims. The 'Black Brochure' stated the figure to be just over 890 million tons of sand and other placer material. This figure was arrived at by multiplying the total area of all the claims by the number of tons of material per claim to a depth of 150 feet.

Stevenson gave conflicting answers on this point. In his report he concluded that the available tonnage of material was approximately one-half of that stated in the brochure; -- closer to 500 million tons of sand based on an estimate of sand to a depth of 100 feet. But, in a later paragraph he opinioned that, "the sands and gravels probably extend to depths of several hundred feet." This fact should have allowed him to conclude that there was significantly more material available than set out in Metals Research's Black Brochure.

On the stand that day in referring to the 'Black Brochure', Stevenson gave the impression that to reach bedrock where there would be a significant increase in precious metal content, one would have to drill to somewhere between 1,550 to 2,300 feet. If placer material were in place to this great depth that would put the available tonnage on the claims in the ten billion ton range -- way beyond anything ever suggested by the defendants.

Other than this incongruity, Mr. Stevenson fared well as a witness in Worsley's able hands. Within half-an-hour, Mr. Worsley was finished and he sat down.

Tony was itching to cross-examine William Stevenson. It is likely that the witness held no animosity toward any defendant but merely saw his role as a professional assisting the court to reach a conclusion. That view wasn't shared by Tony. He felt under attack by a man who could give testimony against them so easily while blithely ignoring much of the important test work on the sands.

Tony began easily, asking some general items about the usual practices in the mining industry in British Columbia. Then he moved to the heart of the matter.

"Mr. Stevenson is it normal for a geological engineer, like yourself, to take your samples to a laboratory for assay by other persons not in your presence?"

"Yes it is."

"And what is your opinion of the standards of assay in British Columbia?"

"I would say the standard of assaying in British Columbia is highly regarded."

"And what is the usual method of assay in British Columbia?"

"The normal method is fire assaying and spectrographic analysis."

"Is there a legal requirement that a mining company use these forms of assay."

"No, if the geological engineer recommends the prospectus and the Securities Commission accepts his recommendations if they seem reasonable, then the method of assay would not be important."

"Are there other methods of assay known to you, Mr. Stevenson?"

"I have always used a different method for lead, zinc and copper. I believe it is known as 'wet chemical'."

"Can this wet chemical method of assay be used for precious metals?"

"I am not aware of this method having ever been used for precious metals."

"Are you saying, Mr. Stevenson, that wet chemical assay is not used for precious metals or are you saying you don't know whether it is ever used?"

Stevenson looked uncomfortable. He exclaimed, "I have no personal knowledge of wet chemical assaying for precious metals. I take the samples and send them for assay. Generally the choice of method is made by the laboratory."

Robert, sitting at the back of the courtroom silently cheered on his brother. It looked like Tony was going to be up two for two against the Crown's so-called scientific experts. Robert knew Tony's knowledge of work on the property. His understanding of the assay process was superior to the witness. Things were about to go from bad to worse for Mr. Stevenson.

"Well Sir, do you know what factors go into choosing a method of assay?"

"Certain procedures are cheaper than others and often that affects the choice."

"What about accuracy? What is the most accurate form of assay?"

"Accuracy is important. Fire assay is the oldest and most accurate method."

"Are there any new methods of assay which may work better than the standard fire method?"

"In my opinion there are no new methods which will extract more gold from a sample than a standard fire assay."

Inwardly, Tony sighed. The man was showing his lack of knowledge about conventional methods. Tony knew that fire-assaying was rarely used to assess conventional placer ore samples simply because one did not want to assay all of the gold. Rather one wanted to quantify only the recoverable metal. If Stevenson wasn't going to cooperate, Tony would have keep asking questions until he got answers he needed. For the rest of the afternoon Tony asked him about other forms of assay; where and when they were used.

Stevenson would admit to only two other methods for precious metals; atomic absorption and one used in the past century known as the sluice box method.

Tony got nothing more helpful from Stevenson that day. The witness insisted, "I don't ... recognize any assay method other than those I have just mentioned."

When four o'clock came, the magistrate asked Tony if he had many more questions. Tony replied that he expected at least a couple of hours more for the witness. "Then, we'll adjourn at this point to reconvene on Monday, the 16th. I trust no one minds missing court on Friday the 13th."

Tony regarded this adjournment as fortuitous. He would have three days to prepare his continued cross-examination of Stevenson. He intended to make the man squirm.

On Monday morning, Tony went directly to the other scientific work Stevenson claimed to have reviewed but failed to mention or consider when coming to his own conclusions. Tony asked him to compare his reported assay figures with those stated by Schellinger and Schmuckler.

Stevenson had to admit there was a significant discrepancy between his figures and the other work. But he proposed a possible explanation, "... Dr. Schmuckler's figures come from a magnetic concentrate, a small fraction of the total sample, whereas the figures in my paragraph 6 refer to the total sample."

Tony asked Stevenson to look at paragraph 5(e) of Dr. Schellinger's report, "He refers there to two tests for determining gold content in a sample, 'Microprobe' and 'Superpanning'. What are these Mr. Stevenson?"

"Microprobe and Superpanning are methods of assaying samples that include wide accuracy variations. This will be even more so if the gold is very fine."

"But, then, you are now saying these are two additional forms of assay, over and above the three forms you recognized under oath last Thursday."

"Well, yes, but as I say they tend to be very inaccurate methods. It would appear that Dr. Schellinger agrees that these methods are inaccurate because immediately following these comments in Dr. Schellinger's report he says, '... the presence of gold can only be confirmed by complete digestion and ion exchange extraction methods, neither of which are done at Stanford ...'

Before Tony could ask the witness about this statement, he added forcefully. "I wish to say I strongly disagree with Dr. Schellinger's statement. I recommend fire assaying to determine the presence of gold -- standard fire assay."

Stevenson was unwilling to bend on this issue but that was okay with Tony. By being unreasonable now, Stevenson was going to look that much worse when Tony finally got what he wanted.

In the afternoon of Stevenson's second day of cross-examination Tony turned to the question of proven reserves and the total tonnage of placer material.

"I would like to direct you to that part of your report headed 'Geology'. From where did you draw your information about the geology of the mining claims?"

"... from my reading of Mr. Kirwan's report, also from my own remembrance of many prior visits to the Lillooet area, and also, from Government reports."

"On the basis of those sources would you agree with an estimate of the depth of alluvial sand on the claims to at least 150 feet?"

"Based on my experience, I would agree that the depth is 150 feet or more."

"Then, Mr. Stevenson, could you give me a rough estimate of the total tonnage of placer material on these claims assuming a depth of 150 ft."

Stevenson shifted in his chair. With his calculator he performed a calculation he was very familiar with. "Assuming full sized placer claims and assuming 1-1/2 tons of alluvium equals 1 cubic yard, to a depth of 150 feet all the placer claims would contain 800 million plus or minus tons." He flushed as he spoke.

"Mr. Stevenson, would you look at the passage headed 'proven reserves' in the 'Black Brochure'. Does the figure that appears there correlate closely with the figure you have just given the court?"

"I see the passage ... and given my hypothesis and calculations, the figure 891,200,000 tons would be about right as a measure of alluvium. But, I do not accept that figure as 'proven reserves' as stated in the 'Black Brochure' ".

"Mr. Stevenson, would you agree that this figure is, at least, a reasonable estimate of total tonnage?"

"Assuming frequent on-site drilling without touching bedrock, I would regard the figure 891,200,000 as reasonable, but ... subject to the qualifications ... full sized placer claims and 1-1/2 tons per cubic yard."

The lawyers in the room began to sit up and take notice. Tony had extracted substantial agreement from the Crown's own expert on a significant piece of evidence. Worsley had claimed this was a preposterous figure like everything else in the 'Black Brochure'.

Tony now switched to another area of questioning. "Would you look at that part of your May 1974 report which quotes gold and silver prices?"

"Yes, I have it. Gold - $150 an ounce, silver - $5.35 an ounce."

"Now, would you refer to your letter of May 27th, 1974 and explain for the court the significance of that letter?"

Tony could see he had Stevenson off-balance.

"That is a letter I wrote to Robert Papalia following a conversation with you, about inaccuracies in my report. Pardon me, I would like to correct the word to 'inaccuracies' to 'misinterpretations' by me of Mr. Kirwan's report ... Following this conversation I sent Mr. Robert Papalia, with that letter, a corrected page 3 of my report, with the new gold and silver prices."

"And if you refer to your corrected prices, what does that tell you about the values of gold and silver present in terms of today's prices?"

"Looking at the prices for combined gold and silver, quoted on the second last line of my corrected page, I see that these values would be about five times higher by today's prices."

From that moment on the witness never regained his composure. As Tony asked more questions, Stevenson was forced to backtrack from his previously intractable positions.

"What about the quote in your report, Mr. Stevenson, which says the complex sand and gravel material did not respond to normal fire assay techniques?"

"That reference was quoting the view of Mr. Robert Craig. It is not my view."

"Mr. Stevenson since you are so certain that the standard fire assay is the most accurate and most reliable method of assay, perhaps you can tell us a little more about it. For instance, would you refer to paragraph 3, page 4 of your report and tell me whether the fire assay used by Delta Smelting and Refining Company was a standard fire assay?"

"I do not know whether Delta used a standard fire assay technique."

"No? Well, can you tell us what the temperature is for standard fire assay?"

"I don't know the temperature. I probably knew the temperature when I was in school but I have now forgotten it."

"Can you tell us the specific procedures for fire assay?"

"I do not know the specific procedures for fire assay."

This was going even better than Tony had anticipated.

"Let's look at page 5 of your report where you've attributed an assay result for gold to Dr. Schellinger, of 0.005 ounces per ton. Dr. Schellinger's later tests on the same samples using Dr. Schmuckler's ion exchange techniques showed 600 times that amount of gold as revealed by fire assay. Yet, your report completely ignores this later finding using the ion exchange technique."

"It was not that I ignored Dr. Schellinger's opinion but I did not accept it. I rejected the results reported by Dr. Schmuckler, the Colorado School of Mines, and Scientific Gold and Platinum Recovery of Princeton University. They are not pertinent to the evaluation of this property."

"Well, Mr. Stevenson, perhaps you can explain what it is about the ion exchange method of assay that causes you to reject it so completely."

The witness had to pause but eventually had to answer. "I am not familiar with the principles of ion exchange. The term is unfamiliar to me throughout my long career."

Tony was unrelenting, he asked Stevenson to comment on Dr. Schmuckler's qualifications in the Crown's evidence bundle.

"Do you think Dr. Schmuckler is capable of performing an accurate assay?"

"Looking at the qualifications of Miss (sic) Schmuckler and the 32 publications attributed to her ... I would think that she would be capable of an accurate assay. These are extremely impressive qualifications."

Under Tony's next series of questions, Stevenson had to acknowledge that an industry magazine entitled 'The Mining Journal' had published an article on Dr. Schmuckler's work entitled "New Process to Recover Precious Metals Developed by Israel Technion Researcher," Stevenson admitted he subscribed to the magazine and had read this article.

"Well, what is your opinion of Dr. Schmuckler's ion exchange technique, having read this article?"

"Reading a magazine will not make me aware of the system and principles used. The procedure of ion exchange described here is beyond my scope, I am unable to pass an opinion about it."

Stevenson had progressed from rejecting the other promising assay results out of hand to admitting that he knew nothing about ion exchange and declining to express an opinion on it. Then he acknowledged that his conclusions about compliance with ecological laws had not considered that mining would be done using ion exchange. He conceded that on the basis of the 'Black Brochure', ion exchange was the only processing method envisaged by the Company.

Stevenson tried hard to maintain his position but with virtually every answer Tony was able to exploit a weakness. He tried to say that he couldn't accept the results obtained from Dr. Schellinger's samples because he wasn't present when the samples were collected. Since Dr. Schellinger's credentials were also very impressive, Tony wanted to know if he was somehow suggesting impropriety on the part of Dr. Schellinger. Stevenson said, "No, but if I were conducting the work I would not allow a principal of the firm to assist me with the collection of samples from his property."

"Really! When you visited the Lillooet mining site on January 7th and 8th, 1975 were you not accompanied by Robert Papalia, President of Pacific Nickel?"

"I am often accompanied to such properties with the owner or principals."

"Did you collect any samples on those dates?"

"I did. I collected two sets of nine samples."

"Mr. Papalia assisted you in collecting one of the sets of samples, didn't he?"

Stevenson was really wishing this grilling would come to an end. He gulped, "Yes, but the other set of samples were collected by me personally and retained under my control and supervision until turned into the assayer."

"Do you recall putting those sets of samples into drums with the assistance of Mr. Swann, Mr. Papalia and their two laborers?"

"Yes."

"Did you seal those drums?"

"I don't recall although this may have been done under my direction."

"And how were the drums shipped?"

"Shipment was made in accordance with instruction from Mr. Papalia."

So much for Stevenson's aspersions on Dr. Schellinger's methods of collection.

The Magistrate, interrupted here, and suggested they continue the next day.

The next day was more of the same. As the two men continued their jousting Stevenson's answers were no longer delivered with the same degree of certainty. Often he qualified his response by saying "maybe I cannot be certain I do not remember I cannot say whether I agree in full".

At one point, the witness stated that a letter from International Nickel of Canada had been skeptical of assay results obtained. So Tony made him read the letter. Stevenson ended up: "I apologize for saying just now that that letter included the word 'skeptical'. This letter dated six years prior to my study expressed considerable interest in the deposit. What I meant to say is, in as much as no action was taken to my knowledge, over this six year period, I am skeptical of the merits of the assay shown in that letter ..." "... Yes, the authors of this letter represent one of the largest platinum producers in the free world."

Returning to the subject of Mr. Stevenson's own expertise in assaying Tony received the following answers: "… I have some experience in assaying but it would not be hard to have more experience than I have." "I know the procedures for fire assaying very generally. I have never, myself, performed an atomic absorption assay."

"How many assays have you performed, Mr. Stevenson?" By now Tony felt very safe in asking this question.

"I have performed one fire assay as was required in University more than thirty years ago. I performed a wet chemical assay about the same period; I have performed panning tests within the last few years."

Tony was satisfied now that he had destroyed any credibility Stevenson might have had as an expert in assay techniques. Since he was certainly not an assayer, the entire basis for his conclusions and opinions were now in dispute.

Tony tried to take Stevenson back to some of the other promising reports and get his agreement with their results. But Stevenson still resisted, But now, his answers began to appear more and more unreasonable.

The Kirwan report contained assay results from drill hole-samples taken from depths between 50 to 100 feet. Stevenson conceded that in his report referring to the Kirwan assays, he had used the phrase "these remarkably high values". He would not admit however, that this phrase was a correct appraisal of the precious metals that were present at these depths.

"… I was very suspicious of Kirwan's assay results …"

"Why?"

"… because, I understand that these assays were obtained from sand unassociated with bedrock. I would describe this as remarkable ...."

"When you visited the property, Mr. Stevenson, did you see any gold?"

"No."

"Did you find any gold as a result of your assay tests?"

"Yes, five of the samples I collected showed 'measurable' gold content, one of them erratically high."

"How deep did you dig to obtain these samples?"

"... within three feet of the surface."

"In 1975 after you gave Pacific Nickel the results of your fire assays, do you recall that I telephoned you and asked you to send part of your samples to the University of Montreal?"

"Yes, I sent part of the same samples, as you requested"

"Which assay lab was employed to test your samples?"

"General Testing Laboratory."

"Now I am going to ask you to compare the Certificates of Assay of the University of Montreal with that of General Testing Labs. Would you tell me what was the result of both assays for sample 0256C?"

"Uh, the result of the University of Montreal reads more than twice as high as the General Testing certificate. The University of Montreal assay reads 0.288 ounces/ton ... but I must add that I have no personal knowledge that the sample tested in Montreal was the same as that tested by General Testing Labs."

"But Mr. Stevenson, didn't you just testify that you sent the sample to the lab in Montreal. And didn't you also state that samples collected by you remained in your possession and supervision until you sent them to the assayers?"

Stevenson protested weakly, "I have no recollection of how the samples were delivered to Montreal." Then resignedly, "I would accept the figure of 0.288 as a reliable reading of the assay done in Montreal."

Tony had Stevenson read the assay results of the other two samples sent to Montreal. In one case the result was three times higher, in the other, four times higher than that of General Testing. It was then pointed out to Stevenson that the University of Montreal had used a modified fire assay procedure employing a higher temperature.

Despite the persistent attack on the foundations to his conclusions, Stevenson would not back down from his 'flat-earth' view of the assay process. His blind acceptance of standard fire assay methods as the only viable technique now looked wholly unreasonable to nearly everyone in the courtroom.

When Tony tried to get agreement from Stevenson that the project was viable and the company had a valuable asset in the ground, the witness disagreed.

"But," said Tony, "in this case, the envisioned recovery method is the same process as the detection method -- ion exchange, and all the gold that is detected can ultimately be extracted, don't you agree?"

"No. The extraction method used has nothing to do with the method used for detection. That is my opinion. I do not regard myself as an expert in methods of extraction. I don't regard myself as an expert in methods of assaying."

After this response Tony decided he had accomplished enough. If the man wouldn't agree with Tony, he had at least gotten Stevenson to disqualify himself as an expert by his own admission. This should mean the court would give his opinion very little weight.

There was one more detail Tony wanted to discuss. He referred Stevenson to his 1974 report and asked him to look at the section entitled 'History'.

"Would you agree, Mr. Stevenson, that there is no mention of any of the testing done on the site between 1966 and 1971 and that this reflects an inaccuracy in your report?"

"There is no mention of any work done at the site or concerning the site between 1966 and 1971. I do not agree that the omission of such facts as inaccuracy. There are several omissions of fact from this history. My history was designed to present what I considered pertinent information having to do with the property prior to submission of my report. "

Tony was thinking to himself, "and the Delta Smelting Labs assay program wasn't pertinent to his view?" Never mind, Tony had made his point about the inaccuracy of the report.

Tony asked a few more questions and then turned to Stevenson's 1977 report prepared for the police. He couldn't resist the sarcasm as he spoke, "Was this report prepared with the same accuracy as your previous report?"

The insult was not lost on Stevenson.

"My report to the police was made with the same accuracy as the previous report. It is just as reliable ..."

By now some of the observers were beginning to feel sorry for the man. There were wry smiles at this answer. He had been set up and knocked down so often by this Papalia character that one wished for the bell to ring.

Tony questioned Stevenson about the retainer he had received from the police and then decided to finish. He had cross-examined the man for four days. If he kept on, he would begin to repeat himself. Tony knew he had accomplished a lot. He told the court he was finished and sat down.

There was a visible sigh of relief from Stevenson. He had stood in the witness box for four days under assault from Tony's questions. He was both physically and mentally exhausted. He believed his ordeal was over and he was glad.

But as he turned to leave the box, Stevenson was to be disappointed yet again. When the magistrate asked if anyone else wished to examine the witness, Frascati, the Defense Counsel for Robert, the Defense Counsel for Mario and Mr. Worsley himself all stood up. During Tony's cross-examination of Stevenson, there had been a significant shift in attitude by many lawyers in the courtroom.

After Worsley's opening speech, the Defense lawyers appeared to be afraid to ask questions of the Crown's witnesses for fear of the horror it might reveal about their clients. They didn't want information to come out that would assist the Crown in convicting their clients. With the four day display of the amateur lawyer, Tony Papalia, they couldn't wait to find out more. It now looked like there were enormous holes in the Crown's case. From this moment on the Defense went on the attack while the Crown played defensive.

Frascati was the first up to ask questions. He stepped Stevenson through the 'Black Brochure' and got the following admissions:

"… I acknowledge that the year 1968 appears both in the 'Black Brochure' and also in the map contained in the research document apparently indicating some work at the site … The picture of gravel shown on page 12 of the 'Black Brochure' could be taken at Lillooet … The photograph on the right shows the kind of work carried out during a drilling program … The picture on the left could be a kind of boat used for offshore drilling."

These admissions were from the Crown's own witness about a brochure that Worsley had tried to characterize as nothing but a pack of lies.

Seeking to clarify Stevenson's position with respect to the Delta Smelting test work, Frascati asked if he used the Delta reports in making his conclusions. Despite having told the court less than an hour before that he didn't regard this work as pertinent, Stevenson now stated, "The conclusions in my November 1974 report have taken into account the material furnished by Delta Smelting."

Next, Frascati asked, "Mr. Stevenson, seeing as you were 'skeptical' of the other work by Delta as well as that carried out by Schellinger and by Schmuckler, did you ever attempt to contact these people to discuss your concerns?"

Stevenson admitted he had not tried to contact these people, although he had made 'strenuous' efforts to speak with Kirwan but was unsuccessful.

Frascati also discussed fire assaying with Stevenson and the witness repeated his view that the standard fire assay was infallible, despite all the evidence to the contrary put before him. At this juncture he was beginning to show signs of wear and tear from the unrelenting drilling. Frascati then asked a question he was surprised to hear Stevenson agree with: "Do you agree that the magnitude of the result rather than the source of the sample had a strong bearing on your reasons to reject the high readings and accept only the low ones?" Stevenson replied, "Yes." This led Frascati to his next question; one that only a defendant would ask of a witness.

"Why are you trying to sabotage the Papalia's work on this property?"

Before anyone could object, Stevenson, his frustration and exhaustion at a peak, went into a long rambling speech. The people in the courtroom sat mesmerized, not so much by what he was saying but because it was clear that he was suffering a breakdown on the stand.

> "The furthest thing from my mind is to sabotage the ongoing work at this property. When I first met the Papalias, they had two things essential for prospectors and mine developers. First, they had enthusiasm for the success of the venture they were working on; and second, a concept that development and exploration could lead to establishing an ore body. It would be a feather in my cap if I could help develop the huge deposit they envisage. I have absolutely no reason or advantage to downplay or

sabotage work at this property."

"... the enthusiasm of prospectors is often advantageously guided by consulting geologists and engineers who recommend programs to follow. The drill program I recommended represents a worthwhile endeavor. The only sabotage is that my program has not been carried out. As to my not having properly attended to this project or the work done by others, my answer is ... my services were no longer desired ... subsequent to delivery of my letter of February 11, 1975."

"This was the last contact I had with the company. As to the suggestion that I neglected the work of many, other reputable experts I would say that I used my best judgment to determine what to include, what to discount, and what to ignore in the preparation of my reports and recommendations ... I wish the very best to the Papalias and the outcome of their project."

With that, Mr. Stevenson, who had been standing for hours, literally collapsed in the witness box.

Tony glanced over at the Crown's counsel table. He was pleased to see Mr. Worsley sitting with his head in his hands. Worsley couldn't stand to watch his witness break down. The proceedings were halted by the Magistrate to instruct the sheriff to provide the witness with a seat. Once seated, he was given a glass of water and asked if he could go on.

Frascati allowed that his questioning was finished but Robert's lawyer and Berton's had one or two questions. Mr. Stevenson chose to finish his testimony and apologizing for his lapse returned to stand in the witness box.

Robert's lawyer had picked up on a detail in the evidence that he knew was important to the defense. The Forensic Lab report of Mr. Facey had shown in amount of gold in the range of 1.2 to 1.5 grams per ton on surface samples collected by Stevenson.

First he asked Mr. Stevenson to describe his reservations about all the assays.

Stevenson replied: "One of the major reservations about the results, except those obtained by myself and Mr. Bacon, is whether transport of samples was free of interference. My second reservation is that much of the assaying has been done by exotic methods."

"Well, Sir, what about Mr. Facey's results from your own surface samples, are these mere traces of gold?"

"The results shown by Mr. Facey establish that there are more than traces of gold in the surface of these alluvial sands. A result of 1.5 grams per tonne is considerably more than a trace. A trace is less than 0.15."

He concluded that despite his reservations about Mr. Facey's qualifications as an assayer, "on the basis that an average of 1.2 grams per ton is a correct measurement, the Lillooet sands are unique in my experience since such an amount of gold appears at the surface a considerable distance above bedrock."

As a final point of clarification Mr. Reide asked Stevenson's opinion of how much precious metal was present on the site.

"I do not really know what gold or silver or platinum there is underneath the Lillooet Delta."

In the world of courts and measures of proof, the Crown's case had been badly damaged by their own witness. The police and prosecutors had talked for months about the fakery of these conspirators. The Crown's position was – there are no precious metals in these mining claims. It was all a big hoax. But now the best they could say was that there was almost certainly some measure of precious metals but the Crown expert simply didn't know how much.

Mario Berton's lawyer asked one last question. Making reference to the CSMRI results using Schmuckler's process he asked whether assays of that magnitude, would interest him.

"If I discovered there was gold present in alluvial sands at 3 ounces per ton of magnetite concentrate ... that would certainly excite me."

Mr. Worsley re-examined Stevenson on several matters, but the damage done to the Crown's case would not be undone. When Mr. Stevenson finally stepped down from the stand the Crown was forced to re-access their case.

The morning after Stevenson's testimony, Mr. Worsley arrived in court with a new motto that he would repeat over and over throughout the preliminary hearing and subsequent trials:

"My Lord, on a kernel of truth is built a mountain of lies."

Tony's response to this was simple and always delivered with a laugh:

"On a kernel of ignorance, is built a mountain of nonsense."

The Crown's next scientific witness was in marked contrast to their first two.

Dr. Gabriella Schmuckler had been brought to London from her research lab at the Technion Institute in Israel to give evidence on behalf of the Crown.

The Crown supposed that this witness, with her impeccable credentials and objective scientific style, would deliver irrefutable proof of the Papalia's fraud.

Mr. Worsley's examination-in-chief was very brief.

Her qualifications were put into the record. Her undergraduate work was completed at the Technion Institute in Chemical Engineering. Thereafter she completed a Masters and Doctoral work in Chemistry also at Technion. She completed post-graduate studies at both New York University and the University of North Carolina at Chapel Hill. She had forty-odd scientific publications to her credit and four patents in the field of chemical recovery of noble metals from solution. Her active research for some twenty-five years was in the area of chemistry and separation of noble metals from solution.

At the time of the preliminary hearing Dr. Schmuckler had been elevated in status from Senior Lecturer to Associate Professor of Chemistry.

Mr. Worsley sought to show that her work was highly experimental, that it had never been used on a commercial scale, that she had no personal knowledge of the true origins of the samples sent to her lab for analysis, and that any preliminary work she had done on the Lillooet sands was long finished.

And so, Mr. Worsley got very much the answers he expected:

"My patented process is not able to detect the existence of precious metals which could not otherwise be detected by other means such as fire assay."

"Ion exchange processes are being used on a large commercial scale, but in regard to my process, one could only discover whether it could work on a commercial scale by trying it with a pilot plant and by experimenting with ever increasing quantities of resin and ore. This has not been done."

He asked about the contact she had with Robert Papalia regarding the Lillooet Project. The doctor produced photocopies of all the correspondence between herself and Robert.

When asked about the last time she had contact with Robert she responded, "My last contact with Robert Papalia was over the telephone early last year. We discussed a possible future meeting in Israel but nothing came of it."

From Worsley's questioning, it was easy to conclude that although the Papalias had listed Dr. Schmuckler in the 'Black Brochure' as a member of the technical staff of Metals Research, her work for the company was all but finished and had certainly never progressed to the stage where her process had any commercial application.

With one question however, the Crown got a response they didn't like.

Mr. Worsley asked Dr. Schmuckler, if during their last telephone conversation, Robert Papalia had expressed a reason for a future meeting.

"Yes," said Dr. Schmuckler, "the purpose of the future meeting in Israel was to make final arrangements for the testing of further samples."

At this point, the examination was abruptly concluded. The Crown had no desire to delve any further into this area.

Robert's lawyer, Mr. Reide immediately took up where the Crown had left off and pointedly asked Dr. Schmuckler to elaborate on these further tests.

"These further samples were to be one to two kilogram samples -- much larger than anything I have so far dealt with in connection with this project."

Here it was again. Each time the full truth was allowed to emerge in the course of the proceedings, it invariably put the lie to the implications of the Crown. They wanted to convince the Magistrate that the Papalias planned to dupe Dr. Schmuckler into using her credibility and her name to lend credence to a bogus creation. But in reality, the Papalias were actually contracting with Dr. Schmuckler to continue her research on a much larger scale than in the past.

Under cross-examination by Mr. Reide, Dr. Schmuckler clarified a number of points. She told the court that methods of ion extraction were known and in commercial use for sometime. Most particularly, the technique was developed during the time of the "Manhattan Project" in the early 1940's for use in recovering uranium. Other metals obtained commercially by ion exchange are the 'rare-earth elements'.

Her developed and patented 'resin' was produced commercially and exported to users in various parts of the world including a gold mine in South Africa. She had visited that mine and observed the process to be essentially the same as in her lab. The main variable in ion exchange is the composition of the resin. A resin is designed to specifically extract the metals to be recovered and for the specific orebody in question.

She believed her finding of 11 to 12 parts per million of gold in the sand was significant and that this assay justified continuation of her work on the Lillooet sands despite earlier negative and inconclusive results.

She presented an explanation as to why some assays of the sands would be so unpromising. First of all, the gold was present in both the magnetic and non-magnetic portions of the raw sand. Gold present in the magnetic fraction could be difficult to assay both by fire assay and by dissolution methods since the presence of iron can interfere with the assay for gold.

Secondly, she made it clear that assaying is to some degree an art form as much as a science. It is important to use an assayer with a very high degree of competence and personal experience with the material being assayed. The need to vary the flux according to the type of material being examined was also important. She told the court that "... under the right conditions, fire assay is a reliable technique. By right conditions, I include the need for the right flux."

Under cross-examination by Tony, she elaborated, "Reliable results of precious metal content can be achieved by fire assaying if the methods have been applied under well-defined conditions. The necessary conditions may vary widely."

Frascati lead her through the 'Black Brochure'. The doctor was able to agree with almost everything stated in the brochure. When she did find something of disagreement, her objection was a matter of degree rather than substance.

In response to questions regarding the 'Chem Bulk' sample, "The analysis of 11 to 12 parts per million of gold is a result repeated many times and reconfirmed by Neutron Activation Analysis carried out at Princeton University. I was in constant contact with these people ... I visited them in March 1973. These people are top scientists of world repute. Dr. Rosenbluth holds the Einstein medal. That is the medal which comes right below the Nobel Prize."

By the time Dr. Schmuckler's cross-examination was complete, the Crown's scientific case looked like it had disappeared.

Once again, Mr. Worsley was forced to get up and re-examine his witness hoping to strengthen his unravelling scientific evidence.

He got the doctor to agree that there was only one mining facility in the world using her process of metal extraction on a commercial basis. Then with some aggression in his voice and his manner he asked, "If it is such a promising process why is it that no other mining ventures anywhere in the world use it?"

Dr. Schmuckler, momentarily flustered by the unexpected attack of prosecutor immediately responded, "I don't know why that is the case."

Worsley also put it to Dr. Schmuckler that her knowledge of the origin of the samples she tested was limited. She agreed that she received all the samples by parcel post from either Ben Swann or Neils Skov. It was these two men who identified the samples to her is coming from the Lillooet mining claims.

Worsley moved his questioning to her previous responses about tests done at Princeton University. The doctor conceded that she had no personal knowledge about who had performed the actual analysis of the samples at that university. She also stated that the samples tested at Princeton were not provided by her.

Satisfied that he was able to underline her lack of personal knowledge of the simple origins, Worsley left his questioning with the implication that the samples had been interfered with; that gold and other metals had been added to and mixed into the sands after removal from the mine site. Worsley sat down.

Umberto Frascati stood up and advised the court that he had some questions arising from Mr. Worsley's re-examination.

Frascati was the kind of man who watched other people closely and was in tune with what they were thinking and feeling. His assessment of the current witness after seeing her demeanor on the stand was that she would do nothing malicious to hurt their case. All they needed to do was ask her questions that allowed the truth to come out -- instead of half truths.

There was another odd shift taking place in the courtroom. During his re-examination, Worsley had attempted to elicit limited yes or no answers from his own witness. He had gone on the attack using his force of will to get her agreement to the propositions he put to her. He attempted to lead her to her answers. He treated this eminent lady as though she were a hostile witness.

Umberto asked, "Dr. Schmuckler, can you think of any reason why your process is in use in only one place?"

The doctor, having time to consider her answer, and not feeling pressed responded, "One of the reasons I would think my system is only in use in one place, is the expense of changing the whole technology of an existing plant. The precious metals industry is also a very conservative industry. It is not quick to respond to change."

Then, Frascati, sensing that this was the right thing to do, moved directly to the heart of the matter, "Doctor, can you tell us whether the ore samples you tested were 'salted' with precious metals?"

There was no hesitation as the doctor answered, "In the samples I received, I would have been able to tell if these samples had been salted ... and I can say they were not salted."

This statement, in no uncertain terms, was a revelation to everyone in the courtroom, except the witness and the defendants. The defense lawyers were excited by the prospect that this scientist was able to give such a favorable opinion with such certainty.

Mr. Worsley couldn't believe it. She couldn't be right about this. How could this woman say with such authority that the samples were not salted? Mentally he admonished himself for not having found out how the witness would answer such a question. He cursed to himself. An already difficult case was now becoming much more difficult. He comforted himself with the thought that at least if the scientific evidence in his case was going 'to pot' he still had the accused own statements to the police wherein they had admitted the fraud.

There was only one question on the prosecutor's mind when he rose again from his seat, "Dr. Schmuckler, what is your reason for saying that the samples received by you were NOT salted?"

The witness was very matter-of-fact in her response.

"I say the samples which I tested were not salted, because if samples are salted they are leached into solution very easily, and my samples are not."

This was not a line of questioning Worsley wanted to pursue. The doctor appeared very certain of herself on this point. The prosecutor sat down. It was a weakness in the case he would try to repair before trial. Perhaps he could find another scientific witness to contradict her. It wouldn't be easy, though, to find someone with credentials as impressive as Dr. Schmuckler.

By now, the Magistrate had questions that he wanted to ask, "Dr. Schmuckler, when you last saw the defendants prior to these proceedings, what would you say the chances were that your system could become a commercial process?"

"At the date of my last contact with the defendants, I would have described my method as having a good chance to become a commercial process."

It was a convenient time to adjourn. The various Defense Counsels, the defendants, Geoff Lines and the other Solicitor's Clerks all met in a corner of the courtroom. The mood was buoyant. The barristers were convinced that the questioning of Dr. Schmuckler had gone better than they could ever have hoped. So far, the entire Crown case had been much in favor of the Defense.

There was still the matter of the police evidence and the defendants' admissions of guilt. But the defense team of lawyers was no longer skeptical of their clients' claims that the police had fabricated their statements. The scientific evidence had essentially vindicated them. Schmuckler's unequivocal statement that the ore samples could not have been salted simply destroyed the Crown's case. The only solid evidence left were the defendant's alleged confessions.

Reaching into Europe

(1976-1977)

WHEN HE ABANDONED the Bahamas, Robert chose Rome as his destination because it appeared to an outsider to be the obvious center of activity in Italy. It was a very important focus for the arts in Europe and had one of the largest movie production facilities outside of Hollywood. He naturally assumed that this was where the Italian business world would be centered.

He arrived at Leonardo Da Vinci Airport in early February 1976. He got a cab from the airport and accepted the cabby's recommendation of a good hotel in central Rome. Robert enjoyed the opportunity to speak Italian again. Other than his family and friends in Montreal he had rarely spoken the language over the years. Yet, given the opportunity, he spoke it flawlessly, better than English, which he spoke with an accent. Now in the cab, Robert found an initial tendency to translate his English thoughts to Italian and occasionally search his brain for an Italian word that wouldn't come.

The cabby asked questions and was very interested to hear that Robert was originally from Calabria but had grown up in North America. Then he helped Robert by answering his questions about Rome; place names, squares, streets and sections of the city where he could best open an office.

After his initial arrival, Robert spent several days exploring the city. He satisfied himself that he understood what Rome had to offer and he found an office to rent on Rome's Via Veneto. At the time he thought being on the Via Veneto in Rome was equivalent to leasing offices on Wall Street in New York.

This Roman Period was to be relatively short-lived and had an air of the comic. Robert began introducing himself to people in the business community. He had a number of long, leisurely lunches that Romans are famous for, with some of his new acquaintances.

When he returned to his office usually after 3:00 pm, he was so stuffed with the wonderful food and wine that sometimes all he could do was take a nap and prepare for the evening's nightlife. As dusk fell, it seemed there was always a party emerging somewhere in the streets of Rome.

As hard as he partied, Robert was a man who kept his commitments. During his month in Rome, he was virtually the only one to keep his appointments or to be available in his office. Planned meetings seemed to evaporate from the minds of his associates along with the champagne of the night's revelry. People were impossible to reach. No one turned up when and where they'd agreed.

Within a month he knew that Rome wasn't working out. He had become wiser about things Italian in the short time he'd been there and it was beginning to look like Northern Italy was the place to be if you were serious about work.

He remembered a fellow he had met at Monte Carlo a few years before. They had spent a long weekend with a group of international types on someone's yacht at the Cannes Film Festival. He still had his name and number somewhere. Robert searched through his business diaries, his wallet and other miscellaneous papers. He had business cards, names and address of people from around the world. Finally he was rewarded with the slip of paper he needed. The name of the man was Mario Berton. He lived in Milan. Robert picked up the phone and called him.

Mario remembered Robert well. Robert told him a little about his difficulties in Rome. Mario laughed, "Rome is for 'la dolce vita', it's not a place for work. That's why we have Milan. It is the Italian capital of business and finance."

Mario, despite his comment on Rome, was himself a proud Roman. His father's background was a mix of French and Italian. His father's family fled from the disruption and horrors of the late Napoleonic era in France and resettled in Rome. His physical appearance reflected his mixed background; tall, sandy-haired and fair-skinned. He carried himself with the air of a patrician.

Although he grew up in Rome, after being educated in Economics, he went directly into work in the financial field in Milan. By the early seventies, he was a partner in a firm of investment bankers and brokers in Milan, called CFA.

When Mario and Robert were introduced in 1972, one of the reasons they talked at length, was because Mario's firm had become the first brokerage firm in Italy to be licensed to deal in Canadian securities. At the time, Robert was President of Pacific Nickel and he told Mario about his hopes for a gold mining property in BC. He also told Mario a great deal about Montreal and how the brokerage business worked there and in other markets in North America.

They arranged to meet in a few days when Robert could come to Milan.

This time, when Robert arrived at his appointment, he found an Italian who was there to greet him. They shook hands warmly. Robert was very impressed with Mario's offices. The premises were not merely spacious and elegant, they were opulent and luxurious. The Italians have a name for it -- "faraonico" meaning very grand and impressive, echoing the architecture of the ancient Egyptian Pharaohs.

Robert looked around Mario's offices, "Very nice, Mario."

"If you are going to do business in Europe, Robert, get used to it. We Italians cannot work in the sterile and soulless little cubicles North Americans call offices. Our aesthetic feelings require our offices be pleasing to the senses."

After this commentary Mario asked, "How is your gold mine progressing?"

Robert was glad to see Mario show an immediate interest in his reason for being here. "That's why I've come to talk to you, Mario. The project is having its ups and downs, and I'm hoping you can help me get it beyond development and into production."

Over the next few days, in several meetings Robert outlined for Mario everything he thought important about the background of this deal. In addition to the test work results on the property, he related their problems with the RCMP in Canada and the reason he had been forced to leave the Bahamas.

The two discussed the mine and as Mario listened, he considered the possible impact of Canadian interference in the development of the property. From the things that Robert told him and the way he explained the geological reports, it sounded as though there was a great potential for profit.

Important decisions were made about the structure of the project once they had put together a budget for taking the test program to the pilot plant stage. Mario knew they would need some partners. They were still looking at a couple of years of development work before the project would generate money.

Mario spent a good part of his working life as a financial consultant and investment banker and it was second-nature for him to put suitable investors together with business proposals.

He began to assist Robert to create a new corporate structure. First, he found and introduced a number of Italian businessmen to Robert. Two people who became involved as investor were Baron Locatelli, who had a mining background and was from an old and wealthy Italian nobility family; and Dario Marruchi, a self-made millionaire looking for investment opportunities. The Baron agreed to become a director of the new company.

A major consideration was the form that the corporate structure should take and where it was best to incorporate, The Italian Stock Exchange even today lists only about two-hundred companies and these are what one would call "Fortune-500" companies. There is almost no provision to raise capital publicly through an exchange for a high-risk company, particularly one as high-risk as a junior resource company. There weren't any options within Italy for the promoters when it came to listing a company owning a non-producing gold mine. They must think in terms of incorporating a new company somewhere in the world where it could become public fairly quickly. For this reason they would need to look outside the said European markets.

So Tony arranged for a new company to be incorporated in Panama. It was called Metals Research Society Anonymous (MRSA). The new corporation bought all the shares of Complex Metals. While it would not be listed initially on any exchange, the shares could be traded publicly 'over-the-counter' and quoted on the Reuters world-wide wire service. Tony would focus on the American side of the company; its dealings in Canada, the USA and the Caribbean while Robert would take care of issues in Europe; financing, investment banking and metal sales.

Once the company was in place, they sought to get the research under way again. Robert contacted Dr. Schmuckler to ask her to serve on the board of the company and act as a Technical Advisor. She agreed to continue her research on the sands and to continue to refine her extraction process.

Putting the project into development was going to require the services of an engineer. They went with Robert Craig. He was familiar with the Lillooet Project from the testwork he had performed on samples over the past ten years. He had already expressed a willingness to design a pilot plant based on Dr. Schmuckler's methods of extraction.

Robert began to rebuild his dream from his base in Italy. He packed up and left Rome realizing that if he was going to do business he needed to be in an environment which nurtured it. He decided to move to Como, just across the border from Switzerland in Italy, which was still part of the fresh, alpine world of central Europe. Como was clean, orderly, and Nordic; similar to the world he left behind in Canada.

He loved waking up in the mornings to the lake and the mountain's but he hated the way the town closed in on itself in the evening. There was no nightlife. The people here were too settled and solemn to let the night impinge on their souls. Robert found himself at the end of the day with nowhere to go and nothing to do. It was just too quiet. So far, Italy struck him as a place of extremes. Rome was all play while here it was no play.

In the end, Robert did as Mario had urged him to do from the start, he moved to Milan. He rented a large and beautiful apartment on the top floor of a three hundred year old building. He had a patio that extended seventy-five meters along the street side of his building. The patio was partially enclosed by vine-covered trellises and became the perfect mix for business and pleasure. Finally, he had found the perfect mix for business and pleasure.

Milan in the mid-1970s was just starting to feel its power, and was emerging as one of the most important centers of business and fashion in modern Europe.

Now, Robert found his world 'in-sync'. He worked for months developing the social and business connections needed to make him a player and deal-maker in the Milanese community. He realized that Italy had a greater depth of wealth than Canada. There were the old-moneyed elite; mega-moguls, often of noble background. And there were the newly-moneyed upper classes arising in the world of European economic growth. It was a time in which a tiding of newly created wealth was boiling to the surface of an exuberant and resurgent Italy.

By October 1976, much had been accomplished. Robert had returned on several occasions to the Bahamas. He was instructing his lawyers about the final absorption of Complex Metals into MRSA and arranging his permanent move to Europe.

Whenever Robert was in the Bahamas, Tony would fly over to meet him from his new base in Miami. Robert relied upon Tony to take care of matters in North America. Robert would brief him on what was happening in Europe while Tony would discuss what was being done in North America. One of the tasks Tony had undertaken was to fly to Los Angeles and speak with Robert Craig about conducting the engineering work to construct and place a pilot plant at the mine site.

When it came time to finalize their agreement with Robert Craig, it was necessary for Robert, Mario, Baron Locatelli, and Dario Marruchi to travel to California. They arranged to meet with Tony and Dr. Craig at the Bonaventure Hotel in Los Angeles. The outcome of this meeting was that Craig was hired to build a pilot plant which relied upon the Schmuckler technique as the basis of the plant's operation.

After their formal discussions were sealed, the group went out for a celebration dinner. The champagne was flowing and the group was expansive, discussing their plans for the future. Robert and Tony, switched back and forth between Italian and English in an effort to include everyone in all aspects of the evening's conversation.

Dr. Craig was a Gary Cooper type; an older, somewhat cavernous, mid-western man who wore string-ties. He listened to Tony talk about the planned gold production. Finally, he interrupted, in a slightly testy impatient way, "You really don't know what you've got here, do you?"

That stopped Tony in mid-sentence, "What do you mean?"

"I mean, I've been hearing you and your brother go on and on about gold tonight as if that's all there was. The reports on the property don't only show gold. They include an array of other precious metals and when it's been tested for, platinum shows in impressive quantities. With the amount of ore available, you have one of the richest platinum deposits in the world. You have so much platinum there, you're going to have to be careful how much of it you put onto the market at one time, because your holdings could actually adversely affect the world market price for platinum."

Robert and Tony looked at one another significantly. Mario could see that he was missing something. He said "Allora?" "What?"

Robert translated what Craig had said.

This is something they hadn't spent much time considering. They knew about the platinum assays, but, at that point, their knowledge of the platinum market was rudimentary. Now they were being told they had so much of the metal, they could influence the market all by themselves.

Another bottle of champagne was ordered and a new series of toasts were drunk. The dinner carried on into the wee hours of the morning as Robert and Tony sought to extract from Craig everything he knew about platinum.

❧

On their return from this trip, Robert and Mario stopped, in the Bahamas.

They talked at length about how best to utilize Craig's information. It made sense if they were going to be producers of noble metals they should protect the value of their assets in times of volatile metal prices by having a hand in the precious metals market. Mario advised Robert that with the kind of wealth they were expecting to produce from the mine they should seriously think about diversifying their holdings. He told Robert they should look for additional investment opportunities when they returned to Italy. Mario also believed they needed a merchant bank as a financial tool to market the gold and platinum.

So while they were in the Bahamas they decided to look into forming a private bank. Robert called one of his old friends, Richard Swinnerton.

"Richard, it's Robert. I'm in Nassau for a few days with business associates from Italy. Do you think you could arrange a car to drive us to the lawyer's office? If you've got the time you can wait for us and we'll carry on afterwards to the Cumberland for some good times."

"Sounds great, Robert. I can be at your hotel in half an hour to pick you up."

The meeting with the lawyers was relatively quick. They gave Mario and Robert some summary advice about how to incorporate a closely-held private bank in any one of several Caribbean countries.

It would be necessary to have a banking office wherever they would be doing business. Initially they thought they should have a branch office in the United States, in Los Angeles and then possibly, in Europe. London seemed a particularly good spot to be based as it was an international financial center and one of the world's most important gold markets.

When Robert and Mario emerged from the law office, they found Richard waiting for them. "On to the Cumberland", Robert said, and they drove off to their favorite Bahamian watering-hole.

When they were seated and drinks were ordered, Robert asked Richard how things were going, Richard replied, "Fine, I guess. But, my contract runs out in a few months and then it's back to England to find some new employment."

As early as the previous year Richard had made it clear that he didn't feel his present career was going anywhere. He had previously hinted he'd be open to accepting a position if something was available. Robert considered this and as always acted on impulse, "You're going to England and don't have any plans?"

"Right!"

"We could use someone in England if we get this bank off the ground. How would you like to become a banker, Richard?"

Richard looked eager but said, "I don't know a thing about banking. I'm lucky if I can balance my checkbook."

Robert laughed at this, "We're not talking about the Bank of England. We won't be taking other peoples' money deposits. It'll be a private bank used as vehicle to market our company's metal production and to reinvest profits."

"Initially, all we'll need is someone in England to take care of housekeeping matters. You'll appear as a director and officer of the bank to give you added credibility, but, we won't ask you to do anything beyond your capabilities. We'll let you grow into the job."

Robert explained about the gold and platinum mine. Richard had heard Robert discuss it in the past but never in such detail. He heard again of the riches this project was expected to generate. Richard thought if he played a part in this company he could expect to become a rich man.

They talked about it some more. Robert told him not to count on it yet. There was no hurry. They were still in the planning stages and they would have to travel to the Grand Caymans to find out more about setting up a private bank. They had the name of a man in the Grand Caymans to see about incorporating a bank. Furthermore, the bank was to be in Tony's purview and Robert would have to verify with Tony whether Richard was acceptable to him. "If you take the position we'll have you working directly under Tony's supervision."

When they returned to their hotel that night, as they entered the lobby, Robert asked the concierge, "What is the fastest way to get to the Cayman Islands?"

"By charter helicopter, the people behind the desk can arrange it if you like."

Robert always had a propensity for the grand gesture and now in the wake of the euphoria of the Craig meeting he thought this sounded fine. "Yes, we'll charter a helicopter. Come with us Richard."

Richard didn't hesitate. It sounded like fun. "Certainly, if there's room."

"Of course there's room." Robert went to the front desk and asked the clerk to arrange the charter. In the morning the three of them found themselves being whisked over the azure Caribbean seas toward Grand Cayman.

Robert had telephoned Tony in Miami and he, too, was on his way and would meet them in the Caymans later in the morning.

Richard was deep in thought as he jumped to the ground. He thought about how much he would like to live like this every day of his life. This was the life that allowed you to rent a helicopter to fly around the Caribbean if you just felt like it. You just did it. He thought there really wasn't much that separated him from Robert, Tony or Mario. He and Robert were roughly the same age and both had middle-class backgrounds. Richard felt himself reasonably intelligent. The only difference between them was Robert's energy and willingness to take chances, to create his own opportunities. Richard thought that maybe this was the one big opportunity he would have in his lifetime. If he took it, who knew where his life might lead, he thought to himself, he was going to become a player. He would learn what he had to about banking and do it.

After discussions with Paul Harris at his Grand Cayman offices, instructions were given to incorporate a bank. Harris suggested that the bank be incorporated in St. Vincent. This jurisdiction was amongst the least expensive and quickest places to incorporate. Several possible names for the bank were suggested to the clients by the lawyers who would do the incorporation. Their first suggestion was "Anglo-American Trade Bank", or AATB. Their clients liked the reference to the English and American connections in the name.

❧

Towards the end of 1976 the corporate structure was in place. Metals Research made an offering to shareholders of Complex Metals. One share of Complex Metals was exchanged for four shares of Metals Research. In this way 'Complex' became wholly owned by MRSA.

The group made arrangements for the shares of MRSA to be traded on the 'Offshore Exchange'. This is a small over-the-counter market operated out of the Cayman Islands. Whenever a company is traded on an over-the-counter market it is likely that trading in such shares will remain very limited. In most cases the only people who would seek to buy shares in a company so listed would be those with knowledge of the affairs of the company and wishing to become involved in it. Nevertheless, it is possible for anyone to buy shares on the over-the-counter market subject to availability. The trading price of shares listed on the Offshore Exchange is monitored by Reuters and quoted on their Reuters Wire Service worldwide.

Metals Research SA needed someone to act as transfer agent for the Company. A transfer agent is the record-keeper of all stock transfer transactions keeping an up-to-date registry of shareholders and doing all necessary exchanges of old certificates for new ones after transfer.

Paul Harris, being a professional accountant and financial advisor, often acted as a transfer agent and registry office for client corporations. It made sense to Robert, that in addition to assisting them in establishing AATB, Harris would also act as transfer agent for MRSA.

Robert had heard of Harris because he'd done some administrative work for one of Tony's companies -- First Montreal Investment Corporation. Harris was a well-known financial expert. He gave seminars in the USA. He had written two books and audiotape speeches of his were marketed in the States. Harris was advising the St. Vincent government with respect to banking laws. Based on his reputation alone, Robert had no hesitation in retaining Harris' company, InterMart Services (IMS), to act for MRSA as transfer agent.

Besides setting up registered offices for MRSA, the group applied for a license to establish AATB. Their plans were set back somewhat when Paul told them their license would be delayed until sometime early in the New Year, since the St. Vincent government had not yet enacted certain new banking legislation. Nevertheless, it was a very satisfactory meeting in the Caymans.

Upon returning to Italy, Mario and Robert began to seek out investment opportunities in new technologies. They found two very interesting products and were able to obtain the rights to them. In the first case they obtained rights to a device which removed and recycled anesthetic gases from hospital operating rooms. A company was formed to develop, manufacture and market the machine under the name X-Laboratories Corp. (X-Labs). They created it as a wholly-owned subsidiary of MRSA.

The second subsidiary company was Sonorama Corporation. This enterprise held the world-wide rights (excluding North America) to a new type of high-fidelity surround-sound technology to be used in movie theaters. This was at a time when a great many movie houses were in the process of discarding old and antiquated sound systems and replacing them with new-technology audio sound to give their patrons a richer, more-authentic experience.

The long term plan was for profits from Metals Research to be channeled into these companies to produce and market these products around the world.

Over New Years of 1977, Robert, Mario and his wife Martine, and Tony and his wife Pattie, got together in Miami and the Grand Caymans to finalize the planning stages of their corporate development and to relax and socialize over the holidays.

When they did discuss business, Tony explained that Craig had promised to have the pilot plant in place within six weeks. He had developed a design for the plant and now it was in the hands of metal fabricators in Nevada.

The Anglo-American Trading Bank still did not have its license but Paul Harris explained that the delay was only a minor problem and they should proceed with their plans for the bank in any event.

Richard Swinnerton had now returned to England, having agreed to work for the bank and to search for suitable premises in London.

At that point in time it was looking like everything would move quickly. Craig's pilot plant should be on the property and functioning by early March. This was to be a small plant processing twenty-four tons of ore per day. The plant was to verify that the Schmuckler process worked on a continuous scale. Although it had been proven in the lab, the commercial potential of Schmuckler's technique was still unknown. Theoretically, it should be very successful and the pilot plant would prove this point. It was the first opportunity to refine the process during on-site production. If everything went well and Schmuckler and Craig were able to prove the process on a pilot plant scale, the company would then move on to the next phase of production.

Within the first three to six months of the pilot plant operation, they should know the viability of the process with a good deal of certainty. Anticipating positive results, it became necessary to think about the second phase of production when the mine would process significant quantities of ore and the company could expect to begin making money. They would want to move to the second stage of production as rapidly possible. But, a mine that could process one-thousand tons per day would be very expensive. The cost of building such a mine would be beyond the scope of their current group of private investors. Before the second stage could become a reality they would have to seek some form of public financing.

To accomplish this goal, Mario and Robert decided to put together a brochure to be used as a promotional tool when expansion to the first level of full production became an imminent reality. If the pilot plant stage was successful they could move rapidly to obtain the necessary financing.

London

(March 1977)

RICHARD SWINNERTON RETURNED to England in January 1977 and began his work for the AATB. His first task was to find suitable premises in London.

Despite his technical knowledge of building plans and structure he knew very little about London properties or the real estate market. Richard was assisted by his brother, Peter, who had many years of experience in commercial real estate in the United Kingdom as a property developer and managing agent.

Richard threw himself into the task but was soon to discover that finding a place wasn't easy. It was very much a seller's market at this time. The Arabs with their OPEC oil money were moving into London and spending money in extravagant fashion. If the son of a sheik liked a particular hotel he might just make an offer to buy that the owner couldn't refuse. Their insatiable appetite for London real estate and their seemingly endless supply of wealth had created a speculative fever in the London property market.

Richard explained his instructions to his brother. He was to find a freehold property in an exclusive part of London. The premises need not be overly large, but they wanted an adjacent apartment, where Richard could live and company executives could stay when in London.

Peter recommended a firm of London property agents to his brother and made introductions for him. With this help, Richard found two possible sites for the bank. He notified Robert who then travelled to London on January 21st.

When Robert arrived, they went to view the two properties; one at Wardrobe Place in the City and another at One Dyers Building, Holburn. Robert found the Wardrobe property unsuitable but was interested in the Dyers Building.

Robert and Richard sought Peter's advice about the amount they should initially offer. Peter advised them to start at £220,000. Robert was a bit shocked as he had been thinking of starting at a price considerably less. Robert instructed Richard to start negotiations at £160,000 and he also asked Richard to look into financing part of the purchase price with a mortgage.

❧

There was nothing exceptional about a private offshore, group coming to London to set up a bank in the mid-1970s.

Like the monolithic state-run banking systems of other European countries, for at least two centuries England had allowed the birth of a burgeoning Merchant Banking system. These private banks served to provide needed capital for commerce, to facilitate trade very much at the heart of the British economy.

After introduction of the Currency Exchange Act of 1945, a system of tax avoidance had grown up in England whereby English residents could avoid tax on international investments by using the services of private international banks with offices in England which could deal in currencies and securities other than those negotiable in Sterling. Some of the better known families that have made or added to vast fortunes through the business of merchant banking in London are the Rothschilds, the Kleinworts, the Hambros, and the Barings.

Merchant banks are devices to mobilize private capital for investment in commercial areas. They grow and survive on their good name. Reputation is almost everything in this business.

In late September of 1976, a young banker, Umberto Frascati, came to London from Milan as an employee of a small merchant bank based in England. The bank was called Bear Securities.

Umberto was hired shortly after his return to Milan from a three year sojourn in New Zealand. He had gone there in 1973, after casting aside a career as a retirement-fund manager for one of the largest government owned investment firms in Italy. In the early 1970s he had wanted to see something of the world after growing disenchanted with the stresses and strains of his career. He was offered an executive position with the largest investment bank in New Zealand. He was not required to report to the bank for several months so he chose to spend the time in itinerant travel. He went overland by car and by sea through Europe, North America, Central America and South America where he hitched a ride on a ship to his final destination.

When he arrived in Auckland and reported to the bank he realized that when the New Zealand group told him what a large concern they were, they were speaking in relative terms. New Zealand was, at that time, a country of some 2,000,000, not counting sheep. While the bank was the largest of its type in the country, it was small by any standard he'd previously known. Umberto stayed a few months but the work mostly involved lending money on mortgage securities which neither challenged nor excited him. So he left the bank.

He had come a long way to settle in New Zealand and was not yet ready to admit that he made a mistake in coming here. He and his girlfriend had romantic notions of living there when they'd planned their removal from Milan. They liked the country and Auckland was a pleasant and quiet place. They decided to open their own business and soon were running a pizza restaurant they dubbed Pinocchio. It was a success but it also became a series of endless days attached to his small business.

Umberto Frascati began to feel something he thought would never happen. He began to miss Milan and all the machinations, stresses and excitement of the life he'd thrown aside. He missed handling big deals and millions of liras or francs of other peoples who entrusted him with turning it into more money.

The thought of growing old running a pizza parlor in Auckland on the far side of the world, began to weigh heavily on him. He missed being at the center of the action.

It was only a matter of time before Umberto sold his restaurant and returned home to Milan in the last half of 1976. When he arrived, he found things had changed during his absence. The economy was on a roll again after a dip in the early 1970s.

Shortly after his return to Milan, Umberto received a call from an old friend, named Pellizzone. He and another financier, Silvera, were directors of a Swiss company, Magica Corvena. In August 1976, this company had purchased controlling interest in a small private English bank, named Bear Securities.

The bank had operated almost exclusively in lending money on the security of land mortgages. When the English parent company, Northland Foods Ltd, agreed to sell 'Bear' they retained their mortgage assets for themselves, and sold the Italians the name, the banking license and the deposit accounts held by 'Bear' at that time. This amounted to less than £60,000 held on account.

The Italian financiers wanted to develop 'Bear' into a merchant bank to attract Italian businesses to use the investment and banking services when doing business, particularly in the UK.

Umberto was one of two Italian nationals hired to develop the bank's business. It was Frascati's job to attract business to the bank. He would sometimes be in London, sometimes in Italy or elsewhere in search of customers for the bank. The official title he was given was co-manager which he shared with an Englishman named Michael Mann.

The directors and officers of 'Bear' were the two principals of the parent company, Pellizzone and Silvera; the bank's English lawyer, Colombotti; Pier-Luigi Torri; and James Maude, an Englishman who acted on behalf of the parent company to negotiate the purchase of the bank in early 1976. He continued to work for 'Bear' in an executive capacity after the acquisition.

The lawyers who acted for the new bank owners were Colombotti & Partners, a well-respected firm of London solicitors who specialized in commercial work and who acted on behalf of the Italian government in the UK.

Umberto was hired by 'Bear' within a few months of his return to Italy in the summer of 1976. He made his first trip to London in September. He was given a tour of the premises that the bank was to occupy at 11-12 Waterloo Place, London. Renovations were still underway at that time as the sale of the Bank to the Swiss-Italian group was only completed at the end of August. Frascati was also introduced to Bear's other employees at that time, including James Maude, Michael Mann and the other Italian employee, Pier-Luigi Torri.

Frascati understood that he and Torri were to have very much the same job. Frascati's first impression of Torri was that of an impressive, but distant character. He arrived at the Bank in a Rolls-Royce and dressed beautifully in British tailor-made suits. He had an air about him that caused the Bank's other employees to treat him with a great deal of deference. Upon being introduced to Frascati, he was gracious but reserved. Unlike most Italians, Frascati had never heard of Torri before, since he had been away from Europe for several years.

It was mid-October before the Bank was fully operational and its premises ready for occupancy. By this time Frascati realized Torri worked exclusively in London. He never made trips to Italy. Apparently, he had lived in London since the early 1970s and now appeared to be thoroughly ensconced in England. He was a very active fixture in the London international social scene; Frascati saw a picture of Torri in the social pages of a London newspaper as escort to Ursula Andress. He heard names like Khasoggi and Prince Faisil el Saud in connection with Torri's name. It appeared that Torri was hired by 'Bear' to attract some of the significant sums of capital floating around the London jet-set deal-makers.

He also heard through the office grapevine that there had been some sort of scandal in Italy and that Torri had left Italy under a cloud, but Torri was not the kind of person that encouraged inquiries and so Frascati never asked him anything about the rumors.

Frascati thought Torri must be quite wealthy. Not only did he live the life of a rich man, but, the work he did for 'Bear' was only a small portion of his activities. He also owned his own small bank in London, called ICB. It was obvious that Torri's work for 'Bear' was primarily a public-relations coup.

He was a high-profile, jet-set personality who could give 'Bear' exposure in London, but he really didn't spend a great deal of time in the bank. He would drop in almost daily, but rarely stayed more than the few minutes it took to inform himself of any new matters for his attention. As for Torri's other dealings and his ICB bank, that was his private affair and had nothing to do with 'Bear'. As long as he continued to act in such a consistently professional manner Frascati had no qualms about working with him.

'Bear' was only in business a little over two months and had not had any major infusions of capital nor handled any sizable transactions, when a newspaper article appeared in the London Sunday Times newspaper. The author of the article, Richard Milner, drew a connection between ICB and 'Bear' alleging that both banks were seriously deficient in many respects. He then profiled Torri as a sleazy derelict playboy. Relying heavily on innuendo and gossip, he concluded neither bank was the type with which any respectable person would wish to do business.

After the article appeared, the directors and lawyers of 'Bear' held a meeting at which they decided to sue the writers and publishers of the article for libel. Colombotti was instructed to begin a lawsuit against the London Sunday Times and Richard Milner.

In the meantime, even with this slur to their reputation hanging over them,

Frascati continued his efforts to develop a client base for the bank. He telephoned and contacted a great many members of the Milan business community to tell them about the bank. One of the people he spoke to was a prominent Italian named Santoro. Santoro mentioned that he had a possible aircraft deal in the works and he would keep 'Bear' in mind.

Frascati made contact with another businessman, Mr. Ghiardelli, who was a client of Mario Berton's brokerage firm.

After Robert returned from his first trip to London, Ghirardelli gave him Frascati's business card after learning he and Mario had business in England.

In early February, Richard contacted Robert by telephone to tell him that he had not yet had a response to their last offer on the Dyer Building but he had found a couple of other properties that Robert should examine.

On their next trip to London in the second week of February, Robert and Mario contacted Frascati and made an appointment at 'Bear'.

Robert, Richard and Mario all went to this first meeting with Umberto. There were introductions all around. The two parties took some time to explain their interests to each other. Frascati explained that 'Bear' had been acquired recently by Magica Corvena. He outlined the services the bank could provide. Frascati noted that 'Bear', did not yet have permission to hold non-resident accounts to develop its services with banks and companies abroad. However, the parent company did, and because Magica Corvina was a Swiss fiduciary company it could provide the services of a Swiss bank.

Robert told Frascati that the company he represented, Metals Research, was a mining company. He told him that MRSA already had two subsidiary companies. They now wished to incorporate an English subsidiary company in order to distribute under license the products of Sonorama.

In the course of explaining their respective positions, the discussion became general and the parties discussed the business climate in the UK, the sterling situation and the real estate market. Robert mentioned to Frascati that he was looking for premises in London on behalf of a bank, the AATB.

Frascati told Robert he couldn't be of much assistance in the London real estate market, but, he thought another of Bear's executives, an Italian named Torri, might be able to help as he had resided in London for some three to four years.

Frascati suggested they open an account at 'Bear'. But both parties had other appointments to attend so the meeting came to an end with an agreement they would meet again and continue their discussions the next day, February 10th. Frascati undertook to have Mr. Torri present at that time.

Frascati was pleased. This group looked like they had potential to become a significant client for 'Bear'. If they could impress these businessmen, the bank would be on its way to handling the kind of transactions that could be very lucrative. And with Mr. Berton's position in CFA, the well-known Milanese investment house, they could anticipate other business coming their way. He was going to do everything in his power to ensure this business would be theirs. He contacted

Torri and let him know he was on the verge of attracting a significant business client to the bank. The company's representatives were Italians and he wondered if Torri could be present at their next meeting.

Between the first and second meeting with the Bear officers, Robert and Richard continued their tour of London properties. They had not yet heard a response to their last offer to the owners at the Dyer Building and they were beginning to think that this offer was unlikely to succeed.

When they met with Frascati the next day, they had a chance to talk with Torri for the first time. Where Frascati's approach was that of the low-key, professional money-manager, Torri's forceful and sometimes, histrionic character dominated this meeting. He pushed the group to invest significant sums with him. He advised that he already had a private 'shelf' company available named Laxall Limited which he would transfer to the MRSA group for their plan to start a British distribution company. Robert and Mario instructed him to transfer ownership to MRSA and to change the name of the company to Metals Research UK Limited. They also agreed to transfer $10,000 US to the credit of 'Laxall' on account with Bear Securities as a start to dealing with the Bank. They would consider further investment later.

Robert had power-of-attorney for a private closely-held investment company, Richfield Investment Corporation. Richfield was the beneficiary of 200,000 MRSA shares. In addition to the matters discussed with Torri and Frascati, Robert decided to open an account with the Swiss company Magica Corvena, on behalf of Richfield and advised that he would send Richfield's 200,000 MRSA shares to Magica Corvena in Switzerland to be held on account.

Robert and Mario left London for Italy. Once they had gone, Richard got word that the offer on the Dyer Building was refused. Richard and Robert discussed the matter at length over the phone. On the 15th of February, Richard was told to offer £180,000 for the Dyer premises but within a week this offer was also turned down. Robert authorized Richard to increase the offer again, but soon after Richard learned that the owners of the property decided not to sell.

It was now off the market and no further offers would be considered. Richard knew that Robert was frustrated about his failure to find a building. He promised Robert that he would redouble his efforts. Poor Richard worried that what had seemed a fairly simple task had become a major problem. Affordable premises on the upscale end of the London real estate market were a rarity.

Robert was frustrated, but it wasn't just the failure to find bank premises in London that bothered him. He had hoped to have the pilot plant in operation on the property by the beginning of March. Robert Craig's last telephone call brought news about delays with the plant fabricators in Nevada. They were waiting for some parts to be shipped before they could proceed with the construction of the plant. He didn't know the exact length of the delay but would let Robert know as soon as possible.

Paul Harris in the Caymans was doing some backpedaling as well. The incorporation of AATB in St. Vincent was delayed by bureaucracy. Paul was promising to stay on top of the situation and do everything he could to expedite incorporation, but the bank was not yet licensed.

In January, several people including one of the Canadian directors of MRSA had assembled materials and put them in the hands of translators and a graphic artist in Milan. Text with pictures for a company brochure had been assembled by these creative people and was being printed. Robert was advised that five thousand brochures were ready for pick-up and the printer wanted the balance of his account paid at that time. Robert was curious, "What are we doing with five-thousand brochures. This is just a draft."

Mario smiled and shrugged, "Ask Fausta, I put it in her hands."

Robert sought out Mario's secretary, "Why did the printer run 5000 brochures? We only wanted a small first run in case we have to make changes."

Fausta was the type of smart, attractive young woman who prided herself on competence and efficiency. "The printer said that virtually all the initial cost of printing would be in the setup of the format. The full color, glossy graphics with translation into four languages was going to be very expensive, and that the same costs would be incurred whether we ordered 500 or 5000 brochures. So, I gave him the go ahead for 5000 copies."

Robert hadn't approved the mock-up version of the brochure before it went to press and he hoped it was what they wanted. As it was, this first draft version of the brochure was the only thing that was coming in on time.

Robert and Mario would have to return to London again. They would see how establishment of the English subsidiary company was going and this time, their primary interest would be to find premises for AATB.

The duo arrived in London on March 7th, 1977. It was on this trip that they found the Dragonara Hotel in Belgravia. They liked its proximity to the City and that it was situated at the end of a square away from heavy traffic. A girlfriend whom Robert had met the previous year in Miami, Sandy Fishman, came with them on this trip. They were hoping to enjoy some London nightlife while dealing with the mundane details of their business.

They toured London with Richard and the estate agent in search of premises. They went to 'Bear' and spoke to Torri and Frascati. Their discussions were a continuation of the matters regarding the English company and the market potentials for Sonorama products. Robert left copies of a London solicitor's memo outlining the legal requirement for corporate operations within the UK.

They mentioned they were having no luck finding offices for their bank. Torri explained, "It will be very difficult and costly to buy a commercial property in London. If you can lease a space you'll save money and have a wider choice."

Then he added, "You know, I'm thinking of moving to the US to get back into the movie business. If I do that I will probably close my ICB bank office here and reopen it in New York. In that event, it might be possible for AATB to take over the lease." The matter was not pursued further at that time.

Torri also advised them that their cheque for $10,000 US had been received at the Midland Bank. He mentioned that because the cheque was non-sterling funds, 'Bear' was unable to deal with the cheque. He had used his own company, ICB, to cash it and convert it into approximately £5,200, after which it was credited to their Bear account. Robert and Mario were satisfied with this. Robert asked Torri and Frascati if they would join them for dinner.

When they met at Mr. Chow's for Chinese food, Robert regretted inviting Torri. The guy had the audacity to come on to Sandy at the dinner table. He was unbelievably arrogant. This was the first and last time Robert and Mario would socialize with Torri, until they were forced together again by circumstances.

On the day that Robert and Mario left London, Richard found another potential property, a leasehold, at 4 Halkin Place. Robert told him to begin negotiations. Again there were a few weeks of offers and discussions. The first offer was turned down but on March 21st, their revised offer of £125,000 was accepted subject to Robert's approval. Richard notified Robert so another trip to London was booked for March 28th.

He was very anxious now to find premises. Early on the morning of the 25th, Paul Harris had phoned him from the Caymans to say he now had the signed banking license in hand and AATB was now a reality. Harris was pleased to make the point that their certificate number showed that the AATB was the First bank to be incorporated in St. Vincent pursuant to the new banking legislation. He sought to impress upon Robert that the delays were not his nor the lawyers' fault, but, merely a result of the St. Vincent government's dawdling in putting the mechanics of their new laws into place.

The evening of their return to London, the group met with Richard's brother Peter. He explained the various steps required before proceeding to close the deal. Robert was surprised by all the bureaucratic requirements for a nonresident company to purchase real estate in London. Richard looked a little taken aback when Peter told him that as a director his personal guarantee would probably be required on the lease. Robert conferred with Mario in Italian and then told Richard and Peter that before any final decision was made, they would have to view the property.

The next morning they made a quick stop at 'Bear' to meet Frascati. Umberto told them it had not been possible to use the name Metals Research UK Limited for their English company. It was too similar to some existing corporate names in England. They would have to choose a new name. Robert gave Frascati a list of alternate names to try.

Torri came in to the meeting while they were still discussing 'Laxall Limited'. He greeted them and then said, "I'm definitely moving my operations to New York. Perhaps you would like to see the ICB premises. If they are suitable for your bank I'm sure the lease could be assigned without any problem."

Robert's response was, "How much money would we be looking at?

Knowing their previous dealings in the London realty market, Torri said with a smile, "This property is available from year to year. You pay £8000 per annum. And, if you're interested I could sell you some of the furnishings at a reasonable price. The space has already been utilized for the purposes of a bank, and so very little renovation would be required."

This looked fortuitous. Robert said, "Certainly we'll take a look at it. We're available right now if you'd like to show us the property."

ICB was, in fact, in-the same neighborhood as 'Bear', just a brief two blocks away at 69 Pall Mall. Frascati bid them good-bye and went to attend to other business. Torri walked Robert, Richard and Mario over to ICB.

Before they even entered the bank, they were impressed by the granite-columned facade and the fancy address. To be able to say one had offices in 'Pall Mall' was to have an address that was immediately recognizable to Londoners as prestigious.

Torri made a flourishing gesture with his hands as he turned the knob on the door and beckoned them inside. He looked to their faces for their reaction as they looked around the room. The foyer was dark and somber, very much in the style of a serious banking concern. Torri could tell they were very interested.

There was a young, pretty, dark-haired woman about twenty year old sitting at a reception desk. "This is my receptionist/secretary, Miss Blot."

It turned out she was French, so Robert exchanged a few pleasantries in her native language. All the men were gracious and polite, introducing themselves and then proceeding on their tour. They looked around the offices and nodded in agreement that this was exactly the kind of building they'd been looking for. Robert, Mario and Torri began talking seriously about what was involved in taking over the lease. Torri had not yet decided when he would move his bank to the States, but, it was a small bank, the representative office here in London was not very active and he could vacate the premises on relatively short notice.

Robert let Torri know they were not yet in a position in which AATB could be a party to a contract or could become operational in London. They agreed in principle to an assignment of the lease and agreed to sign the papers and arrange to pay the buyout during their next visit to England.

Richard felt chagrined. He'd spent months looking, trying to do a job that would really impress the others, and now his efforts were being superseded by their unbelievable good fortune and the fluke of having met Torri.

Robert, Mario and Richard said good-bye to Torri on the steps of ICB. They hailed one of London's ubiquitous cabs and jumped in. "Gentlemen, it's time to go out and enjoy ourselves", said Robert.

He then turned to Richard and said, "You can stop searching, you don't need to look for more properties. We've found premises we need for AATB."

"Driver, take us to the Four Seasons Hotel."

"We'll start there and carry on until we're exhausted, or until we meet at least three beautiful women, whichever comes first."

The next afternoon Robert met with a businessman named Karniol, from

Switzerland who claimed to have contacts in the British mining industry. Robert wanted to find possible companies with both the engineering and technical background together with the financial resources to commit to building the 1000 ton per day plant.

Robert explained to Karniol that they were still very much in the preliminary stages of their work on the property. But they wanted to start planning long term for the second phase of the mine development. Karniol offered to explain the project to at least one major English mining engineering firm. For this purpose Robert gave him copies of the written material he had, the draft brochure and a copy of the research that had been carried out on the property.

He told Karniol that if anyone was interested in going to the mining site, just contact himself or his brother, Tony and the necessary arrangements would be made. He also wanted Karniol to keep in mind the financing of the project. "See if the plant can be built on a leaseback basis."

When they departed, Richard, who had accompanied Robert said, "He sounds like he's very well-connected in this business."

"He says he's a personal friend of the President of Lonrho. I'm hoping he can introduce the project to a company worth doing business with. I can take care of all the detail after the introduction. If not we've lost nothing. Karniol will get a finder's fee if we successfully contract with an English firm."

It was the end of April when Robert received word from Torri that the lease contract for 69 Pall Mail was ready to be signed. Two weeks before, Robert Craig telephoned to say that the pilot plant was now under construction. They could expect that it would be on-site in six weeks.

The plant could be operating by the middle of June. They had already arranged that after Robert Craig setup the plant and got it operating, Bert Swann would take over as site manager with a couple of men to do the actual 'grunt' labor.

Tony was arriving in Italy in a day with his wife and son, He had already arranged with Paul Harris to have the incorporation documents for AATB sent to Milan for review when they got there. They could take these to England to be kept in the offices there. There were some pro-forma resolutions that both he and Richard would have to sign.

Robert made arrangements for Tony, Mario and himself to make another trip to England on May 7th. They could finalize everything on the English end to get AATB operating. Tony wanted to see the premises and he planned to buy a car for use while in London.

❧

At the end of April much of Umberto Frascati's work was beginning to bear fruit. He had succeeded in convincing Santoro, the Milanese solicitor with the airplane deal that 'Bear' was the merchant bank he should use in London.

Santoro's client was the Cessna Aircraft dealer in Italy, a company called CAST.

The principals were a judge from Northern Italy, named Baracchini, and a businessman by the name of Boccardi.

The Italian dealership wanted to buy seven Cessna aircraft for resale in Italy. While the purchase was normally between the American parent company and its dealership, financing was to be handled by the Cessna International Corporation (CIFC); in this case through its Brussels office and the European Regional Manager, a Mr. Van Drunen.

Selling aircraft in other countries requires intervention of government departments whose mandate is to administer civil aviation. All of the parties to this deal expected that the time between delivery of the aircraft to Italy and their subsequent clearance through customs and ultimate licensing approvals and registration in Italy, would take up to three months, possibly longer.

After most of the terms of financing and the schedule of payments had been agreed to, Van Drunen noted that CIFC already carried in outstanding debt of $600,000 US for CAST on their line of credit. With so much money presently outstanding, Van Drunen told the representatives of the dealership that he felt it necessary to get additional guarantees on the purchase price while the aircraft were in limbo, after delivery but before registration in Italy.

CAST fully intended to pay for the aircraft as soon as possible after registration and sale of the aircraft in Italy, but the approximately $1.5 million US cost of the aircraft was too much money to tie up for three or more months with no return. They discussed with Van Drunen what type of guarantee he would require and ultimately the parties agreed that Van Drunen would accept three post-dated bank drafts from CAST's London merchant bank - all amounts payable in US funds for a total of $1,510,000.

Santoro, Baracchini, Boccardi and two of their associates came to London and met with Frascati, Mann and Torri. Bear Securities was very happy to act as bankers for CAST in their purchase of these aircraft. One problem would arise, however. Bear did not have a license to issue non-sterling drafts. Torri had previously used his International Commerce Bank as an intermediary when dealing in other currencies and none of the bankers anticipated a problem if they were to do so again. They met with Santoro and the CAST representatives and it was agreed that ICB would issue the drafts and the drafts would be backed by 'Bear', while 'Bear' held title to the aircraft as security until after CAST paid for the aircraft and the debt was retired.

Van Drunen agreed to all this at the time the matters were discussed.

On April 20th, 1977, Bear Securities placed in Van Drunen's possession three drafts of the International Commerce Bank. The first draft was for $503,333 US payable on March 31, 1978. The second was in the same amount and was payable on April 29, 1978. And the third was for $503,334 US payable on May 31, 1978. When Van Drunen had the drafts in his possession he handed over to Mr. Mann the title documents to the seven aircrafts.

Almost certainly if everything had gone according to plan at this point, once

CAST had the aircraft in their possession, licensed and registered in Italy they would have paid 'Bear' for their financing of the deal and other administration fees owing. They understood from Van Drunen that the amount owed to CIFC would not be cashed unless CAST defaulted on their payment schedule. 'Bear' was covered because the bank was holding the ownership certificates for the aircraft as security.

Frascati was very pleased that he had attracted such a large and impressive client. He hoped this would lead to more business for Bear's banking services.

Torri was pleased because he was able to make an additional sum of money by collecting a fee through ICB's role as issuing bank.

The transaction was not destined however, to end so uneventfully or happily. Van Drunen, rather than holding the drafts for a year until they came due thought he would sell the drafts to a third party immediately for a discounted amount. This type of trade in commercial paper is absolutely normal in the international financial world. A person holding paper having a future value of $1.5 million US may not want to wait to collect his money. Someone else may be willing to purchase the drafts at a discount immediately.

Before offering to purchase the drafts, the potential buyer will consider risk factors such as the length of time between purchase and negotiability, the strength of the currency in which the draft is made out, and the reputation of the issuing bank or financial institution. These factors will determine whether the buyer buys the drafts, and the price he is willing to pay. There is no legal requirement that one merchant bank must discount the drafts of another.

A few days after accepting the drafts and returning to Brussels, Mr. Van Drunen found that his bank would not touch his ICB drafts. He could not get them immediately discounted.

This gave Van Drunen some concern and he flew to London where he visited the main London office of Midland Bank. They told him they would not accept the drafts even if they were fully guaranteed by Bear Securities. When Van Drunen inquired as to why they refused to discount the drafts, he was shown a copy of Richard Milner's London Times article of several months before. When Van Drunen saw the allegations made against ICB and 'Bear', and the portrayal of Torri as a sleazy playboy, he became alarmed.

He left the Midland Bank, and immediately contacted Bear Securities by telephone. He told them he was on his way to the bank to discuss some very serious matters. Mr. Mann was available and he advised Van Drunen that he would meet with him upon his arrival.

Van Drunen told Mann about his inability to get the drafts discounted. Mr. Mann offered to provide whatever additional guarantees CIFC required. Van Drunen said he was unwilling to accept any sort of guarantee on any terms from 'Bear' or ICB. He told Mann as far as he was concerned the entire deal would have to be restructured.

There was nothing Mann could say to this. If 'Bear' was out of the deal that would be something CAST and Van Drunen would have to sort out.

The people at Bear Securities, in the hope of salvaging their role as financiers of the deal remained willing to give him whatever further reasonable legal assurances he desired but to no avail. He wasn't listening.

Van Drunen left 'Bear' and telephoned Italy. After his discussions with Baracchini, who was upset by the things Van Drunen was telling him, he agreed to return to England to sort out the problems that had arisen with the financing.

Neither Santoro nor Baracchini could comprehend why Van Drunen was upset. They had understood he wanted the drafts to "hold" as security. They weren't payable for a year in any event, and the whole outstanding debt was to be paid out as soon as the aircraft were registered in Italy. They did not understand why it was essential to discount the drafts immediately. Baracchini tried to explain this to Van Drunen over the phone, but neither man was able to make himself understood by the other.

Van Drunen sat in his hotel room, bothered by the events of the last few days. He had blundered into accepting a lesser security than he had intended. Santoro and Baracchini wouldn't arrive in London for at least two days. He began to think of everything that could go wrong. To be holding three potentially worthless bank drafts after he'd handed over title to the planes and after the planes were sitting in Italian Customs meant the Italians were wholly in control of the situation while he waited to see if they would replace the drafts. Nothing like this had ever happened before when he had requested additional security. He wondered what he could do to replace those drafts. He badly wanted that security.

It was the very next morning that Scotland Yard approached Van Drunen. They told him they had been watching ICB and 'Bear'. They suspected that these banks were involved in criminal activities. They wanted Van Drunen's cooperation - and they got it.

With the actions of this banker, a series of events began that would destroy the fledgling Bear Securities, would envelope people of vastly different backgrounds in one huge legal morass and would involve the English court system in one of the most useless and expensive, overblown criminal trials in English history, with a cost to the English taxpayer of millions of pounds.

On the afternoon of the next day, Umberto Frascati was at the bank when three suited gentlemen walked in and identified themselves is members of the Scotland Yard Commercial Fraud Squad. These men were unstintingly professional and polite. They proceeded to interview the employees of the bank and undertake what appeared to be an audit of 'Bear'.

While they wondered what could have prompted such an investigation, after discussions with their lawyers, the people in the bank were cooperative and continued their work while the audit went on around them.

The next day the Fraud Squad returned. This was the same day Santoro, Baracchini and Boccardi returned to London to sort out their problem with Van Drunen. They were unable to contact him upon their arrival do they decided to go first to Bear Securities to see what the bankers knew about Van Drunen's complaints. Santoro telephoned 'Bear' to arrange a meeting for mid-afternoon.

After lunch, the police audit continued at the Bank. Frascati and Mann were there awaiting their meeting with Baracchini and Santoro and Boccardi. Just after 2:00 pm a half dozen men came crashing into the bank. Frascati went to deal with them to find out what was causing this disturbance. He was shoved aside and told to shut up. The men were all coarse and vulgar, dressed in casual street clothes. The new group began barking instructions and ordering people about. Frascati watched as the leader of the Fraud Squad hastily conferred with one of his men. He then called to his team to gather up their things. Frascati asked him what was going on. "You're in the hands of the Serious Crime Squad now." Within minutes the first group of police had deserted the bank premises.

Umberto watched in amazement as this second group of officers began turning the place inside out. "What are you doing?" he asked of them.

"We are seizing all your bank records. And don't you go anywhere. You're going to have to answer some questions at the station."

Over the next couple of hours all the employees and papers were rounded up, and taken to a local station. Umberto was questioned for several hours and then released. The police were concentrating on ICB, Torri, and the Cessna bank drafts in their questioning. They also wanted to know about the Italian company that was purchasing the planes. At one point in Frascati's interrogation, one of his examiners mentioned that Santoro, Baracchini and Boccardi were now in police custody. Frascati was horrified.

"You've arrested those three gentlemen? What in the world for?"

"That is what we want you to help us with. Tell us what you know."

Frascati, of course, could do little to 'help' them. He attempted to explain the Cessna deal to the police but to no avail. When allowed to leave, he found a phone booth immediately and phoned the bank's lawyer, Colombotti. Frascati was upset but explained what he knew as best he could. His main concern was that something be done about Santoro, Boccardi and Baracchini right away.

When Colombotti discovered the Italian businessmen were in the custody of the police, he shuddered. Whatever was going on with the bank, it would ruin their business once word got out their clients were arrested by Scotland Yard.

Colombotti found that the Italians were charged with attempting to defraud CIFC. Within about two weeks of their arrest, counsel retained by Colombotti had succeeded in obtaining their release on bail.

On leaving the Magistrate Court in a London taxi, Boccardi, Santoro and Barracchini were livid with anger over all that had happened to them, not the least being their period of incarceration. They were mature, powerful men respected in the law and in business in Northern Italy. They were outraged to be accused of a crime when all they were doing, in coming to England on this trip, was attempting to sort out a financing arrangement with Van Drunen.

Colombotti dropped them at their hotel promising to find an excellent barrister for their criminal trial. As Baracchini descended from the step of the cab he turned toward Colombotti and said, "To hell with English justice."

Within a few days, when the police called to ask him more questions, Frascati heard that the three men had left England on the first available flight after returning to their hotel.

Only a few days after Santoro, Boccardi and Baracchini ended up in a British jail, Robert, Mario and Tony entered England for the final time. Five days later they as well, were arrested by Scotland Yard's Serious Crime Squad while waiting at Bear Securities to speak to a bank officer about their account.

Scotland Yard on Trial

(February 1978)

THE POLICE EVIDENCE at Committal consisted of two major parts. In late December 1977, the police brought the documents they had seized, their observations at the two banks and their physical evidence, photos, notes and recollections of their general investigations. The second part consisted of the "confessions" made by each defendant during their interrogation by CID.

Like other common law countries, Britain allows admission of a defendant's "confession" of a crime as long as the court is satisfied that the defendant gave the statement to the police freely and voluntarily. There was no strict legal requirement that these so-called "confessions" be signed by the accused.

The statements in this case were not in the defendants' handwriting; there was no evidence in the documents that any accused had even seen his "confession". On the contrary, the statements consisted of notes prepared and signed by all officers present at the interview attesting that the defendants had given the contained answers to the questions listed in the prepared witness statements.

Such a system depends on the scrupulous honesty of the police officers who take statements from criminal suspects. Following their arrest, except for Renata Harris and Madeline Blot, the defendants had alleged mistreatment and physical abuse by the police during their interrogations.

Once the police statements were made available, Tony, Robert, Mario and Umberto took issue with their purported "confessions". The statements did not represent a complete or correct version of what happened in their interviews. They were highly edited fabrications of the discussions that had occurred.

The defendant's difficulty is that the court must decide between two versions, one from the police and the other from the accused. With four or five police officers agreeing that it happened in a particular way, a defendant has no chance of being believed if his account differs.

Several months before the Committal, when Tony and the others saw their "confessions", they knew immediately they were caught in a police frame-up.

The statements conveniently omitted any of the words or deeds that would even hint at the atmosphere of oppression and abuse present during each of the interviews, there was no mention of their repeated requests for legal counsel. Many of their answers to questions were deliberately misquoted so that a denial of complicity would read as an affirmative response. For example, an answer such as "I didn't do it" would appear in the transcript as "I did do it."

Mario Berton's confession was written with both the questions and answers appearing in English. But at the time of his arrest, Mario did not speak and certainly could only understand the most rudimentary phrases in English.

When they told their lawyers that they were being framed by the police, the reply was that even if this were true, getting the confessions impugned would be an uphill battle. David Benham and the other solicitors explained that they would have to prove the oppression, the beatings and the lies. In the absence of proof, the police would certainly be believed.

While in prison awaiting their trial, the Italians spent much of their time going over and over the details of their arrest, interrogations and dealings with the police and prison authorities. They found themselves flashing back on their experiences and reliving the horror of their first weeks in custody in their dreams. They were outraged at what was happening to them.

They read and re-read the police evidence over and over again. They found minor discrepancies in the statements and sometimes one of them would recall a minor incident to be discussed with the others to establish the best strategy to reveal the lies in the police statements. When the time came in which their "confessions" were presented to the court, Tony and Umberto were ready.

The first witness was Sergeant Brian George. He testified to a visit to the mine site following arrest of the Company promoters. He described it as, "a wild, isolated piece of land with nothing on it but a half-submerged floating shack."

His testimony was the last bit of sensational journalism to appear in the London newspapers -- the headline read "Gold Mine was just a Shack!" As recently as January 1996, the British press have continued to repeat this lie in reporting on the property.

George reported that he saw no evidence of mining activity on the site but did observe a sign declaring that Metals Research was developing the property. He also found evidence of the previous sampling upon the property. Together with William Stevenson, he had scooped a sample of sand from the surface of a "beach" area to be returned to Scotland Yard's forensic laboratory for analysis.

Another officer, a Sergeant McCusker, told of his visit with Robert Craig in Sun Valley, California. On cross-examination, he admitted he had seen a pilot plant at Craig's place of work. He showed photographs of the plant and told the court that Craig said the plant was to have been moved to the mine site before the arrests. None of this evidence was ever published by the British Press.

Finally, the interrogators arrived to give their evidence. Detective Inspector Edwin Ward was first. Initially his evidence focused on the scope of the Yard's investigation. He spoke of his trip to Italy and the Grand Cayman Islands.

When the prosecutor finally advised the court that the "confessions" were about to be brought forward, the Defense team called for a "trial-within-a-trial" to establish the admissibility of the evidence. If the Crown could prove the statements were given voluntarily, they would be admitted as evidence.

The statements made by Renata Harris and Veronique Blot had been signed and adopted by each of them as true records of their interview. Since most of their statements regarding their roles at ICB and Bear were innocuous and truthful, there was no objection about their introduction as evidence. But none of the remaining defendants would concede that their statements were taken voluntarily. Neither were they a correct account of what had been said.

Initially, the police were highly amused that the Defense wished to claim that the statements were lies. How were they ever going to prove this? They all arrived in court sporting bemused and somewhat arrogant smiles. The prosecution pretended to be outraged at the position being taken by these sniveling foreigners. They had made these statements and now they simply wished to deny the evidence and claim the police were all liars.

Of course, the truth would eventually come out several years later during a Royal Commission on Criminal Procedure in the United Kingdom. The testimony at this investigation would reveal that over 90% of all criminal convictions in England during the 1970s were based on statements of guilt purportedly extracted from the mouths of the accused. These statements were all submitted to the courts by the interviewing officers -- most of the "confessions" unsigned.

This was how things were being done at the time of the Twin's case and the Serious Crime Squad really didn't anticipate this case would be much different than the others. In the early days of the Committal hearing they strutted around the environs of the courthouse like peacocks anxious to give their testimony.

In answering questions from the Crown, Ward stated, "Neither myself nor any other person in my presence held out any inducement, whether by threat or promise … to make a statement or to say anything, to any of the accused."

Robert's lawyer, Mr. Reide, began the cross. He asked Ward for information about the circumstances of Robert's arrest. Ward began reciting the date, time and place of Robert's arrest eleven months before.

Reide asked, "Have you referred to your notes prior to giving your testimony here today?" He was expecting an affirmative answer at which point, he would ask Ward to produce his notes for examination.

Instead he heard Ward state, "I have just a brief note in my notebook about the arrest. The note says: 12/5/77 II Waterloo, 4:10 pm - two Papalias and Berton arrested. See Ernie's notes. That means Detective Constable Pawley."

"Detective Inspector Ward, do your notes contain a record of what you said to Mr. Papalia at the bank?"

"I have no record of what I said or did not say when I arrested Robert Papalia."

"Are you saying there is no record of the arrest and you are relying solely on your memory as to what transpired?"

"The record would be in Detective Constable Pawley's original notes. Both of us arrested all three people at that time."

"What reason did you give Mr. Papalia for arresting him?"

"I told him I was arresting him on the charge of suspected criminal deception."

Robert watched Ward on the stand closely. He had never told Robert the reason for his arrest that day at the bank. It was clear if Ward did have any notes on the detention, the Defense would never get to see them. Instead he was going to give his recollection of times, dates and events from memory. Whatever was inconvenient to be recalled would be conveniently forgotten. All four Italians loathed this man. They felt he was the center from where all the fabrications and lies emanated. Ward admitted he had given numerous press conferences and issued press statements to sensationalize the case over the past year; coverage which led the defendants to wonder if they could ever get a fair trial.

All of them recalled the atmosphere of intimidation and violence that Ward had created with the help of his lackeys. In their view, he was not a man who cared about the truth; he only wanted to secure a conviction. The defendants believed Ward was motivated by his future career prospects which would be enhanced significantly by their conviction.

Tony had been waiting for this moment. He stood up and glared at the witness. Ward glared back. Neither of them blinked or looked away for a long time. It was clear that a contest of wills by two bitter adversaries was about to begin. Had they not been in a courtroom which demanded civility and respect for all persons, both man would have stripped off gladly and battled it out toe to toe.

Tony did not miss out any detail in his questioning of Ward. His recollection of the arrest and interrogation were so divergent from the official police version, it was necessary for the court to determine who was lying. He put his version to Ward and Ward denied it. The questions and answers that day and into the next were a litany of accusation and denial.

"When you first picked me up at Bear Securities do you recall that I asked for an attorney?"

"I recall that you did not ask for an attorney when I arrested you."

"Mr. Ward, I put it to you that the truth is that at Bear Securities you merely asked if we would accompany you to the police station."

"That is not true. I arrested you."

"Do you recall that after arriving at the police station, I again asked for a lawyer or that I be allowed to contact my Embassy."

"I deny that. You never asked for a lawyer nor did you ask for your Embassy."

Ward admitted that between May 12th when Tony was arrested and May 17th when he was first interviewed, Tony had been kept incommunicado, "I do not recall exactly what I said to the officers at Bow Road, but I believe I said that these prisoners were not to contact anybody."

Ward did not make any admissions under cross-examination that he felt were damaging. The particulars of their detention and the hours of their interviews were items on which the police were wholly frank. Ward admitted that each of the Italian defendants except Frascati, had been arrested on the 12th and all had been kept isolated in separate cells until May 18th.

Tony was held in his cell until the 17th when he was taken out and interviewed for eight hours. Robert was interviewed from 11:30 am on the 14th until 12:30 am on the 15th -- over twelve hours. Mario was interviewed on the 15th from 10:30 am until 10:20 pm – slightly less than twelve hours. They had waited in isolation until the evening of the 17th to be charged and were delivered to prison authorities on the morning of the 18th. Ward saw nothing extraordinary with the duration of this isolation and the length of the interrogations. He felt normal police procedures had been followed.

No matter how many times it was put to Ward that the defendants had asked for lawyers and Embassies, he denied that any such request was ever made.

This reply became more interesting once Ward admitted that even had a request been made for a lawyer, none would have been allowed. When Tony asked how it was that he had not been represented by a lawyer at the May 18th bail hearing Ward responded, "You were not represented because you never asked for a solicitor to be contacted."

"But, Detective Inspector Ward, you've already said you gave specific instructions that I not be allowed to communicate with anyone. I asked for a solicitor but you did not allow it."

"Although I gave instructions that you were not to be in communication with anyone, the reason that you were not represented at court was that you had not asked for any representation. Any requests of that kind would have been conveyed through a policeman. I am bound to add however, that even had such a request been made, a solicitor would not have been allowed."

When Tony moved to the issue of violence, Ward virtually spit out his denials:

"I did not come from behind my desk and put a lit cigarette up your nose with two of my men, one standing on one side, one on the other."

Tony kept at it, "Mr. Ward, do you remember your two officers on either side of me, continually beating me up for a period of seven hours?"

"I deny that."

Tony tried again, "Sir, do you recollect that throughout the interview, you and the other three men in the room, under your orders, would feed me a 'correct' response to some questions, and you would all hit, slap or kick me until I recited the answer you wanted?"

"That is not true."

"Do you recall the manner in which you and the other three officers struck me with open hand on the back of the head and other places so it would not show?"

"I do not agree that any such striking ever took place. I do not beat people up when I question them."

As Tony moved through his questions, the people in the courtroom became absorbed in the battle. As they listened to the repeated accusations and denials, there were many people who began to wonder about the truth. Not because Ward was shaky in his replies; on the contrary, he delivered his responses with deadly conviction. The doubt instead sprang from the other side -- from the way Tony put his questions together like pieces in a jigsaw puzzle. Each incident he recounted was filled with startling clarity. Either he was a consummate actor who could create details of a seven hour marathon of abuse from his own mind without notes or prompting, or else he was remembering a personal ordeal that fueled his intensity and directed his questioning.

When someone is not telling the whole truth, there are always items that tend to cast doubt on the whole of the story. It is these inconsistencies that cause highlighting in the minds of the people listening.

Tony found several flaws in Ward's story. No matter how Ward denied it, some of his explanations appeared weak and inadequate.

Tony wanted to know why the Harris, Blot and Swinnerton statements were signed. Ward claimed he had not been concerned with Blot and Harris signing their statements. The orders had come from his superiors. Fair enough, but then he opened a can of worms about Swinnerton: "... as to Mr. Swinnerton signing his record, it was suggested that he might turn Queen's Evidence."

Tony pounced on this admission. How did Swinnerton discover he could turn Queen's Evidence? Knowing he had testified about not offering coercion or inducement, Ward insisted the suggestion had come from Swinnerton.

But when pressed, his best recollection was that in the course of questioning, Swinnerton was allowed to speak to his older brother, Peter, on the telephone and the suggestion must have been first put forward by Peter to Richard and then Richard brought up the matter with his interviewers.

This allowed Tony another area of attack, if as the police claimed, all notes of the interviews were made contemporaneously and unedited, why was there nothing in the statement or any of the police notes made available to the court, about the conversations regarding turning Queen's Evidence.

In the course of Tony's questions, Ward gave the following explanations:

"... I can't recollect why Swinnerton was allowed outside contact. He had asked whether he could turn Queen's Evidence."

"... The suggestion of turning Queen's Evidence came from Swinnerton."

"... As it is not in the evidence before the Court I have no note of it."

"... There probably was a conversation leading up to Swinnerton asking to turn Queen's Evidence but he may have said 'Can I turn Queen's Evidence?' and the conversation would have followed."

Tony asked, "Why didn't you make a record of this conversation at the time?"

"At the time I did not record the incident about turning Queen's Evidence because in my opinion, such an incident was not evidence."

"... there would almost certainly have been a conversation between myself and

Swinnerton when I would have told him what turning Queen's Evidence meant and the fact that it was not my decision."

Several of the Defense lawyers in the courtroom were appalled by Ward's answers on this point. It was very difficult to believe a police officer of Ward's experience and stated concern for correct police procedure, wouldn't know the importance of making a record of such a conversation.

When questioned on this point by Swinnerton's lawyer, Ward said, "I did not think a record of such a conversation would be relevant to this court."

At this, the lawyer very pointedly asked, "Detective Inspector Ward, are you familiar with the Judge's Rules?"

As a competent police Inspector Ward was forced to answer, "Yes."

"Are you aware that the spirit of those Rules clearly state that whatever a suspect says about the matters to which he is being questioned should be recorded so the court can then decide whether those facts are relevant?"

While the lawyer was nicely setting out this proposition to the witness he was really thinking, "You bloody bastard, you know perfectly well that the 'relevance' of any part of the interview isn't for you to decide. It's for the court."

Ward knew there was only one correct response, "Yes, I am aware of that."

The lawyer then wanted to know if the other three officers were present when the unrecorded conversation took place. Ward now began to sound a little less certain in some of his answers. "I cannot clearly remember, but I would have thought the other three officers were present during the conversation ..."

"So each of these other three officers made the same decision as you - that the conversation wasn't 'relevant' and needn't be recorded?"

Ward knew he was being mocked and he lashed back. "The other officers in that room had no say in the matter, it was for me to decide alone."

The Defense raised some important questions about the circumstance in which Swinnerton's statement was taken. Unfortunately the official police version was generally upheld at this stage of the proceedings because Richard did not take the stand and counter what the police were saying.

Another major battle between the Defense and Detective Inspector Ward concerned Mario's Berton's statement.

The Defense lawyers knew when they first met Mario in prison almost two months after his arrest that his command of English was negligible. Even now, after eleven months in an English prison, his English was halting, slow, and less than comprehensive.

On the morning of Berton's interview, Ward testified he had never previously spoken to Berton. Approximately one half-hour into the interview, an interpreter was summoned. She arrived approximately two hours into the interview. The interpreter was present and assisted the police in their questions and answers for the balance of the interview.

Despite this, Ward insisted that he knew before the interview that Berton spoke English and was satisfied, upon interrogating Berton, that he both spoke and understood English perfectly well. He claimed he was aware before the interview that Berton spoke English well because "... Swinnerton told me that Berton spoke English."

It is unclear why Ward insisted that Berton was conversant in English. It is probable that the police were afraid to concede Berton's poor understanding of English to prevent opening a possible defense for him against the charges. They had already acknowledged Berton had never been near the Lillooet mining property. In fact, he had never even been to Canada. If they were forced to admit that he could not read or understand any of the corporate documents, letters, scientific reports and memos printed only in English it might not be possible to attribute the requisite knowledge to him to prove intent to defraud.

For the defendants, this insistence that Mario spoke English was another example of bungling and proof of the police attempt to frame them.

When Mario's lawyer cross-examined Ward, he was concerned with repeated requests made for a lawyer or to contact his Embassy. Ward stated that the four interviewing officers were himself, Detective Constable Pawley, Detective Constable Harrison, and Detective Constable Fowler. Ward's answers to this series of questions included the following:

"Berton was kept at Bow Road Police Station for three days until the 15th May when I and other officers interviewed him at Limehouse police station."

"... At no time did Mr. Berton ask to contact a solicitor or his Embassy."

"... At no time did I tell him he could not contact his solicitor or his Embassy."

Mario's lawyer continued, "At the beginning of the interview did Mr. Berton ask what his rights were?"

"No, neither at the beginning of the interview nor at any time did he ask that."

"Do you remember telling Mr. Berton that he had no rights?"

"I did not tell him that."

The lawyer moved to another area. "Did Mr. Berton ask for a solicitor as the interview commenced?"

"No, Mr. Berton did not ask for access to a solicitor at the beginning of the interview nor at any other time."

"Was Mr. Berton 'cautioned' during the interview?"

"There is a record that Mr. Berton was cautioned after one question at the beginning of the interview, as is shown in the record."

"Who gave the caution and what was the form of the caution."

"I would have given him the following caution: 'You are not obliged to say anything unless you wish to do so but what you say may be put into writing and given in evidence but I am only going from the notes of the interview.'"

Mario's lawyer moved to the point of this question: "Is it your opinion that Mr. Berton understood this caution given to him only in English?"

"In my mind, Mr. Berton understood English as shown by the opening question and answer."

Ward was referring to a question that read: "Do you speak, English?" The answer given was, "Yes, but, slowly please."

Mario's lawyer then wanted to know why they would then call an interpreter, if the police felt he spoke English.

"Did Mr. Berton ask for an interpreter?"

"No, he did not."

"How was it that an interpreter was called to the interview?"

"My recollection is that after about half an hour I decided to get an interpreter. She was called at about 11:00 am."

"Why would you call in interpreter for a man who speaks English?"

"I decided that the interview was proceeding slowly. In my opinion Berton does not need in interpreter but appeared to be pretending that he did."

"Had you ever previously interviewed Mr. Berton?"

"No."

"Then on what do you base your opinion when you say you believed he was pretending to need in interpreter?"

"My opinion is based upon ... several pages of questioning. This man appeared to have no difficulty understanding my questions by virtue of his answers."

"It must have been clear to you the difficulty Mr. Berton was having speaking to you in English."

"No, it was not clear. He did not appear to have difficulty speaking English."

"I put it to you that at the beginning of the interview Mr. Berton asked you for an interpreter and this request was greeted with a slap across the face."

"No, he did not ask for an interpreter. Nor did I slap him at any time."

"You don't recall either yourself or Detective Constable Harrison slapping or kicking Mr. Berton early on in the interview?"

"It is not true that I or Mr. Harrison slapped or kicked Mr. Berton at any time."

"I put it to you that before the arrival of the interpreter the questions and answers were written down without Mr. Berton speaking."

"That is not true. Those questions and answers are truly recorded."

"I put it to you that it was said to Mr. Berton that if he didn't give the answers that you wanted to hear he would be slapped and kicked."

"That is not true. I would like to add that we had no idea what answers or what facts would be given by this man."

"Was it necessary to have four officers present at the interview?"

"No, however, I decided that was the number of officers I needed to assist me."

"How did these officers assist you?"

"I needed one officer to write the note and two other officers to sort a mountain of documents."

"I put it to you that the presence of four officers at the interview was primarily for the purpose of intimidating Mr. Berton."

"That is not true." Never had Edwin Ward been subjected to such unrelenting and repeated attacks on his integrity while on the witness stand. He was a tough person and was still holding up well, to outward appearances, but, inwardly he was finding this verbal assault mentally and physically exhausting. This Committal hearing was giving him a new perspective and appreciation of the effect of harsh interrogation.

"... It is not true that I warned Mr. Berton not to complain when the interpreter arrived. Nor did any of the other officers present make such a statement."

Now his exhaustion and concern not to say the wrong thing became apparent. Almost every answer given was less certain and qualified by words to the effect of "I cannot remember..." "... It is possible that I repeated some questions after the interpreter was called, but I do not specifically remember them."

After giving this answer Ward immediately realized the mistake he had made. It is surprising that if some questions were repeated that it wasn't reflected in the so-called, unedited, contemporaneous notes of the interview and that Ward had to rely upon his faulty memory of what happened.

Then Ward denied recalling almost every detail asked of him.

"... I cannot remember whether the interpreter had a dictionary or not."

"... I cannot recall in which office these notes were read by the interpreter but I do remember it was not the same office in which the interview took place."

"... I cannot remember for how long I was present while the interpreter was reading the notes or at what stage I left the room."

"I am not sure where Berton was while the interpreter was reading the notes."

"I cannot remember whether I signed the notes before or after the interpreter."

"... To the best of my recollection during the interview most of the documents in English were just shown to Mr. Berton and he did not need them translated. I think on one or two occasions the interpreter assisted."

After this marathon of "don't recall" answers by Ward, Mario's lawyer was understandably curious about the interpreter.

"Who was the interpreter, Detective Inspector Ward?"

"A Mrs. Thea Thompson, she is on the central list of interpreters held at Scotland Yard."

The lawyer made a note of the name and, after establishing that Ward had no previous knowledge of or acquaintance with the woman, decided that it might be helpful to speak with her.

The only concession Ward would give about Berton's command of the English language, was when he finally said, "It now occurs to me that there is a substantial difference between speaking and understanding English, but I gathered he understood English from the course of our interview with him."

Berton's lawyer took his seat. At the next break, the Defense team decided to require the Crown to bring the interpreter to court for cross-examination.

More of the same took place when Ward was questioned about Robert's interview and Frascati's interview. He denied the specific instances of violence put to him. He denied either of them had ever asked at any time for lawyers or requested contact with anyone on the outside.

He denied that Robert had asked to know the names of the officers questioning him. He denied that Robert requested that the interview be tape-recorded.

Mr. Reide asked Ward about specific instances of violence Robert had related to him. "Do you recall any occasions when Pawley kicked the chair from under my client?"

"Not true."

"Two officers picked Robert up and rammed him against the wall."

"Not true ... there were no blows at any time."

"... When, at the end of the interview, while putting on his jacket, Robert's arm was seized and twisted up his back by two officers."

"Didn't happen."

Mr. Reide had a special reason for getting the denials on the record. According to Ward it was a perfectly friendly interview. Nothing untoward happened in his version of events.

Scotland Yard couldn't anticipate every possible Defense tactic. So there was a good deal of behind-the-scenes scrambling when Ward's testimony was finished and Robert's lawyers made a request that the suit he was wearing on the date of his interview be produced for the court. Robert clearly remembered that sometime in the course of his interview his waistcoat had been badly ripped while he was being manhandled. He also thought that some of the blood from his nose might have dripped onto the waistcoat. It was essential to the Defense that this article of clothing be brought before the court.

The police officer responsible for possession and storage of property in this case, Det. Const. John Sanger, appeared in court a few days later with Robert's suit. The suit he brought consisted of a suit jacket and pants. No waistcoat.

He testified, "I have been in charge of Exhibits since the beginning of the case ... storing them at the Property store at Limehouse police station. I have never had possession of a waistcoat belonging to this suit. I have never seen a torn waistcoat with bloodstains on it."

Reide cross-examined Sanger. The constable acknowledged there was a record book, itemizing all the property received into his possession.

"Have you checked the Property Book before coming to court today?"

'I have not checked the Property Book to see if it refers to a waistcoat or not."

"Constable, will you check the Property Book and bring your findings back the court?"

"I will most certainly do so."

"Have you bothered to search the Property store for a waistcoat?"

"Yes, I looked in the Property store to make sure there is no waistcoat there."

At the next break, Mr. Reide, the other Defense lawyers, Tony, Robert and

Umberto discussed these revelations. "Can you believe this? The Property man comes to court and not only does he fail to bring the Property Book with him, but he claims he neglected to look at the book."

Tony added, "They're lying. And because of that they're trying to hide evidence that will prove the lies."

Robert stated almost matter-of-factly, "I think I know a way to prove the existence of the waistcoat."

Robert's solicitors asked for Detective Inspector Ward to be recalled to the witness stand. The Defense wanted to establish the line of possession; to discover who had last seen the waistcoat; to find its current whereabouts.

Ward must receive credit at this point, because when he was called to give testimony on the waistcoat, he gave a masterful performance, obfuscating the issue and raising doubt about whether this item ever existed, or whether it was in police custody. He tried to suggest that these pants and jacket were not Robert's but rather, had been in Tony's possession during his escape. He raised the possibility that if there had ever been a waistcoat in the possession of Scotland Yard, it may have disappeared during Tony's time at large.

He said that he recalled this suit being handed down from the attic at the time Tony was re-captured.

"I have no recollection whatsoever of a third piece of clothing to this suit."

"I do not know if the waistcoat is in the store at Limehouse nor do I know if it was ever in our possession, but there are indications that it was not."

When asked to elaborate on what these "indications" might be, Ward suggested that the suit with the waistcoat was either one found in Tony's possession when he was recaptured, or, "based upon a statement made by Maxine Hibbard, a girlfriend of Robert Papalia who describes a number of articles she brought back from the dry cleaners ... she specifically said a three-piece suit."

Ward was asked, "Do you remember seeing the waistcoat in question after your initial interview with Robert Papalia on May 14th?"

"No, I do not remember seeing it."

Now was the time for Mr. Reide to put Ward's testimony to the test.

"On May 17th, Mr. Ward, all the defendants had their photos taken while in custody. Was this a full-figure photo or head and shoulders?"

"This is normally head and shoulders only." Ward was becoming wary realizing the trap that had been set for him.

"Are the photos taken on May 17th of each of the defendants available?"

"Those photographs are available but not at this stage." Ward wanted to give himself sometime to consider how to deal with this problem.

Mr. Reide concluded his examination after a few more questions. But before dismissing the witness, he requested the court to require Ward to search his files and return with the relevant pictures. The Magistrate instructed the witness to bring the photos to court.

Frascati got up at this point to question Ward about the suit and the photos.

He tried a different approach from Reide. At the time of the escape, the May 17th photos of Tony, Torri and himself were plastered all over the front pages of the London newspapers.

"Detective Inspector Ward, have you ever seen the photographs taken of the defendants on May 17th when they were charged?"

"No. However, I did try to find those photographs yesterday because that is an obvious thing to do ... I could not find them at our office in Scotland Yard. I assume they are at the Limehouse police station ..."

"Detective Inspector Ward, would Robert Papalia have had an opportunity to change his clothing between the time of his arrest on May 12th and the time of his being charged on May 17th?"

"No, his clothing would have been unchanged."

Frascati approached Ward and presented him with a newspaper print of the May 17th photos of Tony and himself. "Do you recognize these photographs?"

"Yes, they are the May 17th photos taken of Mr. Tony Papalia and yourself."

Having previously testified that he had never seen any photos it is unclear how he could now identify these newspaper pictures. Despite this, his testimony on this point was allowed. The photos were admitted as 'Exhibit 254'.

Frascati asked him to take a close look at Tony's picture and compare it to the jacket and pants brought to the court from Limehouse Property by Constable Sanger. Frascati was looking for agreement by Ward that the suit Tony was wearing in the photo could not be the one now exhibited in the courtroom.

Ward didn't agree, "This jacket appears identical to the one in the photograph of Tony Papalia."

Soldiering on, Frascati asked, "Are you unable to tell the difference in color between the jacket in the photo and the jacket in front of you?"

"I am unable from the photograph to distinguish any colors except the difference between light and dark."

It was a reproduction photo -- black and white, so it was easy for Ward to be imprecise on the question of color.

Frascati, obviously frustrated, said, "Do you know the difference between a double-breasted and a single-breasted jacket?"

"Yes, I know the difference."

"Tell me, then, the jacket in front of you, is it single or double-breasted?"

"The exhibited jacket before me is a single-breasted jacket."

"Now, Inspector, look at the photo of Tony Papalia and tell me if the jacket there is single-breasted or double-breasted?"

"I have no way of telling from the photograph of Tony Papalia whether this is a double-breasted or a single breasted suit."

"Inspector, look at the photograph, can you see the lapels of the jacket clearly?"

"Yes, they are both equally distinguishable."

"Now tell me, is the jacket in front of you the same is the one in the photo?"

"I am unable to say."

Frascati decided to leave this line of questioning. Ward was being totally uncooperative. Both the jacket and the photo were exhibited. The Magistrate could look at the exhibits himself and make a decision about whether Ward was giving reasonable responses. Anyone who looked closely at the picture and the jacket could clearly see that they were different articles of clothing.

Frascati moved his questioning to the day of his recapture. He wanted to put before the court some of his recollections of what happened. He wanted the court to hear about the guns drawn throughout their recapture, including Pawley's gun in Frascati's mouth.

Not surprisingly, Ward denied any guns were drawn at any time while the two men were being returned to police custody and that "... Mr. Pawley ... did not point his gun in your face. His revolver remained in his holster."

"How could they win against this wall of denial?" That was what Frascati found himself asking over and over again. Asking Ward for the answers was getting him nowhere. If there was a route to the truth, it would have to be found in a more round-about way. When Frascati tried again to get Ward to agree that the jacket marked as Exhibit 253 was Robert's jacket worn during his interrogation, Ward responded, "I cannot say any such thing. First, I cannot remember, as I have said, what his clothing was on that day and secondly, I have searched but have not so far been able to find the May 17th photographs."

This was where the issue was left that afternoon. The entire Defense team wondered what would happen tomorrow. Would Detective Inspector Ward return with the photographs to put before the court or would the court be told that the pictures could not be found? If the latter occurred, the Defense would be unable to prove the existence of the waistcoat, but Scotland Yard would look bad and the Defense could use this as an effective tool to whittle away the police's shrinking credibility. It was obvious the police had the pictures in September when the escape occurred as they had given all the London papers access to them. They would now have difficulty explaining their disappearance.

The Magistrate had shown exasperation on a couple of occasions when police came to testify but failed to bring the necessary records while at the same time saying they couldn't clearly remember details of the situations they were asked to recall. No matter what Ward chose to do he was taking a calculated risk, and the Defense was prepared to make the most of whatever Ward decided.

Next morning, Ward recounted that he had found the pictures of each of the defendants at the Limehouse police station, which he then produced for the court. As soon is the photos were admitted as evidence, Robert's lawyer, Mr. Reide rose and asked that the photo of Robert Papalia be given to the witness and that the jacket, Exhibit 253, be placed before him for inspection. Reide picked up a magnifying glass from the counsel table. He had brought it to court in anticipation of this moment.

Reide gave the magnifying glass to Ward and asked him to look at the original photo of Robert. Ward was cornered. There was nothing to do but backtrack completely from his previous claim that Exhibit 253 was Tony's jacket.

"Looking at the photo of Robert Papalia through a magnifying glass, it appears to me that the jacket in this photograph is identical to Exhibit 253," he said as he examined the jacket draped across the witness box.

Reide wanted one more thing, "In the photo of Robert Papalia, is he wearing a waistcoat and is it similar in color to this jacket?"

"It appears from the photograph that Robert Papalia was wearing a waistcoat of similar color to this suit jacket."

"Now, Detective Inspector Ward, we know that Robert Papalia was wearing a waistcoat on May 17th while in police custody. Has Robert Papalia remained in custody since the date of that photograph?"

"Yes, he has been in custody throughout."

"Well then, what has happened to the waistcoat?"

"At this stage, the photo is the last information we have of the waistcoat."

Reide sat down. They didn't have the waistcoat but they'd proven it existed and that Robert was wearing it during his interrogation. Having initially claimed that it didn't exist, Scotland Yard was suffering a crisis of credibility. With no explanation about the loss of the waistcoat, there were questions in everyone's mind about what the vest might prove if it could be brought to court. Was it torn and bloody? The court would never know because it disappeared without explanation while in the hands of police.

The next witness was Thea Thompson, the interpreter, present throughout most of Mario Berton's interrogation/interview. She was called to the stand at the request of the Defense team.

Worsley established her credentials as an interpreter in the Italian language. The essence of her testimony was that she had witnessed no physical abuse or threats while she was present in the room. And after the interview she read the handwritten notes of questions and answers in English to confirm they were a fair interpretation of questions and answers given. She then signed them.

Mario's lawyer rose to question her. She recalled that the questions asked during the interview were put in English, she would then put them to Mr. Berton in Italian and then she would interpret the response. Detective Inspector Ward had asked most of the questions. She thought she remembered one of the officers taking notes during the interview. She herself did not take any notes.

He was almost afraid to dig too deeply for fear he would not get the answers he needed. So far the witness had said nothing very helpful but there was one last question. He had no idea what the answer would be, but it had to be asked.

They'd accomplished nothing with this witness so far.

"Ms. Thompson, do you recall Mr. Berton asking for a lawyer or his Embassy?"

"Oh, yes. All the time."

"What did the officers present do in response to these requests?"

"I was shocked. I'd never seen anything like it. They told me to ignore the requests and they just kept at him and at him to answer their questions,"

This is as good as it ever gets for a lawyer cross-examining a witness. She was a witness who had nothing to gain by helping the Defense and whose testimony was impartial. She was giving evidence that directly contradicted Ward.

The Defense had effectively put the lie to the police allegation that four intelligent, sophisticated men had never once in five and a half days in custody requested legal counsel.

After the revelations regarding the waistcoat and the requests for lawyers, once again there was a shift in the emphasis of the case. The police had now stopped coming to court to see how the case was going. There was no more cockiness, no running into officers hanging out in the hall. The only police officers present at court now were the ones that had to give testimony. When they saw Tony coming, they looked the other way. There were no more wise-ass comments about "Perry Mason".

Aside from the disappearance of the waistcoat and the revelations about the requests for legal counsel, there were several other telling disclosures. A comic moment occurred came when the doctor who had tended to Tony in his cell the night after his police interview came to give his testimony. He entered the witness box and stated his name, Yogadeva Subramanian. He was sworn in and proceeded to answer Mr. Worsley's questions.

"I am a registered medical practitioner qualified in 1968, practicing in partnership at Bow Road in London."

"On May 17th I was called to Limehouse Station in the late evening. I saw Mr. Anthony Papalia in custody. I did not examine him. We talked in English. He complained of a headache. He did not complain of anything else. He did not say the police had ill-treated him in any way. I gave him a painkiller, Paracetamol. I would say I was with him for five or ten minutes."

"I can't recall if there was anyone else present while I was with him."

"I declared that he was fit to be detained."

"Had there been anything unusual or abnormal I would have made an entry but I have not done so. Had his clothing been disarrayed, I would have noted that and again my records do not show anything of that nature."

"Unless I looked specifically for the effect of a lighted cigarette up one nostril, I would not have noticed this. He did not mention any such thing to have happened to him."

Tony got up to conduct his cross-examination of the witness.

"Doctor, who called you to the police station that night and why?"

"I was called by the police officer in charge of the station to see Papalia, to see if he was fit to be detained."

Tony raised an eyebrow at this.

"Wasn't this interesting?" he thought. The doctor was referring to Tony in the third person. The good doctor, who claimed to have spoken to Tony for five to ten minutes not only didn't recognize his face, but neither did his accent or manner reveal his identity to the witness. There wasn't a flicker of recognition.

Tony walked closer to the witness box. There were just a few feet separating the two men. The doctor was oblivious to the connection.

"Is it customary for you to examine persons in custody to determine if they are fit to be detained?"

"No, I only check on people in custody when asked to do so."

"What reason did the police officer give for wanting you to examine Mr. Papalia in particular?"

"The officer didn't give me a reason. He told me that Tony Papalia had complained of a headache."

"Did you ask Mr. Papalia why he had a headache?"

"No, I didn't. I don't ask a patient why he has a headache. A headache is such a common complaint that one does not make enquiries about it."

"Would you look around the courtroom, Doctor, and tell me if you recognize Mr. Papalia?"

"I do not recognize Tony Papalia."

"Doctor, let me enlighten you on that point. I am Tony Papalia."

The witness looked chagrined with this revelation. He cleared his throat and looked at his feet.

"Doctor, do you remember me telling you that I had been hit for seven hours on my head and wanted to be examined?"

"I disagree that you said that to me."

"Do you remember me saying something might be broken in my head?"

"I cannot remember if you said that to me."

"Do you recall replying to this complaint, 'It happens all the time' and then shutting the door in my face?"

"I did not say that in response to any alleged complaint by you. Nor did I shut the door in your face."

"I put it to you, Doctor that you are lying in your response to my questions."

"I am not lying."

"You testified that you gave me Paracetamol. What kind of medication is that?"

"It is a painkiller, a mild painkiller like aspirin."

"What would cause you to prescribe that medication on the night of May 17th?"

"I would give that type of pill to anyone who comes to me with a headache."

"Was this visit to me at the police station an unusual occurrence for you?"

"No, I go to a lot of police stations in order to examine prisoners."

"Do any of these prisoners ever allege they have been beaten up by police?"

"From time to time."

"Do you keep a record that the prisoner was beaten by police?"

"I cannot say that a prisoner has been beaten by police or anybody else. I do, however, record when a person alleges he has been assaulted by the police."

"Then why didn't you record my complaint of assault when you spoke to me?"

"The reason was that you did not allege such a complaint."

"When you record an alleged assault what particulars do you take note of?"

"When I write these matters up I just put the words 'alleged complaint'."

"And where do you keep these records of an 'alleged complaint'?"

"In Book 83 in the police station."

"Doctor, can you give me one name, one instance when you made a record in Book 83 of an 'alleged complaint'?"

"I can't remember any name I have written down for alleged police brutality."

"In your written statement, Doctor, you said there was no complaint of injuries by Mr. Papalia. Did you enter this information in Book 83 that night?"

"No, I did not."

"You testified that you can't remember what we talked about for five to ten minutes. In the absence of your memory or a written record, why would you say in your statement that I did not complain of any injuries?"

"... When I made my statement I was asked by the officer whether you made any complaint of injury. My recollection at the time was that you hadn't."

"You made that statement one week ago, on April 4th, 1978, is that correct?"

"Yes."

"Who was the police officer who took this statement from you?"

"I cannot remember."

"Do the police officers have access to Book 83 at Bow Road Station?"

"Yes."

"Subject to the Doctor bringing Book 83 to show the court the record he made that night, I have no more questions at this time."

As soon is Tony was in his seat, Worsley raised to his feet.

"Doctor, did you refer to Book 83 prior to making your witness statement?"

"Yes, when I made my statement on April 4th, I was shown a Photostat of my notes in Book 83."

"How did you recognize this entry as your own?"

"I recognized my handwriting."

"If a man complained to you that he had been hit about the head for seven hours, would you conduct a thorough examination of him?"

"Yes, of course."

At this point Worsley stopped his questioning and had the witness stand down until Book 83 could be made available to the court. When the book arrived, Worsley was pleased that he needn't have worried about the note it contained. He didn't want any more unhappy surprises in this case. He advised the Defense he would submit the relevant part of the book as evidence, but would strenuously object to any attempt to go fishing through the book into unrelated areas in hope of finding something incriminating.

Limiting his cross-examination frustrated Tony. The other Defense lawyers told him it wasn't worth pursuing. They were into the fourth month of hearings, making this the longest Committal in English history. To go off on a tangent that might prove nothing would only irritate the Magistrate. Tony was assured he had done an excellent job impugning Subramanian's testimony by showing the doctor couldn't remember details about his statement made the previous week let alone specifics of his meeting with Tony eleven months ago.

When the witness was recalled, Worsley put the Book before the doctor. It was opened to the relevant page with those on either side fastened together with paper clips to prevent anyone leafing through the pages.

"Doctor, I refer you to Book 83, page 141. Can you peruse that page and tell me if you see the entry you made concerning Tony Papalia?"

"Yes, I see my entry. It is the second one on page 141 on the left-hand side. It reads as follows: dated 17th May; given a tablet for headache. Fit to be detained and signed. That is my signature."

This record at least proved after five days of custody following his return to his cell from his interview, his captors had called a doctor for him because of his "headache" complaint. Tony hoped the Magistrate might draw a presumption from this point.

The medical officers at Brixton Prison denied there were any sign of beatings on any of the prisoners when they arrived at Brixton on May 18th.

The best that Tony and Frascati could show was that the witnesses had absolutely no independent recollection of their examinations of the men when they arrived at the prison. The witnesses could not recognize any of the defendants. Their testimony relied on a written record of their admission to the prison and a recital of "normal practice".

"A physical examination is normal practice," said the Hospital Chief Officer.

Tony asked, "In the event a prisoner complains to the Hospital Officer or Doctor that he was beat up by police what would be done?"

"There is a well-tried routine, and I stress the word -- routine, where the doctor notes on a pro forma the exact nature of the injuries."

"And if there were no visible injuries, what would be noted?"

"The doctor would put in the register that the prisoner alleges police injuries and would note on the form 'No visible sign of injury'."

"What notations appear in the record beside my name?"

"I see your entry 'Tony Papalia'. Nothing is written against your name. There is a blank against the four Defendants' names."

"I put it to you that the system at Brixton Prison is to disregard the allegations of injuries caused by police," snapped Tony.

"That is most definitely not the case. Nor do we cover up for the police. On the contrary we note such allegations, and we treat them, whatever the cause."

It wasn't Tony's position that he had complained to the prison doctor about his injuries and that such complaints had been ignored. The truth was as follows:

the men appeared before the doctor who asked a couple of perfunctory questions whereupon they were immediately shunted off to the next place in the admission system. The examination was so brief and mechanical; there was no time or opportunity to complain. The failure to complain is understandable because since the day they had been taken into custody all their complaints had been ignored or derided. Tony's experience with Dr. Subramanian led him to conclude it was pointless to complain to anyone in the system. Now, in retrospect, all he could show was the cursory nature of the examination. The doctor's testimony supported this view.

A doctor faced with 150-200 men per day couldn't possibly get it all done if any of the men were sick and required more than three minutes. Since the doctor admitted there were many complaints and numerous drug problems, those men who came into his office with no visible signs of injury, and without complaint, were given the most superficial exam before being sent off to the prison population, certainly less than three minutes of the doctor's time.

The Defense team looked at what they had accomplished. They had some medical evidence in Tony's case, but overall, the physical evidence of police beatings was unequivocal. The "waistcoat" evidence was also equivocal, but its disappearance without explanation was enough to warrant a presumption of police complicity. It was clear that the police had lied about Mario Berton's requests for a solicitor. The circumstances of their arrests and period of time they had been held without any contact with the outside world suggested an overall atmosphere of oppression. They had made in-roads against the statement but was it enough?

It might have stopped there but the Crown decided to bring in additional witnesses to bolster their case in light of the serious allegations made against the police. Several of the police who had been present as jailors or bystanders at the police station were brought in to give evidence of what they saw between the time of arrest and imprisonment at Brixton. This resulted in a broadening of viewpoints and actually allowed the Defense to win several small victories. They were able to show a number of minor, yet important, inconsistencies.

Principal Officer Hardy, the man in charge of C wing at Brixton Prison told the court of his dealings with the prisoners in the first weeks of their arrival. He testified in a straightforward fashion -- clearly a man with nothing to hide.

He recalled an incident upon arrival of the Papalias and Berton. They applied to make a phone call. They wished to contact their families to let them know where they were. Hardy took the three men to a room and advised the Prison Governor of their request. Their request was denied on the basis that "telephone calls are allowed only on urgent matters."

They were told they could write letters to their wives and family. The first phone call any of them was allowed to make was on June 13, 1977 when Mario called his wife because she had taken ill. At that time Hardy also allowed the Papalias one phone call between the two of them.

When questioned about their ability to speak or understand English, Hardy said, "... Mr. Berton's English was very bad. I did not try to speak to Mr. Berton. It was a waste of time. Neither did Berton try to communicate with me. Papalia was always with him. It is not normal for two prisoners to see me at once. You (Tony) were there to interpret for Berton."

There were also items of evidence which raised questions about the accuracy of police notes. It began to appear that many of the notes were written after the fact. In some cases, there was evidence that the notes brought to court were edited rewrites made well after the interview.

Both Tony and Frascati lead the charge on these points.

Frascati recalled that the officer who took notes during his interview had used a blue fountain pen taken from his breast pocket. Frascati asked the officer if he recalled using a blue fountain pen. Trying to appear cooperative with in excellent memory, the officer was very happy to agree, "Yes, I recall using my blue fountain pen." Later on, when presented with his handwritten notes, he became very flustered. They had been prepared using a green-inked ball point.

The officers who took Frascati to his interview while referring to their notes, alleged he had been transported in a blue Ford car, a police detective's private vehicle. The Defense requested the Register of movement of police vehicles. The Register showed that the detective's car had been in Liverpool on that day.

When Tony cross-examined Ward about the arrest, the witness insisted only three officers had been present throughout the arrest of the Papalias and Berton. Tony tried to get to the bottom of how the three suspects had been transported to two different police stations. If only three officers were present, this meant at least two of the suspects must have been in one car. Ward claimed only himself, Harrison and Pawley were present.

"Other officers did not come to the bank premises at the time of the arrest. The three arrested persons were taken from the premises in our cars to Vine Street police station in two cars."

"I can't remember who was in each car at this stage. There were no other police officers in those cars other than the three officers so far named."

"One car would have only one police officer in it and the other car would have two police officers. I think one officer, Dryden, was alone in one of the cars with one of the prisoners but I cannot say for sure."

Where Officer Dryden materialized from is unclear. A brief minute before, Ward insisted no other officers were present.

Detective Constable John Fowler gave evidence of events that took place on the evening the men were charged. Fowler claimed he was present and had taken notes at that time of the prisoners' response to the charges. He also claimed to have recorded an incident in the finger-print room when Robert and Mario first saw one another again. The note of the fingerprinting incident read:

> 8:30 in the Finger-Print room. About to take F/P's of Berton. I am at table, typing. Robert Papalia entered and began chatting to Berton in

> Italian.
> Fowler, "If you're going to talk to him, talk in English."
> Robert P: "Mario, I've told them about the shares."
> Berton "You have what?"
> Robert P: "I've told them about Metals Research, the other companies and the shares, OK?"
> Berton slapped his forehead with hand, "Mama Mia" and something else in Italian and walked away, shaking his head.
> Signed and dated.

What exactly this note was supposed to prove isn't clear. It seems to have been placed in evidence for the potential prejudice it might cause the defendants, as opposed to its proof of any criminal wrong doing.

Robert and Mario both knew that nothing like this had ever occurred. Certainly they had spoken to each other at the time, but their words were taken out of context and their meaning twisted to suit police purposes. The most interesting point about these notes was that Fowler claimed they were made at the time of finger printing and they were signed and validated by four officers. But the wrong date occurs four times on the face of the note. Fowler had written 18/5/77 8:30 pm and 18/5/77 9:05 pm twice.

On May 18th after 6:30 pm, none of the defendants were in police custody any longer; they had made their first appearance in remand court and been transferred to Brixton Prison. It was put to Fowler on the witness stand that it wasn't possible for Robert and Mario to be anywhere near the finger-print room on May 18th and he had to agree. Now it is possible that a simple mistake in recording the correct date had occurred. But Fowler had been on shift for several hours and was present at Tony's interrogation that same day and had participated in note-taking which would have made him aware that the correct date was May 17th. At the alleged time of the incident, he had prepared finger-print reports, all of which were properly dated.

No matter that Fowler insisted the correct date was May 17th, few people watching in the courtroom were able to feel certain about much of the police testimony. There were too many little slips and the cumulative effect of these "errors" cast doubt on the police version of these statements.

Gittings, the first lawyer fired by the defendants, was brought to court by the Defense to give evidence about his meetings with Berton and the Twins.

"About May 19th, 1977 ... at this first meeting, Mr. Berton did not speak terribly fluent English but was trying hard. The Papalia brothers did the talking for Mr. Berton, and all three men complained about being knocked about by the police when they were arrested."

"As for Robert Papalia, on every occasion I saw him he complained about the police and about his treatment when first arrested. I continually said to him this was the wrong time to deal with this problem."

"... Tony Papalia told me he had been knocked about for a very long time. It went into hours, certainly not minutes ... I think he said he had been hit in the head or slapped in the face."

"... I ... listened to what I was told but ... considered it ... inappropriate to do anything ... at that time."

Tony asked Gittings, "Do you recall we wanted to sue the police?"

"Our discussions involved you wanting to issue writs and me refusing to do it. I was sacked by you because I wouldn't issue a writ against the police."

Finally, it was time for the defendants to tell their version of events; Tony and Umberto would both take the stand. As the 'trial-within-a-trial' drew to a close, it was nearing the end of April 1978. During their brief walks from the prison van into Lambeth Court each morning, the men could feel the touch of Spring. In the courtroom, they began to feel some hope -- a sense of renewal. Things had appeared to be going very well. In their phone calls to their wives and families, the men expressed their belief that the ordeal would soon be over. Frascati believed the Magistrate was becoming sympathetic to them.

If they could get the Magistrate to believe what they had to tell about what the police had done to them, then perhaps they could prevail and their case would be dismissed. All the defendants were hoping they would be walking away from this nightmare as free men in just a few weeks time.

Tony's Testimony

(March 1978)

IT WAS NOW time for the Defense to place its testimony before the court. Tony was first to take the stand. He began his evidence late on a Friday afternoon, and continued his narrative and cross-examination throughout to most of the following Monday. He was sworn in and began.

"Statements obtained from me were obtained under an atmosphere of assault and actual assault…"

Then, without prompting, he gave a complete and detailed account of everything that happened to him while in police custody.

"I was outside Bear Securities a few blocks away from the door when a man came in front of me and told me I should go back to the bank because something had happened there. I did so, walking to the bank. At that point I found a man that months later I recognized as Mr. Ward, and other individuals whose names I do not know."

"There were definitely more than three people at the bank. There were many people in the Bank and many people outside; I met Robert on the steps in animated discussion with Mr. Ward."

"He was encouraging my brother to accompany him to a police station in order to answer some questions. My brother was arguing that he was on his way to the solicitor and was already late ..."

"I agreed to go along. Then we were pushed towards some police cars and I was placed physically into a car with three people ... It was no longer a friendly incident; it was an intimidating incident... I recognize two people in the car, Mr. Harrison and Sgt. George. The third person ... I've seen him sometimes at the Thames Magistrate Court but I don't recognize him at this court."

"When we got to the police station I didn't know where anyone else was. Mr. Berton arrived in the same room as I. We sat down and I said, 'Are we guests or are we arrested.' Harrison simply replied, 'Sit down and stay there'."

"After things were taken from my pockets... somebody came and put handcuffs on me and away I went. I found myself in a car with three people again ... It wasn't the case that I went to the police station and they asked my name and about this and that. I arrived at the back door and was dragged upstairs, dragged to a cell and the door was slammed. "

"Shortly after, I tried to regain my composure and to find out where I was and what had happened. I found the bell in the wall and rang it. A person came to the cell and said 'There's nothing I can do for you'."

"I asked if I was arrested and he said, 'You are not arrested, you are in detention'."

"I said, 'If that's the case I have the right to a lawyer and an Embassy call'."

"He said, 'We can't talk to you, you must talk to the officer in your case'."

"I did not understand what that meant. This went on for five days. Anytime anybody came to the door I asked for a lawyer, asked for the Embassy contact. I asked for people to allow me a phone call. I asked for everything under the sun but nothing happened ..."

"During the night before the 17th and from the very first day I was in the police station, people would come to the door and yell. I was awakened five or six times during the night by a person coming to the cell, opening the little window and screaming."

"... During the nights of the 16th and 17th, the lights were always on in my cell ... someone would come to the door and would scream 'Hey in there' or kick the door. You would wake up because you got disturbed, the door would slam and away they would go."

"On the 17th I was picked up by Mr. Harrison and somebody else. They took me to Limehouse Station where I was placed in a room with Mr. Ward and three other people: Mr. Pawley, Fowler and Harrison."

"... I was told to sit in a chair. They were organized. Mr. Ward went behind me, lit a cigarette and put the blinds down. He started talking coming from the blinds, coming round the desk to me. As he got near me he stuck his cigarette right in here," exclaimed Tony pointing to his left nostril."

"It came close to my skin and I moved my head back. I smelled my nose hairs burning. As I moved my head back, I got hit on one side and then the other."

"Mr. Ward said, 'You have no rights, you don't get a lawyer, you sit there.' I cannot remember verbatim what was said to me by the policemen who were there, but it was all to the effect that no one knew I was there. They could do as they pleased with me, I'd get no lawyers, no Embassies, nobody. I could sit there and answer their questions."

"They said that they would beat me up. They told me they would beat the daylights out of me."

"I was leaning over in my chair and as I moved back I got slapped either side of my face and I got punched on the top of my head and my mouth was open and my mouth went cluck. From this point on for a period of seven hours except for the lunch hour I got punched and slapped mostly slapped in the back or on top of my head. After a few minutes in there I had a headache. I was trying to count from one to ten at all times just to keep my sanity."

"The discussion was 'What are you doing in England, you bunch of crooks.' I was trying to talk to them and give answers. Ward was distorting everything and writing it down ..."

"... There was a lunch break ... I said, 'I don't think I can eat lunch. I don't think I can eat anything. What I would like is a lawyer. What I would like is to tell the lawyer about you guys beating up people in this place'."

Tony continued his narrative. He told the court of being returned to the cell; the brief meeting he had with the doctor that night in his cell; the morning at Remand Court, and their arrival at Brixton.

He spent the better part of Monday telling his story and when he was done Mr. Worsley had at him.

Worsley, of course, was interested in showing that Tony was completely fabricating his allegations of police abuse.

"Mr. Papalia, you claim that you were burned by a cigarette up the nose and beaten for seven hours by police yet a short time later when Dr. Yogadeva attended upon you never showed him any sign of physical injury?"

"I did not show the doctor evidence of physical injury because the doctor was not interested in anything I would tell him ..."

"When you arrived at Brixton Prison, did you still think you had a 'broken head'?"

"By the time I got to Brixton I had survived the night therefore I did not think I had a broken head."

"So your headache was better by the next day?"

"I still felt pain in my head for two or three weeks after, in a decreasing way."

"If you still had pain when you saw the Brixton doctor, then I take it you told him about the beatings?"

"I did have pain, I did not tell him about the beatings as I was only in the room for 30 seconds and he said 'go'. I knew he wasn't interested because he gave me such a short examination."

To this point Tony had kept his anger in check with each of his replies. He had played at being a good witness, calm with sensible responses. But with Worsley's next question, his response heated up. His outrage at having to defend himself against this garbage emanating from the twisted minds of a few self-justifying police officers, finally burst through.

"You've accused a great many people, Mr. Papalia, both police officers and professionals, of lying in the course of this hearing, haven't you?"

"Since I started conducting my own case I have tried my very best to let the truth come out. When someone is lying, I accuse them."

"... I agree I have accused professional people of being liars. I am a man who believes in my rights and I am willing to fight for them."

"Mr. Papalia, if indeed you were beaten by police why didn't you tell any of these people about it?"

"I told Mr. Oxford. I told Mr. Gould. I told Swinnerton, my brother, Frascati,

Berton, and my solicitor from Bischoffs, and my barrister. I told everybody under the sun."

Worsley decided to move to another area of questioning. "At your interview on May 17th, you gave answers to the officers questions, didn't you? And you saw them writing it down?"

"As regards the interview at Limehouse on the 17th May, under the pressure I was put, by the assaults on me, although it was not my intention to give them the time of day, I tried to the best of my ability to explain my position. This was never accepted by them."

"But you saw them writing down the questions and answers?"

"I have no idea what they wrote down or what they put down although some answers and questions could be something that was taken out of context of my discussion with them. I regard the whole thing as a fabrication."

"Have you read the notes of the interview several times?"

"I have read the copy notes of the interview. As to whether I have re-read the notes, I have not done so, as I do not want to poison my mind with false garbage. I read it enough to know it was a fabrication ... a very careful fabrication including sentences that could be factual."

"You responded to the questions put to you, during your May 17th interview, didn't you?"

"Yes."

"If you thought they were manipulating the facts and fabricating answers other than what you gave, why did you bother to speak to them at all?"

"I had no idea at the time that they were fabricating the answers. The only reason I spoke to the officers on the 17th of May was because I was threatened. The fear of violence was from the very beginning. I tried to explain my position to them to the best of my ability, but they contorted everything. The whole thing was done under threat of violence or actual violence; I uttered the words yes and no on the 17th of May because I was forced to do it."

"Can you explain why the police officers would beat you to make you talk if they were then making up the questions and answers that best suited them?"

"No I cannot. No officer explained to me why they beat me instead of just writing down fabricated questions and answers."

This line of questioning wasn't furthering the Crown's case at all. Mr. Worsley handed Tony a clear copy of the typed notes of the interview. He asked him to point out specific examples of fabricated answers. Tony was happy to comply with Worsley's request. He spent the next half hour going through the notes and giving examples of incorrect "answers".

In addition to the factual inconsistencies in Tony's interview there was one page that purported to show questions and answers wherein Tony had "admitted" that they had come to England to sell shares in the Company ..."to the public and to anyone else who is interested."

"I refer to page 11 - top of page - to the question 'Was it found by experts in this field?' I was not asked that question. I did not say 'my brother and I are both experts in the mining field.'"

"I was not asked about the company being in an optimum position. I did not give the reply noted."

"I did not tell the police I was going to sell shares to the public and anybody else who was interested. I do not sell shares."

"It was not part of the venture for me, my brother and Berton to sell shares."

"I did not know about Mr. Karniol. I only learned of him when I got the papers served by you in August."

"There was no attempt to sell shares on the afternoon of my arrest. On that afternoon we were trying to sell a medical machine for hospitals in England. That company has no shares to sell."

"There was no attempt to sell shares in Metals Research to Mr. Singh."

Worsley was feeling stymied. His attempts to cross-examine this accused were allowing the witness a forum to explain his position.

Worsley moved to the issue of the waistcoat.

"If the waistcoat of Exhibit 253 was torn and bloodied, did you bother to advise Mr. Gittings, your first solicitor, of this?"

"I did not tell Mr. Gittings about the suit when he came to see me in Brixton."

"Did your brother, Robert, tell Gittings about the waistcoat?"

"I don't know; he might have."

Worsley thought he was on to something, "Are you saying that Robert forgot, or neglected to tell Mr. Gittings that his waistcoat was torn and bloodied when the police beat him?"

"There was a lot of discussion. I can't remember every word that was said. I think Robert described his position very clearly to Mr. Gittings."

Suddenly the correct answer occurred to Tony, "I am not qualified to tell counsel what Robert said to Mr. Gittings. I was not present at every meeting between the lawyer and my brother."

The prosecutor had asked Tony a question that he couldn't reasonably answer. He didn't have personal knowledge of everything that Robert had told the lawyer at Brixton. Tony could surmise what Robert had said but he couldn't give an authoritative answer. The question was only properly answerable by either Robert or Gittings. Worsley had pounced on the question because it was the first time Tony had exhibited anything less than absolute certainty on the stand. Worsley had wanted to get an "I don't know" answer so that he could make much of it. How could it be that a man whose clothes were ripped and torn during his beatings by police would not mention such a thing to his lawyer at the first opportunity? Tony had smelled the trap and had avoided it.

Mr. Worsley sat down.

Umberto Frascati's Testimony

(March 1978)

FRASCATI HAD A different but no less compelling story to tell about his treatment at the hands of the Serious Crime Squad.

For many months after the initial arrests in May, both the police and Umberto's first solicitor never flagged in their efforts to get him to turn Queen's Evidence. Frascati was problematical for the police and prosecution. He was a bright, well-educated, open and earnest man who obviously had a number of years of experience in banking and the financial services industry. His background appeared wholly legitimate. There was nothing in it that could be characterized as being even slightly sleazy.

He had arrived in London in the Fall of 1976 well after Bear Securities was bought by the Swiss parent company. Prior to that he had been in New Zealand and presumably well out of any conspiracy being planned, Frascati had nothing personal to gain from the alleged conspiracy. He was a mere employee, neither a director nor owner of the bank. Yet, he was the lynch-pin between Metals Research and Bear Securities. If the Crown was going to allege a conspiracy between the principals of the company and the bank, they needed Frascati to connect the two. When Frascati refused to "cooperate" with the police, he too, was jailed in the summer of 1977 with the others.

Frascati took the stand and recalled the events of May 1977.

"On May 6th ... I arrived at Bear Securities at about 10 o'clock in the morning. There were two dozen uniformed and non-uniformed policemen in the bank."

"As I entered, a couple of policemen asked me my name which I gave. Then Mr. Mann showed me a search warrant and explained this as the reason why the policemen were present on the premises."

"In the bank is a very large room and I was shown into that room together with many, many people. I would say I was there more than an hour. During that time we all had coffee. A policeman asked me why in the address book of the bank there were the names of a Swiss bank. I laughed and said 'Because you are in a bank. Therefore you will probably find the addresses of other banks.' Then a conversation took place about different things. I tried to help the secretary who was under stress and crying."

"Mr. McCusker asked me if I would walk with him down to the basement, and we were followed by a uniformed policeman, and I sat with the uniformed policeman for about an hour in Mr. Maude's office. At that point I was left alone with the uniformed policeman."

"I asked for leave to go to the toilet. In fact, I walked to the toilet and the uniformed policeman told me that I could not move unless he received orders. So I asked the Officer-in-Charge if I could go to the toilet and the reply was 'Yes, but the uniformed policeman will stand behind you'."

"I was then asked to go upstairs to the hall and there was Mr. McCusker and another policeman in uniform, and they told me they needed to ask me a few questions. I was the only person in the bank by that time. Everybody else had left. I said okay, my understanding being that I would be taken to a police office and would be asked a few questions about the papers the policemen were carrying from the bank."

"I was taken to a grey-colored Rover by three officers. We drove for quite a long time and went into a police station which I later learned was West Ham."

"I was put against a wall. I was asked to take all my personal belongings out of my pocket. Then one of the policemen told me I had to stay very quiet in my cell to think over everything, and to give cooperative answers when I was asked to go for the interview, as my freedom might depend upon it. So, I was put into an isolation cell and I didn't see anybody except the police station officers."

"In the afternoon I asked one of them to call my Embassy and a solicitor and my relatives. The reply was 'I cannot authorize anything of this sort unless I am ordered by the chief policeman in your investigation.' I asked him to contact the chief policeman immediately and ask him. I did not receive a reply or see the officer again that day. At a later stage, during the night I complained to the same officer that I did not receive any answer. He said that he could not add anything to what he had said before."

"I complained about the toilet water, which was flushing and interrupting my peace for about ten hours. I complained about dogs barking and he said he would try to calm them down. The lights in the cell were kept on all night. I was kept in isolation for three days."

"Then on the 8th of May I was taken by some policeman for questioning to a place I learned later to be Limehouse police station. One of the officers was Mr. Fowler and another one was Mr. Pawley. The third one I don't know who he was. I was asked to be cooperative during the interview about to take place."

"Later at Limehouse, it would have been in the early evening because daylight was still apparent; Cloughley, Fowler and Pawley were in the room."

"The interview took place in the form of questioning. Mr. Cloughley and Mr. Pawley were taking notes of the questions and answers."

"At a certain point, Mr. Cloughley or perhaps I suggested that this be written down in a statement form. So they did."

"When we started from the early stage, I remember that because he was asking about my background. I remember r... explaining to him, going back as far as 1963, when I was working for the UN in New York. In my statement there is no mention of the United Nations. That is just an example that the statement was an edited version of what I said during the questioning ... Later at night, I think about 11:30 pm I was offered tea and Mr. Pawley told me that everybody involved with the bank were crooks, Columbotti, Maude, and everybody else. I remember that one of my replies was, 'I could not believe that.' I remember I said Mr. Columbotti was the Italian Embassy solicitor."

Frascati concluded this part of the narrative by explaining that the interview ended and he was then returned to the West Ham police station. In the police version of events the officers who accompanied Frascati on this trip alleged that he spent much of the trip crying, and expressing great fear of Mr. Torri. Frascati said, "nothing of the sort described by the police took place. I was never crying or frightened by anything."

The next day he had another 'interview'. He was again returned to Limehouse and placed in a room different than before but with the same three officers.

"Mr. Pawley started his interview by asking the hour and saying the word 'Caution'. Mr. Fowler was taking down what Mr. Pawley was dictating. During this interview Mr. Pawley dictated everything. On one occasion which I remember instead of replying, 'You are all crazy,' I actually told them it was a lie. I am referring here to one question about a meeting at the Westmoreland Hotel. Mr. Pawley insisted that myself, Torri, Boccardi, Santoro and Baracchini were present. Mr. Pawley dictated that Baracchini was present. I insisted that Mr. Baracchini was not present."

"By the end of this interview, it was quite short -- about a dozen answers with questions were written down. They are not now in the final edition of the statement. They have disappeared and new answers and questions are now in the text. I think they tried to see my reaction to certain questions, put down my alleged replies and then after having looked at the other people's questioning, added a few things to incriminate me. There was no mention at any stage during the interview, for example, about covering up the sign at the bank. The question and answer concerning the sign never occurred."

At the short interview on the evening of the 9th, they wrote down the word 'Caution' then they put down some question and answers which do not appear in the statement they have attributed to me. They dictated the wrong answers -- Mr. Pawley did. Mr. Cloughley was mainly silent. At the end of this questioning, Mr. Pawley looked at me and said 'I don't suppose you want to sign these'. I was then taken back to West Ham Station."

Frascati's main point was not that he had been beaten or physically abused. Indeed, he was willing to concede that this had not happened. About the first interview, Frascati testified, "During the making of that first statement, the policemen were completely correct in their dealings with me." The problem with the 'voluntariness' of his alleged statement to police was not so much that it was coerced from him, but rather, that it wasn't his 'statement' at all. It was a version of events made up by police sometime after the interview, containing questions and answers which best suited the purposes of the police.

But in acknowledging he was not beaten, Frascati insisted there were other forms of coercion used by the police during their dealings with him. First there was the implied threat that his freedom might depend upon the kind of answers he gave. During the second interview Frascati got the distinct feeling the police were trying to frighten him.

Mario Berton had recounted how at the start of his first short interrogation, the officer questioning him had partially undressed, then started doing push-ups, while speaking to him. They used a tactic much like this during Umberto's first short interview. "Mr. Pawley undressed himself during the second interview."

When Frascati said this, there was a ripple of shock that went through the court. It was almost a worse allegation against the police than the threats of physical violence had been. Mr. Worsley took the opportunity to cross-examine Frascati about these allegations.

"At your first interview with Mr. Pawley and Mr. Fowler, did you tell them what this other detective said, that 'your freedom might depend upon it'?"

"No."

"Did you mention this threat to the policemen who transported you in the car?"

"No."

"Did you mention this threat at the later interview that evening?"

"What little I did say is not recorded."

"Are you saying that some of the things said at that interview were not recorded?"

"It is my contention that nothing that was said was recorded."

"Were you badly treated during the transportation?"

"Yes."

Worsley raised his eyebrows at this, "Oh? Were you hit during the transportation?"

"No, I wasn't ..."

"Were you hit later at the station?"

"No."

"Well, did anyone ever threaten you with violence?"

"Nobody threatened me with violence except the striptease of Mr. Pawley which didn't really scare me."

Worsley wasn't sure what Frascati was getting at. Was the witness going to allege some sort of threat was made to him while Mr. Pawley was undressing?

Worsley thought he had better be cautious about how he asked his next questions.

"Did Mr. Pawley tell you why he was undressing?"

"No, he just looked at me and smiled."

That was enough for Worsley. He had got the witness to admit that there were no physical assaults nor verbal threats, just this rather bizarre allegation that Mr. Pawley took off his clothes for no apparent reason during the interview.

He asked a few questions about the escape. He hoped Frascati might slip up and incriminate Robert Papalia in the execution of the escape scheme. Robert, Tony and Umberto were all to be tried after the committal hearing with escape, and attempted escape from custody. But, Frascati said nothing that could incriminate anyone other than himself and Tony.

That was the end of Frascati's story.

The Defense team had decided that only Tony and Umberto would take the witness stand at this point. In Robert's case they had established the missing waistcoat and in Mario's case the interpreter had contradicted the police on material matters. These four defendants would have liked it if Swinnerton had taken the stand as well, but throughout the Committal hearing he kept his own counsel and avoided contact with his co-defendants.

The others weren't sure what Richard was planning. It seemed he was sitting on the fence. If things started to go bad for them they suspected he was planning to make a deal and turn Queen's Evidence to try to save himself from a long prison sentence. At the Committal stage, neither Richard nor his lawyer contributed much to the Defense attack, preferring to sit back with the other nominal defendants, Renata Harris and Madeline Blot, and watch how the evidence would unfold.

The lawyers turned to their submissions on the statements. The Magistrate asked all parties to be brief. Was there sufficient evidence to establish that the statements were not voluntarily or freely made, and so not admissible as evidence against them?

Mr. Worsley highlighted the evidence most favorable to his position. Most of the accused allegations about the police were unsubstantiated by other independent evidence, or could be satisfactorily explained in ways other than those suggested by the defendants, or at best, were merely equivocal, neither proving nor disproving their allegations.

The Defense counsel reiterated each of the points of evidence that created concern about the making of the statements: The long periods of isolation; Tony's headache and complaints immediately following his interview; the disappearance of the waistcoat while in the hands of Scotland Yard; the clear independent evidence that Berton had asked for a lawyer contradicting the police on this point; both Tony's and Umberto's version of events while in police custody suggesting coercion, intimidation, physical assault, their testimony unshaken by cross-examination; the clear examples given by Tony and Umberto of incorrect answers recorded and evidence that all the interviews were edited; the excessive length of some of the interviews, from morning of one day into the early hours of the next day.

It was the Defense that took the position that all of these things showed a course of conduct that was oppressive. More serious were the problems with the contents of the statements. The Defense contended that the statements were edited, taken out of context, and incorrect. All of the defendants vehemently denied that their statements were correct versions of the questions and answers given.

Other than for the self-serving evidence of the police, how could the court accept that such statements were freely and voluntarily given?

When the submissions were in, the Magistrate told the parties he wanted some time to review the evidence on the trial-within-a-trial.

"There is a good deal of evidence to consider, much of it conflicting."

He turned to Defense Counsel, "Is it your intention to call evidence at this hearing?"

Speaking on behalf of all of them Robert's lawyer, Mr. Reide said, "Yes, Sir, we will be bringing evidence and we have a number of witnesses to call. Perhaps we can now arrange some of the scheduling with respect to presentation of our case."

"Hmm, I think it might be best if we leave those matters until after I have made my ruling on the admissibility of the statements. How I rule on that issue could affect my need to hear further evidence."

Seeing this as a potentially positive sign, Counsel responded. "Yes, Sir, I suppose it might be best to sort out the housekeeping matters after you've made your ruling."

The Magistrate then suggested that the hearing reconvene in one week's time. All parties were in agreement that this be done and court was adjourned to await Magistrate Burke's decision.

Defense counsel assembled with Tony, Umberto and the other clients to discuss their best estimate of where the case was going. The lawyers cautioned their clients, not to be too hopeful, but the fact that the Magistrate wanted to review the evidence before deciding whether to admit the statements might mean that he would rule in their favor. Frascati expressed the opinion that the Magistrate seemed to be increasingly sympathetic to the Defense as the case progressed.

The indication by the Magistrate that he may not need to hear any Defense evidence, gave them more cause for cautious optimism. The decision whether to bring evidence or not is normally left to the Defense to decide. To say to them that he might not need to hear their evidence had everyone wondering whether he was seriously considering not committing the defendants to trial. It was unusual to see a case halted at the Committal stage, but not unheard of. The case had fallen far, far short of the sensational billing given by Mr. Worsley's opening speech and the knee-jerk news rags.

The defendants left the courtroom hoping that soon this case would be finished. They imagined a world where next week the Magistrate would tell the prosecution that he had fallen so far short of establishing a case of criminal conspiracy that it would be a waste of taxpayer money to take the case to trial -- a world where next week they would walk out of the courtroom free and vindicated men.

The Magistrate's Decision

(April 1978)

TONY, ROBERT, UMBERTO and Mario spent a relatively quiet week at Brixton. Frascati, like a gambler who believes he can't lose, was telling his wife that he thought it would soon be over. Things were looking good. He asked her to tell his parents that he expected to be a free man in a few weeks.

The others wanted to believe they had won, but they were more wary of being disappointed. They tried to contain their hope in one small compartment of their mind while trying to plan the questions they would ask of their own witnesses if it became necessary to bring further evidence. Tony felt it was important not to let the possibility of a quick victory overrule the need to develop the best strategy for proving their innocence. He tried not to let himself become distracted. He told the others that even if the Magistrate admitted their statements they could and would put together such a strong case in their own defense that the Magistrate would have to believe them. The week away from the courtroom seemed to pass quickly as they busied themselves with thoughts and plans for the future.

On the morning of April 25th, 1978 everyone assembled at Lambeth Magistrate court to hear Mr. Burke's decision. The judge entered the courtroom in a flurry, with robe flying, a few minutes late. The barristers bowed as a sign of respect, and the Magistrate returned their bow, before being seated. The case was called and Mr. Burke began to speak.

"I have reviewed the evidence pertaining to the admissibility of the defendant's statements to police. Without making a specific reference to the credibility of the various witnesses, I find that the defendant's attacks on these statements fall far short of impugning the voluntarisms of their statements. Accordingly, I find that all the statements are admissible evidence in this hearing."

He continued, "Having made that determination, I have this to say about the defendant's desire to prolong this hearing further by introducing a considerable amount of evidence on their own behalf. It seems to me that the Crown has brought sufficient evidence that, if believed, could sustain the charges of conspiracy laid against each of the defendants. The defendants, on the other hand, are disputing the truth of the evidence brought on behalf of the Crown."

"To allow further evidence on behalf of the defendants at this stage of the proceedings, would put me in the position of determining a great many matters of credibility, and that I will not do. I am satisfied that the Crown has established a prima facie case. That is all I need decide."

"The credibility of the various parties is better left to the judge or jury. Judge and jury can decide who they will believe when determining the guilt or innocence of the defendants."

"Therefore, I decline to hear any further evidence, but will allow each of the parties a brief opportunity to make their final arguments to me. I'm hoping we can be finished here before the end of the day. If counsel for the Defense would like to make submissions I recommend they keep it brief, perhaps not more than an hour each."

Tony and Umberto at the front of the courtroom, and Robert and Mario at the back, were stunned. This was a scenario that none of them expected. Always they had been told by their lawyers that it was their right to bring evidence at the Committal hearing. They had made the decision months ago that they would put forward a positive defense at this hearing. Now all their carefully laid plans were being turned to nothing.

The hearing proceeded quickly to a conclusion after this speech. Mr. Worsley gave his final argument, keeping it brief, reading the mood of Mr. Burke.

Each of the Defense lawyers got up and said a few words, but their speeches had little heart. Burke had admitted the statements and said that he wasn't going to hear Defense evidence because it wasn't for him to decide credibility between the two parties. He may as well have said that he'd already decided to send the case to trial. The committal hearing puttered to an end. Mr. Burke finally asked Tony if he had anything to say.

Devastated by what was happening, Tony got to his feet, "Over the period of the last four months, every time there was an explanation to make I was told by this court that the point should be made to this court at a later date. To this time I have not been able to do so. I have been asked to explain a case that has lasted four months in this court, in one hour. It is impossible for me to explain my case in one hour, and I really wonder where we are going from here."

Reluctantly he took his seat.

The submissions were finished, and the Magistrate spoke again, "I think I've given counsel a fair idea of my thoughts in this case and I've heard nothing today to dissuade me from my initial impression."

Burke turned to the clerk of the court and asked him to read each of the charges laid against each of the defendants. After each name was read by the clerk, he paused and in every case, Mr. Burke ruled the defendant be committed to stand trial on the charges. There were other matters. Those defendants who were in custody would remain in custody. A trial date would be set at a later date.

That was it. The Committal was concluded; the Magistrate rose and left the courtroom. None of the defendants could quite believe how the morning had gone. They sat in their seats with blank faces looking as though they expected something more.

Mr. Worsley was collecting his bundles of paper at his counsel table. He had a grin on his face and his step was bright. No one could remember him looking so well, so upbeat, at anytime during the past four months. The results were his pay-off for all the hard work he'd put into this case. He'd won the first battle. He and his peers, the Defense lawyers across the floor, knew he would now have the opportunity of several months respite to think about, adjust and hone the elements of his case.

There was a bitter contrast between the obvious joy of the prosecutor and the abject disappointment of the defendants and their counsel as they left the courtroom. Their lawyers tried to minimize what had happened to them. Tony, Robert and the others listened to their explanations.

"It is unusual not to be allowed to present our own evidence at Committal, but a lot of what we were planning to do would simply have to be duplicated at trial. It's seldom that a Magistrate doesn't commit to trial, and with a case of this magnitude, with the sensationalism that surrounded the laying of the charges, it was probably too much to expect a Magistrate to put a stop to it at this early stage. It was too hot, too political."

They were told not to be disappointed.

"The Crown hasn't won yet. There is a vast difference between being made to stand trial and being convicted of charges."

The men heard their lawyers telling them these things, but after the drubbing they had just taken none of it sank in. Mostly they felt betrayed by the system.

Until that point they had known that the police and the prosecutor were against them, but now, they did not understand what had happened to them in court. They thought the system was stacked against them. They believed they could not get a fair trial in England.

❧

Less than three weeks after the abrupt conclusion of the Committal hearing Robert, Tony, Umberto and Mario passed their first anniversary in jail at Brixton Prison.

Their solicitors were visiting the jail several times a week trying to get their client's instructions on a multitude of matters in anticipation of the trial.

For at least two weeks after their loss at Committal, the group sank into a kind of lethargic hopelessness. As they talked about it, they got angry and it wasn't long before their fighting spirit returned. They knew even if they felt betrayed by the British justice system, their best chance to win meant they mustn't give up the fight.

David Benham as well as Tony's and Mario's solicitor were busy planning for trial. His was a unique perspective, devoid of any previous criminal legal work. He examined the exhibits, documents, and testimony of the case as it had so far developed. He was struck that while the case was nominally a criminal one, all of the elements of proof and many of the possible Defense strategies were in the commercial realm. There were gold assays, technical data, expert opinions on scientific reports, patent considerations, contracts, banking practices and laws, stock transactions, company law and numerous variations on many of these themes.

Normally Benham let Geoff Lines make the trek to prison to meet with the clients when it was necessary. But on one eventful day in May, he drove himself from his office in the bustling financial district of London across the city to the shabby, baleful edifice of Brixton Prison that was home to his clients.. He wanted to speak with Tony about their plans.

Upon his arrival he waited in a solicitor's meeting room for Tony to be brought up from his cell.

When Tony arrived he was at his most taciturn. He no longer wholly trusted his own lawyers. His demeanor bordered on rudeness. Declining to shake hands and not smiling, he sat at one end of the table with his hands folded on the table. "Why are you here?" he said.

David shrugged off the lack of greeting and got right down to business. "I believe our case requires a much different approach than the normal run-of-the-mill criminal trial."

Still barely responding, Tony muttered, "How's that?"

"We and the other solicitors are in the process of lining up a new leading counsel to act at the trial. So far, several barristers we have contacted have expressed interest in acting on behalf of each of you. All of these people are first-rate lawyers; that's not the concern. I've been thinking that this case needs the services of a top-notch barrister who normally specializes in commercial cases. I already have someone in mind, a Q.C. amongst the best there is. He will be able to grasp all of the commercial aspects of the case without having to do acres of research. He will be one step ahead of all the other lawyers in the courtroom -- especially Worsley."

"The usual criminal cases involve answering the following questions:

Did he do it?
If so, did he mean to do it?
Does self-defense or insanity play a role?

However, it is not that simple in this case."

"We need someone who can convince the jury that the gold exists; that the company had reasonable prospects at the time of your arrest; and that the share value of Metal Research stock was a reflection of a realistic market price."

"All of the allegations of fraud against you, Mario and your brother, can be laid to rest if those facts are established to the satisfaction of the jury."

"What do you think? Do I have your approval to take this step?"

Tony was not yet willing to soften up for his lawyer. The idea sounded good but, in truth, at this point he wasn't yet certain what the best move was. He finally spoke, "Listen, David, you are the lawyer. All I know is that I want you to make the right choices so that we win this case. If you think we need a different kind of lawyer; then get one. Just let me meet with him and I will then decide whether I can work with him or not. Okay?"

Benham decided to put a dose of reality into his client's view of the world.

"Tony, the only reason I am able to ask this man to represent you is because I am not some sleazy, little criminal solicitor with an office on Broad Street."

"Whether he will act for you or not isn't for you or me to decide. It will be his choice. If we are lucky he will say -- Yes! So if he does agree to act for you, I strongly urge you to take him up on this offer."

Impassively, Tony stood up and knocked on the door to be returned to his cell. Before he left the room, he turned to Benham and said, "David, I look forward to meeting him."

More Time in Brixton

(May 1978 - August 1978)

WHILE BENHAM AND the other solicitors were busy coordinating their Defense strategy, their clients were not idle in their cells. They were feeling very resentful about their current circumstances. As they expressed their anger to their families and friends, they focused their efforts on fighting the battle on a new front -- in the court of public opinion.

Fueled by a sense of outrage, those who were close to these men who were not members of the British establishment began concerted efforts to sway the public. The right was led by their new patrons -- Fortuna and Bombara.

Fortuna held a press conference on the steps of the Thames Magistrate Court. He spoke of the slander, the lies, the innuendoes propagated by the police. He referred to the incarceration of his clients as a travesty of justice. Fortuna was about to be appointed Vice President of the Italian Republic and his press conference threatened to spark a serious international incident. The British press regarded Fortuna's action as the worst sort of meddling by a foreigner and an insult to the integrity of the British people and their institutions.

On the other hand, the Italian press and some European journalists reported the contents of the press conference and the plight of these men with some sympathy. This marked a turning point in the reporting of the case in Europe. The stories now dealt with human rights violations by the British justice system toward foreign prisoners. The British press went suddenly silent.

Petitions were collected and the case was explained to passersby in the streets of London. A series of press releases summarizing the Committal hearing were disseminated but most of the major British papers declined to publish them or, in that matter, anything else to do with the case.

Lawyers were retained to bring a case before the Human Rights Tribunal at The Hague. The men wanted this international court to assess their treatment by them and their continued incarceration as an abuse of their human rights as defined in the United Nation's "International Treaty on Human Rights".

In Canada, the McDonald Royal Commission began to hear evidence about the actions of the RCMP and other security forces operating in Canada and Quebec during the early 1970s. Tony sent many briefs to the Commission describing their treatment by Kesley Merry and the RCMP without receiving even an acknowledgment of receipt of any of his submissions. It was clear to the Twins that their homeland had abandoned them completely. They were being regarded as "personae-non-grata" by all Canadian government agencies. In point of fact, it is now known that the word was sent out from the highest levels in the Canadian government to "... ignore these criminals".

As the summer approached, there was a glimmer of hope that their message was beginning to get through. Articles were in evidence in the Italian, French and German newspapers about the sensational nature of the case and the extreme bias that seemed to be working against these men. Their "foreignness" appeared to be preventing fair and impartial treatment. There was concern they were being "railroaded" and that a fair trial was not possible in England.

Perhaps none of this really mattered. Perhaps none of the questions being asked by the defendants created the least concern for the British Establishment. But from the prisoners' viewpoint, it was reassuring to see that somewhere, there were people prepared to speak up about the injustices being meted out on them.

Robert and Tony knew the British pride themselves on the "rule of law" -- the notion that no man is above the law and every person will be treated equally by the law. The British view their country as a bastion of human rights. Attacks on this ideal were repugnant to British sensibilities. As the questions were raised again and again, the Twins could feel the pressure mounting to ensure they received a fair trial.

They were pleased to learn of the judge selected for their trial. Judge Lawson was considered one of the most honest and fair judges available. He wasn't a push-over, but was intelligent, witty and strict in the conduct of a case in his courtroom. He was his own man and would not shy away from making an unpopular or difficult decision if it had to be made.

There were better news, Michael West, QC, a criminal barrister of considerable knowledge and experience, had agreed to be leading counsel for Robert. And the man that David Benham had hoped to persuade to represent Tony, Roy Ward, QC, had agreed to take on the case.

Ward's expertise was in commercial litigation and this case would put a few new wrinkles in his usual courtroom appearances. He liked the challenge of that. The solicitors tried to convey to their clients how lucky they were to have such excellent leading counsel and a fair-minded judge to hear the case.

But no matter how well the case seemed to be shaping up, the men in their jail cell were nervous and concerned. They felt the aborted Committal hearing was an example of poor English justice and so they did not hope for much.

While all the men were testy, Tony in particular, was being as difficult with his lawyers now as he had been during the Committal hearing. He was very familiar with the role he had played in the first courtroom case. He had taken it on himself to mount his own Defense at Committal and during the entire time he was imprisoned he had read and reread every scrap of paper in this case. This was no mean feat as the case set records for the volume of paper it produced. Tony had a familiarity with and command of the documents and evidence that none of the lawyers could ever hope to match.

During his meetings with clerks, solicitors and barristers, Tony was often frustrated having to review basics with them. He felt like he had told his story a thousand times and still he had to tell it again.

Michael Spencer was brought back to assist Ward. His earlier experience with the case would help considerably. When Tony became exasperated, Spencer could step in and explain the facts to the senior barristers new to the case.

Roy Ward was not bothered by Tony's moodiness and unfriendly manner. He was accustomed to handling difficult and demanding clients and had mastered the art of dealing with such people over many years of experience. He had the knack of responding to Tony's pique with a soft, but forceful voice. Never hurried, never raffled, always in command, Roy Ward had the patience to allow his client to rant away and then steer him back to the subject at hand. His manner had a distinctly calming effect on his client. But the solicitors worried that Tony was taking a wait-and-see attitude-with his new barrister.

David Benham had already told Geoff that if Tony had the audacity to fire Ward as he had done to Michael Spencer at Committal, he would have to consider withdrawing from the case.

The summer was a flurry of activity as everyone prepared for the case to go to trial. David Benham and Geoff Lines worked late into the evenings seven days a week. The men's wives joked that they had been widowed by the case.

Of course, the "real" widows were the wives of the defendants. They had not been with their husbands for almost 15 months and still the trial had not started. The defendants now spent their time in Brixton reviewing the evidence of the Crown in minute detail. They went over their supposed "confessions" again and again looking for inconsistencies and errors that could prove or enhance their position that these documents were fraudulent. They timed the speaking of the words written to see if the length of the statements coincided with the admitted schedule of these "interviews".

Much of this exercise allowed the prisoners to feel in control; to be able to do something that could gain them their freedom. As the trial date approached they grew strong with the knowledge that they had many ways to fight this case and that there would be little the prosecution could do to refute their attacks. They awaited the trial now with anxious, but eager, anticipation.

The Trial

(September 1978)

THE FALL ASSIZES at the Old Bailey were announced and a date was set for the trial to start. On September 12th, 1978, all the parties convened in Courtroom 5 at the Old Bailey in Central London. The trappings of this court were more formal than those of Magistrate Court.

The barristers were all be-wigged and be-gowned, as was Judge Lawson. The courtroom allowed no interaction between the participants and observers. The general public was confined to a gallery above and to one side of the courtroom. The defendants were seated against the back wall. In front of them sat the solicitor's clerks in a row, then the line of barristers. In the front row sat the senior counsel. At the front of the court, facing them all and looking down from bench the English coat-of-arms perched Judge Lawson.

On the floor of the Court directly opposite the public gallery was the jury box, as yet empty. Across from the jury, was a long table where the police sat. This table was the only part of the courtroom not visible to the public as it was directly below the gallery.

The first item of business was to impanel a jury. Picking a jury is not the contentious or strategic issue that it is in an American trial. The lawyers are allowed to ask only one or two innocuous questions of each prospective juror and each defendant is entitled to a maximum of two objections.

The Defense strategy was to look for jurors who appeared intelligent. If the jury could stay interested, there was a good chance to gain an acquittal. On the other hand, if the jury got lost and couldn't absorb the mass of evidence or if they failed to appreciate some of the finer points of evidence, it was difficult to predict the outcome. Wanting an intelligent jury and getting one were not the same things. The lawyers' objections to certain jurors were made very much in the dark. The only useful information available was each person's occupation. With that in mind, objections were made to a few people who might not have had the capacity to follow such a difficult case for several months. Overall, the jury selection was accomplished very quickly.

Once the jury was chosen and seated, Judge Lawson welcomed them and explained their purpose in the Court process. It would be their job to listen to and evaluate the evidence. They would be looking at the facts and with the Judge's instructions on points of law; they would determine the guilt or innocence of the accused.

The Judge outlined the nature of the case, There were seven defendants, all charged with conspiracy to defraud. The two female defendants, Harris and Blot, together with Frascati were charged with attempting to defraud Cessna Aircraft Corporation of $1.5 million dollars US by issuing false bank drafts. Frascati and the other four men, the Papalias, Berton and Swinnerton, were charged with conspiracy to defraud investors in Metals Research SA shares. It was alleged this was to be achieved by inflating the value of the shares beyond any legitimate fair price on world markets, selling newly issued shares to the public at the inflated price, and siphoning off money from the company treasury.

Lawson was a man of obvious intellect with considerable wit and much personal warmth. The jury listened intently as he spoke. By noon, the Judge finished his explanations and so, Mr. Worsley began his opening speech after the lunch break.

Worsley had reworked his speech since the Committal hearing, placing greater emphasis on some things and less on others. In one respect though, his speech did not change. He made every effort to blow-up the importance of the alleged crime. He highlighted the monetary figures involved in the case. He pointed out how these foreigners had come to the United Kingdom from abroad to perpetrate their frauds on innocent English investors.

He told the jury how some of the conspirators had perpetrated a smaller fraud on Cessna International Financial Corporation by issuing bogus cheques for $1.5 million dollars US. That scam paled in comparison to the much larger swindle planned by these sophisticated criminals through Metals Research SA and several 'fringe' banks. These men were trying to persuade people to invest $300 million dollars US in their bogus company.

Metals Research was a Panamanian-registered company, which the promoters claimed, had title to land in British Columbia, Canada with gold, silver and platinum in the ground worth $288 billion dollars. Worsley repeated this figure for the benefit of the jury exclaiming, "Quite a sum of money. A company with assets in the ground worth billions of dollars was certainly a good investment."

"That is what the Papalia brothers and their accomplices wanted prospective investors to believe. They plotted to issue 25 million shares at $1.00 US to be sold at the inflated price of $12.00 US to investors who were to be told to expect a return of $346.00 US on each share."

"During this trial you will see many corporate documents and scientific reports that will make you think this company is a legitimate business enterprise. But, of course, that is part of the sophisticated plan hatched by these men. The case is so complicated it makes the mind boggle."

"The Papalias wanted to grab the money that would flow from the sale of shares in Metals Research and they wanted to retain the 'appearance' of legality until substantial sums could be put into their own pockets."

"They hired auditors, managers, and office juniors. They brought into being forged documents for bogus expenses so that people would think they were genuine. In due course, much of the proceeds of the sale of the company would have become the personal wealth of the brothers."

"Part of this elaborate scheme required establishing several bank branches in London as well as approaching Reuters for their stock price monitoring service. It was all done to make the corporate activities appear regular."

As at the Committal hearing, Worsley emphasized the "Black Brochure". He picked up the publication from his table. With its glossy black cover and the gold embossed logo and printing, it was an obviously expensive publication.

"These confidence tricksters were planning an expensive advertising campaign for their criminal enterprise." Worsley flourished the brochure and leafed through it. Then he pointed to the front cover.

"Across the bottom in bold gold letters it reads 'Metals Research'. Above that is a pyramid and a scripted motto derived from the US dollar bill. The company motto differs from that on the dollar bill in one important aspect. Instead of reading 'In God We Trust' it reads 'In Gold We Trust'. I imagine the perpetrators thought themselves quite clever in twisting and perverting the meaning of that phrase for their own purposes."

Worsley blatantly overstated his case in outlining the contents of the Brochure.

"The gold mine showed in this brochure as being in production, turns out to be nothing more than a waterlogged shack in the back woods. Sergeant George of Scotland Yard visited the property in British Columbia and will testify there is no sign of development anywhere upon the property."

"The Brochure states the mine was processing 24 tons of ore a day through its pilot plant, but that is a deliberate lie. Sergeant George found mountains, lakes and forests virtually untouched 60 miles (sic) northeast of Vancouver."

The Defense lawyers listened impassively as Worsley stated his case. They knew the Brochure didn't really contain statements that could be characterized as lies. They knew the evidence fell short of what Worsley wanted the jury to believe. This could only work in their favor when they would show a factual basis for virtually every statement appearing in the document.

Mercifully, Worsley did not continue his speech for most of the week as he had done at Committal. He tried to state his case simply and concisely for the benefit of the jury. His opening had the desired effect. By the time he finished several jury members were casting suspicious, covert looks at the accused. He portrayed the defendants as highly sophisticated, cunning, immoral characters with probable connections to organized crime who preyed upon innocent and trusting members of the public with a few pounds to invest. Worsley knew there were substantial weaknesses in the Crown's evidence. To overcome these shortcomings, he would color the jury's view of the defendants. If the jury thought them nasty characters, they would be more likely to convict. Worsley did all he could to reinforce this view of the men standing trial.

The prosecutor followed the advice given him by the Magistrate at the Committal hearing and called a stockbroker from one of London's largest brokerage firms as his first witness. This man was to give expert evidence about share prices of public stock. He would also express an expert opinion about the price of Metals Research stock.

The witness testified that a $12.00 US trading price for Metals Research shares was not supported by any underlying value in the company and was an artificially inflated price for these shares. Once Worsley had this opinion on the record he concluded his questions and sat down.

From his seat at the back of the room, Tony watched with interest to see what his Counsel would do. He would accept nothing less than all attack on all fronts of the Crown's case. Judge Lawson asked Defense counsel if any of them had questions for the Crown's first witness. Several lawyers declined but Roy Ward got to his feet, "I have a few questions, My Lord."

"We are talking about shares in a 'publicly-traded' company. Is that correct'?"

"Metals Research shares are not listed on a stock exchange either in England or anywhere in the world. I understand they are sold 'over-the-counter' worldwide. So yes, in that sense they are publicly-traded shares. "

"Generally, what determines the trading price of publicly-traded shares?"

"Primarily the market, of course."

"By the market, you mean what?"

"The market consists of several factors including availability of any demand for shares, or the price at which sellers will sell and buyers will buy."

"So, the price of such shares is not writ in stone?"

"No, not at all, share prices move up or down as the market for them changes."

"One of the factors that would cause the market price of a share to change, would be speculation in those shares would it not?"

"Yes."

"How would you define 'speculation' in stocks?"

"It would generally refer to an investment in shares that carry a good deal of risk but also a chance of a sizable profit on investment."

"Mining companies such as Metals Research, which are traded publicly, do they tend to be a 'speculative' type of stock?"

"Yes, an unproven mining company is regarded as a very high risk."

"I wish to put the following hypothetical to you: If there is a short supply of sellers wishing to sell shares in Metals Research but a large number of people wish to speculate in these shares, could this cause the share price of shares in the company to rise to $12.00 US per share or higher."

"Yes it could, if there were investors willing to pay that price for the shares."

"So, the price of a publicly traded stock does not always reflect a company's current earnings or assets, but is subject to fluctuation from market forces."

"Yes, that is correct."

"One more question, Sir. When you looked at Metals Research, did you examine or consider the assets and prospects of its wholly owned subsidiary companies, Sonorama Corporation and X-Labs Inc.?"

"No, I was unaware of any subsidiary of Metals Research SA. My opinion regarding share value does not encompass any enterprise other than the non-producing mining claims in British Columbia."

"Would your opinion of the value of Metals Research shares change if you were to consider the subsidiary companies as part of the package?"

"If Metals Research is the parent of two wholly-owned subsidiaries, then my opinion of valuation is incomplete and meaningless until I have had an opportunity to review the workings of those companies. My opinion of share price might be unchanged depending on the value those companies represent."

"You have not yet had an opportunity to familiarize yourself with those subsidiary companies?"

"No."

"So then, you cannot give us your opinion of the total value of MRSA?"

"No, I cannot."

"Those are all my questions."

With the Crown's very first witness, Roy Ward had managed to get agreement on every proposition he put to the man. Whatever the Crown had wanted to prove about the value of Metals Research shares with this witness had been wholly undone with Mr. Ward's ten minutes of cross-examination.

Michael Spencer, the man who Tony had dismissed during Committal, looked back at his client. Tony was sitting with a semi-smile on his face. He appeared visibly relaxed and Spencer knew Tony would be a much less difficult client from this day forward.

Much of the trial re-hashed what had taken place at Committal. The Crown brought their witnesses and the Defense punched holes in all their theories. The scientific evidence about the grade of precious metals was no better than at Committal. Not surprisingly, Mr. William Stevenson was not called back as an "Expert" witness at the trial.

After Scotland Yard's forensic scientist took the stand to explain the results of his assays, the Defense was able to show that his results revealed enough gold (approximately 2 ppm) to assume a workable mine. Some of the other assayers called to the stand expressed amazement that a non-assayer, such as Mr. Facey, performing an assay in an ill-equipped lab, could find any gold in his samples. The collective opinion was that the result was nothing short of amazing.

The Defense found scientific publications by both the US Bureau of Mines and the Canadian Department of Energy, Mines and Resources. These publications delineated the problem of inaccurate results when using standard fire assay techniques upon ore deposits high in platinum.

It seems the use of standard fire assays upon platinate-bearing ores results in false readings often masking the true amount of gold and silver in the placer deposit. Several of the expert assayers; confronted with the literature admitted they were aware of this problem and that the usual approach to solve the problem was to vary temperatures and fluxes to arrive at a more accurate assay.

The Crown continued to present its case and the Defense continued to rip it apart. The jurors had looked fearfully at the defendants at first, but now they smiled or shook their heads knowingly as each piece of the Crown's case fell flat. The Judge did much to set the tone of the courtroom. Initially Lawson had appeared to be a harsh but fair man. Once the Crown's case had been underway for more than a month, he was alternately amused and irritated by many aspects of their case.

After the evidence regarding Metals Research had been placed into the record, Worsley set about to prove his case against those defendants charged with issuing false bank drafts to Cessna International Finance Corporation.

One of the key non-police witnesses at this stage was Ferdinand Van Drunen. He came from Belgium to tell how he had requested the bank drafts totaling $1.5 million dollars US as a collateral guarantee from the Cessna dealership when they purchased the aircraft. He gave evidence of his unsuccessful attempt to have the drafts discounted and his dealings with the people at ICB and Bear Securities when trying to resolve the problem.

Mr. Worsley took considerable time with this witness, ensuring all relevant parts of the story came out. It was late on the last day of the week when Worsley finished his questions. Van Drunen's testimony to this point had been relatively uneventful.

Unknown to the Crown, the Defense had learned about certain damaging information regarding Mr. Van Drunen's credibility and the Crown's case.

Frascati's lawyer, Mr. Harmon, stood up and requested permission to ask one question before the witness was dismissed from the stand for the day. The lawyer didn't give his reasons for this request and the Judge agreed since one question shouldn't in all likelihood take too much time.

The lawyer picked up a document. "Mr. Van Drunen, are you aware that a warrant for your arrest has been issued out of Brussels ... "

Before Mr. Harmon had finished speaking, Worsley was half-way to his feet. The prosecutor looked flustered, "I must object, My Lord!"

The witness was talking too. He looked very surprised. It wasn't clear whether Van Drunen knew of the warrant before that moment, but he was now most anxious, "No. I cannot answer such a question. I won't. I must catch my plane." Worsley started again, "My Lord, perhaps the witness can be stood down so I can discuss this matter with my learned friend to establish the relevancy of this line of questioning."

Defense Counsel smiled, "My Lord, I assure you the question is most relevant to these proceedings."

Mr. Van Drunen was still repeating, "I can't answer that. I must go."

Judge Lawson was visibly amused by this turn of events. It looked like Defence Counsel had lit a fire under the Crown. Worsley was obviously surprised.

The Judge addressed the witness, "Mr. Van Drunen, as a witness before this court you are required to answer all relevant questions. However, I'm quite satisfied that Defense Counsel gave no notice to the prosecution about what is obviously going to be a contentious line of questioning."

"So I think it is appropriate that you stand down for the time being. I must remind you that you are under oath and must not discuss the evidence you are to give with anyone prior to returning to the witness stand."

"Meanwhile, Defense Counsel can discuss the matter with Mr. Worsley. On Monday, Mr. Worsley can let us know whether he still objects to the question and then we'll hear argument on the point, if need be."

Mr. Van Drunen asked, "May I go?"

Judge Lawson nodded yes and added, "You are to return to this court on Monday morning at 10:00 am to continue your testimony."

"Oh yes," said Mr. Van Drunen as he stepped down and ran from the room.

Mr. Worsley added his assurances to the court, "Mr. Van Drunen is certainly prepared to return to finish his testimony."

The door was already shut behind van Drunen as he dashed out. Judge Lawson began to laugh, "It will be most interesting to see if Mr. Van Drunen reappears on Monday."

The jury, the defendants and their counsel laughed along with the judge, while the red-faced Worsley and his minions sat with pinched and worried faces.

When court was dismissed, Frascati's counsel produced a copy of the warrant for Worsley's inspection. The document was very relevant to the case. The warrant had been issued since Van Drunen was wanted for questioning in an investigation into his possible misappropriation of funds from his employer, Cessna International Financial Corporation.

Frascati and his lawyers were apprised of this investigation by lawyers on the Continent acting on behalf of the three Italian men, Santoro, Barracchini and Boccardi. Umberto believed that Santoro and the other two accused Italian businessmen were somehow involved. After their arrest in London, they had retreated to Italy where they worked to clear their names.

They wondered why Van Drunen had attempted to negotiate the bank drafts. When they had set up the deal with him, they believed they had already put the terms of payment in place. The bank drafts were suggested by Van Drunen late in the game. He told them he required post-dated bank drafts for $1.5 million dollars US as 'collateral'. These drafts were to be cashed only in the event of a default by CAST. But, the moment Van Drunen had the drafts in his possession he had used his signing authority to try to discount the drafts. Why?

Apparently Van Drunen was using this collateral security for his personal benefit. Here is how the alleged scam worked:

Unknown to his employer, Van Drunen would "require" some clients to provide additional "collateral" security by way of post-dated bank drafts. For example, if Van Drunen received bank drafts totaling $1.5 million dollars US, he could take those drafts to a reputable third party bank and immediately have them discounted. Suppose the bank took a 5% discount, Van Drunen would receive the sum of $1.125 million dollars US. He could now invest this money on his own behalf at an interest rate in excess of the discount rate, say at 7%. This would give him a gross return of $99,750 on his investment. At year end, he could return the sum of $1.5 million dollars US to the issuing bank to cover the bank drafts and pocket the net profit for himself -- a sum of $24,750 US.

On the Monday morning following his abrupt departure, there was no sign of Van Drunen in court. Mr. Worsley stood up to explain that the two officers who had gone to the airport to escort Van Drunen to court reported that the major airports were completely socked in with fog. No aircraft could land. This non-availability of a witness meant the morning was wasted. Counsel set about to arrange the next witness as an adjournment was granted.

During the adjournment, Frascati asked his solicitor's clerk to phone the airports to discover if there really was fog at the airports and if the flights from Brussels had been unable to land. When the clerk returned, he was grinning.

"It looks like the police are doing their best to keep old Worsley in the dark."

Frascati asked, "What did you find out?"

"Both Gatwick and Heathrow report no fog. All flights from Brussels this morning arrived on time. There were no cancellations."

Frascati replied, "Let's show this to Harmon."

He spent the next ten minutes arguing with his barrister to advise the court that planes were landing. He wanted the judge and jury to understand that Van Drunen failed to show for reasons other than the weather. He wanted the court to realize that the police were manipulating the facts to suit their own purposes.

Frascati's lawyer felt Van Drunen's real reason for not being there would be understood by all when he failed to return at all. He didn't want to make Worsley appear to have misinformed the court. He respected the prosecutor's integrity and was sure he had relied on the police when he told the court that Van Drunen's plane was unable to land. Eventually however, his client's insistence won out and Mr. Harmon agreed to argue the matter.

When court was called back into session, Mr. Harmon asked permission to speak to the matter of Mr. Van Drunen's failure to attend that morning.

"During the break I received information from verifiable sources that all scheduled flights from Brussels have arrived on time at both Gatwick and Heathrow airports. Perhaps the police officers who advised the court about fog at the airport were mistaken."

Someone piped up, "They don't have the foggiest idea where Van Drunen is."

There were chuckles in the court but Judge Lawson quickly settled the issue, "if Mr. Van Drunen should re-appear to finish his evidence I expect he will have a satisfactory explanation of his failure to attend today. Should he not re-appear and in the absence of a verifiable explanation for his failure, I will instruct the jury at the appropriate time about the weight they may give to his testimony."

He continued, "I expect we have seen the last of Mr. van Drunen. We need not waste any more time on this matter. Call your next witness, Mr. Worsley."

Judge Lawson was right. Van Drunen never came back to finish his testimony, or to subject himself to further cross-examination.

This incident was one of many small victories on the road to failure of the Crown's case against the defendants. Although the case in Brussels never made it to trial, Van Drunen resigned from Cessna shortly after his return from England and reportedly retired to the South of France.

The Crown's case continued through September, October, and into November. Most of the documentary, expert and scientific evidence presented were consistent with a legitimate business enterprise.

So once again, the Crown had to rely on the defendant's police admissions.

The jury was dismissed so Judge Lawson could also conduct a "trial-within-a-trial" to determine admissibility of the statements. Each of the police involved in the arrest and interviews came before the court again. The same evidence heard at the Committal hearing was now brought before Judge Lawson.

The Defense barristers were able to use much of the Committal evidence to highlight the inconsistencies in the police version of events. One of the most effective areas of attack was an analysis on the content of the statements. By counting the total number of words contained in each statement and the time elapsed at each interview, they were able to show that much more time elapsed than should have. For instance, even reading through Tony's statement in the slowest manner possible and allowing time for pauses and breaks, there must have been an inordinate amount of 'blank' time during his thirteen hour interview when supposedly, no discussions took place. The Defense was able to show that Mario Berton, with his language problems and need for translation, responded more quickly to his questions than did either Robert or Tony.

The police never provided satisfactory explanations about the several hours of "blank" time in each of these interviews.

There were days during the "trial-within-a-trial" when Judge Lawson would leave the courtroom looking troubled after observing the demeanor of the of the police officers when they failed to explain some perplexing inconsistency.

As their second Christmas in custody came around, each of the defendants took the stand to recount their remembrance of their arrest and "interview". All the men alleged some degree of intimidation. Tony and Robert told their stories of being slapped, kicked and punched. Each of the defendants said they had requested lawyers but their requests were ignored.

When all the evidence was in and arguments on the point were finished, Judge Lawson adjourned the court. He wished to review the evidence as he intended to give written reasons. The matter would be contentious whichever way he decided the issue. Written reasons would be best in the event of an appeal. He would ponder the question over the Christmas vacation and render his decision in the New Year.

On January 4th, 1979, the court reconvened. This would be a major turning point in the case. At Committal, the Defense believed they had effectively cast plenty of doubt upon the contents, veracity and circumstances of taking the statements but nothing had been achieved. This time there was less blind faith and more hard-edged realism as the defendants awaited the judge's decision.

Judge Lawson entered the courtroom from a side door and acknowledged the bows of the assembled barristers before taking his seat.

Court was called into session and Lawson began to speak. With the orderly deliberation of a seasoned jurist, the Judge prefaced his remarks by noting the extreme length of the "trial-within-a-trial" -- 42 days; 30 days of which involved testimony. He remarked that in the course of this hearing, all the defendants had given evidence.

There were three legal arguments put forward by the Defense:

1. The conduct of the police was oppressive;
2. The police had breached the "Judge's Rules" in several instances, most particularly by denying right to counsel; and
3. The police had induced the confessions by using force.

The Crown's answer to these arguments was there had been no inducement, beatings or otherwise, and no oppression. The defendants had not requested lawyers, so there was no breach of the "Judge's Rules". But, even if they had requested lawyers, the police are entitled to disallow contact with lawyers since allowing counsel at that stage would have 'hindered' the investigation.

The main argument for the Papalias and Berton focused upon the denial of 'right to counsel' because that is where their proof was strongest.

Unlike some other common law countries the 'right to counsel' in England is not an absolute legal right. Instead, these 'rights' are set out in the 'Judge's Rules'. These are rules of practice, not of law, approved by judges of the Criminal division of the High Court, to guide police officers in the conduct of their investigations. Failure of police to comply with these rules may result in statements being excluded from evidence in subsequent proceedings.

As Judge Lawson turned to the substance of his decision, all of the defendants and counsel were on the edge of their seats. The courtroom was utterly still except for the voice of the judge.

"I have five separate defendants to whom I have to consider what the law is, and how it applies … The general principles are abundantly plain."

"I must be satisfied beyond reasonable doubt that a statement is voluntary and I must consider the situation of each interview separately..."

"This court readily accepts that officers carrying out an investigation have a difficult task. If there is interference at an early stage, justice may escape. On the other hand, a detainee suspected of a crime is entitled to the protection of the court ... Judges faced with balancing the requirements of investigating officers and the investigated have a difficult task to perform."

"The first allegation we will deal with is ... 'inducement'. The inducement is ... said to have comprised ... a degree of force -- cuffing. In the case of one defendant, it was suggested that a lighted cigarette was put up his nostril."

"I do not accept ... the evidence against the police that force ... was used ..."

"But that is not the end of the matter ... On the one hand, having rejected the evidence of brutality; I have to consider the defendants' credibility and that of the police officers, because this goes to the question of refusal of solicitors."

"I will deal with Swinnerton ... separately ... As for the other defendants, it is claimed they never asked for a solicitor. Mr. Worsley says if a solicitor had been asked for and there was a general policy not to allow solicitors to be consulted in these circumstances, why would the police make up a story that no solicitor was asked for? I do not know why a story was made up, but I do not accept that two voluble Canadian gentlemen or the two Italians ... did not at the earliest opportunity demand their rights ... to see a solicitor."

"Indeed, that is actually borne out by evidence called on behalf of the Crown. On the 12th of May, Police Constable Fowler heard Robert Papalia read out the notice on the wall in the charge room about telephoning a solicitor. That was the first day Fowler was involved in the investigation."

"It is clear that when Mrs. Thompson came upon the scene ... that Berton said to Mrs. Thompson more than once, 'why can't I have a lawyer'. Although she cannot specifically remember, this is the sort of thing she would translate."

"I have the credibility gap between the rejection of the evidence of the defendants about the use of force on the one hand and the rejection of the police officers' evidence about the requests for solicitors on the other. That is a matter which I have to deal with in this case since there is a good ... argument that refusal of the right to a solicitor is a matter which brings in the discretion I have ... to exclude certain evidence."

"I have some criticisms to offer in this case because the decision in relation to solicitors was taken on either the 5th of May or some days before the raid was made on Bear Securities. The policy was continued thereafter."

"While I can understand an initial decision that nobody be allowed to consult a solicitor -- investigations of this kind by the police force are by no means simple. But whether a blanket view can be continued through to the 12th of May is a different kettle of fish. Insofar as police officers are justified in taking a decision that nobody would be allowed to consult a solicitor ... that is something which ought not to have taken place, and certainly would not take place at present. Without some justification it should never have taken place. The only justification is that there may be hindrance to the investigation. Again, I accept that problem might well have existed at some date around the 5th or 6th of May, but not by the 12th.

"

"I do not accept that there was an unlawful arrest ... there was ... a lawful arrest, although it may be that the expression used by the police officers to describe the crime might ... be ... a statement of the offense but not the particulars."

"In the case of Tony Papalia, there is no doubt that he was kept in custody without being seen for a period which extended from 4:10 pm, Thursday, the 12th of May...until 11:50 am on Tuesday the 17th of May. This is grossly excessive notwithstanding the difficulties which the police had to deal with in the vast matters of this case."

"Detective Inspector Edwin Ward said that he would not trust any solicitor. He was given various names of well-known distinguished solicitors, none of whom he was prepared to accept."

"I take the view that the Papalias and Berton requested a solicitor but were refused. I exercise my discretion with the Papalias and Berton ... it was suggested there might be hindrance in this case and therefore the refusal of a solicitor was justifiable. I do not accept, in the case of any of these defendants, that that situation existed when they were arrested and interviewed ..."

"That leads me to the case of Frascati. It seems what happened in this case was quite wrong. There is no doubt he was arrested. He was then interviewed and that interview took the form of a 'witness statement'. Never in my personal experience has such a situation ever occurred before."

"There would be no objection to questions being asked of Frascati for the purpose of investigation. But, what ... disturbs me and gets up my nose is that the statement was taken in the form of a 'witness statement' on the basis that his evidence was going to be used by the Crown in the trial."

"So I exercise my discretion in favor of exclusion and so all subsequent discussions with Frascati must be excluded."

"Swinnerton is in a rather different category ... in relation to a 'right to a solicitor'. Mr. Rawley says it does not matter whether requests were made; the fact is there was a blanket refusal. I think the issuing of a request is important."

"The question is -- did Mr. Swinnerton ask for counsel? He says: he said something to the Sergeant on the first night of his arrest. He says there was a subsequent discussion in the company of two uniformed officers on the 16th after the first interview conducted that day and before the last interview on the 16th at Limehouse Station between 3:15 pm and 9:20 pm. When he spoke to the two officers while sitting on a bench, he was told, 'it has nothing to do with us.' Since this occurred outside the interviews I do not find that Mr. Swinnerton asked for a solicitor in a manner that would breach the Judge's Rules."

"There is no doubt that later on when talking to his brother on the phone, he was told by Detective Inspector Ward that all he could say was that he was all right. Then, when his brother asked, 'Are you all right?' 'Do you want any help?' His reply was 'Yes'. That is very much different than a request for a solicitor so I cannot treat him like the other defendants."

"It is clear Swinnerton was anxious to give ... assistance ... to the police and wanted to make clear what he knew about this matter ... He offered to give evidence on behalf of the prosecution. In these circumstances even though the blanket provision still persisted, it seems to me that in Swinnerton's case there was no ... request ... for a solicitor ... I can not exercise my discretion in his favor."

"... As to the question of whether his statement is voluntary, I have found Swinnerton's ... written statements were voluntarily given ..."

"The length of questioning is also referred to ... and ... I entirely disapprove of such long questioning. To go to the finish, as Ward said he wanted ... seems to be entirely wrong and is a practice which ought to be stopped immediately. I understand there are cases where it is necessary to go on into unreasonable hours, but I doubt that the circumstances of this case justified it."

"Despite this, I do not regard the length of questioning as constituting oppressive conduct on the part of the police officers concerned. And so, the result is that Swinnerton's statements should be admitted."

"The statements of the other four defendants should not be admitted."

Having the statements excluded was an important victory, since it simplified the issues in the trial. It meant the Defense did not have to spend days going through each statement with the jury, explaining which parts were made up and which were incorrect. Whether the jury could remember or believe each instance was a concern. This was a complicated and highly technical trial. Admission of the statements would only obscure the evidence.

No one could yet tell the impact of Richard Swinnerton's statement on his own Defense or that of the other defendants.

Mr. Worsley's case was running into difficulties. The police had taken a calculated risk when they ignored proper practice while in charge of the defendants. They threw the dice and lost. Now their alleged 'confessions' were wholly neutralized in four of the five cases. Van Drunen was gone. He was the only person who could claim to have been victimized by Bear Securities.

The other side of Worsley's case tried to prove the non-existence of the mine and the corresponding intention to defraud those investors induced to put their money into this bogus enterprise. Try as he might, his proof fell short.

He tried to claim that favorable assays were the result of 'salting' the samples. That was seriously called into question by Dr. Schmuckler's opinion that this did not happen with the samples she received.

Scotland Yard's efforts to discover disgruntled investors also drew a blank. The Crown decided to bring a witness to court to show that she had been induced to invest in MRSA shares. The witness was Robert's girlfriend in London, Maxine Hibbard. She held a total of $300 worth of shares. She was required to come to court to testify that she owned the shares. During her examination, she testified that she had insisted to Robert that she wanted to invest in the company so he had given her $300 to buy the shares. This was not really the kind of evidence that showed any intent to defraud her of money.

With his case failing on so many fronts, Worsley continued to try to convince the judge and jury that these were very tricky, sophisticated con-artists. At every chance, he tried to malign their character or their motives. When the Crown failed to bring any of the directors of Metals Research SA to testify, it was because they were obviously in league with the defendants. Being as sleazy is their colleagues on trial, they would be hostile to the Crown's case.

The Crown wanted all the questions and doubts raised by the Defense to be ignored. As the trial stumbled into the Spring of 1979, the judge and jury were having increased difficulty in taking such a leap of faith.

Near the close of the Crown's case Judge Lawson showed some irritation when he said to the prosecutor, "Mr. Worsley, where are you going with this case?"

Worsley's response served to exasperate the judge even more, "Trust me, My Lord. It will all become clear very shortly."

When it became obvious that the Crown had no more evidence to present with respect to the Cessna fraud, Judge Lawson released both Renata Harris and Madeline Blot. The Judge was satisfied there was no evidence against these two women to be considered by the jury.

For the first time in months, some London newspapers reported on the case. Buried in the back pages, a short terse article noted that two of the defendants in an on-going fraud trial at the Old Bailey had been released by the Judge after eighty-six days of Crown evidence. This left only the five male defendants, the Papalias, Berton, Swinnerton and Frascati.

One grey morning in March 1979, the Crown's case limped to a close. Judge Lawson, upon being notified that the Crown's case was completed, raised an eyebrow and then requested to see Counsel in his Chambers.

At this meeting, a number of matters were discussed. Judge Lawson said that had he known at the beginning of the case what he now knew, he would never have allowed the charges dealing with the Bear Securities/Cessna fraud to be tried together with the MRSA fraud. He made it clear that he was not impressed with the Crown's evidence. He was disposed to direct acquittals with respect to all charges concerning Bear Securities. So, the jury subsequently returned with Not Guilty verdicts on all charges related to the Cessna/Bear Securities fraud charges. Blot and Harris were free to go while the charges on the Cessna fraud against Frascati were similarly dismissed.

One of the most problematic issues in the Crown's case was the allegation that the Papalias had knowingly bought into a fraudulent company when they initially became involved in the Lillooet project. But many of the scientific reports, the variable results of fire assays, the Schmuckler and Schellinger tests on the sands preceded any of their involvement in the mine. It was hard to believe that the originators of the project would create fraudulent reports and assays and then tell the Papalias that what they were buying was a fraud and not a legitimate mining venture. It was far easier to believe that Robert and Tony believed what they had read and been told about the project.

When queried on this point, Worsley's response was "This case is difficult, because at some point these people took over an existing fraud." Of course, to present this rationale, the originators of the Lillooet project also had to be characterized as sleazy criminals.

But David Benham and Geoff Lines had traveled to British Columbia themselves when planning their case. They went by boat up Harrison Lake to visit the mining claims. They spent several days in Vancouver interviewing a great many people. They met with Pattie, Tony's wife, now living in Vancouver awaiting the return of her husband. They reassured her that although the case was difficult, things were moving slowly in the right direction.

They met with Bert Swann and felt immediately he would be helpful to their case. They asked him if he would be prepared to testify at the trial in London. At this time, there was certainly no guarantee about the fate of the defendants.

Bert was told that he risked considerable exposure to allegations of criminality if he came to London. He could expect no indulgence from the Crown. As a director of Metals Research SA and one of the originators of a project which the Crown was calling a scam, he might be charged with fraud himself if he came to England. Listening to Benham and Lines explain the allegations, Swann was struck by the absurdity of the case. His natural instinct was to go to court and tell his story; it was the right thing to do. He agreed to come to the Old Bailey and tell the history of the project from the perspective of someone involved with it from the beginning.

Bert Swann was one of the first witnesses for the Defense. Traveling half way across the globe to appear in court of his own volition, Swann made a favorable impression even before he opened his mouth.

This perception was further enhanced as he related his story. He told how the small group of investors had come to stake their mining claims in the 1960's. He described the formation of the Zyrox and Platinate companies as vehicles to develop the claims. He explained the assay problems and corresponding extraction problems and their attempts to find a solution. He told about Dr. Schmuckler's work and the promise of her methods followed by the frustrations of a lack of development money and the need to find a financial partner. He explained how, he had met Tony to setup Pacific Nickel's involvement as a partner in the venture. He explained how Pacific Nickel became Metals Research to allow on-going continuation of development work.

Swann's evidence was the first from someone with an overview of the entire history of the Lillooet project. He had first-hand knowledge about events of which even the defendants had no personal knowledge. As he gave his testimony, his open, earnest manner and his complete command of each part of his story sounded much more plausible than the Crown's incongruous theories.

"Mr. Swann," asked Roy Ward, "Is that tie pin you are wearing made of gold?"

While giving his evidence it became very noticeable that Swann was wearing a most distinctive tie pin. His occasional movements caused the gold-colored pin to sparkle brightly as it caught the light.

Swann replied, "Yes, it is."

"Do you know the source of the gold contained in that pin?"

"Yes, I do. I had this pin custom-made from gold taken entirely from the Zyrox mining claims in the Lillooet River Delta."

It was a memorable moment. There was a perceptible reaction among those present in the courtroom. This was the first time in the trial with all its talk of gold and precious metals that the values had been made real. The reflection of light from that gold pin flashed in each of the jurors' eyes.

Swann stood up well to Worsley's cross-examination. He provided detail and plausible explanations in response to the prosecutor's questions. When he was finished, the Defense was at a high-water mark.

Judge Lawson, who had heard for so long about this sleaze, Bert Swann, let the Court know that he found Swann a very credible witness. He again called for a meeting in Chambers and told the assembled Counsel that if the jury should find any of the remaining defendants guilty on any of the remaining charges, he would be disposed to granting minimal sentences, limiting jail time to that already served in custody during the trial.

When the day's proceedings drew to a close and the lawyers were gathering their briefs and bundles of documents from the counsel tables, one of the younger barristers couldn't resist an aside to the prosecutor. The Defense lawyers in the protracted trial had coined a pet name for their adversary. The young lawyer used it now when he said, "Worsley, your 'difficult' case is beginning to look hopeless."

Worsley resented the fellow's attempt to make light of the trial. He had invested the last two years of his life into this case and was not able to do anything, but take it seriously. He didn't respond to the jibe, he merely glared at the lawyer.

Trials are fickle things. No matter how a lawyer prepares strategy and agonizes over how to present the case, the trial may take twists and turns that no one can plan for or anticipate. Just when a lawyer thinks the case is well-in-hand, he is liable to be blind-sided by an assault from an unconsidered source.

The morning after their marvelous success, the defendants arrived at the Old Bailey in their prison van to be told by worried solicitors' clerks that they would be requesting a brief adjournment so the barristers could seek instructions from their clients on an important matter. When asked "What important matter?" the clerks said they would let the barristers explain it to them. Geoff commented, "It may affect the course of the whole trial."

The defendants looked at one another mystified, wondering what they were dealing with now. A few minutes later, having retired to a conference room in the courthouse, their lawyers showed them their cause of concern: an article in the Guardian newspaper.

❧

A few days earlier, Torri had been recaptured in New York and was being held by the FBI. The British were seeking his return from the States and the extradition hearing was set for early April. All this had hit the papers in the last day or two. But this was not what concerned the lawyers.

That day's edition of the Guardian was what had them worried. There was an article telling of Torri's apprehension; it re-hashed his spectacular escape from custody and the story clearly identified the others involved in the escape; Tony, Umberto, Robert and Mario.

The Defense lawyers didn't know if this article would have a negative effect. There was danger that the story of the escape would color the view of some jurors. Their lawyers advised them that because the story may have prejudiced their trial, they should apply for a mistrial.

Robert spoke first. "What is a mistrial?"

"If the motion were granted, it would have the effect of stopping the trial. It would be as though all the proceedings of the last six months were erased. Then a couple of things might happen. The Crown would either seek to re-try the case or they might review the matter and stay the charges. That would mean you would be free to go."

This sounded like a gamble. Robert asked, "I thought we were going to win this thing. If there is a mistrial, does that mean we could sit in jail for another year waiting for another trial."

"I won't lie to you. That is a possibility. We've discussed it and our general feeling is that we should make the motion for a mistrial, but we don't expect it will be granted. The newspaper article won't help our case, but it isn't blatantly sensational. It is difficult to gauge the prejudicial effect of the article. For that reason we think, our motion will be denied."

"It's really a question of strategy. In the event of your conviction on any of the charges, if the mistrial motion is denied, we will have additional grounds for appeal. This could be a significant trump card. So even if you are convicted at this trial, you could be granted a new trial later."

The defendants stood resolute. They believed they had won the case and would soon be vindicated. They insisted that a petition for a 'mistrial' should not be made but despite this request, they were soon to be over-whelmed by circumstances. Judge Lawson had already become aware of the article.

Furthermore, he had personally observed members of the jury coming to the court that morning with copies of the offending newspaper under their arms.

When court opened that day, Judge Lawson, looking very grave, announced his concern about the newspaper article in the Guardian. He was deeply offended that such a reputable newspaper would print such an article which clearly brought great prejudice toward the defendants in this case. He asked for submissions from both Defense and Prosecution counsel.

The Defense Counsel was stunned when Worsley said he had no position on the application. There was a buzz at the counsel tables. The Crown wasn't objecting to the motion. What did this mean? Could it be that the Crown wanted a mistrial to be granted? Their submissions were to the effect that the trial should still go to the jury despite the obvious extreme prejudice that the article brought to their case. When the lawyers were finished, the Judge announced that he needed some time to consider the matter. Court would reconvene that afternoon at 2 o'clock, and he would deliver his decision.

It was an anxious time of waiting for the defendants. For almost two years their lives had been consumed by police, courts, prisons and lawyers. They had become very wary of the justice system. Even the possibility of being taken back to prison, for months of waiting for a new trial, was unbearable to them.

Two o'clock came and Judge Lawson returned promptly to his court. He looked even less happy than he had that morning. He spat out some scathing words for the newspaper that printed the article. He expected a newspaper of the Guardian's caliber to know better than to publish an article of the sort that had appeared, knowing the damage that could be done to an on-going trial.

In the past, everyone had seen the judge display moments of irritation, but generally he was a man of excellent good-humor. Today, that was not the case. He was visibly angered by what had occurred. There would later be evidence that the Crown and the Police had planted the story about Torri's recapture.

The Judge's decision on the Cessna/Bear Securities fraud together with his sympathies for the remaining defendants posed significant concern for the Prosecution. They probably believed their only hope at that point was to get a mistrial and attempt to organize a new case with a new Judge. Eventually, the Guardian would be fined in excess of £5 million pounds to be used to offset the tremendous expense of the case.

The rest of the courtroom remained hushed and quiet as Judge Lawson rebuked Fleet Street for having interfered in the conduct of a trial in which dozens of people had invested countless hours. In the interests of a fair, impartial trial he felt he must declare a mistrial.

With the next words emitted by the judge, Worsley leaped to his feet to object.

"I am immediately granting bail to these gentlemen, and I do mean gentlemen, Mr. Worsley."

Worsley was sputtering, "My Lord, these men previously escaped or attempted to escape custody, they're ..."

The Judge cut him off, "I don't want to hear any more of your objections, Mr. Worsley. I'm not sure I wouldn't have done the same thing in their situation. They are immediately to be granted bail. I'd like to hear from Counsel about what bail terms should be imposed."

"Gentlemen, you are free to go."

The lawyers scrambled to prepare themselves to speak to this new issue.

At the back of the room their clients were both elated and unbelieving -- the thought of walking out into the street instead of returning to Brixton, couldn't have made the four defendants feel any better than if they had won the case.

When the terms of bail were sorted out, there were some questions about when there might be a re-trial. Judge Lawson said that decision about a re-trial would be made by the Attorney-General. "I will certainly be making my own recommendations to the Solicitor General. Whether a re-trial is in the public interest is a question that still needs to be decided."

The conditions of bail were not problematic for Mario and Robert. All that was required in their cases were sureties. For Tony, however, there was still an outstanding arrest warrant in Canada. When Judge Lawson was reminded of this fact, he very nearly had a change of heart.

Finally it was decided that so long as Tony surrendered his passport, agreed to remain in Britain, and stayed under the supervision of a responsible person, he could be freed as well. But who was a suitable 'supervisor'? This problem was resolved when Geoff Lines volunteered to be personally responsible for Tony. During the time Geoff had entered into the case, he had come to respect Tony a great deal. He regarded these men as more than clients; they had become his friends. He had no hesitation in accepting Tony's "safe-keeping".

It took about three days to put the necessary sureties in place and to satisfy all the terms of bail. Then suddenly, the four men who had shared cell space for twenty-two months found themselves free.

There were a myriad of details to arrange. Without strong roots in London, none of them had any of the trappings of daily life immediately available. They had to arrange living accommodations and money.

All of them, except Tony, applied for and received permission to travel abroad. Robert and Mario made arrangements to return to Italy. Tony moved in with the Lines family until other accommodation could be arranged. As Judge Lawson had suggested, there was no immediate re-trial. The lawyers as well as the judge were preparing opinions for the Attorney General.

In their first week of freedom, there was a considerable note of caution in everything they did. All of them were paranoid that the Serious Crime Squad officers who had leveled the original criminal charges would be out to "get" them. They made sure that they were in the presence of other people at all times. They never went anywhere alone.

Frascati in particular, was very disoriented in being on the outside again. He had been thrown together with the Papalias and Berton by circumstance. He stayed with his junior Defense solicitor for the first week of freedom in London never leaving the side of his patron. When he was permitted to leave Britain, he immediately boarded a plane for Italy. Until he stepped off the plane in Milan and was greeted by his family, he never relaxed for one moment.

Robert, Mario and Tony's response to freedom was much different from Frascati. While Frascati had kept a low profile, the other three sought to make up for some of the life they'd been unable to live while in prison. To ensure they stayed out of trouble and harm's way, they hired one of the toughest characters they had met in Brixton to be their chauffeur/bodyguard and shepherd them around London's finest restaurants and clubs.

Robert had befriended Robin Wood months before when the fellow was about to beat-up Mario for taking too long in the bathroom. Robert had stepped in and smoothed over the situation, by drawing the man's attention to the lies being printed about them in the British press at the time. Since that date the fellow had been devoted to their protection and continuing well-being.

With Robin driving them around and watching over them, they made the scene all over London for several days until Robert and Mario were allowed to leave.

The Final Battle

(April 1980)

THE TWINS DECIDED that Tony would keep in touch with the lawyers and stay abreast of their case while he remained in London. Robert and Mario would go to Italy to regain some semblance of normalcy in their lives. Mario would return to what was left of his stock brokering business. He would try to rebuild his home life with his wife, Martine, and get to know his infant daughters. He and his wife had been apart longer than they had been together. He wondered if he still knew Martine after all this time. He wondered if either of them could ever understand what the other had been through over the past two years.

Even it the worst of times, Robert was an optimist bursting with energy. His intense creativity had been simmering for too long. Now his mind filled with new plans. He had a multitude of things to do. In Italy he wanted to find new projects and revitalize old ones. He had to start making money.

There was still the matter of the Italian investigation instigated by Edwin Ward in 1977. It had been sitting in limbo, partly because the Italian authorities were waiting for the outcome of the English case and partly since so much evidence was unavailable as long as the English trial continued. When Robert arrived in Italy, he tried to move the Italian investigation forward with the assistance of Fortuna and Bombara. He visited the Magistrate conducting the investigation and gave him a lengthy account of events up to the mistrial. Eventually, the Italian authorities decided to drop all their investigations.

Robert looked over the projects he had been promoting prior to their arrest. The Lillooet mine development could not begin producing until the fraud trial was behind them. Over the long term though, it looked like a better project than they had initially thought. While they were in prison, gold prices had climbed to previously unprecedented highs, at around $350 US dollars an ounce. This was over three times the price used in the infamous 'Black Brochure'.

But two years of standing still had seriously affected their subsidiaries. Sonorama, although a viable technology, had been left at the starting line by 'Dolby' stereo sound, which had become the industry standard. X-Labs' anesthetic gas collection machine was feasible but the product was still in the development stage and did not have a marketing or production plan in place.

When Robert thought of the opportunities lost by being completely out of contention for two years together with their current world-wide reputations as bosses of organized crime, it made him sick. He decided he must re-establish himself as a promoter and entrepreneur quickly since the threat of a re-trial still hung heavily over their heads and further delays were likely.

In May, Tony phoned Robert to tell him their lawyers had filed a joint opinion with the Attorney-General and were awaiting a decision, something else had arisen which formed part of the opinion. Roy Ward had been appointed a Judge. If the case was re-tried, he would not be available as Tony's barrister to deal with all the technical aspects of the case. It would be difficult for a new lawyer to become conversant with all the business complexities of the case.

Tony delighted in telling Robert about how he was rubbing the cops' noses in his newly-found freedom. Whenever he reported to the police station to comply with the terms of his bail, he would arrive in an expensive car, sometimes a Rolls Royce, on other occasions a Mercedes sedan or perhaps, a classic sports car.

His "buddy", Robin Wood, would drive him to the station where they would act out an elaborate ritual of parking the car. Robin would pull up to the curb. He would rush to the rear curb-side door to hold it open and bow while Tony emerged from the interior of the vehicle. Once he had reported in, Tony would return to the car where Robin stood at attention to open the door once again. Generally, there would be several well-endowed and scantily-clad models in their accompaniment. The police were very upset by this charade and some of the "gossip" newspapers got wind of the show and published pictures.

Whether in London or Rome, the brothers were enjoying the luxury of their renewed freedom. Like Mario, Tony had a family to get to know again. His wife and son came to England, but their trip was only a visit. There was some concern that Scotland Yard might still try to draw Pattie into the case as a defendant. So after a two-week stay, she returned to her parent's home in Montreal to await word on the disposition of the charges. Tony and Pattie had decided she and Anthony would move permanently to Vancouver to establish roots prior to Tony's return to Canada and the re-opening of their attempt to develop the Lillooet Project.

Robert was working on a number of new business ventures in the hope that he could revitalize his fortunes. On the personal side of his life, he had met a new woman almost immediately upon his return to Italy. Her name was Alba Rosa and he nicknamed her Abba after the famous Swedish rock group.

She was from Northern Italy; a fair-haired beauty with strong aquiline lines and curves. She was one of the few women Robert had ever met as quick-witted and strong-willed as he. The couple was striking in their contrasts; Abba was reserved and cultured while he was exuberant and effusive; she was fair while Robert was dark; Abba liked quiet times while he thrived on parties and people. In many ways, Alba Rosa provided the stabilizing force that Robert knew he needed to rebuild his life. He fell madly in love with her and later married her.

Alba Rosa's life had been devoid of intrigue until she met Robert. To that point she had lived the quiet life of a university student from an upper-middle class family. For her, Robert's initial charm was the mystery of someone who lived on the edge; a man who courted danger. She soon realized how little he resembled the criminal ogre created by the police. The more she got to know this sensitive, eccentric man, the more bewildering became the notion of Robert, the criminal mastermind.

Towards the end of their first summer of freedom, Tony informed Robert that Torri had finally been extradited to Britain. It was splashed over all the newspapers. As the authorities began their plans to prosecute Torri, the Twins wondered what the Crown might still have in store for them.

On a bright summer afternoon in late August, Tony was sitting in the garden of Robin Wood's home. It was in a nice area of London with detached houses and full private yards away from the roadside of the house. He and Robin were having a couple of drinks. They were soaking up the rare sunshine, listening to some newly released rock and roll tunes when the phone rang. It was David Benham. He had received word. The Crown was going to re-institute the charges and there would be a new trial, probably in the New Year. The news hit Tony as if a large rock had dropped to the pit of his stomach. He arranged to visit David to examine the latest charges.

He thought to himself, "So, we are going to do it all over again." Tony picked up the phone and called Robert. As he dialed, he looked over at Robin. "Go get the rest of that bottle from the house and pour us two more drinks. Tonight we are going to tear up the town."

Robert was just as disappointed as Tony. Since leaving England, the case had become a bad memory. He had begun to believe their troubles were over. He was becoming comfortable again in his life in Milan. He told Abba the bad news. He would have to return to London and face a trial on a new set of charges. That evening they did not go out. They stayed at home in Robert's apartment. Alba Rosa saw another side to her man. Robert sat in his chair in the living room. His stony silence and his stare had an intensity that previously was unknown to her. She could see that he had retreated to a place in his mind in which she could not share. Now was the time to simply provide comfort.

The Crown's new approach was soon revealed to the accused through David Benham's office. There was no longer any attempt to link them to Bear Securities or ICB. So in that way the case was simplified. This was good news for Umberto Frascati. All the charges against him had been stayed and he could now put this part of his life behind him.

The Crown had reassessed its case against the remaining defendants, Robert, Tony, Mario Berton and Richard Swinnerton. They were going to place greater emphasis on share-price "rigging". They would minimize the role of the scientific evidence, the geological reports and assays, and attempt to show that the price of the shares had been artificially inflated by the actions or the defendants and their agents with the intention to defraud investors.

There was a new twist to the Crown's case this time. A new charge of "exaggerating in an advertising brochure" was being laid based on the contents of the "Black Brochure". When they first heard this new charge, they had to laugh. The case had gone from allegations of a scam of several hundreds of billions of dollars -- the largest planned fraud in the history of the world -- to a simple charge of "exaggerated advertising". It appeared that the Crown hoped they would plead guilty to this lesser charge to end the case early but that was not the way innocent men such as Tony and Robert operated. They were not guilty of any of these charges and would never admit to such lies.

Robert remembered the impression Bert Swann's gold tie pin had made at the original trial. One small bit of physical evidence spoke volumes more to a jury than mountains of documents and days of testimony. It reminded him of their plant plans and so he decided to travel to the United States to take a look at Robert Craig's pilot plant. It's placement on the Lillooet property had been aborted by their arrest and detention. Instead, the equipment had been held in storage in Nevada for the past two and a half years.

Shortly after arriving in Las Vegas, he received a message from Bombara to telephone him in Italy. When Robert called, his lawyer sounded excited. One of Italy's largest daily newspapers, Corriere Della Sera, had taken a renewed interest in the case and was rehashing every inflammatory and sensational story that had ever been written about them, MRSA and Torri.

Bombara suggested Robert should sue for defamation or libel. Robert listened as the article was read. It was the same old crap about the Mafia and about Torri. He became infuriated. This kind of story had stopped in England but now it was starting again in Italy. He decided to send a message to the reporter who had written the story. He went downstairs to the hotel desk and dashed off an angry telegram, telling the reporter he didn't know anything about what he was writing. He felt much better and went to look at the pilot plant, where he took some pictures and measured the dimensions of the equipment.

Two days later as he was preparing to leave Las Vegas, he received a second phone call from Bombara. The lawyer was just as excited as the last time they had talked. The reporter had published a second article suggesting that Robert had sent a very threatening telegram to him. The article indicated that the telegram had originated in Las Vegas, which, "as everyone knows, is the headquarters of the American Mafia".

The thrust of this second article was clear; the telegram was positive proof that the Papalias really were Mafia. Robert was immensely frustrated. He might have to spend the rest of his life trying to protect his reputation. He realized now how fragile a reputation can be. Even if they won their cases in England and Italy, he wondered if they would ever be truly vindicated or freed from the smear of these bogus charges.

He instructed Bombara to write a strongly worded lawyer's letter to the paper and let that be the end of it. They would save their energies for the courtroom.

❧

In England, David Benham and Geoff Lines were reviewing the new case. They no longer had Roy Ward, QC and the Crown was taking a stream-lined approach to the trial trying to set an early date. There would be no more Bear Securities or ICB to confuse the issues. They were not going to bring the accuseds' statements as evidence except for that of Richard Swinnerton.

Many of the Crown's scientific witnesses who had testified at both the Committal hearing and the first trial and whose evidence proved favorable to the Defense were not going to be called back by the Crown. This posed a problem for the Defense. It meant they would have to call these witnesses themselves. They wondered if any of these people would balk at making a third trip to London to testify. They could not compel anyone living outside the UK to come to give evidence and they had limited funds to pay their expenses.

When the Crown's original case had focused on the amount of ore reserves, the Defense had highlighted all the evidence that showed there were probably significant reserves of precious metals in the mining claims.

Since the Crown had scrapped that approach and was now alleging share-price rigging, Benham felt they had better look for an expert opinion regarding the value of Metals Research shares. He told Geoff to do some research into what type of firm could best render an expert opinion.

Late in the Fall of 1979, Tony called Robert with the news that the Torri trial had started. He was going to be tried alone for issuing false bank drafts, the Cessna $1.5 million dollars US cheques. Predictably, the case was receiving much attention in the press.

Tony also reported that a Judge for their trial had been chosen and none of their lawyers were happy about the selection. Judge Abdela was the antithesis of Judge Lawson. He had the nickname, "Black Jack" and was referred to as the "hanging judge." He had the solid reputation as being a prosecutor's judge leaning towards conviction whenever he could find a way.

Christmas and New Year's were the first holidays in three years that the Twins were outside of prison. Despite the news about the Judge, both brothers found themselves toasting the new decade on New Year's Eve with a wish for an end to their legal battles and a hope for a fresh start.

At the beginning of 1980, things began to take shape for the impending trial, David Benham had found a well-known firm which specialized in "mineral industry consulting". HF Ditchburn & Associates Ltd. worked out of Toronto, Canada. Herb Ditchburn, or 'Ditch' as he was known in industry circles, had worked in the mining field for some forty years. In addition to being a Mining Engineer from Queen's University, Kingston, Ontario, he had an MBA, from Harvard. He consulted on matters of "... geology, mining, metallurgy, metal marketing, financial analysis, and mineral economics."

Ditchburn reviewed the relevant information and provided Benham with a written opinion on the "speculative value of Metals Research SA."

Michael Spencer told Benham of an acquaintance who worked for British Oxygen. While the source was unwilling to testify, he had told Spencer that British Oxygen was aware of the anesthetic-gas collection machine owned by X-Labs. The machine appeared to be viable. It was causing his company some concern, as it had the potential to take up a large segment of the anesthetic gas market.

Benham felt the information important enough to get an expert opinion of the machine. He convinced a knowledgeable anesthesiologist to accompany him to Italy to look at the machine; observe it in operation; ask relevant questions of the people who had developed it; and generally ascertain whether the machine did what it was supposed to do. Following the trip, the doctor was willing to testify on all of the above points.

In early Spring, the barristers appeared before Judge Abdela to work out when to start the trial. No date was agreed to at this meeting and things did not go well for the Defense barristers. Abdela refused to listen to their submissions regarding scheduling. The Crown was prepared to proceed. However, the Defense consisted of four leading barristers and several juniors, most of them with prior, unmovable, court commitments. Besides the fact that some of the barristers were unavailable on dates being suggested by the Crown, there was another concern. The Torri case was proving to be a media circus. The papers followed it slavishly. Every day they reported on his courtroom antics.

The Crown showed that when Torri incorporated his private bank, ICB, he had listed one D. Soto as a shareholder and Director. Soto's signature appeared on the bank drafts to the Cessna International Financial Corporation. The Crown claimed that Soto was in fact, Hugo Ramirez Soto, a deckhand on one of Torri's yachts. It was claimed that Torri had appropriated the name and used it whenever he acted on behalf of his bank. In his defense, Torri tried to show that the signature was genuine and was a name used by an Italian multi-millionaire named Ferruzzi who was actually backing the drafts.

Unfortunately, Ferruzzi had been killed in a plane crash in December 1979 and could not be called to verify that Torri had the authority to use his signature. The Crown was able to show that at the time of the transaction, Ferruzzi was in the United States and couldn't possibly have signed the documents.

Much of the evidence presented by Detective Inspector Edwin Ward was filled with innuendoes and claims of a massive and complicated swindle with Mafia-inspired backing. The trivial association between ICB and Metals Research was used to establish credibility for the assertion that this was the world's biggest fraud ever attempted $288 billion dollars.

Just like Tony and Umberto, Torri became disenchanted with his lawyer and so he fired him and attempted to conduct his own defense. He was far less successful. His poor command of English and melodramatic mannerisms together with his disrespect for the English justice system, muddled his case very badly. The Judge and jury lost any sympathy they might have held for him. When the jury retired at the end of March, it took them little time to return a guilty verdict.

When it came time for sentencing, Torri brought to court a 21-year old attractive woman named Ada Basquez, with babe in arms. She submitted a letter to the court to show the former playboy was now a reformed family man

The child was their baby, and they had been living together quietly in New York until Torri's extradition had taken place. She hoped the Judge would not send her Pier-Luigi away for a long stretch in prison as it would cause her and her baby much hardship to be without him.

The young woman wept as Judge Gwynn Morris, unmoved by her plea, sentenced Torri to prison for seven years. The judge was quoted in the newspapers as saying he found Torri to be "... an utterly bogus person".

When Torri was convicted, the newspapers in Italy and England renewed their coverage of the story, writing wholly fanciful and libelous articles linking Torri to Metals Research. The Corriere Della Sera, after Robert's telegram, was one of the worst offenders. David Benham tried to stem the tide of libel by sending his own telegram to the Italian paper on March 27, 1980:

> **TO CORRIERE DELLA SERA:**
>
> We refer to your article concerning Pierre Luigi Torri dated 22nd March, 1980. We act for Tony Papalia, Robert Papalia. Mario Berton, and Metals Research. The contents of your article are extremely libelous in that it raises matters concerning our clients which are demonstrably untrue and in any event are in no way connected with the charges against Torri and the result or that case; in the event that you do not publish an immediate revocation of nil matters relating to our clients they must take legal action against you.
>
> **BISCHOFF AND CO. - LONDON**

With all these innuendoes being gleefully splashed across international newspapers every day, the Defense team was understandably concerned that their clients' case might be tainted by their tenuous connection to Torri. They objected to a jury being impaneled while there were stories circulating in the newspapers of the Torri/Papalia escape from prison. The Defense tried to get the date of April 9th, 1980 changed.

Judge Abdela viewed this matter differently from Judge Lawson. He failed to understand the basis for their objection. He felt the trial should proceed as soon as possible. He wanted to begin in early April. When Defense Counsels notified him about prior court commitments on that day, Abdela suggested it would be alright to impanel a jury and allow Mr. Worsley to do his opening with only junior counsel present. In his view, senior counsel need not be there. The juniors could take notes and handle anything that might arise.

When their lawyers reported on this development, their clients were aghast. They believed they were being, steam-rolled towards a conviction. Tony knew he must do something and he decided Abdela should be removed from the case. He began plotting to bring this about and soon settled on a course of action. He worked for weeks preparing a document called a Petition to the Court.

He tied the petition with a pink ribbon, as is the custom in the United Kingdom and attended Abdela's court himself to present the petition to the Judge while he was hearing another case. Tony entered the courtroom, approached the bar, bowed, and advised the court that he was Tony Papalia and was there to petition the court on an urgent matter. The Judge was somewhat surprised as he received the document entitled "Petition for Removal of Judge Abdela and for Investigation into the Conduct of the Crown in R. v. Papalia and Others".

Momentarily confused, the Judge exclaimed, "What is this?"

Tony replied. "I think it is self-explanatory, if you read it."

Then he left the courtroom.

At the same time he delivered his Petition to Abdela, copies were sent to Judge Lawson, all the Defense barristers and solicitors in his case, the Canadian High Commission and Italian Embassy, the Attorney-General, two daily London newspapers, several Members of Parliament, the Lord Chancellor of the Exchequer, the Law Society, the Bar Council, and London Weekend TV.

The petition outlined the history of their case with an emphasis on the defendants' allegations of police impropriety. It went on to explain why the defendants had little faith in Judge Abdela or the Prosecution:

"Since the conviction of Mr. Torri, the Crown has sought to re-introduce the defendants statements to police, which Judge Lawson had already ruled against. In particular, we are worried that the Crown will still imply that Bear Securities and International Commerce Bank were set up in order to facilitate the promotion of the 'Metals Research Fraud', a point which Judge Lawson specifically said was not supported by evidence ..."

"Judge Abdela knows about the conviction of Mr. Torri and we consider that he is prejudiced against us ... because of that conviction."

"Despite three applications to change the fixture because of the adverse press reports surrounding the Torri case, Judge Abdela has casually dismissed these by saying he disregarded these reports'. He has insisted on the 9th of April."

"Eventually at the third application, Judge Abdela ruled that the trial could be delayed until the 21st April, despite the fact that on this date, two Defense QC's must be absent for nearly all of the Prosecution's opening while attending to other court cases. His Lordship considers that the junior barristers can substitute ... His Lordship said it is 'convenient' to start the case as soon as possible so that the trial will be over by August 1st ... we don't believe that the administration of British justice should turn on mere convenience. "

"... we are entitled to full representation by Counsel and to an unbiased Judge.

We unanimously consider these rights to have been violated and that Judge Abdela by his rulings and reasoning has shown himself partial. We demand that Judge Lawson re-try our case."

"We want the trial delayed until our Leading Counsels are available and until the news about Mr. Torri's conviction has subsided ... we would be content for the trial to begin in September, assuming no further adverse press ..."

"... the Italian press has ... printed huge inaccuracies ... extensively quoting Mr. Worsley saying that we are Mafia and that there is no gold in our land. The rules of justice must prevail if we are to receive a fair trial ... we consider that the Crown in its enthusiasm to put us in jail and to justify the huge expense of bringing this action, is using the press... to this end."

"Judge Abdela has dismissed these press reports... which appeared in Italian publications freely available in London ... we have no doubt they have been read by the large Italian population of this city ..."

"... we consider our treatment at the hands of the English police and the Director of Public Prosecutions appalling. The Italians defendants were imprisoned for nearly two years without bail while an English co-defendant, Richard Swinnerton, was granted bail immediately ... We have been branded by the police as 'Mafia' simply because we are Italian ..."

"We have now been put through the ordeal of two major court cases, the latter one being prematurely terminated because of the Guardian newspaper... and what action was taken against this paper, whose interference now forces us to face a third lengthy hearing ... at the Old Bailey? None!"

"... The above ... is only a small portion of our grievances ... we refuse to be tried under these circumstances in the absence of Leading Defense Counsel. We demand that the trial be set back and that Judge Lawson be re-appointed."

"... This matter has so far cost the English taxpayer approximately £3 million pounds and yet no one in this country or anywhere else in the world has lost money because of our activities."

"Judge Abdela has shown himself to be affected by the powerful publicity created by Scotland Yard and Mr. Worsley, as he has shown no regard for our rights and the safeguard of justice."

"We implore the reader of this petition to come to our aid and to see that we are given the same rights as English nationals. The democratic and constitutional measures that exist to protect individual rights must be upheld in our case."

The petition concluded by noting that one of the senior Scotland Yard inspectors in charge of their case, Detective Inspector Bennington, was under suspension from the force for corruption charges in an unrelated matter. Another police officer, Detective Pawley, had not given evidence at the first trial even though his presence was desired by the Defense. The court had been told the officer was sick and unable to testify.

Tony ended as follows:

WE, THE UNDERSIGNED DEFENDANTS DEMAND JUSTICE."

Needless to say, Judge Abdela was not impressed or amused with the petition.

The reaction to Tony's petition was predictable. The document was ignored, especially by the media. The petition was stuffed into the "kook" file and forgotten. Neither did the Press take the opportunity to interview the defendants, although the "Torri" story was still in the headlines for several days. Perhaps it wasn't "exciting" enough to print a story denying Mafia connections. Despite the legitimate concerns set out in the petition, Tony and the others were sent to trial on April 21st in front of Judge Abdela.

The Crown was ready to obtain a conviction from these Mafia warlords. They had now achieved Torri's conviction and his connection to these defendants swirled about in the media as this new trial approached. This was their third opportunity to present their "theories" in a court of law. It was now strictly a matter of showing that the promoters of MRSA had embarked on a course of conduct designed to bilk potential investors. They had a judge now who definitely had a tendency to side with the prosecution.

A jury was impaneled and the case began. Mr. Worsley gave his opening with two of the leading Defense Counsels being absent.

The Defense Counsel remained unchanged, except for the loss of Roy Ward. Tony's new lawyer was Brian Leary, QC. Some continuity was provided by the presence of Michael Spencer as junior counsel who had taken on an ever expanding role with increased responsibilities.

The Crown had eliminated seventy-one witnesses from the previous trial. There would be no scientific witnesses to give their opinion to the jury. The Crown was now relying almost wholly on the 'Black Brochure' and the geological reports done on the property prior to 1970, to prove that Metals Research was a fraud. They would also use Swinnerton's 'confession' in which he admitted that he had suspected the whole thing was a fraud all along.

The Defense had one new piece of evidence to present; Herb Ditchburn's report on his speculative evaluation of the company. It was a conservative report in its terms and very favorable to the Defense. Ditchburn had delivered his draft several days before the trial began and he was quite willing to testify.

It wasn't long into the trial before distinct personal animosities begin to grow between Judge Abdela and the Papalia brothers. The judge deeply resented the petition Tony had disseminated all over London alleging bias. Now, in court, at various junctures, when he would comment upon or ask a question regarding something that had just transpired, his words were greeted by derisive laughter from the two defendants.

Tony and Robert had observed Abdela in action for sometime. They had come to the conclusion that the Judge intended to assist the Crown at all costs. The Twins took great delight in laughing out loud whenever Abdela said something they regarded as inane or which showed a lack of understanding of the case. In fairness to Judge Abdela, nearly every other person involved in the trial had literally worked on the case for years, and those things that were regarded as self-evident to others were not always immediately clear to a fresh mind.

Their lawyers tried to get their clients to behave a little better, but this wasn't to be. Brian Leary was less able to control Tony than Roy Ward had been and it led to some friction between lawyer and client. Tony told his counsel "I respected Judge Lawson's courtroom, but if I'm going to get a 'kangaroo court' trial, then I'm not about to let anyone think I respect that process."

The Lawyers' demonstrations to behave went unheeded; On the contrary, the defendants went even further in their disrespect. All of them rented luxury cars to take them to court each day. They hired a bevy of young women to drive and attend their cars. Jurors and police, arriving at the Old Bailey in the morning, were treated to the sight of an entourage of attractive, well-dressed women and men, pulling up in expensive limousines. They looked as if they were going to Ascot rather than defending themselves in a major criminal trial.

As the trial progressed their light-hearted approach to the trial did not appear to alienate the jury. Their demeanor together with the glaring weakness of the Crown's case seemed to have an effect opposite to what their lawyers feared. Sometimes when the defendants laughed, the jury laughed with them.

One morning Detective Inspector Edwin Ward, seated at the police witness box beside the defendant's bench, got up to deliver some evidence to Mr. Worsley. He walked directly in front of the defendants as he proceeded towards the Crown Prosecutors. As he passed by, Robert couldn't resist a jibe. He whispered, "Hey, Ward! Traffic! I hear you're going to Traffic."

To suggest that a Detective Inspector of the Serious Crime Squad would be sent to traffic detail was extremely insulting and generated an immediate response from Ward. His face went red and with a murderous look, he moved threateningly toward the defendants. Robert wondered if he was about to be throttled by Ward right here in the courtroom, but the Inspector quickly regained control and backed away. The incident was not lost upon the jury. They hadn't heard Robert's comment but they had witnessed Ward's response.

Robert motioned with his forefinger circling it beside his ear, smiling and shrugging at the jury as he pointed at Ward's retreating figure. Several members of the jury appeared to understand his intent, "What can you do? The man's insane." and they smiled in complicity at the joke.

The Crown theorized that there was nothing underlying the value of $12.00 per share for the company stock. The impending plan for Metals Research at the date of their arrest was to increase the capitalization of the company to 25,000,000 shares. This was the key element used to shore up their assumption of an intention to defraud investors of $300 million dollars.

From the start, there were significant weaknesses in the Crown's evidence. The Crown's 'experts' were always assailed by the Defense. Often Crown witnesses would be in total agreement with the Defense on cross-examination. On other occasions, Worsley would overstate the qualifications of his witnesses. In one instance, he mistakenly elevated the weight of one of his experts by constantly referring to him as 'Doctor'. The Defense was able to show that the man was a measure -- technician in an assay tab. One must wonder at such desperate measure -- Worsley was clearly uncertain about the details of his case. Why would the Crown press forward in such an unprepared fashion? Who was manipulating the prosecution (read: persecution) of these individuals behind the scene?

The pre-eminence of the Defense experts was to continue at this second trial. Herb Ditchburn, with forty years of experience in the mining industry, his Queen's University Mining degree and Harvard MBA and his conservative approach to giving evidence, made a most favorable impression with the jury.

Ditchburn put Metals Research and its shares into context. To paraphrase his testimony, "development is an extremely speculative, high-risk business at the initial stages ... When a mine is only a 'mineral prospect' it is almost impossible to state its value with certainty. Yet, if the mineral industry is to survive and thrive, it is essential to attempt to formulate a value for the purpose of generating the necessary financing. In North America and Australia ... about one-thousand mineral prospects will ultimately result in only one profitable mining venture. The cost of examining these thousand ventures, including the one profitable venture out of the one-thousand, is somewhere in the neighborhood of $35-40 million US dollars in 1980."

"All mining companies and entrepreneurs must ... determine the speculative value of mineral prospects, since the generation of many mineral prospects is absolutely necessary...New mines must be found to replace those being mined and depleted ... Over a period of time, companies that do not generate new prospects and find a few mines will ultimately go out of business."

"A mineral prospect is a long way from becoming an assured, profitable mining enterprise ... To develop a profitable mining venture requires spending huge sums of money initially at a very high risk, but when a profitable venture is achieved it usually will pay for all those prospects which were abandoned."

"Doing a speculative valuation of a new enterprise is in itself a risky business, but even in a situation where there is a scarcity of information; an expert mineral industry evaluator ... can use his experience and judgment to arrive at the speculative value of a mineral prospect."

"There is a common and accepted method for all enterprises in arriving at a benchmark. That is, to estimate the net cash flow generated by the enterprise, on a per share basis, over the expected life of the enterprise. Future earnings are discounted by applying a suitable interest rate to arrive at the present value of the business and each share in the business."

"The market value is often 2 to 3 times the net present value of the shares. The price paid by speculators in such companies is comprised of two parts - the net present value plus the anticipation that the enterprise will be successful."

"In high risk enterprises such as mining, share prices usually follow a three stage pattern: 1. initially, very high prices due to euphoria of speculators, media, etc.; 2. as a mine nears production, the price falls back below the speculative net present value; 3. after successful financial results are announced and the mine is a 'fait accompli', there is less business and technical risk and so, the market price rises to a level close to the real net present value."

"In looking at the Lillooet Project, I assumed only 1000 tons of ore per day processed over a life of ten years. The tonnage of ore to be processed over this period represents 6% of the total tonnage. This level results in a calculated speculative net present value of between $4.18 and $8.41 US dollars per share depending on the discounted price of gold."

"I have also examined the subsidiary companies of Metals Research in considerable detail. X-Labs as its primary asset a patented anesthetic gas recovery machine while Sonorama has a licensed movie theater sound system. Considering potential sales and marketing of these products, I have arrived at a 'speculative' net present value of between $21 and $25 per share."

His final conclusions took into account the values of these subsidiaries together with the speculative nature of the mining opportunity to forecast that "it would not be unreasonable in my view if Metals Research shares were changing hands in the region of $12 US in early 1977. Such a value is a pure speculative investment but that is in fact what every share is."

Worsley was unable to refute this evidence. Mr. Ditchburn's analysis was entirely reasonable as he had stuck to what he knew and carefully delineated the limitations of his opinion.

❧

The denial of the defendant's statements by Judge Lawson was carried over into this new trial, but Swinnerton's statement would finally be used. The effect of his 'confession' remained an unknown factor. Throughout the past three years, Richard had kept his distance from Robert, Mario and Tony. It was clear he had been put under considerable pressure from his lawyers and from certain members of his family to turn Crown's evidence. To his credit, so far he had resisted that pressure.

At the first trial when it appeared they were going to be victorious, Richard loosened up with them but following Judge Lawson's decision to admit his statement he once again became aloof. Robert and Tony sensed that he was taking a 'wait-and-see' attitude. It seemed that if Richard thought things were going badly at the new trial, he might take the stand and corroborate his 'confession' in exchange for a plea bargain with the Crown.

So there was an air of considerable anticipation when Swinnerton's statement was put into evidence by the Crown.

The first few pages of the statement dealt with several preliminary matters -- he told the police how he had first met Robert in the Bahamas in 1975. Initially their relationship was merely social. His contract with the Bahamian government as an architectural assistant was due to expire in March 1977. In December 1976,

Tony called from Miami and asked him to come over for a visit. During this visit, Swinnerton told Tony he was planning to return to England to look for work and Tony then offered him a job.

Tony advised him he had a company that was forming a bank and they wanted premises in London for the bank. Richard was to help find a suitable location.

"My function would be to survey, purchase and acquire premises suitable for banking premises, a field in which I had considerable experience."

Richard did not immediately accept this offer although a salary was agreed to. He told Tony he would consider the offer over Christmas during a holiday sojourn in the UK. While in England, Richard received a call from 'one of the Papalias' to join them in Miami after the New Year.

"... I did in fact join them. At this stage I was in two minds as to what to do but to return to Nassau via Miami was of no inconvenience. I got to Miami and they invited me to stay with them for a few days to help make up my mind."

The statement asserted that Richard believed he was better off with a job than to be unemployed, so he took the position, resigned his Bahamian post and returned to London to look for premises for the bank. All his efforts over the next three months to negotiate a purchase or lease on a property were itemized.

To this point, virtually all of the statement was accepted by everyone as being true and correct, although the document confused Robert with Tony and vice versa on several minor points.

The statement then turned to his directorship. "I had been told in January that I would become a Director of Metals Research. I knew the Papalias owned the company. They gave me all the documents relating to the company. I handed these documents back at the end of March to Robert never having read them."

"Upon seeing the MRSA brochure in March 1977 in which my photograph appeared as director, treasurer and banker, I became suspicious. I had a discussion with Robert in which I denied ever agreeing to be a banker. I concluded I was involved in an organization instituted purely for fraud; however, I declined to do anything about it. I went to Bear Securities with Robert at the end of March. By the way everybody jumped when he came in, I gathered Torri was the boss at Bear Securities."

"I had the impression at that time that our purpose was to seek the assistance of Bear Securities to purchase the lease of a property at 4 Halkin Place."

"At subsequent meetings with Torri and Frascati at the hotel, a great deal of discussion took place which I know nothing about since it was all spoken in Italian. After about two or three meetings, I was informed that the AATB was to be located at 60 Pall Mall (Torri's ICB Bank)."

Whenever the statement dealt with items in which Swinnerton had personal knowledge, the truth shone through. But when he was pushed into areas in which he had no knowledge or in which he had to make, an inference, Swinnerton was clearly forced to give incriminating 'evidence'.

"… My previous suspicions of fraud were strengthened; in fact, I now knew it was a fraud. I didn't like the people involved or how things were being done, was I aware that any transaction for Metals Research was at least highly irregular and fraudulent. I wasn't happy with the brochure at all. I didn't know if the oil rig (sic) on Page 1 ever existed. I was sure the company was not multinational is shown on Page 2. I didn't know if the tests shown on Page 12 had actually been carried out or if the shares were good. Most importantly, I didn't know anything about banking and here they were asking me to run one."

Swinnerton also answered questions about selling shares to innocent investors. He claimed to have prevented Sandy Fishman, one of Robert's 'rich' girlfriends from investing heavily in Metals Research. "She asked me if she should invest money and I knew if I advised her to do so, she would have invested millions. I knew this was a fraud but I did not wish to reveal it to her because she knew I was associated with these people. I therefore told her not to invest more than $1000. I knew ... she would lose it but she had plenty of money and at least she wouldn't lose too much."

The remainder of the statement dealt with details of the last trip to London by Robert accompanied by Mario and Tony. It contained several examples of corporate legal activities that Richard was asked to perform -- none of which incriminated any of the defendants.

"... Robert was on the phone, and when he finished he said he had been speaking with Bear Securities. He told me Umberto had vanished and that Metals Research stock had been used to raise cash in some way. Tony said they were going to Bear Securities to sort out the matter."

The statement clearly showed Robert, Tony and Mario were all very concerned about getting their money and stock deposited at Bear returned to them. Richard says, "I arranged a meeting with lawyers in London for that Thursday afternoon. They planned to visit the lawyers after going to Bear. They said the reason for this was that if they could get no satisfaction from the bank, they would take legal action."

"But it turned out they were arrested at Bear that day. I stayed around the hotel wondering what had happened. Later that evening, I was also arrested."

If the statement as made is a true representation of what Swinnerton said, it is an indictment of his character. Swinnerton was not a bad or evil person, but if he did state these things in his 'confession', he was clearly a moral coward.

In his own words used in the statement, he sought to take "the easy way out". So he said that despite his suspicions about the company, he chose to stay involved. If he had concerns, he never aired them with the others but hid them instead. When asked to do something, Richard simply did what he was told, regardless of whether he understood why. Presumably, he believed by staying totally ignorant, he would be absolved of wrong-doing if it turned out he was involved in a scam.

His lawyer put Richard on the stand to answer questions about his statement and to explain why he had said the things he did to the police. All of Richard's gratuitous comments about 'fraud' and 'Mafia' had been problematic for the defendants since the, first day of their arrest. Judge Lawson had found Swinnerton to be the least credible of all the defendants especially as he had never asked for a lawyer throughout all of his interviews with the police.

The Crown treated Swinnerton with disrespect. During his cross-examination, Worsley put it to Swinnerton that he had told the police he was involved in a fraud. Richard replied, "Well, yes, but it is not quite as simple as that."

Worsley replied with almost a sneer, "Mr. Swinnerton, no matter what you did or did not know about the company, you certainly made it very clear to the police that you knew you were involved in a fraud. Isn't that so?"

"Now look here, you're trying to put words in my mouth just as the police did."

"Did you tell the police it was a fraud?"

Richard was struggling. He knew he was being manipulated but could only concede in this struggle of wills. "Well, yes, I did, but ..."

The prosecutor cut him off, "Those are all my questions."

Richard's lawyer, Mr. Rawley, arose to re-examine the witness on several points, "What do you mean, Richard, that it is not that simple, that the police put words in your mouth?"

"You have to understand, I'd been living in the Bahamas for several years. Things are simpler and easier there than here. I guess I'd gotten used to the way things were there. Then I came back to England, and I wasn't used to rough or harsh people like those types in the Serious Crimes Squad."

"That evening at the hotel when I was arrested, Robert, Tony and Mario had disappeared. I didn't know why or where they were. That was playing on my mind when the officers picked me up at the hotel. They told me I was being arrested and when I asked 'what for?', they wouldn't tell me. I sure didn't know why I was being held, but I certainly got the impression that it had something to do with Bear Securities and Metals Research."

"So there I was, wondering what I had gotten myself into. I'd avoided asking questions of Robert and Tony that I should have asked. I hadn't liked that Torri fellow on the few occasions that I had met him. I didn't trust him and now the police were telling me it was all a fraud."

"I tried to cooperate, but I couldn't tell them very much. That's when they started intimidating me and saying things like, 'you know what these kinds of people are like don't you?' 'What do you think they will do to you once we tell them you have confessed everything?' The police were warning me about the others implying they were dangerous people. I thought, 'Well, they are the police, they must know what they are talking about.'"

"After four or five hours of this, my mind had imagined just about every possible terror. I was afraid of the police and of not cooperating with them. I was now fearful of the people I had been working with. I no longer knew which way was up. I was telling them what I knew and agreeing with their suggestions that it was all a fraud."

"... they terrorized me, setting up all the answers ... that are in my statement."

"I was so far gone by the time they finished with me, I would have sold out my mother as being part of the 'Mafia' if they had asked me."

Richard was quivering all over as he related the story of his interrogation. His emotion rose to the surface and bubbled over. His sincerity was apparent to all in the court room.

Robert, Mario and Tony were relieved. Richard had finally found his backbone and had admitted that the police had made him very afraid. His statement to the police had been his attempt to save his own skin by telling them what he thought they wanted to hear just as the Italian defendants had been forced to say things that weren't true.

At the end of the day, when counsel and clients got together, they all felt the damaging effect of his statement had been minimized by his heart-felt explanation on the witness stand. Richard's statement contained no proof of fraud, but mere speculations by a terrified man in a very suggestible state.

The Crown was far from finished however, despite the softening of Richard's statement by his testimony. Although seventy or so witnesses from the first trial had been dispensed with, the Crown had redoubled its efforts regarding documentary evidence.

First, it was alleged that the defendants had deliberately and systematically filtered out the less favorable scientific reports on the property from public scrutiny from a Company bundle of documents entitled 'Research Documents'. But the approach to presenting the evidence achieved exactly the opposite of what they were asserting -- any document favorable to the presence of gold at high levels was not presented. Only those reports which supported their case were highlighted. The Crown was being as selective about the evidence as they were accusing the defendants of being.

The Crown was relying heavily on one particular document as an example that the defendant's corporate dealings were simply a 'house of cards'. Out of tens of thousands of pieces of paper, someone in the Crown's office had read this document and realized the potentially damning impact of its content.

The item in question was a Certificate issued on Anglo-American Trade Bank stationary. The form had been supplied by Metals Research to its auditors to assist in the preparation of the company's annual financial statement.

In entering the certificate into evidence Worsley said, "Let's look at this paper in more detail. You can see it is a printed form -- an AATB Certificate of Deposit, dated April 30th, 1977 for $598,280. The form is signed at the top ... by Richard Swinnerton."

"Members of the Jury, no document or other evidence has ever been found to show that any deposits had ever been made by Metals Research with AATB. After an exhaustive search by the police, we have failed to find any bank account held by MRSA containing anywhere near this amount of money. It is clear this is a false, fraudulent document issued for the sole purpose of misleading the Company's auditors."

As this issue arose, the Defense Leading Counsel asked Geoff Lines to canvas the defendants about the document. The allegation needed to be addressed by the Defense team if they wished to avoid doubt in the minds of the Jury.

The certificate had been completely ignored by the Crown at the first trial so this was the first time that the defendants had put their minds into explaining the issues surrounding the document. Swinnerton's position was simple and not particularly helpful to the Defense. He claimed that Tony had told him to sign the certificate and so he had done so, no questions asked. He claimed to have no idea whether the document was legitimate or not.

Geoff Lines went to Tony to discover where MRSA had deposited this sum of approximately six hundred thousand dollars. During his three years of working on the case with the Papalias, on each occasion that he had discussed contentious issues, both Tony and Robert had answered his questions directly and provisions, first rate explanations for the complex nature of their corporate dealings. He believed it was their ability to address each and every allegation with such detail that proved their innocence.

But this time, Tony hesitated when asked "what about this $600,000 deposit?"

Geoff watched Tony's expression as the question was put forward. His eyes look on a veiled look and his mouth became a resolute straight line. It was obvious that he considered the matter a serious one. If Geoff tried to pull the answer out piece-meal with a series of probing questions, he knew he would get a fit of Italian anger. So he sat quietly and waited for Tony to speak.

After several minutes, Tony turned to Geoff and said, "Geoff, when you need your answer, I will tell you what you need to know."

Geoff was stunned. "What?" He found himself thinking that maybe, just maybe, the Crown had finally stumbled onto the 'smoking gun'. Maybe there really was a fraud committed with the issue of this certificate. "Tony, I can't take an answer like that back to Counsel."

Tony just stared stone-faced at Geoff, "I'm telling you that the question will be addressed -- but at the appropriate time."

"But, Tony, we need to refute this issue right now while the document is on the table submitted into evidence."

"I'm sorry, Geoff, but I can't tell you the answer just now."

Geoff was very uncomfortable as he returned to relate this response to the barristers. This was not a matter of petty cash that had gone missing from a desk drawer at company offices. They were considering a sum in excess of a half million dollars which the Crown alleged, had never existed. Brian Leary told Geoff he wanted an explanation at this time with no options.

It was a most distressing situation for the solicitors. A lawyer likes to conduct a trial with as little interference as possible from the client. He prefers to be in control of planning the appropriate strategy to present evidence or answer allegations. But here was Tony, once again wrestling, control of the case from his lawyers. Brian Leary exclaimed to Geoff in exasperation, "He better have a satisfactory explanation for this matter or what we are doing here in court every day will be for naught!"

Geoff returned to Tony to repeat Brian's words but the response from Tony was a simple smile. "Damn you Tony, you can be a most infuriating individual."

So the trial continued with the Crown emphasizing this document as absolute proof of the deceptive, intentions of the defendants. Presenting the remainder of their case went much quicker this time with their considerably abbreviated witness list. By June, it was time to begin the case for the Defense for the first time in three trials. They began by introducing as Defense evidence all of the documents and reports that had been left out this time by the Crown.

They went through the 'Black Brochure' step by step refuting each of the so-called lies alleged by the Crown. They brought Dr. Gabriella Schmuckler from Israel to testify on their behalf. On her two previous appearances in Court, she had given her evidence as a Crown witness. This time, the Crown decided her testimony was too supportive of the defendants. This time, although she gave essentially the same evidence as she had on the previous two occasions, the order in which she was questioned was reversed. She was now to be subjected to cross-examination by Worsley.

Worsley pursued Dr. Schmuckler with extreme vigor. He attempted to get her to agree with certain of his 'theories' about the case. He tried to place her 12 gram per ton gold assay of the 'Bulk' sample into disrepute. He repeatedly badgered the witness on this point trying to get her to admit that the result had been inflated by at least four times. Finally after the witness denied the accusation at least three times, Judge Abdela advised Worsley to accept her answer and get on with his questioning.

Worsley refused to leave the point however and demanded that all of the relevant documents and reports be reviewed to 'prove' that his 'recollection' of earlier assay reports was correct and that Dr. Schmuckler had forgotten the facts after so many years had passed. But following such a review by the Court and by the witness with the Jury dismissed, Worsley was forced to let the 12 gram per ton assay stand in evidence before the Jury. It is still unclear whether or not Worsley was ever satisfied about this point but there was little he could do in a legal sense.

Worsley then moved on to another area. He said to her, "... you expressed the view in 1975 that it was desirable to have about ten thousand samples ..."

Dr. Schmuckler disagreed, saying she was quite certain she had said no such thing. Again Worsley refused to accept this response and continued to pester her about the number of samples need. Schmuckler replied that while she had wanted many more samples to produce statistical results, "... thousands would be an exaggeration."

To help strengthen the Defense claim of the presence of significant gold in the

Lillooet sands, Brian Leary decided to question the witness on re-direct about the findings of other groups. He began with the assay reported by Scotland Yard's Dr. Facey. At this trial the Crown had declined to present him as a witness but it was still a matter of record and available for examination as evidence. It was a comic moment when Mr. Worsley jumped to his feet and objected to this line of questioning on the basis that Dr. Facey had not been called by agreement of the parties. He claimed the Defense Counsel was trying to put Dr. Facey's competence as a scientist into disrepute.

Mr. Leary responded to this objection is follows, "On the contrary, My Lord, I have no intention to demean Dr. Facey's expertise as a forensic scientist. I simply wish to examine if his work corroborates the results of this witness."

Judge Abdela allowed him to ask his questions provided he stick with the facts of the Scotland Yard forensic report.

Mr. Leary continued, "Dr. Schmuckler, are you aware that Dr. Facey found 1.8 grams per tonne of gold from the surface sample provided to his laboratory?"

Dr. Schmuckler replied, "... I think it's good news that other people found gold. You need not rely only on my evidence that gold is on the property."

Very pleased with her response, Brian Leary hammered home the significance of this point to the Jury, "Yes, and isn't it even better news that it was found by one of the scientists at New Scotland Yard's laboratories from a sample of soil gathered by a police officer who went there with a shovel?"

Following his point with interest, Schmuckler exclaimed, "In the Lillooet?"

"Yes."

"Yes," she agreed with Leary.

This is one example of how absurd the trial had become -- the Crown had objected to the admission of a report prepared by their own scientist from evidence gathered by the police.

Dr. Schmuckler's testimony had gone so well toward proving that gold was actually found in significant quantities at the Lillooet deposit that the Defense decided to shorten their case. Originally they had planned to bring Robert Craig to testify about his assays, but Craig was bilking. He complained that the police had threatened him with arrest if he came to London to present evidence. Craig had good reason to believe that this would happen, since when Ward and Pawley had traveled to interview him at his home in California; at the end of the interview, Ward was not liking what Ward had to say about the mine in Canada nor about the Papalias, started to insult Craig and put in doubt his credibility, integrity and professional work. Craig got very upset and told them both to leave his property. As Ward and Pawley were on their way out and walking through the yard in front of the house, Craig was behind them to close the gate, Ward made some other remark and Craig walked up to him and punched Ward sending him crashing to the ground.

Craig was a Gary Cooper look alike, 6 foot 2 inches tall and an ex-colonel of the US Air Force in Korea. He could not believe the audacity and twisted mind of Ward. He was not going to be insulted by Ward in his own home and let him get away with it. Upon leaving, Ward threaten to arrest Craig if he would show up in London to testify at the trial and present evidence.

They had intended to use this claim to explain Craig's failure to show up, and it was clear that such a scandalous allegation would be met with vigorous denials by the Crown. Such a debate in Court might prove to be as damaging to their case as it was to the Crown's so the Defense decided they no longer needed Craig's testimony.

Next it was Robert's turn to take the stand and testify. This was a re-match between Robert and Worsley. In the first trial with Judge Lawson, Robert had been on the stand for twenty-five days fighting it out with Worsley. Worsley had come out badly beaten by Robert. So, Worsley wanted this time to do better and teach Robert a lesson.

After two days of examination by Sir Michael West, Robert was left to be re-examined by Worsley. It became a memorable marathon that lasted twenty-eight days; a record for a legal proceeding anywhere in the world. This time Worsley got a worse beating than their previous match. Robert knew the tens of thousands of pages of evidence by heart. He knew all the affairs of the companies and found himself very often during the questioning of Worsley having to lecture Worsley on numerous points. Worsley tried everything in his bag of tricks to confuse Robert; asking questions about points already covered on previous days or presenting parts of documents or out of context, etc. There was no way, Robert was too concentrated, Worsley was not able to prevail. Worsley in his twenty-fifth day of cross examination could not get one point to his favor.

On one occasion, eighty judges from the USA visiting the Old Bailey spent all day in the visitor's gallery to watch the match between Robert and Worsley to see how an accused was standing head to head with one of the best prosecutors of England. Word of this incredible match had spread and it became an event within an event. The spectator's gallery was full everyday while it was taking place and people would go hours before to stand in line to make sure they would get a seat.

By the twenty-fifth day of their fascinating match both Robert and Worsley were exhausted, like two boxers who had punched and punched for fifteen rounds. It had gone on for twenty-five days non-stop. At one point Worsley was so tired that he asked a question that he had asked thirty minutes before and Robert replied, "I have already answered that."

Worsley insisted and Michael West objected, checked his notes and Robert was right. Robert looked at Worsley and said, "Mr. Worsley, I guess we are both tired." Shortly after, Worsley stopped his cross-examination, sat down putting a white towel on his forehead as he laid his head back. Robert remained standing in the witness box and Michael West asked him a few more questions to tidy up some points that had arisen in the twenty-eight day marathon. After that, Robert was allowed off the stand, exhausted but happy. Robert knew he had prevailed.

Robert actually had made Worsley look silly. Worsley had become too obsessed to score some points and just would not stop. After this Worsley did not get up for two days, he had his assistant carry on for him while he was recovering from the ordeal. The intensity of this battle, its length, and ferocity will probably never be repeated in an English courtroom.

The final piece of the puzzle for the Defense remained the question of the unaccounted six hundred thousand dollars. Brian Leary prevailed upon Geoff Lines to have Tony provide them with his answer on this matter immediately.

Tony agreed that now was the appropriate time to give them the information they required. He advised Geoff that someone would have to travel to Switzerland to confirm the truth of what he would tell them. Tony told him about the relevant banking transactions and accounts and gave Geoff a letter with the authorization to verify the information with a particular bank in Switzerland. Within 24 hours, Geoff Lines was on a flight to Milan.

From Milan, he traveled to Switzerland and visited the bank specified by Tony. He was given access to a file pertaining to a trust account held on behalf of the company, MRSA. The data in the file showed details about shareholders and provided proof that the money said to be held on account of Metals Research was available to the company at the time in question. Geoff made copies of the relevant parts of the file and had them certified.

When he returned to Italy, he was stopped at the border and directed into a small office where his briefcase was seized and opened for examination by the Italian border guards. When they discovered the documents, Lines was grilled at length about their contents. Geoff explained they were needed as evidence in a trial in England. The guards did not appear to accept this account and pressed him for more details for about four hours. Finally after several phone calls and many other minor delays, he was allowed to leave with the photocopies intact in his briefcase.

Upon his return to England, Geoff related to his clients what had happened at Swiss-Italian frontier. Tony snorted, "I'm not surprised and neither should you be. The reason I delayed in telling you about the bank account was because I anticipated police attempts to interfere with the evidence."

Geoff now realized that Tony's reading of the situation had been correct. Once he provided the information to his lawyers, they would feel bound to give notice of the facts to the other side providing greater opportunity to the Crown to anticipate their case.

Geoff Lines took the witness stand the day after his return and provided his evidence which included the certified copies of the accounts showing the company had cash assets available in the amounts contained in the AATB Certificate. The entire Defense team breathed a collective sigh of relief once his evidence had been placed before the Jury.

It was late in July 1980 when the Defense case drew to a close.

Each day after court, the defendants and their Counsel met to sort out their final steps. There was general agreement they had countered every element of the Crown's case, But the defendants were concerned that the Judge and Jury had not heard the whole case because of the deletion of so many witnesses from the earlier trials. They had been subjected to piecemeal bits of evidence, but not once had they been presented with the whole case laid out in a coherent fashion by a single person.

During one of these discussion sessions, the defendants learned they were entitled to give a "speech from the dock" at the close of their case. A "speech from the dock" is a very loosely defined procedure in British jurisprudence. A defendant is allowed to say anything he wishes without a time limit. He can make a plea for mercy or he can tell the Jury what is in his heart.

This was a concept that Mario, the proud Roman, and Robert and Tony could relate to with the passion of their race. All of them loved the idea. Tony decided that he would make a speech instead of taking the stand to testify. This way he could put all the case into proper perspective without Worsley's interference. Besides there was no need to have another battle with Worsley similar to Robert's and go through the same evidence all over again.

When Brian Leary learned about his defendants' plans, he wanted to work together with Tony on his speech. But when Tony began to explain what he intended to say, Leary realized that Tony would not be giving a short statement of a few minutes duration. Instead he was going to summarize the entire case in detail with plenty of editorial comment thrown in for good measure. Leary told Tony, "As your lawyer, I can't allow you to do this."

"The court will take the position that there is suspicion in presenting evidence in the manner you propose without subjecting yourself to cross-examination, Abdela will come down hard in his instructions to the Jury and you will end up damaging our case."

Tony does not accept another viewpoint unless he is thoroughly convinced it is correct. In this case, knowing he had the right to speak freely in a court of law on his own behalf was too much to give up. He insisted that he would exercise his right to give his "speech from the dock".

Brian Leary and Tony clashed heavily on this point. Finally, Leary told his client, "If you are determined to do this, then I can't stop you. But neither can I be party to something I regard as so destructive to our case. I am forced to withdraw as your Counsel."

Tony was disappointed with this position of his lawyer, but if that was the only way in which he could act freely then so be it. He would give his speech with or without Leary's presence. Michael Spencer had been with the case from the beginning and had become a seasoned barrister during the course of this long and complex trial. Tony was satisfied that Michael's presence was all he needed at this point.

So on the fateful day, Tony appeared in court with Michael Spencer as his representative. Leary was there as well but only to explain to the court that he had been forced to withdraw from the case because of strategic differences with his client. Spencer got up and informed the Judge that Tony wished to make a "speech from the dock" before the case was passed over to the Jury for deliberation. Tony was called to the front of the court to stand in the Prisoner's Dock and to say what he wanted to say.

Tony looked at the Jury and began, "Brian Leary and I have had a row about me giving this speech today. That is why he is no longer representing me. As much as I respect Mr. Leary, it is my life on the line here -- and I cannot allow this case to go without having a chance to tell you about it from the beginning to the end."

Several jurors appeared to nod in agreement with this sentiment. This trial was a frustration to Tony, for he saw the truth being hidden; bias rulings by Judge Abdela and constant disagreements with Leary on the conduct of the case.

As the defendants gathered with their lawyers outside the courtroom at the closing of the prosecution case, Tony asked the lawyers, "Would it be possible to have a few days adjournment before the Defense starts its presentation?" They replied that it would be unlikely the Judge would go for it.

Court was adjourned for a few days anyways as Tony caught a terrible cold during the night. A doctor declared him unfit to be out of bed. During this period, he packaged thousands and thousands of pages of evidence in bundles, six inches thick, all bounded in red ribbons.

On the third day, court resumed. For forty-five minutes, bundles of paper were being delivered into the courtroom by clerks and chauffeurs of luxury cars parked in front of the court house. As the court came to order, Tony rose on his feet, looking straight at the Jury. "Good morning, ladies and gentlemen, of the Jury. In the last many months in this courtroom, we may have come to the conclusion that Judge Abdela is here to administer justice, but little do you know that you are looking at a Jekyll and Hyde, who has not got an honest bone in his body. For throughout this case he has hidden facts from you, misdirected you and outright tried to make falsities the truth in your eyes."

Judge Abdela screams, "If you continue that line of thought, Mr. Papalia, I will make you disappear."

"What are you going to do, My Lord, are you going to leach me?"

"What? What?"

One of the Queens Counsel gets up and favours. "My Lord, it is the system of the solving solids into liquid."

Judge Abdela looked flustered. Tony looked straight at him and respectfully bowed.

"My Lord, with all due respect, you are the most dishonest person I have ever met in my whole entire life. You are nothing but a travesty of justice and your attitude throughout this case has been beyond obscenity. It is my turn to speak, My Lord, in these proceedings and I have had the patience to listen to your nonsense throughout the case, so please, do not interrupt me while I am speaking, with all due respect, sir."

Tony bowed again to Judge Adbela and he looked startled. People present in the courtroom would swear that the Judge turned blue in the face. While Tony was slowly turning towards the Jury, the Judge had his head down and was taking notes. There was a silence and intenseness in the courtroom that seemed to bring the proceedings into slow motion; at the same moment, the tension was at its highest.

Tony began with the mining claims. He gave details about the ore and the precious metals contained in the river delta. He discussed the production methods and the equipment needed to obtain and refine these values.

Tony pulled out Dr. Schellinger's amended ended report -- the one in which the Colorado School of Mines had replicated Schmuckler's results and produced similar assays. This was the report that the Crown preferred to ignore relying instead on Schellinger's earlier report in which no gold had been found.

He referred the Jury to the flow sheets at the end of the report. One assumed a production level of 400,000 ounces of gold per year, while the other was based on an annual rate of 800,000 ounces. "These assumptions were made by a man who visited the site, who had knowledge about the complexities of the prospect and who is regarded as a world renowned authority in the field of metallurgy."

Tony listed Schellinger's qualifications and then said, "... the Crown has tried to divert your attention by high-lighting those reports that gave the worst results."

Tony took this opportunity to blast the Crown. "... The Prosecution has continued to repeat stories that have no foundation in the context of all the facts. They have returned again and again to Schellinger's first report which contained findings of only trace amounts of gold using conventional methods. Once Dr. Schellinger was satisfied that he had a method for discovery and extraction why isn't this sufficient proof that the gold is there. I feel like I'm wasting my breath trying to explain this to the Prosecution ..."

He talked about the 'Black Brochure'. "Mr. Worsley says it was a false representation that I do not appear in this document. British Airways or any other company you can think of, does not necessarily have a picture in a brochure of the Chairman of the Board so why should my picture be in this one when I am just a shareholder."

"But you know, I agree with Mr. Worsley on one point -- this is a badly compiled brochure. However, it was a brochure that was never released to the public by the company. The copies that the police found in our possession had a number of corrections and changes, marked in them. We were reworking the brochure at the very date of our arrest."

He explained how he had discovered the project in his search for a mining opportunity for his brother's company Pacific Nickel. He then talked about the many delays that had occurred -- things beyond the company's control the years of vicious attacks by the RCMP. Despite this, the project still persisted because the people behind the project believed they were on the right track.

"The fact that the Crown maintains that it can't be done is nonsense, Dr. Schmuckler came to court and told about the various mining enterprises using ion-exchange resin technology."

"... from the reports prepared, I believe there are about 800 million ton of ore in the Delta. I also believe that the grade of ore set out in the brochure is a fair average value of all the assay results. Even should the total tonnage of ore be much less, say 100 million ton that would still represent about $18 billion dollars of reserves in the ground at a gold price of $300 dollars per ounce."

"If you divide that total by the 5,000,000 outstanding shares that figures to be about $3600 per share."

"Maybe I'm wasting my time, but I feel I must show how ridiculous the Crown's allegations are, otherwise my son will never forgive me."

Tony then repeated his saying developed from Worsley's dictum.

"The Crown has taken some subjects that were based on a kernel of ignorance and have built on them a mountain of nonsense."

Geoff Lines eyed the Jury. Many of them were smiling but all of them looked intent. They appeared to be paying close attention to Tony. He was no longer the dispassionate observer that they had seen so far. He was a man with his life on the line just as he had said. The Jury would have to judge this man and so they were assessing him very carefully.

Tony turned to their arrival in London in March 1977. He had first seen the brochure about two days before coming to London. The various people involved with the company, including Baron Locatelli, a director whose picture appears in the brochure, had had several discussions about how the brochure had been messed up at the printer. It was common knowledge to all that the brochure would be re-written and they had not given the matter another thought. From London, Robert and Mario planned to travel to North America. Robert had thus brought along a packet of brochures to distribute to the officers, directors, lawyers and mining consultants for review in-house. They would then decide on the necessary changes before having it reprinted.

"However, our being in London with a packet of brochures seemed highly suspicious to the police investigators. The police say that when we were arrested they did not know who we were or anything about our company, yet we were regarded with suspicion just the same."

"So ... we were thrown into Brixton Prison on a holding charge that never came to court. The charges were changed again and again -- my solicitors couldn't even keep up with the flood of papers in this case."

"... and the Crown was making unsubstantiated allegations with no basis in fact. One example: the Crown alleged we sent many telexes around the world to create a false impression of the value of the company. Eventually, they were able to prove two telexes were actually sent. The Prosecution would never accept that this was all, even in the absence of proof."

"... The Crown alleged that while we were in the Cayman Islands, my wife was typing up items for inclusion in the brochure. This was based on a statement extracted from Richard Swinnerton's so-called 'confession'. My wife has never typed anything for me. In fact, she has refused to ever type anything for me."

There were chuckles from the Jury as Tony went on, "Before we were married, my wife worked for the Royal Bank of Canada. She has never been a typist."

"The Crown alleges that Paul Harris who we met in the Caymans is a co-conspirator with us. When these charges were first laid, Mr. Harris was arrested and extradition proceedings were begun. This is preposterous. I first met Mr. Harris in 1975 or 1976. I don't recall the exact date. He was an internationally recognized authority in the field of tax law. All of his dealings with respect to AATB and Metals Research were in connection with his capacity as a professional advisor in corporate banking and tax law."

"The Crown has suggested that you should draw a negative inference from our utilization of companies incorporated in Panama and in the Caribbean. Well, there are legitimate reasons for incorporating in those regions."

Tony read from a tax guide and quoted Lord Clyde: "It is not a crime for any man not to be taxed of everything he has."

"We have a right to protect our interests by legitimate means. Today, one looks for ways to avoid taxes and minimize the tax burden on oneself and on the companies with which one is involved. Neither is it unusual for a company involved in large, numerous financial transactions to incorporate an in-house bank to minimize the cost of financing and other banking transactions. There are many corporations in England and elsewhere that have done exactly this."

"Metals Research is a Panamanian company that operates under Panamanian law just as a British company operates under British law. It is not proper for the Prosecution to refer to how a British company should operate since the company in question is Panamanian. When a company starts up business in England it must respect the law of the land and get the best British legal advice. Metals Research had the best Panamanian legal advice and in beginning to conduct business in England we were attempting to set up legitimate vehicles to interact with our other international interests."

"I resent the attacks on companies with which I am associated without basis of fact. Since we have been able to survive and the companies continue to grow, this shows they are based on strong foundation from the beginning."

Tony now switched to the very heart of this current case.

"The key question in this case is 'Are the shares worthless?' followed by 'Did these people try to sell worthless shares?'."

"So first thing then, we must establish that the shares are worthless."

"But if the mine is not worthless then neither can the shares be worthless. There has been no evidence that the mine is worthless."

"With reference to Mr. Ditchburn's report, in the financial community there are certain measures used to determine what a valid buy is. Using conservative parameters estimated by a mining professional, the shares should trade between

$21 to $25 dollars. The mine was commercial in 1977 and it is commercial today. In 1968 I guessed the price of gold would go up and it did. I'd be willing to bet it could go higher still."

"The conflict in this court is either:

1. the Prosecution is correct and the gold is not there, or;
2. I am right and the gold is there."

"I say the Prosecution has no backers. We have many people who have believed in us, our company and our mine over the past many years. A great wrong has been done to us. Using innuendoes and theories based on misinformation, the Crown has fabricated a ridiculous story about us."

"An issue which has bothered the Defense throughout this trial is that the Crown will only accept pieces of the whole. No matter how many times the surface has been tested, one gets the same answer -- there is gold present on the property. Some find a little more, some find a little less. When you examine all of the documents, the presence of gold is unquestionable."

It was now late in the day so the Judge asked him to stop there and resume his speech in the morning.

As Tony left the dock, he and Robert wanted to meet with their solicitors and law clerks to prepare for the next day. Tony could tell from the grudging remarks of the barristers that they felt he was doing a good job. They urged him not to get off track next day and to avoid going on to the point where the Jury would lose interest.

The next morning, Tony moved immediately to the conduct of the original police officers and the mistaken assumptions upon which the investigation has been based.

"In February of 1978, Detective Constable Pawley prepared a written statement stating that MRSA shares were worth only $11.50 cents each, virtually worthless. This statement was made by the officer ten months into the investigation. Under cross-examination at committal, Pauley stated that he had reached this conclusion from information supplied by the Reuters monitor service which quoted this low share price in response to his inquiry. When it was pointed out to him that this number was in error, Pawley insisted that this was the correct price quote. He could not however identify the police officer who had taken down the original quotation."

"But Pawley was wholly mistaken. The Reuters price quote at that time was between $11.50 and $12.00 per share. During this trial, the $12.00 quotation we have claimed makes up one of the cornerstones of the Crown's case. The Crown states that we 'rigged' the price of the shares to arrive at the $12.00 per share value on the monitor service."

"So this was the level of understanding of this officer ten months into the investigation and Pawley was a 'key' individual in this case. He was present at Bear Securities when we were arrested and at each interrogation of all of the defendants.

He was the man Detective Inspector Edwin Ward entrusted with taking notes of what occurred throughout this investigation."

"Clearly he was confused. He could only say the shares were worthless because this is what Reuters had told him but he was even wrong about that. "

"Now, I have nothing against the police," at this remark Tony heard much laughter in the court, "... but certain individuals in this situation have been quite wrong. Ten months after our arrest, the police were still under the mistaken impression that the shares were worthless. The only conclusion I can draw is that the officers misunderstood the figure when the quote was taken from the Reuters wire service. The figure was never rechecked and the mistake continued with the police trying to prove the shares were worthless."

"... When we were arrested, we were held for six days before appearing in front of a Magistrate to hear the charges. During this period, we were denied access to lawyers, to Embassies or to anyone else but the police."

".. Then we were denied bail and held in custody in Brixton Prison. Seven months later, our Committal hearing got underway lasting almost five months. The Crown presented its case but the Defense was denied an opportunity to put forward any evidence."

"Then we waited another year in custody at Brixton until the case proceeded to trial. Finally in September 1978 the trial commenced lasting until April 1979. Once again the Prosecution presented the whole of its case while the Defense had only started their case when the trial was aborted because of the action of the Guardian newspaper. It wasn't until then, after almost twenty-three months of incarceration, that we were released on bail."

"That is a brief history of this case prior to the start of this trial. Throughout all of this time, the charges against us have changed many times. Originally we were charged with circulating a false prospectus. There never was an actual prospectus but perhaps the police viewed the brochure as a prospectus ..."

"... that charge was changed and new ones added over the summer. First the charges were altered to prevent our obtaining bail in September 1977. Again at the Committal hearing, the Magistrate modified the charges. At the trial they were modified back to what they were before the Magistrate modified them."

"Following the Crown's case, Judge Lawson threw out three of the charges against us on the grounds of insufficient evidence. He actually directed the Jury to return a verdict of 'not guilty'. Only two charges remained but we were denied an opportunity to present our case because of external events."

"Once again the two remaining charges were modified before this trial began. Every time we appear in court it seems as if a new set of papers are served."

"In the beginning, the Prosecution began their case by saying there was no gold in our mining property. They began by accusing us of being alchemists -- of attempting to change iron into gold."

"After Committal, the story became 'perhaps there is a small amount of gold but the overall claims of the Papalias are exaggerated -- a mountain of lies'."

"Then during the first trial after over eight months of evidence and over seventy witnesses, 25 to 30 of whom were mining or technical experts, at the end of the day all the Prosecution did was to prove itself wrong -- but they still cannot accept this result."

"So here we are again; this time all of the technical experts have been eliminated from the case. Only shallow words are left for them to play with."

"... I'm puzzled why I am still sitting in the Prisoner's dock. During the Committal hearing I spent four and a half months explaining to the Prosecution and Police what they were doing wrong -- but they would not listen. And so, while the Prosecution has scrambled to adjust its case at every turn, to try to make the facts fit their theories, our case has never changed from the first day. It does not need to change because it is based on facts and truth, not nonsense."

"... At the opening of this case, the Crown claimed we were conspiring to get money out of would-be investors ..."

"When we were arrested, Metals Research was moving towards the production phase of its endeavors. There has not been a single investor anywhere in the world who has lost money because of our plans. The Crown has looked for duped investors but they never found even one."

"This case is the result of some policemen who got mixed up at the beginning of an investigation and then were forced to cover up their confusion and justify their allegations of fraud. But there was no conspiracy to defraud. In fact there was no crime at all."

"When Edwin Ward took the stand he told the Court that 90 percent of the papers in this case were patently worthless and false. This is the type of remark that typifies the police conduct throughout the case. It is a provocative opinion that offers no proof of anything. If that allegation and others like it are to stand, then the Crown must prove which papers are false -- and that they have not done! Remarks such as those of the Detective Inspector should not be permitted in a court of law without any backing."

"I believe the papers are true and my belief is based on personal knowledge and the weight of expert opinion. It is your job to decide if the Prosecution has proven its case. Those are all my remarks."

As Tony finished, Robert wanted to get up and give his performance a standing ovation, but he restrained himself until court was adjourned. He moved quickly to his brother's side and gave him a vigorous hug, "That was great, Tony, simply great!"

Tony was pleased. He knew he had done well. Congratulations were coming his way from all the ranks of the Defense team -- even those lawyers who viewed the speech with trepidation expressed their appreciation for his efforts. He was exhausted after his marathon presentation. It was now out of his hands but he felt better knowing he had been able to present his view about the case directly to the Jury.

It was the first week of August when Judge Abdela began to summarize the case and direct the Jury. Brian Leary was correct about Abdela's instructions to the Jury about Tony's speech -- he came down like a ton of bricks on the defendant. The Judge directed the Jury to regard the entire speech with extreme suspicion since Tony had not taken the stand and had not subjected himself to cross-examination on anything he said to the court. They must give his speech very little weight in the context of the evidence presented.

Robert too was listening very carefully; as the Judge kept speaking he could feel blood rushing to his head and started to say, "No, no, no! That is not so." On his third remark on what the Judge was saying, Judge Abdela stopped and looked across the courtroom at the accused and asked who was making remarks. Robert stood up, "It was I, my Lord."

Judge Abdela then said, "If you don't stop, I will ask you to leave the courtroom."

At this point Robert replied, "My Lord, you won't have to ask me to leave. I'm leaving." And he started to walk to the door that led to the underground cells below the courtroom. As he got to the door, which was on the side of the Jury's box, he opened the door and stopped. He turned to Judge Abdela and said, "Your Lordship, you are twisting the truth. You should summarize the facts of this case not the prosecutor's fantasies. I will not sit in this court and listen to this."

The case was halted and Robert was in a cell below the courtroom. The Defense lawyers went down to see Robert asking him to come back to court and apologize to Judge Abdela. Robert would not have it. So, negotiations were done at a distance between Judge Abdela and Robert with the lawyers acting as messengers. This went on for three hours and finally Robert went back to court in the afternoon, bowed to the Judge as if nothing had happened and the case resumed.

The Defense listened very closely to Abdela's directions. If there were any convictions, an appeal of that decision would most likely be based on the assertion that the Jury had been misdirected by the Judge. But as they listened they found little help in what the Judge said. While his directions were clearly one-sided, he was careful to never go beyond what he was justified in saying. His instructions were proper from a legal viewpoint and there would be great difficulty in appealing what he said to the Jury.

When the Judge finished, everyone in the courtroom watched as the Jury filed out to retire to the deliberation room to make their decision.

Now the Defense team had to wait. The barristers retired to their chambers but the defendants hung around the public areas of the courthouse with their solicitors, friends and supporters. No one knew how long it would take but there was a good deal of speculation that it might be quite a while since there was so much evidence for the Jury to consider.

After several hours, the group began to talk about leaving the courthouse to get some dinner and then retire to their hotel rooms until suddenly the side door to the courtroom snapped open. A clerk stood facing the group in the hall, "The Jury has made a decision. They are ready to return to the courtroom now."

Everyone jumped up and moved to re-assemble in the courtroom. When all the players were in attendance, the Jury was led back into Court. The defendants searched for a sign of their fate in the faces of the Jury members but there was nothing to see. The Jurors maintained poker faces giving nothing away.

The Clerk of the Court began the process of determining the verdicts:

"My Lord, the Jury retired at 10:20 am, returned at 4:47 pm and has been deliberating in all for six hours and twenty-seven minutes."

"Will the Foreman please stand? Mr. Foreman, will you please confine yourself to answering my first question either yes or no? Members of the Jury, have you reached verdicts upon which at least ten of you are agreed?"

"Yes."

"Members of the Jury, on count one of this indictment, conspiracy to defraud, do you find the first defendant Richard Swinnerton guilty or not guilty?"

"Not guilty."

"On the same count, do you find the second defendant Robert Papalia guilty or not guilty?"

"Not guilty."

"On the same count, do you find the third defendant Tony Papalia guilty or not guilty?"

"Not guilty."

"Again on the first count, do you find the fourth defendant Mario Berton guilty or not guilty?"

"Not guilty."

"On the second count of the indictment, conspiracy to contravene section 13(1)(a)(i) of the Prevention of Fraud Investments Act 1958 as amended, do you find the first defendant Richard Swinnerton guilty or not guilty?"

"Not guilty."

"On the same second count, do you find the second defendant Robert Papalia, guilty or not guilty?"

"Not guilty."

"On the same second count, do you find the third defendant Tony Papalia guilty or not guilty?"

"Not guilty."

"And again, finally on the second count, do you find the fourth defendant Mario Berton guilty or not guilty?"

"Not guilty."

When all the acquittals were in, everyone reacted. Mario, who was always the dignified gentleman quiet and composed, leapt from his seat and his voice boomed throughout the courtroom, "Justice has prevailed."

Robert and Tony were smiling and congratulating one another. Richard Swinnerton had tears of joy and gratitude in his eyes. All members of the Jury were now beaming at the defendants and the response their decision had received from the accused men.

Mr. Worsley stared down at the papers on his desk in total dejection. He looked to be in shock. Judge Abdela looked like he had just swallowed a bitter pill.

"Before I adjourn these proceedings there is one more matter which must be dealt with and that is the matter of costs."

"By some estimates, the trials of this matter have cost the British taxpayers as much as four million pounds. Throughout these proceedings, all four of these men have been in receipt of Legal Aid certificates."

"Part of my mandate under the Legal Aid system is to determine those instances when it is appropriate for a defendant in a criminal proceeding to be required to pay a contribution toward the cost of Legal Aid."

"I find that circumstances exist here for such a contribution. In the case of Richard Swinnerton, he is without employment and significant assets. I order him to pay the sum of £100 pounds."

"As for the other three defendants, I understand they are all men of significant means. Therefore I order Robert Papalia, Tony Papalia and Mario Berton to each contribute the sum of £10,000 pounds towards the cost of their defense."

One of the Jurors gasped when she heard the sum specified by the Judge.

Michael Spencer was on his feet immediately and everyone could see his outrage, "My Lord, this is a most unusual order. It has never before been the practice of this court to require acquitted men to pay such sums in aid of their defense. This will be a black day in the history of British justice if such an Order be made."

"Mr. Spencer, it is wholly within my jurisdiction and within the terms of our system of Legal Aid to make this Order. My Order stands. Court is adjourned."

While all of the acquitted men were momentarily stunned by this exchange, once the Judge had left the Courtroom, it no longer mattered. They were too elated by their acquittals to be put off for long by this Order.

Today when they walked from the Old Bailey courthouse, for the first time in three years they would walk out as free men. Judge Abdela's attempt to add insult to their ordeal by making them pay for the injury inflicted upon them by these trials and imprisonment was just another example of the extent to which the British justice system was blinded by its initial errors. But it would be to no avail because Judge Abdela no longer had the power to hurt them further.

They had won.

www.ingramcontent.com/pod-product-compliance
Lightning Source LLC
Chambersburg PA
CBHW030821310726
48980CB00006B/578/J

* 9 7 8 1 4 2 6 9 1 6 6 8 7 *